About the

Jeanine Englert's love af_____
romance began with Nancy Drew and her grandmother's
bookshelves of romance novels. When she isn't wrangling
with her characters, she can be found trying to convince
her husband to watch her latest Masterpiece/BBC show
obsession. She loves to talk about writing, her beloved
rescue pups, as well as mysteries and romance with
readers. Visit her website at jeaninewrites.com

The Historical Collection

The Historical
Collection:

The
Highlander's
Heart

JEANINE ENGLERT

MILLS & BOON

First Published in Great Britain 2023
by Mills & Boon, an imprint of HarperCollins*Publishers* Ltd,
1 London Bridge Street, London, SE1 9GF

www.harpercollins.co.uk

HarperCollins*Publishers*
Macken House, 39/40 Mayor Street Upper,
Dublin 1, D01 C9W8, Ireland

The Historical Collection: The Highlander's Heart © 2023 Harlequin Enterprises ULC.

The Lost Laird from Her Past © 2022 Jeanine Englert
Conveniently Wed to the Laird © 2023 Jeanine Englert

ISBN: 978-0-263-32120-3

MIX
Paper | Supporting
responsible forestry
FSC™ C007454
www.fsc.org

This book is produced from independently certified FSC™ paper to ensure responsible forest management.

For more information visit: www.harpercollins.co.uk/green

Printed and Bound in the UK using 100% Renewable Electricity at CPI Group (UK) Ltd, Croydon, CR0 4YY

THE LOST LAIRD
FROM HER PAST

To my grandmother, Joanne.

You always made me feel like the most loved person in the world. Thank you for always reminding me that I was enough, even when I didn't believe it myself.

I love you and miss you.

Chapter One

Road to Westmoreland, near Loch Linnhe, Scotland, November 1743

The acrid smell of smoke filled the air as Garrick Mac-Lean, Laird of Westmoreland, reined in his horse and crested the final steep incline on the dirt road to his home just beyond Loch Linnhe. The grey puffs buffeting amongst the rising full moon blocked his view of the majestic profile of Westmoreland, giving him a longer reprieve from facing the painful truth seeing his ancestral home would rouse in him. That he had failed his family and failed in his duty as laird to protect his sister.

As his horse climbed, Garrick slid back in the saddle. The cool weight of his sister's silver crucifix pressed against his neck where it hung from a loose chain. The solitary heirloom was a heady reminder of what he had lost and of what little he could bring to his mother to grant her peace. He knew it would be no comfort, but he had nothing else to give. At least his sister, Ayleen, had been buried in the place she had given her life to protect, even if he hated God for it.

The smell of smoke intensified and heat flushed his limbs as it triggered the memory of his arrival in Perth a year ago in search of his sister...

'Ayleen!' Garrick yelled at the burning abbey. He ran towards the structure and hit a wall of heat and flame he couldn't pass. He jogged alongside it, searching for an opening, any opening, in the fire.

His heart sank. There wasn't one.

Panic screeched along his limbs. What if he was too late?

He heard a scream and turned.

Ayleen.

Reivers had her. Their faces were covered in blood and etched in cruelty and hate. She was kicking, flailing, and trying to fight them off. He froze, his legs tree trunks he couldn't move, his limbs stone. She met his gaze and smiled at him, the relief at seeing him evident in her eyes.

His chest tightened but still he couldn't move. He just stared and her smile faltered.

'Garrick!' she yelled.

Finally, his legs gained feeling and he ran to her. A reiver sank his blade into her gut and fled. Agony rippled along her face and her eyes closed as she crumpled to the ground. Garrick ran and ran, skidding to her in the grass on his knees. Please be alive. Please, Ayleen. *Scooping her up into his arms, he knew his prayer had been discarded. She was dead, her eyes wide and staring into the heavens above.*

His scream burned his throat. What had he done? He could have saved her, but he'd done nothing. When it had counted most, he'd frozen.

'I'm sorry, sister,' he whispered in her ear as he rocked her in his arms. 'I failed you.'

Garrick shifted on his mount, clutching the reins to smother the tremble in his hands as well as the shame and horror of that day. If he'd not encouraged her to follow her heart and calling to the church, but had arranged a marriage for her as he should have as her older brother and laird of the clan, his sister would still be alive. Perhaps even happily married with her own bairn by now, and he an uncle. His gut tightened and he ground his teeth. Only fools followed their hearts. He knew that now.

Yet another reason it should have been him rather than his elder brother Lon to die of fever years ago. Garrick didn't know how to be laird, just as his father had long suspected. His heart was too soft, his feelings too deep. But not any more. He'd learned his bloody lesson.

His dark stallion continued its steady plodding along the dirt road and Garrick attempted to shake off the ghosts of regrets surrounding him. Dusk pitted the sky with shadow and the Highlands began to hide her secrets, one of the things she did best. He flipped up the collar of his overcoat to block the wind from his neck and shifted from the road to the grass to avoid the slick pockets of ice shimmering in the gouges of the worn road. The crunch of the frozen stalks beneath his horse's hooves was a signal December was near. The budding winter winds and first snows of the season would press mercilessly upon them in the coming weeks.

Not much had changed within the villages and towns he had passed on his return from Perth, but he had. When he'd left Westmoreland over a year ago, he'd believed himself invincible, and that his will alone would help him rescue his sister from the bloody skirmishes along the Borderlands, but he'd been wrong. He'd arrived too late to protect her from the heartless reivers who had risen like ash from the forsaken land and destroyed it once more. Nothing had been the same since.

As Garrick began to descend, he spied the shell of an overturned carriage resting precariously along the grassy slope of the glen below. He narrowed his gaze. Flames licked down the sides of the wide wooden frame as the fire burned itself out. Empty horse tethers rested along the ground. Gooseflesh rose along his skin. Something wasn't right. He slackened his hold on the reins, scanning from left to right, his gaze sweeping methodically over the scene as it would on a battlefield. Caution and instincts kept a man alive, not weaponry. He'd learned that early on.

When he spied a shadowy mound at the edge of the path half covered in grass and overgrowth, Garrick guided his mount to a stop. It could be part of a planned ambush. Or it could be a wounded man in need of assistance. There was no way to know until he got closer. Shifting the reins to one hand, he pulled a dirk from his waist belt. So much for an uneventful return home this eve.

He dismounted, tethered his horse to a small sapling nearby and approached, his eyes fixed on the dark form, the edges of it sharpening into focus with each step closer. His heart picked up speed. The man had been cleaved in the chest and gut and stripped of anything of value. He was sprawled without shoes or coat like a large X upon the ground. The awkward and unnatural twist of his limbs left little doubt. He was dead.

What Garrick had first thought an accident from afar now appeared otherwise. He scanned the area and found another body in the grass not far away from the first. It looked as if the man had attempted to outrun his attackers, to disappear into the glen and forest below for cover. The man hadn't got far but had been downed by a single blade to the back by a skilled thrower, or perhaps a man schooled to kill quickly, as he was. Garrick turned the body over and cursed. The lad looked the age of his younger brother, Cairn, who was scarce old enough to take a blade to his cheek.

The boy's wide, glassy brown eyes stared back at him, unseeing and full of fear. *Poor lad.* He'd not been dead long. His limbs were still floppy and loose. Garrick guided the boy's eyelids closed with his hand, saying a brief soldier's prayer for a quick release of his spirit to peace. He sighed. Such a loss for no reason. Years ago, he might have felt a twist of anguish in his gut at the sight of the dead boy. Now, he accepted it as a part of existence. The Highlands had changed, England had changed and he had changed along with them. He wasn't the same man who had left this hillside over a year ago, full of certainty for his future.

Now he was certain of...nothing.

A noise stilled him. He paused and listened, closing his eyes to determine the direction of the sound. A soft whimpering, almost like a gentle mewling from a wounded animal seized his ears and he held his breath, concentrating on only the plaintive cry. He opened his eyes. It was coming from the carcass of the overturned carriage that still smoked. He crossed the road with his dirk poised and ready.

He slid down a patch of slick grass and landed on a bevy of boulders that appeared to be holding the carriage in place. Careful to avoid the weak, winking flames, he peered through what was left of the window of a once fine carriage. He could smell and see the remnants of black varnish paint and the faint outline of a gold crest on the door.

He frowned. Such finery wasn't often seen in the Highlands this far north, and the fools within had made themselves a target by travelling so late and without adequate protection. People in the Highlands were desperate, hungry and willing to take what they needed these days. Moonlight winked against the shattered glass, glittering along an ice-blue silk gown. He sucked in a breath.

Deuces.

There was a woman inside. Why had she been abandoned? He froze. *Unless she was dead.* He shoved the thought aside. He sheathed his blade and yanked on the carriage door, but it was jammed shut. Cursing under his breath, he rammed his shoulder into it once, then twice, until the wood gave way, splintering from the force. The carriage yawned under the shifting weight and threatened to roll down the hill, crushing them both. He leaned his weight against it and forced himself half inside. He'd not leave her to be scavenged by animals, even if she was dead.

The woman appeared lifeless, but the moaning from her lips convinced him otherwise. *Saints. She was alive.* His heart picked up speed. Westmoreland was not far. If he rode hard, he could be there in less than an hour. Bloody, dark, matted hair from a head wound obscured part of her face, but otherwise she seemed unharmed. Perhaps he could save her yet.

Sliding his arms around her torso and the billowing folds of her silk skirts, he scooped her up as he held the weight of the carriage at bay using his leg. She snuggled against him and wrapped an arm around his neck. The feel of her faint whisper of breath along his cheek awakened a small seed of worth and want in him. After a very long time of not feeling needed by anyone, and falling short of those who had, it filled him with a sense of purpose. Maybe he could save her, even if it had been far too late for him to save his sister.

He pulled her out of the carriage and quickly shifted out of its path, shielding her with his body. Without his steadying weight, the wooden carcass of the carriage rocked and then careened past them down the hillside before crashing into the bottom of a ravine, splintering into bits. If he'd been seconds longer, they would have been crushed with it along the forest floor. He shook off the thought and continued, clutching the woman as tightly as he dared due to her unknown injuries. She smelled of lavender and rose... He stilled, arrested by the flash of memories the fragrance provoked.

The woman's size and hair colour were familiar.

He breathed in again. His body tightened in longing. He shifted her in his arms, desperate to get her face in the moonlight for a better look. It couldn't be, could it? Surely time was playing tricks on his senses and crushing fatigue confusing his mind? His heart pounded, his mind demanding to know if his fear was true. Finally, a cloud passed and the moonlight allowed him to see her more clearly.

Lord above.

The sight of her landed a solid punch to his gut and his legs tingled. He stared down at the woman in his arms as his heart slammed into his chest.

'Brenna?' he asked. 'Is that you?'

There was no answer but that of his heart. He knew it was her, as he knew this road and the smell of the Highlands in winter—the pert tip of her nose, the single mole along her neck and the feel of her in his arms. But how could it be? She lived south-west of here at Glenhaven with her father and brother. And who were these men escorting her? Where was her chaperone, and why weren't Laird Stewart's men guarding her? He gently pushed back some of the matted hair from her face. None of it made any sense.

'Wake. You must wake,' he pleaded, gripping her face to rouse her.

I cannot lose you twice.

He leaned down to kiss her cheek but checked himself and pulled away in time. He didn't dare.

It had taken all of his strength to let Brenna go the first time. And he'd done so with calculated and deliberate force after Ayleen's death, when he'd realised he couldn't truly protect anyone or be of use to her as a husband. He'd not sent word to Brenna, as he'd promised when he'd left, had but stayed away long after he'd planned to return.

He'd enlisted his honed skills as a soldier to fight along the Borderlands. It suited him far better than his new role as laird, and he knew that. Rage had fuelled every cut of his blade into the enemy, and with each death he'd been able to pull back further into his armour as a warrior and away from his life in the Highlands. He was good at killing. Good at detaching. At least, when it didn't matter. When it mattered, he choked and did nothing, as he had with Ayleen. And, as the days and weeks had ticked by, the old Garrick had fallen away like an old skin shed by a snake.

He'd wanted Brenna to believe him dead and seek out a new life without him, and the only way to do that was to disappear from them all. Should he have written to her and helped her let go of any hopes she still had in him and their future? Aye, he should have. But he'd not been strong enough to lie to her and pretend he didn't still care for her. So, rather than lie, he'd denied himself all feeling and attachment to her, and it had worked. For the most part, anyway.

He'd been a coward. Yet another thing to hate himself for. He'd add it to the bloody list of his failings that was becoming as long as a scroll. He was no longer the man that could love, cherish and protect Brenna for the rest of her days, as he'd believed but a year ago. He'd given up any hopes of a future with her the day he had lost his sister. Brenna deserved to live the happy and full life he had once promised her with a man who could protect her.

His chest tightened. Even if such happiness rested with another man.

She didn't wake or move. Panic clawed along the edges of his spine. He had to get her care. And quickly. Who knew what additional injuries she might have sustained other than her head wound? The gulf between them now didn't matter, only her life.

If he could save her, he could redeem some small part of the man he'd once been and make up for the pain he had caused her this past year. All he needed to do was maintain his distance. He'd done so for a year already, and he'd have to face her soon enough. Once she was at Westmoreland, he would send word to her family. They would come to collect her and then they could continue on without one another, as he'd planned.

No doubt she would be filled with ire at the sight of him alive. And he would use her rage to maintain their estrangement. He deserved her hate and disdain.

He carried her to his stallion and rested her across his mount before untying the reins from the small tree. Then he gently pulled up behind her, readjusting her in his arms with an extra tartan wrapped about her for warmth and protection. She was chilled to the bone.

Who knew how long she'd been exposed to the elements?

He held Brenna tightly and rode as fast as he dared to Westmoreland. The sharp wind in his face was an intoxicating reminder that he was alive, as was she, and that all was not lost.

Not yet, anyway.

Chapter Two

Brenna Stewart woke and had an immediate desire to retch, yet she was too exhausted, and the pounding in her head demanded she keep still with her eyes closed. But all the jostling, all the blasted jostling which would not cease, made the nausea worse. *Curses.* She clutched her head, wincing from the pain. Where was she? A flash of a memory of fire startled her, breaking through part of her confusion amidst the fog of her mind. But it faded away before she could seize upon it, like water running through her fingers.

The harsh smell of damp earth, horse and smoke surrounded her, and she stifled a gag. 'Arthur?' she asked in a raspy voice, trying to clear her burning throat. A wave of dizziness threatened and she clung to his coat sleeve. Perhaps something had happened to the carriage, for she was on horseback now, she was sure of it. But why? And why could she not remember how she'd got here?

'Arthur, stop the horse,' she pleaded in a thready voice that sounded little like her own.

'Nay, I cannot. You're hurt. Be as still as you can. We must get you care.'

She froze. That wasn't Arthur. Yet, the voice sounded so familiar. She clawed through her mind to find the name but couldn't. She concentrated and was finally able to open her eyes and attempt to peer up through the mounds of tartan wrapped around her. She pressed her fingertips to her temple to stop the throbbing and discovered the bloody wound there. She hissed out a breath from how tender it was to her touch. No wonder her head ached.

'Blast,' she mumbled, trying to push herself up and away from the man who was definitely not Arthur for a better look at him. Had she been kidnapped?

'Best save your energy for something other than curses, Brenna.'

She stilled. She *knew* that voice. Even in a wave of confusion, his voice anchored her, as it always had. But it couldn't be, could it? He was dead. She fumbled her way through the wool covering her. Finally it gave way, and a strip of moonlight revealed the rugged, familiar shadowy profile of a man, a man she had once loved. She sucked in a breath. Gripping the horse's mane, she turned closer to him for a better look. Everyone had believed him dead, including her, but here he was. Alive.

'Garrick?' she asked, still uncertain if her injuries and confusion filled her vision with delusions and memories of the past.

'Aye,' he answered. 'Glad to see you awake. Who

is Arthur? And why were you travelling without your father's men? You could have been killed.'

'You are not dead.'

He met her gaze. 'Nay,' he answered. His words were flat, lifeless things floating in the air.

'Am *I* dead?' she asked. It sounded more logical than being here in his arms after so much time had passed without a single word. After long believing him dead. After grieving him for months and forcing herself to move on and let go of her hopes and dreams of their life together.

'You are alive, as am I.'

'You've been gone over a year without a word. Where have you been? Why did you not write?' Shock drowned out her logic and reason.

They continued on in silence.

'I did not think I needed to.' His words chiselled through her confusion. She stared at him blankly as a muscle worked in his jaw.

'After all this time, *that* is all you have to say to me?' she asked. Her joy at seeing him alive and confusion over his manner with her quickly gave way to anger. She swatted him on the shoulder.

She stared up at him. His strong profile, chiselled features and prominent Adam's apple were so familiar. Dizziness made her body sway and he steadied her.

'Best you lean back against me before you topple off. You've a head injury.'

'Where have you been? Why did you not write?' she demanded, the fog of her mind cleared by her frustration. 'Why did you not let me know that you were alive and well?'

He stared off into the distance.

His silence lit her ire like dry tinder. 'You will answer me,' she demanded.

'It was for the best for you to be without me. It still is.' His words chipped away at her understanding of the world.

'What? We loved one another. We'd planned to marry. How was allowing me to believe you were dead and grieving you for the best?'

'Perhaps you can tell me who you were travelling with. And why. Only a fool would travel in such finery around these parts so late without guards.' His words cut through the night air.

Fool? She pushed away from him to lash out, but the world flipped over on itself. She settled herself back against him until the spinning stopped.

'Where are Arthur and his son?' She'd try a new tack to get him talking. Something that would help her get the easier answers. Such as where she was, how she'd got here and what had happened to them on their journey. She'd get to why he'd abandoned her and allowed her to believe he was dead later.

If she didn't throttle him before then.

'The men travelling with you?'

'Aye. Where are they? Answer me,' she demanded, a wave of panic washing over her at the thought of something having happened to them.

He said nothing.

'Where are they?' she asked again.

He shifted on his mount and avoided her gaze. She felt for his trews, found the spot behind his knee that she could reach and pinched him. Hard. Just as she used to when he'd tried to keep a secret from her.

'Saints be,' he cursed and grabbed her hand. 'Stop.'

'Then tell me. Now.'

He hesitated and sighed. 'They're dead. I wanted to wait until you had rested and been tended to before I told you.'

She froze. *Dead?* 'How? What happened to them?'

'I don't know what happened, but they were killed. I found your carriage overturned on my way to Westmoreland. All were dead except for you.'

How in the world could Arthur and his son be dead?

Her ears buzzed, then a deafening silence. Then slowly came back the clomping of the horse's hooves, the feel of her lungs rising and falling and the tingling of her fingers.

Guilt assaulted her and she gagged. She covered her mouth and another dry retch seized her as she clutched the plaid to try to hold on.

He slowed his horse. 'Easy,' he offered, pressing a strong hand to her back while holding her arm to steady her.

'I shouldn't have asked them to take me. I should have known better.' Tears threatened and anger burned the back of her eyes. Making a muck of things seemed one of the only things she was truly good at, and she hated it.

'You always were useless, Brenna. This union has great import. Stop asking questions about Mr Winters

and do your duty, like your sister and your brother, by
securing this arrangement. Be pleasing and obedient.
If you cannot do such, then leave me be.'

The memory of her father's harsh words before she'd
left for Oban a week ago to meet with her now fiancé,
Mr Stephen Winters, sent a flurry of trembles through
her body. Why had she been in such a hurry to return
home? Now Father would truly be furious with her, and
with good reason. She should have heeded his soldiers'
advice and waited to return tomorrow morn. This was
all her fault.

Garrick held her, but at a distance, as if careful to
touch her as little as possible. Yet another man who
thought her distasteful and lacking. Otherwise, why
would he have abandoned her and pretended to be dead
to escape her attentions?

'It is not your fault,' he assured her. 'It appeared to
be an ambush. I have seen them before, and there is
nothing you could have done. You are lucky to be alive,
as I believe they left you for dead.'

She wiped at her eyes, clutching his shoulder to balance herself as another wave of nausea passed. 'I…'
she began.

You were always so useless.

She shivered again and squeezed her eyes shut to
will the loop of words to stop their dull echo in her
head. No wonder Garrick had not come back for her.
Father was right. She was useless, and now she had
caused two men to die. All because she wished to be
home and sleep in her own bed rather than stay in Oban
another night with the dull and disinterested Mr Win-

ters. In a half-day, she could have safely ridden back in the family carriage with the Stewart caravan of soldiers.

'Quiet,' he stated, and pulled his horse to a stop.

His body tightened and he stilled. She opened her eyes. Something was wrong.

After studying something that Brenna couldn't see for far too long, Garrick turned his mount, and she felt herself sliding away from him as he guided the horse down the hillside. 'Hold on to his mane,' he whispered. 'We have to hide. *Now.*'

She remembered that sharp edge in his voice that he used only when he was serious. She clamped her mouth shut and gripped the horse's neck tightly. Something *was* wrong. They hid behind a large cluster of trees and waited.

Soon she saw shadows, a series of dark forms casting protruding profiles against the night sky. They were above them on the main road. One, two, three men, that she could see. Were there more? She clutched at the horse's mane and held her breath even though her heart hammered unevenly in her chest.

'Can't have gone far,' one man said. 'Why didn't you check and make sure she was dead?'

'Probably is dead. A foolish waste of time trailing after them. Just let the sot bury the girl. Even these bastards deserve to bury their dead, especially a pretty one like her.'

She swallowed the fear crawling along her skin. *They were English.* And brutal, by the sound of it. Pain gnawed at her nerves as shock roiled through her. How close had she come to dying? Worse, Arthur and his son were already dead. If Garrick hadn't saved her, she would be as well. She gripped his forearm and he rested his hand on hers and squeezed.

The men turned their mounts in their direction and began a steady advance towards them. Brenna froze. Garrick pulled the tartan back over her to shield her from view.

'Stay here and hide,' he ordered.

She heard the swish of a weapon pulled from its sheath and the mount shifted as he slid off the horse. What was he doing? Was he leaving her? She peeked out from the plaid and frowned. He was approaching them, and he was outnumbered.

Just like Garrick. He'd not back down from any-thing. Except for love. Except for her. He hadn't fought for them. He'd let her go without as much as a word. He'd allowed her to believe he was dead, he'd been so anxious to be rid of her. How had she not seen it be-fore? Had she imagined their deep attachment? She bit her lip to squelch the emotion welling within her. Had she driven him away somehow?

She wiped her eyes. Father was right. She mucked up everything. Why could she never do the right thing? Now her foolishness and need to come home early had cost two men their lives, and maybe even Garrick's now.

The clickety-clack crunch of hooves along the rocks grew louder, closer. Her heart pounded in her chest. Where was Garrick? She clutched the blanket over her face once more and her body trembled.

'Adams?' One of the men spoke.

'I see it,' the other answered.

'Could be the girl.'

'Aye.'

Footfalls edged closer and closer still. The horse shifted on its feet.

Anger and fear tangled within her.

What was she supposed to do now? Had Garrick left her as bait? *Where was he?* She shivered again and her breath came out in irregular spurts. She had no weapon and was still dizzy. What was he thinking? A groan and then a loud thud startled her, and she gripped the horse's mane. Was that Garrick or the other man? She peered out from the blanket and saw him battling two men, while a third lay splayed out on the ground.

Did he honestly expect her to stay here and do nothing when their very lives were at stake? *Blast.* Anger flushed her body. She'd not let Arthur and his son's deaths be for nothing. They deserved justice. Even if she didn't know how to fight, she could try. What did she have to lose now? She'd ruined everything already. She reached into the saddlebags, feeling for any sort of weapon she could find.

Finally, her hand closed over the leather-wrapped grip of a small dirk. She slid from the horse to the ground in a rather ungraceful flop and winced as she landed on her backside, covered in layers of blue silk. Once everything ceased spinning, she made her way through the cold, dewy grass on all fours, cursing her choice of dress as she dragged the heavy, soiled material behind her. The men battled as she crawled along the freezing ground. Once she was close enough, she sat back on her haunches, shut one of her eyes to try to focus the blurring forms into a single one and threw the blade. It hit the man in the back. She gasped and covered her mouth with her hand. He staggered forward before collapsing to the ground.

She didn't know if she was more shocked that she had hit him with the dagger at all or that she had killed him. Perhaps it didn't matter for, in the end, she'd saved them both.

Garrick knocked the other man out cold and then glared at her. 'What are you doing?'

'Helping.'

'Well, don't.' He stomped down the hillside, pulled her up to standing and supported her as they made their way back to the horse.

'You'd prefer I watch you get killed?'

'Aye. I'd rather that than *you* being killed.'

She shook her head. Perhaps she had been a bit impetuous, but it worked, hadn't it? Not that he would ever admit it. 'Just as mule-headed as you've always been.'

'You're one to say. You've suffered a head injury yet insist on thrusting yourself into a situation I clearly had in hand.'

'Did you?' she challenged, crossing her arms against her chest and lifting an eyebrow at him.

'Aye,' he griped, levelling his gaze at her.

He lifted her, plopped her unceremoniously on the horse and mounted behind her. He wrapped his arm around her waist, pulling her flush against his hard, muscular chest, before loosening his hold and sliding further back on the saddle as if he couldn't stand to be any closer. As the horse began its journey up the hill back to the main road, she wondered why she'd ever grieved this detestable man at all.

Chapter Three

'You could just say thank you,' Brenna grumbled.

Garrick would have preferred to swallow a handful of nettles. It didn't matter if she might be right. She exasperated him as finely as he remembered, and he clenched his jaw until it ached.

The woman could have got herself killed. And he couldn't lose anyone else. Why couldn't she understand that? The sooner he reached Westmoreland to deposit her for care under someone else's watch, the better. Until then, he'd try to understand how the hell she'd got herself into such a fine mess.

'Care to tell me why a band of English mercenaries are hunting you through the Highlands? And where you learned to throw a blade?' Garrick tugged the reins for his mount to set off for Westmoreland once more.

They were safe. For now.

'As much as I don't wish to admit it, the throw was luck. And mercenaries? How do you know that is who they were? There is no reason for them to be after us.

Perhaps we were just in the wrong place at the wrong time.'

'Mercenaries do everything with purpose. I've seen many similar scenes over the last year. It was intentional. You were targeted. I want to know why.' His words were tight and clipped. Anger and upset at almost losing her bubbled in his gut.

'I can't imagine why. Arthur and his son were merely bringing me back home.'

'Who are they? Why were you not travelling with your father's men with proper protection? Those men didn't look capable of protecting you. One of them was just a boy.'

Brenna squared her shoulder and shifted further away from him. 'Father selected a husband for me. He sent me south to meet with him one final time to settle the terms of our engagement and pending marriage. A Mr Stephen Winters. He divides his time between London, Edinburgh and Oban. His driver, Arthur, and his son agreed to take me back to Glenhaven this eve rather than tomorrow. They worked for him, this man I am to marry.'

Every fibre of Garrick's body tightened and ached. *Saints be.* She was to marry another man *and* he was English? How much could a man take? He shook his head. While he knew he'd purposefully and wilfully given up on the idea of marrying Brenna, knowing she was promised to another made jealousy bloom tight and full in his chest. And anger too. She had moved on quite easily from the idea of him once she'd believed he was dead.

'And what of us?' he asked. 'What of *our* understanding?'

'What understanding? We were not officially engaged. I waited for you, but you never came home.
You never wrote. Nothing. It is as if you are a ghost
returned from the dead. It's been over a year without
a word from you to anyone. Not me, nor your family.
What else was I and everyone else to believe?'

'As you can see, I'm not dead, nor a ghost.'

'Aye, here you are,' she added under her breath.

'What does that mean?' he asked, irritation sharpening the edge of his words once more.

Silence was his answer.

'Why did you not wait for me?' The words surprised
even him as they fell from his lips. He'd intentionally
let her go. He had no claim or demands he could make.
Not really. Heat flushed his face. He sounded like old
Garrick. Lovesick and hopeful.

It turned his stomach.

She scoffed, facing him. 'Wait! I did. It's been over
a year. What were we all supposed to think, especially
me? Should I have waited for ever?'

Aye.

But he knew it was a foolish and faulty answer. He'd
let her go by not promising her something, by not writing to her—to anyone, for that matter—and he knew
that. Each time he'd tried to put his heart on the page
and pen such a letter to let her go, he'd batted the parchment into a ball and tossed it in the rubbish. He couldn't
let her go, but he also couldn't face his shame.

He couldn't admit he wasn't the man she deserved. He still couldn't.

How could he tell her his sister was dead because of him? He hadn't been able to bear to tell his family or her of his failure. Then he'd stayed away because of guilt and had joined up again as a soldier, despite the duties he had as laird. And now? He didn't deserve happiness after all he'd done. Not any more. He'd killed too many, lost too much, and the colourful beauty he used to see in the world was now a fitful array of charcoal and grey.

'Answer me,' she demanded. Her words yanked him back to the present. Her eyes narrowed on him like a quiver, which he didn't like at all. He was not the one who'd gone and got engaged, now, was he?

'Why? Does it matter what I wished now? You have made your choice.' He shifted on his mount and grunted involuntarily before sucking in a pained breath.

She patted his forearm, and he winced, pulling away from her touch on instinct. He'd taken a blade to his arm, as well as his side during his struggle with the men, and they pained him like the devil. 'You're injured,' she stated, tugging up his tunic sleeve to reveal the wound.

'As are you,' he answered blandly. 'A fine pair we make.'

'We must stop. Wrap it, at least.'

'No time.'

'Wait. Where are we going?' she asked, scanning the road ahead. A thread of uncertainty unravelled in her voice.

'To Westmoreland. Where else would I be headed? I am finally returning to see my family. They can tend to you until your brother can collect you, and I can tell them of my journey.'

And that I failed my mission to rescue Ayleen and that she is dead. Because of me.

'You have not heard?' Her words were quiet and hesitant.

'About...?' he asked, his heart picking up speed in his chest.

She pressed a hand to his uninjured arm and turned in his hold to face him. 'Garrick, the King and his men seized Westmoreland. Your family isn't there.'

What?

He'd heard her words, but they were nonsensical. 'Why?' He chuckled. 'I don't understand. Where else would they be? Cairn wouldn't have just abandoned it without a fight. And mother...' The more he thought of it, the more he couldn't understand what Brenna was saying, and his fingers began to tingle.

'Let's stop for a moment. I...' The way she said the words and the sympathy in her eyes chilled his blood. His legs numbed. Gooseflesh rose along his arms.

'Tell me what has happened,' he demanded, bringing his mount to a stop.

She hesitated and he gripped her shoulders tightly, almost shaking her. 'You will *tell* me. Tell me all of it. *Now*,' he commanded, his voice sounding harsher than he intended.

'I... I don't wish to,' she stuttered, her voice just above a tremble. A single tear ran down her cheek.

He loosened his hold, closed his eyes and lowered his voice. 'Please. Tell me.'

Finally, she released a shaky breath and her light blue gaze held his. The emotion in it cut him to the quick. He knew her words would break him further. He prepared himself to absorb what he was sure would be a heavy blow.

'Your brother would not give in to the tax collector's demands. They were made an example of by the King's men. By the time we heard of the dispute and the outcome, it was too late for anyone to intercede.' She dropped her gaze and sniffed. 'I am so sorry. We all are.'

He swallowed and cleared his throat to ask the question he needed to. The one he dreaded. 'Are they dead?'

'Aye. It has been almost six months.' She worried her hands in her lap. 'Westmoreland was seized and many of the clan sought refuge with the Camerons and other clans farther north.'

He pressed his lips together and commanded himself to breathe and not scream in anguish. He would one day, but not now. Not while they were still in danger. While he didn't care much for his own survival, he did care for Brenna's. He always had. And now she was all he had left in this world. She could still live and be happy, unlike him, who had nothing and no one.

Not any more.

Moments ago, he'd only been bemoaning the loss of Ayleen. Now, he realised his absence from Westmoreland had cost him everything. What had remained

of his clan, his family and his heritage, was now lost
for ever.

Because of him. Because he hadn't been there to
protect them. He'd been off wallowing in his shame and
guilt over Ayleen, telling himself they were better off
without him. How had he been such a fool once more?

He steeled his heart and pushed down his sorrow.
How had this happened? All of them were dead. And
he'd not been there for them as laird, brother and son.
His throat ached, his chest squeezed and what grief
he'd felt this morn was now compounded. By staying
away, he had killed them all. What was he good for?

Nothing, it seemed.

He stilled.

Or maybe one last thing.

Purpose flared in him like a winking candle battling the breeze. He didn't have time to grieve. Keeping Brenna alive was now his sole focus. After that,
he would have his revenge on those who had killed his
family and scattered his clan to the ends of Scotland,
or he'd die trying.

He sucked in greedy breaths to quell the rage and
deep ache of regret filling his chest. After a few more
moments of silence, he stared off in the distance, counting to slow his heart as well as his grief. It worked
on the battlefield, so he hoped it might anchor him
now. He could feel Brenna's gaze on him like the sun
warming his face. He dared not meet it. Otherwise,
he might crush her in his arms and seek the solace his
soul craved. And, if there was one thing he no longer
deserved in his life, it was her.

He tightened his jaw and clenched his shaking hands on the reins. He would keep his anger close for now. Feed on it and focus solely on getting Brenna home to Glenhaven safely.

Her life and happiness was all that mattered now.

Suddenly, a piece of logic slid into place for him. 'Is what happened to Westmoreland and my family why your father was in such haste to arrange a union for you with an Englishman?' Garrick asked as he tugged down his coat sleeves.

She nodded. 'He hoped it would offer us some protection after what happened to your clan. Father is ailing, and Ewan has not settled into his role as future laird yet.'

'Has your brother taken no wife?' Garrick could not keep the surprise from his voice. Ewan was well beyond the age for marriage, especially as the future laird of his clan.

'Nay. As you know, he has long been reluctant to tether himself to anyone, much to Father's annoyance.'

'I do remember that.' Garrick shifted the reins in his hands and stretched them.

'Aye. After losing Emogene, he fears making a poor choice, so he makes none.'

'And he has a right to fear such,' Garrick answered. He knew all about mistakes and regrets. One poor choice could haunt a person for a lifetime. And he seemed to be making one poor choice after another, with no end in sight.

'Where will we go?' Brenna shivered and rubbed her arms.

'Shelter for now. It is too dangerous to travel at night, especially if those men are still after you,' he answered.

Then, he'd return her to her family in Glenhaven. After that, he wasn't sure. He was now a man without a home or family. All he had left in the world was her, and he didn't have her at all.

Chapter Four

Brenna leaned back against Garrick as they travelled across an open meadow into the cover of the edge of forest that would lead them away from the road to Westmoreland, and south towards her home of Glenhaven. How many times had she ridden up this final stretch of road by coach eager to see Garrick emerge from the castle doors, and ridden away with a twinge of sadness on her heart for missing him before she'd even exited the drive? Too many to count during their courtship. Now, it seemed a painful reminder of all they had both lost. The road didn't lead to anyone's home any more.

Brenna struggled to fully sit up. Fatigue and her throbbing skull made wakefulness a challenge for her, but she didn't dare drift off. Arthur and his son Roland were dead. Garrick had returned. The world she had woken to this morn had flipped on end, and she had no idea what would happen next.

She shifted forward to keep space between Garrick and her, but the pull of her body to his and the heat emanating from his solid, muscular frame made it difficult. When he cinched his arm tighter around her waist, she had no choice but to relax against him, and the familiar warmth of his body pooled slowly through her fingers and toes. Soon the chattering of her teeth ceased, reducing the hammering in her head.

'Where have you been?' she asked, her words loud against the backdrop of a rippling stream and a low hoot of an owl. She had kept her question at bay as long as her heart would allow. He'd just learned he'd lost his family and his clan, and she should have heeded that and waited for another moment, but her mind would not let loose of its need to know and understand why he had left and abandoned her.

Had they not been in love? She'd thought they would live the rest of their lives together as man and wife and build a family. But then he'd left to rescue Ayleen and had never returned. No word, no letter, not a hint of where he was or if he was even alive. She had grieved him for months before giving in to Father's demands for her to wed.

Yet now here he was, without a word of explanation.

She deserved an explanation at least, didn't she?

But he said nothing.

The horse crossed a bevy of water, splashing through what would be iced over in a few weeks. They began an ascent and her body pressed more tightly against Garrick, causing his words to edge across her cheek like an intimate whisper when he finally answered. 'It might be easier to say where I haven't been. Here.' His voice dripped with regret, but her own hurt at being left made her unable to let it drop.

'That much is obvious. Answer me. I deserve at least that, do I not?'

She felt his chest rise and fall against her back, and what might have been a curse escaped his lips. They slowed at the edge of a cave. He dismounted, drew his blade from his waist belt and handed her the reins.

'Wait here. If someone comes, ride to safety. I'll find you if need be.'

Before she could utter a word, he disappeared into the dark mouth of the cave. He was gone so long, she feared he had been swallowed by it. Finally he emerged, took the reins and guided his mount to a nearby tree. Close enough to a stream to get water, the horse walked over and drank its fill. Brenna rubbed the stallion's neck, revelling in the animal's simple satisfaction. If only she could be pleased so easily.

She turned and found Garrick staring at her, his eyes haunted and lost as they caught a shaft of moonlight. His breath coiled up into the air. He broke the moment and came to her, taking her hand to help her dismount. She landed and grabbed his wounded forearm by accident. He winced but held steady as she gained her footing on the uneven ground.

She relented on getting an answer. For now.

'We need to tend to your wound,' she said, gesturing to his arm.

'Aye. And your head. All in good time. Let us get settled inside first. While we can't build a large fire without attracting attention, it will be warmer in the cave away from the wind, and we've access to water from the stream.'

She nibbled her lip, narrowing her gaze at the dark mouth of the cave. 'Animals?'

He smirked. 'None. I checked. I remember what happened the last time we were in a cave.'

She chuckled and shivered. 'Aye. I still twitch at the thought of those tiny bats whizzing by my hair.'

'While we might encounter a shrew or two, we'll be fine.'

Would they?

She hesitated. He gestured for her to enter ahead of him.

'If you sit on the western side, you'll avoid the wind,' he offered as they walked into the dark, damp mouth of the cave. 'Stay here.' He left without another word.

She wrapped the wool tartan around her and let the dark, dismal space cocoon her. She knew she should be grateful, and she was. They were alive. She just wished she didn't have to spend the night here with Garrick. Alone. She wished Arthur and his son weren't dead. That Garrick's family and home hadn't been lost. That she could be brave and stick up for herself, like her sister Moira.

But wishes were empty, useless things young lasses clung to for hope and were not for her any more. Practicality would serve her best, and marrying Stephen Winters was the option that would provide her family and her the most favour with the King and the most protection going forward. Even if he was dull and not the man she'd once hoped to marry.

But Garrick didn't seem to be that man any more either. The man she'd known wouldn't have abandoned her. He would have fought for her, for them, for their future, and not hidden himself away.

Her eyes adjusted to the darkness as she sat at the mouth of the cave. Soon, Garrick entered carrying an extra plaid, his saddlebags and a small lit torch that he wedged between two rocks to illuminate their space. He unfurled the plaid and laid it out on the ground, and Brenna settled on it with her back to the cave wall. He sat beside her, dumped the contents of his saddlebags on the plaid and went through them. 'We've enough food for two to three days if needed, but we'll have to find some hay or a place for Montgomerie to graze.'

'You named your horse Montgomerie?'

He shifted items around and avoided her gaze. 'Aye.'

She nibbled her lip. 'For me?'

He didn't answer, which was all the answer she needed.

'Do you still remember the poem?'

'Nay. I've long since forgotten such foolish things. Have some dried meat.' He began to pack the saddlebags with great care.

Her cheeks heated. Well, she had not. Alexander Montgomerie was her favourite Scottish poet and, while Garrick might pretend the name of his horse had little significance, she was not daft. He did everything with purpose. He was calculated and precise, as a soldier should be. He always had been. Even though many things about him had changed, she doubted that had. He had cared for her as she had cared for him, despite the chasm between them now.

She bit into the salty meat and forced herself to eat, as she'd not had a bite since breaking her fast this morn. They sat in silence and ate as a light rain began to fall. If it had been a year ago, the night might have been beautiful, intimate and romantic. Now, it felt almost unbearable to be sitting here beside him. She swallowed the last bit of meat, unable to taste it at all, and pulled her legs up hugging them to her chest.

Garrick ripped a strip from the plaid and held it out in the rain before kneeling before her. He reached for her chin, his calloused fingertips skimming her smooth skin, igniting a rush of heat, awareness and longing through her, and she flinched.

'I'll not hurt you,' he said, frowning at her. 'Your injury needs to be cleaned so I can assess its seriousness.'

She relented, facing him in the flickering light. He began to wash her temple with one hand while clutching her chin with the other, and that achingly familiar thrill her body had always felt from his warm touch spread through her until it became hot and bright. She gripped his wrist and he stilled.

'Did I hurt you?'

Aye. Over hundreds of days.

'Nay,' she lied, removing her hand and releasing a breath. She commanded her body to cease its intense response to his touch, but it was hard to unwind the tight coil of attraction to him she'd always had despite what he'd done. Even now he was still the most handsome man she'd ever known. Fine lines flared out around the corners of his pale green eyes, his sandy hair covering part of his face. She could remember the feel of the stubble on his cheeks against her fingertips, and the way he would sigh when she'd press her lips to his angular jawline.

How many nights had she dreamed of his face and prayed for his return? So many that her body ached for him even still, even now when she knew he had abandoned her. But it no longer mattered. The past was just that. Now, she was engaged to another, and Garrick had let her go. He was simply following his duty as a soldier by protecting her now. He didn't love her. Perhaps he never had.

Her stomach lurched at such a realisation, crushing the trill of awareness she'd felt moments ago from his touch.

'Are you finished?' she asked.

'Patience.'

Blast. She shifted under his hold, willing time to pass more swiftly.

'Tell me more of your journey,' he commanded, continuing to clean her wound.

'We were travelling from Oban back to Glenhaven. Mr Winters has shipping interests in that area, so Father agreed for us to meet there for our final terms of engagement, even though Father was too ill to join us. While he sent Stewart soldiers down to accompany me to Oban earlier in the week, they stayed to gather supplies for Father, and had a plan to travel home on the morrow. I was eager to return. Stephen offered his driver Arthur and his son to escort me home today in his carriage, so I could tell Father of the news that my marriage was settled. I hoped it might ease some of his worry to know it had been secured.'

She didn't add that she hadn't been able to bear to stay a day longer. Stephen was not exactly the doting, interested fiancé a woman dreamed of. He was arrogant and drear at best. She doubted he held any interest in her beyond her lineage. His union with her was an arrangement born of necessity to please the King, nothing more. He'd made that clear upon her latest visit.

At least she had made a decision to please Father. He had to acknowledge her worth and willingness to help him and her clan now. She could hardly wait to see the pride on his face when she showed him the finalised terms of her upcoming marriage. He would finally see her value, and she clung to that hope even now.

'Why Oban?' he asked.

'It was halfway between Glenhaven and where Stephen resides in Edinburgh half of the year. Father suggested it and Stephen agreed.'

Garrick frowned. 'Not quite halfway between the two, if you ask me.'

She nodded in agreement, and then winced as he touched a tender spot along her scalp. 'You know my father. He is formidable. Stephen also knew it was nowhere near halfway between the two, but he allowed Father to win that round of battle.'

'Did you see your sister and brother-in-law while you were visiting in Oban?'

'Nay. I knew Moira would not approve of the match. She does not know.'

Garrick stopped and met her gaze, lifting his brow to encourage her to continue. Brenna shifted and fussed with the tartan draped around her. 'Moira never gave up on the idea you would return.'

Nor did I. Not really.

But Brenna refused to concede such an idea aloud. It did not matter what she felt or wanted now. She had made her decision, and so had he.

Garrick nodded and returned his attention to her wound, albeit his touch seemed harsher now. 'Ow!' she said. 'I believe it has been rubbed raw. That is enough.'

He ignored her and moved her hair back. 'What about while you were on the road? Where did the men come from that attacked your carriage?'

'The weather was fine and I remember listening to Arthur and Roland chatting above on the driver's bench. The scenery rolled by, and I fell asleep to the lulling motion of the carriage. I woke to the sound of raised voices. When I peered out of the carriage window and enquired about what was happening, a man with a scarred face approached, opened the door and hit me before I could do anything. That was the last I remembered until I awoke on horseback with you.'

It didn't seem real. It was as if it had all happened to someone else, but it hadn't.

'Nasty gash you earned for your trouble.' He kneaded his fingers gently through her hair and her breath stuttered from his touch. 'And quite the egg-shaped lump. Do you still feel dizzy?'

'Nay,' she answered. 'Not like before. I think the food, water and rest has helped.'

'And you've no idea why they attacked?' he asked.

'I can't think of any.' She extended her open hand. 'The cloth?'

He shook his head. 'Let me rinse it and get more water. Then you can repay me for my efforts.'

She felt along her temple and winced. It could have been much worse. Perhaps it had been best that she'd not seen Arthur or his son on the road. Her pulse quickened. 'When can we return to collect Arthur and Roland? We can't just leave them there unburied.'

Garrick returned and sat in front of her. 'For now, we must. Those men might be still looking for you and watching the scene. They seemed eager to make sure you were dead. Perhaps they believed you could identify them.'

'Why would they care if they are just thieving?'

'Good question. I think a band of thieves wouldn't have been searching for you to make sure you were dead but would've moved on to their next target. That is why I believe they were mercenaries and hired for their trouble.'

She paused. He had a point. 'Do you think there are any more? You killed two of them.'

'If I oversaw an attack on such a carriage, I would have had at least five men. Two for lookouts and three for execution of the task. If that is the case with you, then that leaves three. The one I left unconscious but not dead, and the other two we didn't see.' He handed her the cloth, newly rinsed and soaked with water.

She gestured to him. 'You'll need to remove your coat and tunic.'

He hesitated.

'I have seen your bare chest before, if you remember.' Her cheeks heated at such memories, and she clutched the cloth tightly. 'Now is not the time for modesty. We're sleeping in a cave together, after all,' she added.

Slowly, he attempted to remove his coat but stilled, his face scrunched up in pain. 'Let me help.' She rose to her knees and eased the coat sleeve off. It was then she saw that the front of his tunic, not just his sleeve, was soaked in blood. 'Garrick! Why did you not stop so this could be tended to? I thought you had a mere cut to your arm. This wound to your side is sizeable.'

'I've had much worse.' He grunted, pulling the tunic off in one deft movement with his good arm. His breathing was laboured from the effort, and the wound began to ooze blood.

She scrambled, tore a strip of fabric from her shift and pressed it to his side. He sucked in a breath at the force of it and attempted to pull her hand away.

'If you don't leave me to tend to this, Garrick Mac-Lean, by all that's holy...' she muttered.

He chuckled and let his hand drop away. 'Forgot about the crinkle you get in your brow when you're riled up.' He stared at her, and the smile he'd shown but a moment ago fell away. 'I've missed it.'

She held his gaze, her pulse quickening from his words. *And I you.*

He cleared his throat, his neck flushing with colour as he looked away, as if he'd just realised what he'd said and regretted it.

'You'll not distract me with your flattery,' she added to break the current in the air between them. 'You need stitches to close this or you'll bleed to death.'

'And you'll be the one to do it, will you?' he challenged, still looking away.

She squared her shoulders. 'Aye, I will. Anything in your bag of use for that?'

'Unfortunately.' He sighed and moved the bag closer to her.

She smiled and rummaged through it with her unoccupied hand. When she spied the small kit, she opened it. 'Quite the medicinal kit you have here.'

'As a soldier, I learned to be able to tend to my own wounds or others under my care. Otherwise, one doesn't last too long in battle.'

She found the needle and thread and set it aside.

'Where have you learned such skills?'

'A woman in the village. She came to us after her own clan, the MacDougalls, had been relocated by the King and his men. Used to be a healer. I asked her to teach me. You could say that I grew weary of being useless.'

He balked. 'What are you talking about? You were never useless.'

'Wasn't I, though?' she asked, threading the needle and avoiding his gaze. 'I sat about that castle waiting to be married off. Moira had her interests in botany and herbs, Ewan spent time learning the duties of being a laird and I sat absorbed in gowns, bows and flirtations without a true care or interest in the world.'

At least, that was what Father always said.

Garrick gripped her arm. 'You were never such to me.'

'But not useful enough to return and lay claim to, was I?' She pulled her hand away. 'You might want to find a stick to bite on before I stitch this up. It will hurt like the devil.'

Chapter Five

Garrick bit down on the stick he'd found and groaned. While he'd oft dreamt of Brenna's touch on his skin while he'd been away this past year, this was not quite the caress he'd hoped for. Sweat beaded his forehead and upper lip with each movement of the needle in and out of his skin. *Deuces*. When he thought he couldn't take a moment longer, he felt her tug once more to tie off the stitching. Then her lips skimmed along his skin as she bit off the end of the thread. His body quaked from the feel of her lush lips on his bare flesh, and he sucked in a breath commanding himself to focus on their survival.

This was not the time to be distracted. Too much was at stake. Namely, Brenna's life.

Her fingertips lingered along his side, and he thought he might die from the combination of agony and bliss. 'Lord above,' she murmured. Her hand trailed along the raised scars puckering his body. He swallowed hard. They were a permanent memory of a time he'd like to forget. He clambered for his blood-stained tunic and attempted to shrug it on. He didn't want her sympathy.

'Let me help you,' she whispered, edging closer to him, guiding the fabric over and down his torso. He was shivering. From shock, her touch or the memory of that day of his injuries, he didn't know. Nor did it matter. He closed his eyes, began counting and took in deep breaths to slow the hammering of his heart in hopes it would also quell his trembling. She didn't need his weakness.

He slid back beside her to lean against the cold but solid cave wall. He would collect himself like he always did and move on. Feeling and remembering would not change the past. Those men were still dead. His sister was still dead. Hell, his mother and brother were dead, and most likely countless other men and women of his clan. All because of him and his bloody weakness. While he'd not thought it possible to despise himself more now than he had this morn, he did. He was responsible for more than just Ayleen's death now. His hands were soaked in blood and loss.

Brenna settled a blanket over both of them and sidled up to him, her side pressed against his own. He should have moved away, but he didn't. She was all he had to link him to the past. The only flickering flame of light left in his life. Although he didn't deserve her and wouldn't allow himself to love her, he needed some small seed of comfort at this moment to keep himself from screaming aloud in anguish and grief. He clenched his jaw and blinked back the emotion that threatened. He didn't deserve to live, but she did.

'Cold,' she whispered.

He thought about wrapping his good arm about her for a moment, but he didn't dare. He didn't trust himself. 'Staying together will help,' he said.

As will keeping my distance. But he couldn't have both. Not today.

Not ever, it seemed.

'What is our plan?' she asked.

A good question. 'We can't go to Westmoreland.'

'What of Glenhaven? Surely we would be safe there?'

'Aye,' he answered. 'It is the best and closest option to get you the care you need. We will have to stay here the night, though. Then, we can pack up in the morning and journey there. I'm sure your father will be thrilled to know I am alive,' he added dryly.

Brenna woke with a dull, pounding ache at her temple. She squinted at the winking rays of sunshine sparkling at the opening of the cave. Garrick's warm arm was wrapped around her back and shoulder, and she was snuggled against his chest with her arm draped across his waist. She should have moved. It wasn't decent. She snuggled closer instead.

Decency had got her nowhere so far. She'd done all that had been expected of her in her role as the youngest daughter of a laird. She had dressed well, been polite and preened herself to within an inch of reason to get the attention of the right men for Father's sake— all to end up here in a cave with the man she had once hoped to marry, while engaged to a man who by all accounts would forget her name if it weren't a requirement. Stephen Winters had not been an impressive man in any way when she'd met him. Truth be told, he was a bit of a gomeral.

She snuggled closer to Garrick, savouring what would most likely be her last time to do so. She smiled at the steady, even rise and fall of his chest as he slept and the solid, safe feel of him holding her. He'd always seen and valued her in a way others hadn't, and she had believed he'd loved her. But how could you love someone and not return? He'd allowed everyone to believe he was dead, even her. Losing him had set her adrift, and she'd grieved him and the dream of the life she'd thought they share together. How had she been so wrong? Why had she not seen the truth? That he hadn't cared for her at all.

She shivered.

'I can almost hear you thinking,' he said, his voice husky with sleep.

'How long have you been awake?'

'Just a few minutes. I stayed awake most of the night to make sure we hadn't been followed. Drifted off for a few hours in the early morn. Did you sleep?'

'Aye,' she answered, her mind still full of confusion and uncertainty.

He rubbed her arm absently for a few moments and then stilled, as if he realised he shouldn't be. He shifted and sat up, removing his arm from her waist. The feeling of loss was instantaneous and made her body ache, much to her chagrin. She shouldn't miss the touch of a man who didn't want her or love her, but she did all the same.

'How long will it take us to get to Glenhaven?'

'Longer than I'd like,' he answered. 'We need to move before the sun is fully up. If you need to…' He gestured to the woods.

'Aye. I won't be long.'

'Don't go far,' he answered as he followed her out of the mouth of the cave, heading in a different direction for privacy.

The woods sighed around her, as if the ground was also waking slowly this morn. Dew dusted the plants that poked through the dirt of the forest floor, and a few lone birds hopped from branch to branch in search of food. A doe off in the distance was grazing along with its mate. Brenna finished her ablutions and headed to the trickling stream. The feel of the cool water on her hands and face refreshed her despite the early-morning chill.

A branch snapped behind her. 'You're quite a difficult woman to find. Although the dress did help. Not many blue silk gowns out here in the woods.'

She froze. *That voice.* It was one of the men who had been searching for them last night. She would recognise it anywhere. She curled her palm around a large rock and hid it in the dense folds of her gown. Her heart hammered in her chest, and she rose slowly, catching sight of Garrick out of the corner of her eye outside the mouth of the cave. He saw her and knew she was in danger.

She turned to the stranger and he grabbed her arm,

yanking her close to him. So close, she could see the wide, dark pupils of his eyes and the unmistakable hatred in them as well. But she didn't even know the man. Why in the world did he hate her so?

No matter.

She'd not wait to find out. She lifted the rock in her other hand and swung until it made contact with his jaw. He cursed and his hold weakened long enough for her to break free and run from him, but she wasn't fast enough in her thin slippers on the slick ground. He lunged for her legs and caught her ankle, which brought her crashing flat onto the cold, hard earth, knocking the wind out of her.

She squirmed, clutching at the dirt and moss to gain purchase as she struggled for air, but he dragged her back. Kicking hard, she connected with his shoulder and he let go. Before she could rise, a blade flew by her in a whish and the man fell to the ground.

Finally, her lungs filled with the cold morning air, and she gasped in relief. Panting for breath, she clutched the leaves, attempting to rise.

Garrick rushed to her, sliding onto his knees into the wet grass and leaves. He clutched Brenna's face in his hands. 'Are you hurt?' His eyes searched her own.

'Nay,' she answered. Her voice and hands shook. She'd almost killed a man. Again.

He released a breath and relaxed. 'What were you thinking? Why did you not wait for my aid?'

'I couldn't afford to wait. And I might have been

dead before you reached me.' She accepted his hand and allowed him to pull her up to standing.

He paled and she realised the error of her words.

Blast. 'I am sorry. I didn't mean...'

'You could have got yourself killed. *Again.*' He ignored her earlier implication and shook his head. 'Come on. We need to leave in case there are others, which I believe there are.' He grabbed her hand and tugged her along.

'Shouldn't we see if he has something on his person that might help us find out who he is and why he is after us?'

They rushed to the dead man and Garrick tugged at his coat. 'He's still alive, but barely.'

'Why are you after me?' she demanded.

The man smiled at her as blood oozed from the corner of his mouth. 'You'll know soon enough, lass. I'd hate to ruin the surprise.'

And with that he was dead.

Garrick cursed and let go of him. The man's body flopped back to the ground.

'You search the left side of him and I'll search the right,' he commanded. 'Quickly.'

'I can't help but notice that you have great ease with searching a dead man,' she said, staring hesitantly at the man's body.

Garrick stilled and said nothing.

Her cheeks heated. Why had she said that? 'I'm sorry. That was a foolish thing to say.'

'No matter.'

She tugged some papers and correspondence bound with a ribbon out of the man's coat pocket.

'You might want to look away for this next bit,' Garrick suggested. 'There's another place I need to look.'

She blushed and turned away. While she didn't know exactly where he was searching, she had a fine idea of the general area.

'Ah! As I thought. It doesn't matter if you're a mercenary, soldier or farmer. You use the same practice for subterfuge. Done?' he asked.

'Aye,' she answered and faced him, extending the papers she'd found in the man's pockets.

He added them to the small dark satchel he'd found. 'We'll put them in the saddlebag and look at them later. But, for now, we must go.'

Saints be.

She paused.

He watched her face. 'What?'

'I'm not sure we should go to Glenhaven.'

'Why not?' he asked.

She pointed to his hands. 'We could be putting my family in danger. That is the satchel Father gave me as a gift for Stephen. I gave it to him myself when I arrived.'

'Surely not? One satchel looks much like another.'

'Is there one gold piece and all of the rest silver?'

He tugged open the bag and poured the contents into his hand. One lone gold coin shone amidst a sea of silver ones.

'It could be a coincidence.' Garrick frowned at his own statement.

'You heard the man. He said I would know soon

enough why they were after me. That he didn't wish to ruin the surprise.' Her voice shook as she said the words.

'Let us go,' he whispered tugging gently on her hand. 'We'll work this out, but not here in the middle of the woods, out in the open. Come.'

She blinked back at him. None of it made sense—the carriage attack, these men hunting her and the pouch of coin from her father on the dead man's person.

Nothing made sense any more.

He tugged her hand once more. 'Trust me.'

Meeting his gaze, Brenna nodded. She didn't trust him. Not really. Not after all that had happened. But what other choice did she have? She was being hunted for reasons she did not know and by men bent on seeing her dead. Her family could be in danger or...

Her steps faltered at another idea that cropped into her head. Could her father be involved? But why? How? Neither theory made a whit of sense and the latter was beyond unsettling to think upon. She picked up her skirts with her free hand and kept up with Garrick's furious pace through the forest.

Her heart pounded in her chest as they climbed the small incline back to the cave. She packed up their meagre belongings and Garrick readied Montgomerie, who had been grazing along a tuft of grass off to the side of the cave. Brenna attempted to wipe some of the mud and blood from her gown but gave up and wrapped a wool plaid around herself instead. She stepped into Garrick's open palm as he offered to help boost her up and onto Montgomerie. He swung up easily behind her.

'Ready?' he asked.

'Nay,' she answered, unable to keep the tremble out of her reply.

'Neither am I, but we go anyway. We'll head south, but off the main road to Glenhaven, until we can stop to look at those letters and the pouch and we're certain it is safe to do so. We'll not risk putting your family in danger in case there are others still following us.'

'Aye.'

She glanced back at the cave and where the dead man lay amongst the morning sunlight and tried to work out why and how she'd even got to this place. How had a carriage ride home turned into this? And how had her father's pouch of coin ended up in the hands of a man trying to kill her?

She stared down at the small garnet ring on her fourth finger. This simple engagement to an Englishman to help protect her family was becoming anything but.

Chapter Six

The western Highland terrain was as unforgiving as his past, and Garrick slowed Montgomerie as they began a steep incline along the narrow, rugged pass that hugged the coastline of Loch Linnhe and would bring them into the outskirts of Glencoe and if needed on down to Oban to Blackmore.

Even during the day, it was a far more dangerous route, riddled with unforgiving climbs, shifting rocks and high winds, but a less travelled one. They had a better chance travelling this route than the main road where they might encounter more men still looking for them. If they could reach Glenhaven in a day's time, they would be safe but, if they ended up needing to travel to Oban to seek refuge with Brenna's sister and brother-in-law at Blackmore, there would be at least two more days of travel, most likely three, before they would reach the outskirts of Oban, especially along this terrain.

Unease settled into Garrick's bones. There was something he was missing. He knew that. His care for Brenna, losing what remained of his family and his own fatigue blocked his reason and logic. He cared for her too much, and the loss of Westmoreland, his family and his clan only clouded his judgement further. He cursed himself. He had to keep his distance physically and emotionally so he could protect her, but how could he do that? They were travelling together, pressed limb to limb, and the contact and memories it conjured within him were as pungent as they'd always been.

Always were too soft to be laird. Why God struck yer brother down and not ye, I'll ne'er understand.

The memory of his father's words after his brother's burial cut through Garrick deeply, for he feared the old man was right, as he had been about most matters with the clan. It was the other parts, of being a father and husband, that he hadn't quite got right.

Garrick couldn't afford to make any mistakes with Brenna. Her life depended on his decisions and the burden of that weighed upon him like slate in his veins.

Montgomerie skidded along the slick moss and small rocks, and Garrick shifted his weight to help offset the strain on his beloved stallion. Soon, they would need to dismount and walk, as the next section appeared more treacherous, especially in this weather, and far too dangerous for them to ride through even on a horse as experienced as his.

Brenna had not spoken a word since their escape from the man in the woods earlier in the morn. They rode on in an eerie silence. A silence that he found unsettling as the hours passed one after another. He frowned. The woman he'd known a year ago would have chatted away to avoid silence about the latest fashion, the exploits of her sister or whatever else she'd found of interest in the latest broadsheet. But this woman, this Brenna, he found he didn't know at all. He couldn't help but wonder what had happened while he'd been away.

She knew how to down a man with a blade, didn't hesitate to assist him in a fight and had agreed to marry an Englishman she didn't know for the sake of her clan and to please her father. The last year had changed them both, it seemed.

He batted away what role he'd played in such a change. Had his absence pushed her to this? To choose a future with a man she did not know to please a father who had never really respected her or her worth? While Garrick's regrets and guilt wouldn't keep her safe, his fierce resolve to protect her would. He would focus on that and that alone. He could grieve his family and recriminate himself for his mistakes later, but for now he would be present and alert. Getting Brenna to safety and discovering what had put her in harm's way in the first place was all that mattered.

As they reached the bottom of the ravine, he spied a small stream. It was a perfect spot to rest after such a long journey this morn. He narrowed his gaze and scanned the horizon. It was also an ideal area for an ambush, but they had been riding for hours, and a break would do them all good, especially with them both wounded. They needed to reach safety alive, and the best way to do that was to keep their wits about them by resting when they could and by taking a few minutes to look over what they'd found on the dead man. The turn in the road towards Glenhaven or Oban was ahead. A decision had to be made. And, once made, there would be no turning back. They had to be certain of their choice, as it might save or endanger their very lives.

'We'll stop here,' he said as they rounded a section of tall boulders.

Again, she said nothing in response.

He brought Montgomerie to a halt, dismounted and offered Brenna his hand. She slid her chilled petite hand into his, the sweet friction of her touch sending a gentle hum through his body. She avoided his gaze, hopped to the ground and let go of his hand.

'I'll return shortly,' she stated and began to walk off into the edge of the clearing behind a tree.

'Wait,' he commanded and jogged over to her. 'After what happened the last time, let me check the area first.'

Even though Brenna rolled her eyes at him, she paused, allowing him to pass. 'I *am* able to fend for myself. Perhaps you've noticed?' She crossed her arms against her chest.

'Aye. I have,' he called from behind her in the trees. 'I'm interested to know how you gained such skills since I've been away.' He emerged from the trees and set his gaze upon her.

Colour filled her cheeks and she walked past him, ignoring him entirely. 'One does what they have to when they have been abandoned.'

Her words cut him, no doubt as she had intended. He

kept his cursed response to himself. Squabbling with her would not help their cause, and if he was honest with himself she had reason to be angry. He had abandoned her by never sending word. In truth he had been a coward, but he was not quite strong enough to admit that to her out loud.

Brenna returned not long after and knelt by the stream to splash the cool water upon her face and take her fill of drink. He unpacked their saddlebags and knelt beside her, with a groan as his stitches pulled, to hand her more dried meat. As meagre as it was, it was far better than nothing.

She shook her head.

'You must eat. You'll not get far without sustenance. Eat. Please.'

Her gaze flicked up to him at the 'Please,' and a notch formed between her brows. 'How did you know that man would be carrying something hidden among his...?' She paused and gestured to his crotch.

It was his turn to blush. He cleared his throat. 'A soldier's hiding place. A necessary evil to protect what is most valuable to you.' He rose and scanned the area to ensure they were alone.

'That pouch you found was from Father. I am sure of it. I gave it to Stephen when I arrived in Oban to visit. The coin was an early dowry gift meant to hasten our union. Father was in quite the rush to secure the arrangement. He never said exactly why. I assumed it was due to his illness, but now I am uncertain. There may have been some other reason than the attack on your clan. One he did not see fit to share with me.'

'Such as?' Garrick asked, sitting down next to her with the saddlebag and strips of meat.

'At first glance, I could tell the packet of letters and correspondence had a variety of seals on them, but I didn't get a chance to take a good look. It's an odd thing for a stranger to have along with a pouch of coin, isn't it?'

'Not if they were a mercenary or hired soldier with a specific duty to fulfil. They may have been instructions and payment.'

She paled. 'Who would want to kill me?'

'I don't know.'

Garrick bit off a hunk of meat and then grabbed the stack of bound letters from the saddlebag. He tugged the ribbon off and split the stack in two, placing another strip of dried meat on the pile before handing it to her. 'You take half, and I'll take the other. Perhaps when we share what we have each found we'll have a clearer idea of what is afoot.'

She took the letters as well as the meat, nibbling off smaller bits as she opened each letter and read the contents. Garrick opened the top one of his stack of correspondence and read with interest.

Dear Sir,
Time is of the essence as we finalise our merger.
The coin we require is past due. You will need to
secure your position by sending us proof of your
commitment to the cause.
M

He frowned. Vague, odd and not of great use, Garrick set it down and continued to the next letter. The contents sent a chill through his bones.

Dear M,
My interest is sound and payment will come to
you as soon as I am wed. I am sending proof of
my commitment until the rest has been secured.
SW

'What did you say this Mr Winters' business interests were? Shipping?'

Brenna shrugged. 'And assorted investments.' She nibbled on another piece of meat and continued reading from a letter.

Garrick picked up the next one and the dread he had been feeling in his gut only increased. By the time he'd finished his stack, the dried meat tasted like ash in his mouth, but he swallowed it down anyway.

Brenna finished the last of her stack and met his gaze. 'All business letters. Yours?'

'The same. Who are the letters from and to?'

She frowned. 'Although I cannot be absolutely certain, it appears to be a series of letters back and forth from my Mr Winters, Father and some other person signed off as "M."'

'Mine as well. When were yours dated? This stack is very recent. Within the last month.'

'These are older, dating back to the beginning of talks of my engagement three months ago.' Her gaze dropped away and a bitter laugh fell from her lips.

'Father was in talks about this engagement well before mentioning it to me. Made me believe it was my choice, and I thought I was doing something to please him and make him proud of me by choosing to marry Mr Winters for the sake of the clan.'

She handed Garrick the letters, her fingertips skimming his palm. 'I was a fool. He had set our marriage in motion before I even knew of the possibility of it. He set the stage and I played into it as a fine, yet unwilling, actor.'

Sadness pulled down the corners of her eyes when she met his gaze. What could he say to that? This was not the first time Bran had used his daughters as pawns in a game of gaining more power for his clan in the Highlands. He'd done the same with her older sister Moira, with rather dire consequences. Garrick wasn't shocked at the revelation, but such words would not lessen the blow to Brenna. Despite all, she loved her father, and had always sought his love and approval.

A gift the man seemed incapable of giving her.

He swallowed hard. It was a gift Garrick had stolen from her as well by wilfully abandoning her. Did that make him as horrid as her father? He wouldn't allow himself the time to puzzle through to an answer. He needed to manage one crisis at a time.

He resisted the urge to reach out to comfort her. 'You are no fool. Just a daughter in search of approval from her father. I did the same with my own. Became a soldier to please him. I believed it would help him see my worth.'

She met his gaze. 'You never told me such. Did it work?'

'Nay. Hamish MacLean was always more impressed by my eldest brother, Lon. While I was jealous of Lon for the love and praise he earned from my father, I never resented him. He was a great man. He would have been a fine laird if the fever had not claimed him. Father never recovered from his loss. He rather resented it wasn't me or Cairn who perished, and we found it hard to compete with my eldest brother's memories. In the end, we gave up our efforts and focused our care on Mother. When Father died, we found we had already grieved him long ago.'

'How long did that take?'

'I'll let you know.' Garrick smiled at her. 'Give yourself credit, Brenna. You are a fine, talented woman. This Stephen Winters is lucky to have you for a wife. My hope is that he endeavours to deserve you, no matter what ideas your father has put in your head about your worth.'

Brenna edged away from him, wiping a tear from her cheek before tucking her legs under her. He forged ahead with his findings and swallowed back the tight ache at the base of his throat. He knew the hurt she felt, and no further words from him would change it. No gentle touch from him would make it better either, but merely make it worse for them both. He'd focus on her safety instead.

'Was he supposed to accompany you back to Glenhaven?' he asked.

'You mean Stephen?'

He nodded.

'Aye. He was. He was even packed and had planned to stay a day or two at Glenhaven, but he received a note by messenger before we were to set out. He went to his study with the man and then, when he emerged again, he said it was imperative he stay and sort out an issue with a shipment that had arrived early at the docks.'

Garrick stilled. 'That makes little sense. Why not simply delay your departure a day?'

'I was in a hurry to return to Glenhaven. I was rather bored, and with Father so ill I thought it best. When Arthur and his son offered to transport me home, I eagerly accepted.'

'And Winters allowed it?'

'Without hesitation. I thought nothing of it at the time but, now that I think upon it, he was behaving strangely. He was rather preoccupied when I left. He sent the messenger out to the docks with a package. Now, I am wondering what exactly was in it.'

'Could it have been the pouch?'

'It was larger than the pouch. About the size of a milliner's box.'

Her comparison made him smile. She had always loved hats. He could remember taking her to the milliner's shop in Edinburgh more than once over the months of their courtship.

'I've been puzzling over it all this morning. Why would he have Father's pouch? Was it his or for delivery to someone else? Did he steal it, or did Stephen give it to him? And why? Did he owe them coin and he was repaying a debt? And what's the importance in all of those letters?'

'All fine questions.' Garrick chewed upon the meat, although he couldn't really taste it. His gut was plaguing him. He couldn't resolve what she had told him in his mind. They were missing something.

'How did your father even come to meet this Mr Winters?' Garrick asked.

She shrugged. She'd either ignored or hadn't noticed the edge in his voice regarding her fiancé. 'Father met him through an acquaintance of the King.'

He balked. 'Why was he meeting with the King? I've never known your father to want to spend any time with the man.'

'It was not by choice, I assure you. Fear made him do it, and Father does not fear much, as you well know.'

Garrick studied her as she braided her hair into a long dark plait and tried to comb out the tangles with her fingers. Despite how focused her hands were upon such a task, she stared out at the stream unseeing, her thoughts consumed elsewhere.

His gut tightened again. She was omitting something by choice, but what?

'You didn't ask for more information about this man you were to marry?'

She tied off a ribbon at the end of her hair and set a glare upon him. 'Of course I did. I'm not daft. I want to know about my future. I am not merely a decoration.' Her words were sharp, tiny splinters sent his way. They hit their mark with ease, and he felt like a bastard.

'You know you are far more than that. I wasn't implying…' he began, attempting to soften the cut his words had made.

'Weren't you?'

'What has happened to make you believe I think so little of you?'

She met his gaze and the hurt in her eyes stole his breath. He had his answer. He'd abandoned her. Left her to believe he was dead.

Aye. He'd been a selfish bastard.

She didn't need to say it for him to know it. He cleared his throat and swallowed the emotion knotted up there. The wind whipped along the hillside and he turned his body away from it, only to see clouds rolling in off in the distance. 'Looks like rain will be moving in well before nightfall. Best we hurry. If you agree, I think it is safer to travel to Blackmore. If these men were intentionally tracking you or your father, they will go to Glenhaven next. It is a more obvious choice.'

'Will Father and Ewan be in danger?' Brenna asked, alarm lifting the pitch of her words.

'Nay. They would not go to the estate outright. Most likely they would wait for you along the road and intercept you there. Make it look like a band of thieves.'

'Like last time,' she mumbled quietly.

'Aye. I am quite certain those men were hired to track you, and either capture or kill you, but I am not certain by whom or why.'

Although, he feared it might be her beloved fiancé. The dead man had Winters' coin in his pocket with correspondence between Bran, himself and some other man. The real question was, who had given it to him with the order to attack? Had it been Winters, 'M,' or another man that Winters had paid? Either way, he didn't trust this fiancé of hers, not a whit. The man was involved somehow, or daft as driftwood. Neither was good enough for Brenna.

Although the need to continue their travels to avoid the weather had spared him from having to discuss the horrid possibilities of who was behind the initial attack on her, as well as her anger at him, Garrick knew they'd have to talk eventually. They needed to work together to get to Oban safely and they couldn't do that while keeping a bevy of secrets between them.

But he wanted to do that as much as he'd like to walk across a field of thistles with bare feet covered in open sores. He'd avoid it as long as he could. She would think him jaded to imply Winters was behind the attack, which would lead to them discussing their own past. He clenched his jaw.

'Best we walk alongside Montgomerie for this next pass. It's quite narrow and steep.'

'As you wish,' she muttered, the edge in her voice unmistakable.

Perhaps he should have been grateful for the previous silence.

They plodded along at a steady pace. The temperature dropped sharply as they neared the edge of the cliffside. Garrick watched for sites to serve as possible shelter as they went up and down hill after hill, the sun lowering at every turn. When he saw an abandoned shell of a church as an early dusk clawed along the horizon, he groaned, but decided it was the best protection they had for the night. The irony was not lost on him. Ayleen would have had a grand chuckle, seeing him walk across the threshold of a holy place so soon after promising he never would again.

'We'll stay here for the night,' he grumbled, leading them through the waist-high crumbling rock wall surrounding the old, abandoned building. The sight of it sent a shiver along his spine. He hadn't been in a church since the night he'd lost Ayleen. The crucifix he wore felt like ice against his throat. He pinched the bridge of his nose to push back the memories of that night.

Focus on Brenna.

He released a breath and rolled his neck. He was weary and his side and arm ached. He settled Montgomerie in the courtyard shaded by a large tree that had grown through the dilapidated remnants of the roof and came back to Brenna. She sat on the rock wall, gazing out at the sea.

'A rainbow,' she murmured. 'Just past the break in the cliffs to the west.'

He followed her hand, the petite fingers looking as if they were dancing upon the array of pastels that arched across the sky. It looked more to him like a sunset than a rainbow, but he smiled just the same. If it gave her a moment of pleasure, he wished for it to be a smattering of rainbows.

He frowned. He was being a fool. He shook his head and turned away. His stitches pulled and he winced. 'We need to change your dressings,' she stated, glancing at his side.

The last thing he wanted was to be fussed over,

but he knew she was right. Otherwise, he might get an infection and slow their journey to Oban, or leave her exposed to attack, which would be even worse. He shrugged, which was as close to an agreement as he could muster.

'I'll take that as a yes,' she answered and patted the rock wall next to her.

He sat down with a thump and pulled up the side of his tunic.

'I'll get your kit,' she said and returned. She pulled out what she needed and set them out on the ledge.

As she unwrapped the makeshift bandages, he winced and then focused his attention out to the sea. The more he stared out, the more he began to see that rainbow.

Bloody rainbow.

He needed a plan, not hope. It was just like God to send him a rainbow rather than a fellow soldier with reinforcements to protect them. A rainbow would help him as much as a bucket of rotten fish.

Brenna cleaned his wound without a word. She rinsed it with water and covered it with salve from his kit, which numbed some of the pain. He closed his eyes in relief. He hadn't realised how much it had been plaguing him as he'd ridden until the throbbing began to fade.

'Whose crucifix is that?' Brenna whispered. The words set his heart thundering and his eyes shot open.

'Ayleen's.'

Her touch softened as she continued to wrap his side with care with a new strip of linen torn from her underskirts. Saying Ayleen's name made his throat ache. Regret burned like acid as he swallowed down the memories.

'What happened to her? To you?' She smoothed the last wrap around his side and tucked an edge gently under it to keep it in place.

Her blue eyes settled on him like the summer sky, and he faltered. She was another beacon of hope that God kept sending him, and it became harder to bat her away, even if it was for her own good. When she was here beside him, all warm, soft, kind and comforting, all he wanted was to touch her.

He dropped his gaze from her and reached for his tunic.

She was meant for another man. Not him. He had never deserved her, especially not now.

'I didn't get there in time. It's as simple as that. I failed her. I failed all of them.'

Before Brenna could say a word, Garrick rose from the wall and shrugged on his tunic and coat with a wince. 'I'll find some wood for the fire. Stay here.'

She opened her mouth but then closed it. She knew *this* Garrick. The man who ran from the past and pushed himself through pain. Pain so deep it had no bottom, no end. Part of her knew she couldn't bring him back from it—not alone, anyway. He'd have to want to come back to her and she wasn't sure he wanted to. And, with all that had happened between them, she wasn't sure she did either. He had chosen to allow her to believe he was dead.

His silhouette cut into the night sky behind him, obliterating the stars in his path. Her body still sung at the sight of him, just as it had that cool autumn day years ago when they'd first met at Glenhaven at the tournament of champions—the yearly assemblage of lairds and their first sons to show their strength and prowess. A man of duty, strength, and honour. She'd never met a man like Garrick before or a man of his equal since.

He disappeared from view, and the familiar loss began as a slight tingling in her fingertips. He'd been gone for over a year, and she had worked hard, very hard, to forget him, grieve him. She'd almost succeeded.

She frowned at the realisation that she couldn't let go all of him and the hope she had had for their future. She still clung to some tiny gossamer thread of hope for them, which was ridiculous. He didn't want her. He'd made that as clear as the summer sky. And she was engaged to another man.

She was being a fool to let his reappearance change any plans she'd already set in motion, wasn't she? She'd grieved him and accepted her fate as part of an arranged marriage proposed by Father to provide their clan protection as the tensions in the country grew. But now, knowing that Garrick was alive and that Father had all but manipulated her into this arrangement, she hesitated. Could she embrace a marriage and a future without love, knowing Garrick was alive? Could they even try to love one another again after all that had happened between them?

She didn't know.

He had deceived her, just like her father.

He'd allowed her to believe one thing while he'd made a decision about her future without her consent. Why had he done it? Did he not believe her capable of making her own decisions?

Garrick came back into view carrying a load of wood and tinder. A slight hitch in his step and grimace along his brow were the only signs of his injury, but she knew he was hurting. The man she had once loved, still loved, was buried under that shell of wounds and guilt over the agony of the past. She approached him to offer to carry some of the weight. To her surprise, he allowed it, and his fingers feathered along her own lightly, accidentally. She clutched the dead branches and twigs to her chest.

'Is it safe to start a fire? Will we be seen?' she rushed out. The confusion over her feelings for him and the tremble of awareness his touch had stirred in her made her words trip over themselves.

His hands faltered as he arranged the tinder along the dead branches of the fire he was building. He shrugged. 'It's a risk, but a storm is coming. I can feel it in my shoulder. It aches before the first snow. And based on that...' he paused, setting the last of the tinder beneath it '...there'll be snow in the morning. We may freeze without the warmth of the fire.'

She shuddered involuntarily and rubbed her arms. Snow would only hamper their progress and make the journey that much more treacherous and uncomfortable. They had scarce enough clothing and food between them to manage to Oban as it was, which was at least two more days out. And her blasted slippers. Her toes might freeze and snap off if she had to walk in the snow for that long.

Garrick walked over to her, removed his coat and draped it around her, his palms skimming the round, soft slope of her shoulders. 'We'll make it. I promise.' The intensity and certainty of his words made her eyes tear up, and she was grateful he couldn't see her blink them back. How did he always know what she was thinking and exactly what she needed to hear?

The warmth of his coat, and knowing it had come from his body, made her shiver once more and he rubbed her arms. She didn't want to give it up, but he was wounded and, despite everything, she still cared for him, even if he had been cruel by staying away.

'Nay,' she said, clearing her throat and thrusting herself back to the present. 'I can't take your coat. You'll freeze.'

He chuckled. 'That's why I'm building the fire.'

'How are we going to make it all the way to Oban in the snow without help? You're wounded. You need to rest before you collapse.'

His cheeks had lost colour since yesterday, and the pinched expression in his face grown more distinct. He was pretending all was fine, as everyone always did around her, as if she were a fragile dandelion that might lose all of its petals if a strong wind came. She wasn't her sister Moira, but she could withstand a great deal more than her family gave her credit for. She picked up some kindling and handed it to him, awaiting an answer.

'I don't need you to fuss over me,' he grumbled, shaking his head.

She lifted her chin. He'd retreated once more. 'Maybe you do, Garrick. Have you not ever thought upon that? We're stuck with one another until Oban. You might as well let me help keep *you* alive. We need each other, no matter how you may feel about it.'

He squatted by the fire, which was beginning to wink with life. They both watched the flickering flames come alive. She grabbed a tartan from Montgomerie and spread it out before the fire. The warmth was as delicious as the coat still wrapped around her shoulders. She sat down, crossing her legs so her feet were close to the fire, and put her chilled hands palms out. She sighed as the warmth began to seep into her hands and frozen toes.

Garrick rose and joined her on the tartan. They sat in silence, watching the fire continue to burn, sending smoke into the midnight-blue sky. Clouds were coming in slowly, blocking out patches of stars and soon the moon.

One thing he was right about. A storm was coming.

Chapter Seven

Brenna's logic was sound. Garrick knew in his mind that they needed to work together to survive. He was injured, as was she, and the weather would hamper their journey, but his heart hated the idea. He didn't want her to need him, as that left room for him to fail her as he had already failed everyone else he loved.

He swallowed hard as the flames curled up and down the dry tinder, casting shadows along the crumbling walls and half-exposed ceiling of the abandoned church. He hated the dark. It always had a way of letting in the past. No matter how hard he tried to keep the reality away, he couldn't.

They were dead. They were all dead. Because of him. Hot tears burned the back of his eyes and his throat constricted. His sister, Ayleen. His younger brother, Cairn. His beautiful mother. And here he'd thought losing his father and eldest brother were the only losses he would have to bear! What an arrogant fool he had been to stay away. And being here with

Brenna, the one woman who had softened the sharp edges of the world into something smoother, more beautiful and manageable, was promised to another?

Saints be. How much could a man take? Especially when he knew he had caused it by staying away. And now he wasn't even sure he was strong enough to protect her.

He blinked back the tears that threatened and cleared his throat to loosen the cry of anguish that hung there waiting to be released. It couldn't be today, nor tomorrow. He had to be clear and alert, not clouded by heartbreak. And, besides, his tears wouldn't change anything. Nothing would bring them back. Hope was a belief for foolish men, and he wouldn't be one of them. Not this time.

The twig he had been holding snapped in two in his hand, forcing him back to the present. He turned his head, only to find Brenna staring at him. The concern and care in her gaze irritated him, so he turned away, ignoring her unspoken questions. If she'd truly loved him, she would have waited. But she hadn't, and he couldn't forgive her for it. Or himself, for daring to let her go.

They'd both been fools.

He tossed the two tiny twigs into the fire and savoured the snap and crackle as they were eaten away by the flames. Nature, he understood. The elements, he understood. People and the ways of life, he didn't. If he'd only left a day earlier or later, he wouldn't have encountered Brenna at all. He would have returned and found her promised to another. He would have grieved, but he could have avoided her until the wound had healed.

He stilled. But she'd also be dead if he'd not come along when he had. No one would have found her before the men doubled back to kill her. He shivered. He would never have wished that, never, but by all that was holy why did it have to be him to have found her and be charged with keeping her safe?

'My mother died on a night like this. Cool, haunting and full of stars.'

Brenna's words were so soft, so light, Garrick wondered if he'd imagined them. He turned to her. She continued staring far off into the distance through the large gaping hole in the battered stone wall before them.

'One moment she was alive, laughing and full of joy, and the next she was gone. Some limp, lifeless creature on the floor I did not recognise. Everyone else reacted, did something, anything, but I just stared. I could not reconcile that it was her. I kept waiting for her to wake, but she never did. It was the only time I'd ever seen Father cry. And I was so unnerved by it that I sat staring at him. Moira offered him comfort, so did Ewan. But me?' She shrugged. 'I sat on the floor next to Mother's still form, running her hair through my fingertips. Praying that life from my touch would flow into her like fairy magic.' She shook her head. 'Ridiculous, I know.'

'Nay. No more so than me wearing this cross of Ayleen's, wishing it might bring her back to me.' He met her gaze and then looked at her hand. 'But it does explain why you rub the ends of your hair between your fingers when you are restless or worried.'

Her brow furrowed and she let go of the end of the plait of hair that she had been absently running her fingertips through. 'Do I do that?'

He smiled at her. 'Aye. I always found it endearing, even more so now that I know the cause.'

Colour rose in her cheeks and she looked away. 'I still miss her. And I wonder about all of the things she would have taught me and what advice she would have given me, especially about Father.'

'Oh?' Garrick asked.

'He is a difficult man, as you well know, but even more so now that he has been so ill and not himself. She always knew how to calm him, settle him, when he was angry or agitated.'

Garrick sat up and moved closer to her, his hand resting on her forearm. 'When did this happen, these changes in him?'

She pulled the coat around her more tightly, causing his hand to fall away. 'Six months past, perhaps a bit more. The doctor says it is his heart, but I wonder if it has affected his logic. When I think about how this arrangement came to be and those letters, it is nonsensical. I'm sorry. I am blathering on.'

'Nay. All we have now is time and the cold. Talking may help the time pass and the cold lessen. It may also help us figure out what is truly going on.'

Brenna clenched her teeth. *Ack*. Why did he have to be so kind? His kindness could be a weapon if used well, as it was now. She shifted and continued on in hopes it would distract her from the biting winds.

'Father tires easily and sleeps much more than he used to. He had quite a serious episode several months ago, and he has never quite recovered. He is determined to have all of his affairs in order and Ewan and I settled before he passes. Men of the clan roam in and out of Glenhaven at all hours with his orders. Since all that happened with your family, he is driven to secure our clan's status within the King's eyes as well, no matter the cost. It is why he is so desperate to finalise my match with Mr Winters, despite hardly knowing the man at all.'

She didn't dare snatch a glimpse of Garrick. Nor did she need to. She could feel the heat of his displeasure on her as if his gaze was the sun. Moments ticked by before he responded.

'How does he know such a match will secure anything for him? Assurances and alliances are far from certain. Those along the Borderlands can attest to that.' He threw another small twig he'd found on the ground into the fire.

'He is certain, despite no further assurances other than the man's word. And, in my haste to bring him peace, I agreed. I did not know he already had made the agreement. My word didn't matter a whit.'

Perhaps I am as useless as Father said.

She batted away the thought.

'And Ewan and Moira have agreed to such a union?'

She shifted and brought the coat collar up to cover her ears. 'Neither of them has any say against Father, and as I said, Moira does not even know of it. I did not wish to tell her until it was finalised.'

'I cannot wait to see her reaction when she finds out.'

Brenna squared her shoulders, a flare of jealousy budding within her. Garrick respected Moira, and they had always had some silent understanding between them since they'd met at the Tournament of Champions years ago, one that she could never quite get to the bottom of. Of course, she'd also never asked either of them. Directness was not one of her strengths. She fiddled with the end of her plait and then batted it away once she realised she was doing it. She glanced up to see him smirking at her.

'What?' she asked.

'Why did you not tell her? Plead for her help or interference? She knows first-hand the ill effects of your father's matches. She would have come to your aid, and so would Rory. They would have assisted you without question.'

Garrick was right. Moira did understand. She had scarce survived her first husband, a match made by Father. Peter Fraser had been cruel in the worst ways a man could be, and she'd suffered in silence until his death. Rory was the husband she had deserved the first time around, despite Brenna's own initial reservations about her sister marrying him.

But that would not be her fate. Stephen Winters didn't seem a cruel man, merely a disinterested and arrogant fiancé, and there were worse things than that, weren't there?

'Because I could not bear to,' she muttered. 'I am trying desperately to make my own way and to not be quite so cast under her shadow.'

'What?' Garrick asked. 'What on earth are you talking about—her shadow?'

'I—I cannot make you understand,' she faltered, fiddling with the end of his coat sleeve instead of her hair. 'You are...*you.*'

'Aye. Is that bad?' he asked.

'Nay, but it makes you completely unable to see my position on the matter.' She lifted her chin.

'How so?'

'You are a laird. A soldier lauded for your achievements on the field, respected for your rank and skill. You are a man who does not doubt himself. You do not know what it feels like to be the one that has no impact on the world. If I disappeared or blew away in the wind tomorrow, it would not matter. I have made no claim, no imprint. No one would even notice my absence.' She hated the quiver of desperation she heard in her voice, but it was the truth. Being nothing scared her far more than being married to an Englishman she did not know.

He studied her. A war waged in his moss-green eyes. She didn't know what it was about, but she could see it. Finally, he nodded. 'I do understand that. More than you know.'

She scoffed at him. 'I doubt it.'

The mask fell back in place, and before her eyes the emotion in him disappeared like an animal hiding in a forest. He shifted away from her and closer to the fire.

A pit opened in her stomach. Perhaps he did know,

but she'd batted his attempt to connect with her aside like a pesky fly.

Blast.

'Garrick, I did not mean to...'

He didn't answer but gestured behind her to the saddlebags. 'Can you gather the letters and pouch we found this morning on the man who attacked you? Reading through them again may help us get to the heart of why those men were after you and how we can ensure your safe return back to Oban.'

She let the matter go and turned to gather the items from the bag. Why was she always mucking up the important bits? He'd almost opened up to her, which she knew was hard for him, but she'd truly thought he was joking and had batted his statement away. She never imagined he would understand how small and insignificant she felt at times. Why would he ever doubt his self-worth, with all he had achieved in his life?

Now she'd never know. Garrick had receded back into his armour of safety like a turtle into its shell. Who knew when he would feel safe enough to try again, if ever?

She handed him the items, letting her fingertips linger along his hand. 'I'm sorry,' she murmured, attempting to build a bridge of words back to the moment that had been severed between them.

He stilled and then pulled his hand away. 'No matter,' he answered and set to the task at hand. Just like Garrick—always focused, logical, neutral. Emotion rarely clouded his judgement.

Reason always ruled.

It was enough to make a woman go mad.

She knew the moment he reached the end of the notes she had read, which held her father's signature, as his neutral mask fell into a scowl.

'This is from your father,' he stated, as if that was new information to them both rather than just her.

'I know.'

'Care to share how and why that man would have had it?' Garrick frowned at her.

She raised her hands in confusion. 'I do not know why he has it. I believe it was the same note, paired with the coin that I brought from Glenhaven and gave to Mr Winters, that ensured our marriage was secured to move forward, as it was a fresh deal. Or at least that is what Father said. That terms had been agreed to, but it could be an older letter. I could be wrong. I don't know why these men would have it. Perhaps he was repaying a debt to them, and the note was included to show the marriage was official, and more coin would be coming their way for whatever endeavour he was working towards?'

'That would explain the coin, but not why they would have the note. It is an invitation for him to visit Glenhaven upon your return. No mercenary would need such a note.'

'Mr Winters does seem rather distractable. Maybe he gave him them both in error?'

Garrick gifted her a droll look and she flushed. 'I know. It sounds ridiculous, but I can think of no other reason why that stranger would have had it and gone to such measures to secure it…hide it…as he did. And then to track me, Arthur and Roland down, only to try to kill us.'

'Did you meet anyone there on your visit? Walk in on a conversation or meeting you shouldn't have?'

She paused and recollected her days at Winters' estate. 'I cannot recall anything of that nature. I spent more time with his household staff than him. In fact, I got to know Arthur and Roland rather well. They were both very kind to me.'

Garrick scrubbed a hand through his hair as he stared into the fire. 'I have an idea, but it also makes little sense. Unless there is a more complex reason at play.'

A gust of wind made her shiver. 'And that is?' Brenna enquired, shifting closer to him.

'Has Mr Winters ever visited Glenhaven before?'

She paused. 'Nay. We have always travelled to him. He does not enjoy the Highlands. Something about it being too cold.'

'Sounds like a real prize,' Garrick muttered under his breath.

She rolled her eyes. 'You were saying possible reasons?'

He continued. 'He may have brought it with him to gain quick entrance at Glenhaven if needed. The man could have merely shown the letter with its seal to the guards at the door, given the name of Stephen Winters and been admitted without question, since he is your betrothed.'

Her heart thudded against her chest. 'Aye,' she replied. 'I suppose.' She bit her lip. 'Only Father has met him, other than the soldiers who escorted me there this time. He sends the same few trusted men with me during each excursion to ensure my safety.' She paused. 'And…they are still gathering supplies and have not yet returned home, so the servants would have no idea if the man was Mr Winters or not, and allowed him in.' Nerves chewed along her skin. 'Garrick, no one would have been aware. Ewan wouldn't even know. But why would the man bother with such a ruse if Father would know immediately of the deceit upon seeing him?'

Garrick paused and pressed his lips together.

'Tell me why,' she pleaded.

He faced her and his grim features warned her that she wouldn't like his answer. Not one bit. 'It wouldn't matter if your goal was to kill the man you met with.'

She recoiled. 'You can't mean that. Why would Stephen… Mr Winters…or anyone send men to kill Father?'

'It would be a great way to incite a maelstrom of discontent and sew more discord and unrest in the Highlands, which would then require the King's men to come and subdue us. It may not have mattered which clan leader, but merely a prominent one. And Bran fits that requirement.'

She gasped. 'What if there are others? How can we get word to Father and Ewan?'

'There may be others, but I don't believe they will be able to gain entry without these items before the Stewart soldiers return with supplies. And, even if we could send word from here, it would not reach Glenhaven in time. We must trust that stopping this one man will keep them safe.'

For now.

It was little comfort. She clutched her hands together in worry.

'What are your terms in the marriage contract?'

Her mind raced and she hid her face in her hands. 'I didn't ask,' she grumbled.

She cursed herself. Why didn't she ask? Why had she trusted these men with her future and not enquired?

Garrick caressed her head, and it lingered down to the nape of her neck, sending a trill of awareness through her. 'Brenna?'

'Aye,' she answered. Heat flushed her body. Had she been a fool once more? Had her lack of involvement left her father and brother at risk?

Useless.

'Look at me,' he urged, rubbing her shoulder.

She forced herself to drop her hands, much as she didn't wish to. The last thing she wanted was to be shamed once more for her mistakes, but she saw no judgement in his eyes.

'It does not matter. If this man was eager to dispense with your Father, or at least gain entry into Glenhaven without detection, he would have found whatever means of entry he needed. This may have just been the avenue they chose to take. And we don't even know if that was the reason. As you know, I am jaded and a sceptic. The past has made me that way. I could be wrong on all counts. We both could be.'

'What I fear is that you are right. Your judgement is sound…' She paused, unable to keep the next words from falling from her lips. 'About most things.'

He stilled and removed his hand, as if he'd only re-alised he was consoling her, and her barb had added impact.

Old patterns were so easy to fall into. She could physically drop back into being comforted and cared for by Garrick as easily as she'd shrugged on his coat, but the past had severed her emotional trust in him and shredded it into ribbons. Her heart couldn't forget or forgive him for showing her a future as bright as a sea of rainbows, only to leave her empty-handed and out in the blinding rain, unable to see but an arm's length ahead of her.

Chapter Eight

Garrick woke with a shiver. Despite being partially protected by what was left of the roof of the abandoned church, he was covered in a light dusting of snow. Brenna was snuggled against him, and his body had curved around her limbs in a protective and unconscious shell. Only small flakes had settled in her hair and along the slope of her back. He should move. *Now.* She was engaged to another. His body ignored his mind's command, so he studied her, memorised her features for later, when all he could do was dream of her and remember this moment when she was tucked in against him.

The imperfect curve of the tiny lashes along her closed eyes fluttered and her slightly parted lips moved. She was dreaming. Of him? Probably not. Even the nasty bluish purple gash along her temple veiled in black wavy hair was beautiful. She could have been his. She *had* been his. As he had been hers. His body trembled, knowing full well what it had lost, what he had consciously given away: his happiness.

But when he'd heard of the reivers rushing along the Borderlands, knowing full well that Ayleen's abbey was along its path, all he'd been able to think of was going and rescuing her. And then he'd arrived and, when he'd had the moment to protect her, he'd frozen. He'd watched his baby sister die at the hands of raiders who cared nothing for her kind heart and generous soul. The memory of her hand reaching for him as the life emptied from her eyes was as clear and terrifying as it had been the moment it'd happened.

He swallowed hard and shuddered, snow tumbling off him. Her death and the death of his family were a reminder of why Brenna was best without him. When it counted, he hadn't been able to protect them. While he was effective on the battlefield, when it came to matters of those he loved, he fell short. He froze and wasn't there for them.

So far, he'd been lucky in being able to keep Brenna safe and alive, but each moment when she'd been thrust in danger his heart had stopped, the dread of past losses hot along his skin. And if he ran out of luck…it would cost her life.

Carefully, he separated his interwoven limbs from hers and brushed the snow from his clothes. He thought about doing the same for Brenna, but that would require touching her, which seemed a poor idea. He fisted his hands at his sides, stepped outside the remnants of the church walls and watched the sun struggling to pull its weight up into the sky.

He knew exactly how he felt. Tired.

His body ached and he was growing weaker. The

lack of food, demanding journey and blood loss would continue to take its toll. But they'd need to travel at least two more days, and the snowfall might make it three. He scrubbed his hand down his face. How in the world would they make it three more days out here with such meagre supplies and enemies possibly still giving chase?

He frowned. They wouldn't. Another opportunity would present itself or he'd make one. That was their only viable option.

'How did you sleep?' Brenna asked. He turned to see her covering her mouth as she yawned. She was sitting up in front of the remnants of the fire that had long since gone out.

'Like the dead again, which might have got us killed.' He had fought off sleep for as long as he could last night, but fatigue had claimed him. He'd used more luck he didn't have.

She frowned at him. '"Quite well" would have been an acceptable answer.'

He shrugged. 'Just being honest.'

'Sorry I asked,' she muttered and shifted to standing. She brushed off the snow.

'Do you need to…?' he asked, pointing to the woods.

'Aye,' she answered and headed towards him. Her skirts were a bedraggled mess of dirt and fabric, and she dragged them behind her. He hit his palm to his forehead. Why had he not thought of it sooner?

He rushed to the saddlebags, where he had an extra tunic and trews rolled up, and returned to her. 'Change,' he ordered, extending them to her.

She glanced down at the clothes and back at him. 'What?'

'Change into these. The men are following a man and a woman in a blue dress. If we both appear to be men from a distance, our chance of survival will improve tenfold. I forgot I even had them.'

'Any chance you have boots in there as well?' She pointed to her thin slippers.

He frowned. 'Nay.'

'Worth asking. These should be a might warmer and drier. Thank you.' She accepted the clothes and clutched them to her chest. He followed her to the woods at a distance.

'Turn,' she commanded, lifting an eyebrow.

He lifted his hands. 'Only trying to ensure your safety.' He turned and quirked a smile. He did wish to look. She had always had a fine form, but she was his no longer.

The idea would take a while to get used to.

Minutes later she returned, having finished her ablutions and changed into his spare clothes. His body heated as she drew closer. She seemed more naked than ever before. His thin tunic revealed the exquisite shape of her breasts and her tiny waist, as she had tucked it into his trews. Despite being far too large, his clothes gave him a clear idea of her shape. His throat dried.

'What's happened to your...erm...?' He gestured to her chest area.

'Corset?' she asked, holding up his trews, far too large for her, with one hand.

'Aye.' He cleared his throat. 'You seem…' Again he gestured to her breasts.

'Comfortable? Able to breathe?' She popped a hand to her hip and the sway of her breasts threatened to strike him dumb. 'Are those the words you are looking for?'

He didn't move. There seemed a right and wrong answer, and he didn't wish to choose the wrong one, so he shrugged, before adding in a final word. 'Liberated?'

She smiled. 'Aye. My breasts have been liberated so that, if I need to run from an attacker, I can take a full breath, so I don't pass out. Have you an extra belt or length of rope, by chance?'

'I can use a rope for your belt.' He grabbed a section of rope from his saddlebags and cut a strip. He started to tie it over her trews, so she could roll it over and secure the material in place, but thought better of it. Being too close wasn't good for his focus. She still affected him. Deeply. He handed her the length of rope that remained and stepped back as she cinched it around her waist. She rolled the excess material and tucked it in place. He draped the plaid back over her shoulders and secured it around as much of her body as he could to block the wind and to obscure her figure.

'Best we get moving before another round of snow comes upon us. You'll ride while I walk. And, if you see anyone or any livestock, tell me. We need to find food for us and Montgomerie.'

'How are we going to pay for it if we do find it? We could use Father's coin.'

'Nay. We'll barter. The coin will only draw more unwanted attention.' He packed up their meagre belongings and helped her to mount.

'What can we barter with?' she asked.

'With whatever we can. Our possessions will matter little if we're both dead.'

Garrick never had been one to mince words. But he was right. Her possessions wouldn't matter if she was dead, so there was no need to worry over what they would trade if they encountered anyone along their journey. Staying alive was the goal. She wouldn't be of much worth to her father, her family or the clan if she were dead. And, deep down, she wanted desperately to live and find a purpose greater than being a bargaining chip or game piece to be manoeuvred by the men in her life.

She just wasn't entirely sure how to go about it. She'd never been terribly good at anything except being pretty. She had dabbled in learning of herbs, as well as sewing, but she wasn't terribly good at either. The fact that she had thrown that blade and downed a man had surprised her as much as it had Garrick.

They set off south once more, taking extra care as they traversed up, down and through narrow passages. Some sections were enclosed on each side with large rocks and boulders worn smooth by the wind and rain, while others were precariously close to the cliff's edge. The waves crashed against the shoreline as the wind blew what was left of the light snow around them. The sound was a heady reminder of the sizeable drop it would be if Montgomerie lost his footing. Even with Garrick guiding the fine stallion by the reins as he walked alongside, Brenna still sat rigid and held her breath.

'Must we travel so close to the edge?' she asked, a quiver evident in her voice.

'Aye,' he answered, continuing. 'There is no other trail until we cut back through this section and join a path that runs parallel to the road.'

Montgomerie slipped on a stone and a few loose pebbles skidded off the side, disappearing into the water below.

'Curses,' she murmured.

He glanced back at her. 'Do we need to stop? Are you unwell?'

'Nay, nay. 'tis just the height. Keep going,' she urged. 'The last thing I want to do is stop at the cliff side. Just get us through this pass. As quickly and safely as possible.'

'Aye,' he answered. 'I had forgotten. Hold fast. We'll be through quickly.'

Brenna clutched at the reins and forced herself to breathe in and then out. She would be fine. Heights still bothered her no matter how she tried to move past it. The memory of almost falling to her death when she'd been but a wee lass was still as clear as if it had happened yesterday.

'Take my hand,' Ewan pleaded over the loud crashing of the waves below. The spray of the waves hit her

calves, and she clung to the roots on the ledge she had fallen to.

She looked down and shrieked. It was a long, long fall into the cold waters of the sea.

'Bren,' he said firmly, his voice confident and certain. 'Hold on to the root with one hand while reaching up to take mine with the other.'

'I don't know if I can!' she cried as she studied the distance between his hand and her own.

He edged further over. 'Don't! You'll fall!'

'Nay,' he answered. 'Moira is holding onto my legs. Trust us, sister. We won't let you fall.'

And they hadn't. Ewan and Moira had pulled her to safety. And, soon, Garrick would bring them to safety too.

A horse whinnied nearby and Garrick brought Montgomerie to a halt and pressed a finger to his lips. Brenna wanted to scream. The cliff was just to her right and now they weren't moving at all. A wave of nausea crushed her. The horizon tilted. She clung tightly to Montgomerie's neck. She drew in a slow breath and the smell of the horse's mane steadied her.

Garrick hadn't moved, his body tense and alert. He stared off to his left, but she couldn't see over the high boulders that blocked her view.

The neigh sounded again, and Garrick eased his blade from its sheath along his waist belt. She ran her fingers along Montgomerie's mane and looked about her for a weapon. It seemed her only real weapon was the horse she sat on. All else was either out of arm's reach or too dangerously close to the edge to risk shifting her weight on Montgomerie for.

Garrick stooped, edged around the lower set of boulders and studied whatever was on the other side of the stretch of rock. Had the attackers found them? Was it another band of soldiers hiding in wait? A band of reivers headed north?

She squeezed her eyes shut for a moment and hoped it was a sweet family travelling to visit relatives in the north, even though she knew it wouldn't be. No family would travel this route. It was too steep and dangerous.

Which was exactly why they shouldn't be trapped here along the precipice.

She bit her lower lip, opened her eyes and prayed. *Provide us an escape. Please.*

After far too long, Garrick's shoulders relaxed and he sheathed his weapon. He nodded to her and tugged Montgomerie along. Soon, they were past the boulders and heading towards the land far away from the cliff's edge. She sighed in relief.

Thank God. She was tempted to jump off the horse and kiss the ground. She hugged Montgomerie's neck instead, and for a moment she could have sworn he pressed his neck back against her as a small sign of reassurance.

She frowned. Lack of food and rest was getting to her.

As they rounded the bend, Brenna started. An old woman was gathering what appeared to be herbs as her horse nibbled on some exposed grass tufts poking out from the snow. What on earth would be growing way up here that one would want to harvest after the first snowfall?

She narrowed her gaze. Was it a trap?

Garrick called a greeting and the petite grey-haired woman stood. She might weigh seven stone in soaking wet wool tartans. Brenna berated herself for her suspicions. She was turning into Garrick and now saw everyone as a threat.

The woman watched them approach. 'Bit far from home, are we?' she asked. Her gaze took in Garrick and then flitted to Brenna. She smiled. 'Wish I could have dressed like such when I was a lass.'

Brenna flushed when she realised the woman was referring to her trews and tunic. She wrapped the plaid tightly around her.

'We're hoping to trade for some supplies and then be on our way. Do you live in these parts?' Garrick asked.

'Depends on what you hope to trade,' she answered, crossing her arms against her chest.

Brenna smothered a smile. She liked this old woman.

He hesitated. 'We have a cross.' He gestured to Ayleen's silver necklace around his throat.

'Nay,' Brenna called out and moved the reins to bring Montgomerie and her closer. 'I have a ring. We'll not trade the necklace.'

Garrick frowned at her.

The old woman eyed it. It was the garnet ring Stephen had given to her as a gift upon her last visit.

Garrick shook his head at her but she ignored him, slid the ring easily off her finger and met the woman's gaze. ''Tis yours if we can have a warm place to sleep for the night, food for us and our horse and something to break our fast in the morn before we depart.'

The woman studied her and then looked to Garrick, as if assessing just how much trouble they might be. 'Aye.' She took the ring, slid it in her dress pocket and nodded. 'We have an agreement. Follow me.'

Garrick came to Brenna and grabbed the reins. 'What are you thinking?' he muttered.

She shrugged. 'The ring can be replaced. I could not allow you to trade away Ayleen's cross. And, like you said, possessions matter little if you are dead.'

He said nothing but took the reins in his hand and began to lead them behind the old woman. She'd tucked away the herbs she had gathered neatly in her saddlebags and clicked her tongue. The mare fell in step beside her as if they'd travelled this very journey a thousand times which, by the grey along the mare's nose, might be true.

The narrow path was well worn and, the deeper they went into the woods, the more Brenna realised that they were on the edges of a small community nestled away from the rest of the world. She spied a granary, drying shed and a well, and then the tops of small stone cottages and makeshift barns. It wasn't a large village, but they seemed to be thriving, despite being nestled so close to the cliffs.

'This is a surprise,' she murmured, and Garrick nodded in agreement.

'Never knew there was a settlement nestled up in here, but I've also never drifted from the trail the few times I have taken it.'

'Who do you think they are? A fractured clan? I see a mixture of plaids.'

'As do I. Let her introduce us to them. I'll not startle them, as we are far outnumbered.' As they entered a more densely settled area, a few men and women paused in their work to watch them walk by.

'Seems a fine plan,' she answered, meeting the uncertain gaze of a woman with a babe snuggled in against her breast. They had enough troubles. The last thing they wished to do was upset the people who might stand between them and survival.

Chapter Nine

'Wait here,' the old woman stated, leaving them in the heart of the small village, and approached a man who looked to be the leader of their community. The man's dark eyes watched Garrick as she spoke to him, never taking his gaze from Brenna or him. Garrick held his stare, wondering where he'd seen the man before, as he seemed familiar. He was tall, medium built with thick brown hair that shielded his eyes. The scars along his left cheek were unique, and the haunted look in his eyes as recognisable as Garrick's own in a looking glass. Why could he not place him?

Probably due to lack of food and rest. His mind was not as sharp as it had been in the days before he'd stumbled across Brenna. Before his world had been turned on its blasted end.

The man nodded once, signalling the end of his conversation with the old woman. He walked over to them, stopping at arm's length from Garrick.

'What is your purpose here?' His gaze darted to

Brenna and then back to Garrick. It wasn't lost on Garrick that each of the man's hands rested along his waist belt, at the ready to pull a dagger and defend himself and those in his village if needed. He moved like a soldier, yet Garrick still couldn't place him.

'We are travelling to Oban. We need food, shelter and a night's rest.' Brevity would serve them far more than any details.

'Odd to be travelling along this route.'

'A necessity,' Garrick added. 'We were attacked along the main road to Loch Linnhe. I need to bring her back to family in Oban where she'll be safe.' He chose to leave out any specifics of her clan or family.

'Safe from…?' The man's gaze narrowed on him.

Garrick cursed himself. He'd said too much already, and this man didn't miss the implication that they were in danger. And that the danger might also become their own if Brenna and him were still being followed as they came further into the forest to their village.

He risked the full truth. 'I found her along the road left for dead in an overturned carriage. The attackers have been chasing us since then. I'm trying to protect her and bring her to her family in Oban alive.' He neglected to add that they knew one another. It was important that his attachment to her not become a weakness of his that could be exploited later.

The man's eyes widened, and he shifted in gaze to Brenna. 'Come, then. Flora will get the woman settled. We will talk.'

He turned. Evidently, that was the end of the conversation. Garrick still didn't even know the man's name or if he was friend or foe. Garrick helped Brenna down from Montgomerie and whispered in her ear, 'Do not tell them more than you have to. I'm not sure where we stand.'

She nodded and fell in step with the old woman named Flora as a lad took their horse away to be brushed down and fed. Garrick followed the man to a small cottage made of stone, ever watchful of the other men in the village. None of them followed them inside, but he was being assessed, and he knew it. He steadied his walk, even though he doubted it would disguise his injury.

The man stooped to enter the doorway, as did Garrick. They were of equal size and build. The cottage was warm and well-tended, and he almost sighed aloud when the heat hit his body. The space was sparse but orderly. And everything of import was either near the door or on the small nightstand near the man's bed. He was a soldier, or had been. Garrick was certain of that now.

'You do not remember me, but I remember you.' The man spoke with his back turned to Garrick, exhibiting a show of trust. He wouldn't turn his back on a man he thought might be a threat or deceitful. He added a small log to fuel the winking fire and it glowed back to life. For whatever reason, this man trusted him, even though he couldn't place him. He waited for the man to continue.

'Perth.'

'Perth?' Garrick asked as the man turned to face him.

'Aye. I'm Doran Adair. You saved my life.'

What?

Garrick stilled and set his gaze upon him. After studying the stranger, he shook his head, rubbing his hand over his neck. 'I think you are mistaken. I would remember.'

Doran prodded the embers with a poker to stoke the fire. 'I am not surprised that you don't remember. You were crazed with grief. I believe you saving me was an impulse, a gut response of a seasoned soldier that you thought nothing of. As you might imagine, it meant a great deal more to me.'

He placed the poker aside and leaned against the wall, crossing his arms against his chest. 'Dragged me from the field where the reivers had left me for dead.'

Heat flushed Garrick's body and his heart thudded in his chest.

'Ayleen!' Garrick yelled at the burning abbey. He ran towards the structure and hit a wall of heat and flame he couldn't pass. He jogged alongside it, searching for an opening, any opening, in the fire.

A log popped as the flame consumed it and thrust Garrick back into the present, his heartbeat pounded in his ears.

'I see you remember after all,' Doran observed.

Garrick blinked back the grief threatening to choke him after the intense flash of memory. His breathing was uneven and rapid. He cleared his throat, swallowing the feel of the smoke burning his throat, and shook his head. 'I remember Perth, but not you.' He scrubbed a hand through his hair.

'Aye. Well, perhaps one day you might. Tell me more

about these men following you. I'd like to repay my debt to you.'

Repay me?

If anything, he owed the world for his mistakes, not the other way round.

'I wouldn't trust me either,' Doran added. 'But you are wounded. You and the woman need help if you are to reach Oban alive. It will take you at least two more days by foot and horseback. And if we have more snow it will be longer. And, by the look of you, I do not believe you'll last that long.'

He didn't mince words, which Garrick appreciated. He nodded. 'I know. The past has left me reluctant to trust my instincts.'

Doran laughed. 'I struggled as well after Perth. I ended up here by accident, half-starved, half-dead. Flora's husband took me in, and after he passed I stayed on. I have no family any more, so it seemed the right choice to repay them all for their kindness. They brought my body and soul back from the dead. Since then, I have begun to believe in my instincts again.'

I have no family any more.

The ugly words echoed through him. Nor did he. They had a great deal in common.

'So?' He gestured to the small table and chairs beside them and sat down. 'Will you at least tell me your name? More of what has happened to you and the woman with you? You and I both know it is the only way we can possibly protect you.'

Garrick hesitated, despite feeling ready to collapse.

Please let this not be a mistake. Otherwise, it may

cost Brenna her life, as well as my own. While mine holds little import, hers does. Above all else, I want her to live.

He nodded and walked to the chair. As he sank down and settled in against the smooth wood, relief coiled through him. Doran was right. If they didn't start trusting someone soon, they would both be dead.

Brenna followed Flora at a distance, catching glances of other men, women, and children as she passed. She hugged the tartan around her, self-conscious about wearing his trews and a tunic rather than a gown, as she would and should as a woman in the Highlands. Colour heated her cheeks as many of them took note of this as she passed, their gazes drifting to her legs and then back to her face.

Blast. How much further was it?

Please let Flora have an old gown she could barter for. She still had a nice hairpin that might be worthy of such an exchange. 'Hurry along,' Flora called over her shoulder.

Brenna shuffled and increased her pace, despite her flagging energy. With all of the travel and little food and rest, she was weary. Bone weary. She tripped on a root and almost fell but caught herself before she landed face-first on the ground. Flora paused and waited for her to catch up.

'Best we get some food in ye before ye topple over.' She shook her head and then smiled. 'I've just put on a stew, but I've a loaf and goat cheese for ye until it's ready.'

'And Garrick?' Brenna asked finally, walking side by side with the old woman, who was moving remarkably fast for her age.

'The man yer with?'

'Aye.'

'Doran will bring him round when it is time. 'Til then, ye can eat, bathe and change.'

The implication of a bath and set of fresh, clean clothes made her sigh. 'Thank you. That sounds lovely.' She couldn't keep the wonder from her voice. Had they only been on their own for two days? It felt like a month.

'Name's Flora Hay. Ye are?' she asked as she opened her cottage door.

'Brenna. Brenna Stewart.'

The woman stopped cold in the door frame and faced her. 'Bran's daughter?'

'Aye.'

She shook her head and continued inside. 'Difficult young man.'

'You knew him?' Brenna asked. How could that even be possible?

'Aye. Came through these parts long ago, trying to convince us to be a part of an alliance with his father and clan. Rather sore about it when we declined.'

Brenna chuckled. 'I can imagine he was. He is rather accustomed to getting his way.'

Flora shot Brenna a soft look. 'Not a great lot for a daughter of a laird such as him.'

'Nay,' she answered quietly. 'Not a bit. I find it hard to voice much of anything. 'Tis easier to agree and be agreeable.'

'For the short term, but not the long, lass. Ye are the one living out the rest of yer days, not him. Best ye remember that.'

Brenna bit her lower lip. The truth hurt to hear, and she had no other response than a nod of agreement. She would be living out her days with an Englishman she didn't know, to please Father and her people. Her happiness was a sacrifice she had agreed to. Now, she wasn't even sure why. She should have fought for her happiness, like Moira, or resisted the match, like Ewan. But she had folded to his demands to feel valued.

Now she only felt more worthless.

Flora opened a trunk and pulled out a wool dress, shaking it out. ''Tis wrinkled and a touch big for ye, but it will do far better than being seen in those, even if they are a might bit more comfortable.' She grinned at her. Brenna noticed the gap in her bottom row of teeth and couldn't help but smile back.

'Thank you. I am so grateful.' She pulled a hairpin from her plait. 'Can I repay you for it?' She extended her hand with the hairpin to Flora.

'Nay, child. I'm glad to see it come to some use. My daughter's.' A wistfulness came into her face, and Brenna's stomach tightened. She knew what the face of loss looked like.

'I'm sorry.'

'She is still alive but chooses to live with her husband and new clan up north near Inverness. I'm too old to travel so far, and she doesn't wish to return here. Still misses her father. As do I. Being here makes her sad to remember. I stay because I do not wish to forget.'

Brenna hugged the dress to her chest. What could she say?

'I'll heat some water for ye to bathe with and prepare ye some bread and cheese.'

'Thank you,' Brenna rushed out. The woman was so kind. She reminded her of her mother.

Soon, the basin was filled with hot water and Flora gave her a bar of soap and a small cloth. She stepped behind the hanging sheet for privacy as she bathed. While she couldn't manage to wash her hair, having the chance to wipe off the mud, dirt and stench of the last few days was heavenly.

'Nice looking lad ye have with ye.'

'Aye.' Brenna hesitated, reminding herself not to say too much, as Garrick had warned.

'He give ye that fine ring?'

'Nay,' Brenna answered. 'But he rescued me. I'm grateful of his help to get me to Oban.'

Focus on the truth and only add details if you have to.

'I'd say be warned. The way he looks at ye is familiar. He may be wanting more of a thank ye than ye wish to give.'

Brenna chuckled. 'Flora!'

The old woman gave a hearty laugh. 'I'm not daft, girl. I may be old, but I'm not dead. Not yet anyway.'

'You truly think he fancies me?'

'Aye. And, if I'm not mistaken, ye do too.'

Blast. Do I?

She cringed and squeezed water from the cloth. Aye, she did. More than she wished to admit. She was trying not to care, and to let him go as wilfully as he had her, but her heart pleaded otherwise. Her fingertips tingled at the memory of waking in his arms this morn.

Careful, Brenna. She was meandering into dangerous territory. She shook away the memory that heated her blood.

'As I thought,' Flora said after an overly long pause.

'I didn't say anything,' Brenna sputtered out.

'Ye didn'a have to.'

She cursed and dried herself off. Crafty old woman. Sliding the wool dress over the stays with which Flora had also provided her, Brenna sighed. She was clean, had on fresh clothes and was warm.

While a new pair of shoes might be nice, her slippers would have to do. At least the wool stockings helped. She hadn't realised how numb her toes had been until now. They tingled as she wiggled them and began to get the feeling back.

'Care for yer bread and cheese?'

'Aye,' Brenna answered. Her mouth watered at the sight and smell of it as she emerged from behind the hanging sheet.

She sat at the small table and gulped down a slice of bread before she even realised it. Then she tore another piece in half and ate it with the soft goat cheese. She sighed at the sweet taste of it as it melted in her mouth, thankful for the blessed distraction that filling her belly offered.

Chapter Ten

'We are grateful for your kindness and hospitality,' Garrick said as he and Doran joined Brenna and Flora at the small table in the old woman's warm, cosy cottage. His heart slowed at the comfortable scene of a fire burning in the hearth and the welcoming smells of stew and fresh bread. How long had it been since he'd sat at a table and enjoyed a meal such as this?

He couldn't remember. He sat at the table, met Brenna's gaze and smiled.

'We find that the people who need to find us do,' Flora added, before bringing a spoonful of stew to her lips.

'How so?' Brenna asked, her brow crinkling in curiosity. 'I had no idea this village was here. Nor did Garrick.'

Garrick bit off a chunk of bread and set his gaze upon her. The candlelight flickered along her features, and his chest tightened. He'd almost lost her twice in so many days. Them being here warm and safe with these people was nothing short of a miracle. One that he was thankful for.

'We prefer it that way,' Doran added. 'We call ourselves "the lost village". We are a collection of clans, all displaced or lost by grief. Everyone here has lost a clan, a child, something of significance that drove them away from their home to here. Together, we have found our way back to a life, one we had not imagined for ourselves.'

Garrick swallowed hard. Perhaps his loss, his grief, had led him here. Such a thought seemed ridiculous, but was such a thing possible? Wasn't arriving here a miracle of chance? Or fate? His heart wanted it to be true and wanted to believe that perhaps he had been guided back to Brenna, even after making such efforts to wilfully give her up and set her free, but the warrior in him balked at such a romantic notion. Life didn't work that way.

'A beautiful sentiment,' Brenna murmured. 'I am glad you all found one another and that we found you.'

'Aye,' Garrick added.

While he knew as a soldier that he shouldn't feel so relaxed amongst them, as they were all but strangers, knowing that Doran understood him and his losses, as he'd lost a brother of his own during the battle of the reivers in Perth, set him at ease. Being here with Brenna, knowing that she was warm and cared for, also helped him. They'd been on the run for two days and both of them were bone-weary and starved. He could see it in her drawn features.

'Since the care and aid we were given upon our arrival saved our lives, we like to help others when we can. Such as you.' Flora smiled.

'We will repay you,' Garrick added.

'You have no debt with us,' Doran replied.

Brenna met Garrick's gaze, her eyes narrowed in confusion. He looked away and nodded to Doran. Some debts could never be settled and, while Garrick understood that, he didn't know how to explain it to her without admitting his shame over what had happened to Ayleen, and he was far from ready to do that. Not yet.

If ever.

After enjoying a hearty stew with Flora and Doran, Brenna and Garrick took a walk outside to the barn to check on Montgomerie. Brenna picked up a brush and ran it along the stallion's coat.

'Seems you are being well tended to as well, old boy.' Garrick rubbed the horse's nose, and Montgomerie pushed back his palm in search of more food. 'And yet still greedy for more.'

'Can you blame him? I also ate far more than I should have this eve. My belly is full. They are kind. Perhaps too kind.' Brenna stilled and met Garrick's gaze.

He shifted closer to her. 'I thought the same at first, but it is genuine. I think it is because of how much they have lost.'

Brenna scrunched her brow. 'Aye. Knowing how they all have suffered such losses pains me. It also makes me wonder why they wouldn't feel vulnerable and more prone to protect themselves from strangers like us.' Brenna set the brush down and snuggled deeper into the borrowed cloak that was several sizes too large, making her appear smaller and younger, like when they'd first met.

All he wished to do was hold her. He answered her question instead. 'I think we are both unused to kindness without expectation.'

'You do not believe they will demand something further from us or steal our horse?' she whispered.

'Nay. I don't. My gut tells me so.'

'Are you not nervous to sleep out here alone? Shall I join you?' When she met Garrick's gaze, realising how it sounded, she added with a blush, 'To help you keep watch on Montgomerie, of course.'

Garrick's throat dried. He shoved away the feelings that stirred in the base of his gut that wanted him to say aye. Too much had happened, too much was still standing in the way of getting her to Oban safely. He slammed back his desire for her, and the loneliness that made his longing as sharp as a blade and his limbs prickle.

'Nay,' he finally answered, his throat dry and husky. 'It wouldn't be appropriate. You are engaged.'

And not to me.

'Shall I be worried about staying with Flora?'

He chuckled, relieved by the easy turn in their conversation. 'Are you scared of the old woman?'

She ribbed him in the gut. 'Stop teasing me. We have been through an ordeal. I do not know whom to trust. People are not always as they seem. You know that.'

He cupped her elbow, regretting his words. 'Aye. I

shouldn't jest. You should be wary. I will sleep outside your door to put your mind at ease, if you wish.'

And he would. He would do anything for her. *Always*. And he hated himself for it. She'd chosen another and had already let him go, as he had her. Or at least he thought he had, but seeing her, being with her, was chipping away at his defences.

Letting her go when she was hundreds of miles away had been one thing. Letting go of her now when she was within his grasp was quite another.

'Now who is being addled? You will do no such thing. You will sleep here, where it's warm, and rest. We'll have the opportunity to freeze to death tomorrow after we leave.'

His smile flattened into a line. 'Aye. We will.'

They had at least two more days to Oban, perhaps three if Doran was correct, and the man didn't seem prone to exaggeration. If anything, he might be understating the danger of their journey ahead.

'Then I will see you in the morn.' She gave Montgomerie a last pat and turned to leave.

'I will walk you back.' He rushed out, not wanting to be separated from her yet. He hadn't mustered up the courage to say what needed to be said, and he'd not be able to rest until he did.

His gut churned with each step closer to the cottage door. *Just say it, you coward.*

'Thank you,' he sputtered out.

She turned to him as she walked. The winking light from Flora's cottage cascaded along the fresh coating of snow on the ground a few lengths in front of them as they approached. 'What for? For not asking you to sleep outside in the snow?' A small chuckle resounded in her throat.

He shoved his hands in his trews and cleared his throat, which tightened with every step. Why was it so hard to speak of anything about Ayleen? He clenched his jaw.

'For offering up your ring in place of Ayleen's cross. It was generous of you. I should not have let you do it.'

She halted in front of Flora's cottage. 'The ring is nothing, while I know the cross means a great deal to you. I would never have let you give it up.' Her eyes glistened in the moonlight as she looked up at him. They held all the wonder they used to have when she'd looked at him long ago before he'd left her and disappointed her. And, for a moment, he wanted to seize it and yank them both back to the past, before he'd lost everything. Before they'd lost each other.

When he'd believed in something, and when she had believed in him.

He ran a fingertip around the edge of her ear, the touch of her warm skin sending feathery whispers through his body as he trailed the pad of his finger down the lobe to skim the side of her neck. Every part of his body tightened. *Deuces.* He wanted to kiss her. Needed to kiss her. And the way her lips parted ever so slightly told him he could. Just once more. Then he could tell her why he'd never returned. He could make right all the things that he had done wrong, but he froze.

Just as he had on the day of Ayleen's death. When it counted, he couldn't act. His mouth, his body, were immobilised by emotion and the fear of loss.

A weakness she didn't deserve.

He had to let the past be and let her go. He swallowed all the words his heart wanted to say and let his hand fall away. Emotion flashed in Brenna's eyes before she blinked and stepped back. In a few days, she wouldn't need him. Not in any way. He'd do well to remember such.

'Where are we headed in the morn?' she asked, glancing away.

'We will try a route Doran suggested. He said it is shorter than journeying along the cliffs and less exposed to the weather. It is more travelled, but my hope is that it might be safer for us, as it is wooded and has much cover. If any men are still after you, I doubt they will have any inkling of where we are travelling to.'

'Do you trust him?'

'Aye.'

'I'm surprised. You are not given to trust so easily.'

'Aye. I decided to take a risk and ask for his guidance, since he knows this land.'

'Why? You told me to be as secretive as possible.'

He shrugged. 'Aye. I did not tell you, but I recognised him when Flora brought us to the village. I didn't say anything to you because I could not place him. Once he told me where he knew me from, it came back to me.'

Even though I did not wish to remember.

'Who is he? How do you know him?'

'From my time in Perth along the borderlands. We suffered...equal losses. I dragged him to safety.'

'You saved his life.' Her features softened, and he hated the way she looked at him. As if he was a hero when it could not be further from the truth.

'He saved himself, but I gave him a chance to do so.'

She shook her head. 'You are so unwilling to let anyone thank you, Garrick MacLean. Why is that?' She crossed her arms against her chest and edged closer to him. 'There is no weakness in acknowledging the good you have done.'

'There is if I failed in the most important aspects of my life when it mattered most.'

'Blazes. You are so bull-headed.'

'No more so than you,' he added.

She scoffed. 'I am not.'

'Aye. You are. You need no one. Least of all me.'

She stepped back and her mouth gaped open.

He'd landed a blow. He hadn't intended to, but now that it was said he wasn't sorry. It was the truth. She didn't need him. No one did.

Instead of recoiling and pushing him away as he'd hoped, she came back to him slowly, like a predator stalking its prey—slow, deliberate and with her gaze locked on his. Fire, passion and something else burned bright in her eyes. His heart pounded in his chest.

'One day,' she began. 'You will realise all you have given up. All that you could have had. That we could have had. I *did* need you. I have since the day we met, but it was you that decided you didn't need or want me once you left for Perth. You are changed. You will not allow yourself happiness.'

'Nay,' he finally answered. 'I may have left but it was you that moved on. *You* gave in to your father's demands in some desperate attempt to please him and win his favour, and got yourself engaged to a bloody Englishman who may or may not want you and your family dead in the process. You showed me you didn't need *me* by moving on. Best you not forget that.'

Hurt shone on her pinched features, and she blinked back the emotion filling her eyes.

'I will see you in the morn. The sooner we reach Oban, the sooner I will be away from you. Then, you can wallow all you wish on your own.' She turned and left him.

He followed at a distance to make sure she reached Flora's cottage safely. She exasperated him, but he still…loved her.

His steps faltered at the realisation. Even though she was promised to another. Even though he didn't deserve her. Even though she hated him, all he wanted was to crush her into his arms and kiss the life out of her until she became as soft and willing as she used to be in his arms.

He cleared his throat.

Nay. Think of Ayleen. Your family. Of what happens to those you love.

She was far better off without him.

Perhaps her hate and rage would make it easier in the end. It would make it easier for her to let him go.

He wished it could be the same for him. He would suffer every remaining moment of their journey.

'Come in, child.' Flora slipped her arm through Brenna's and guided her inside.

Garrick nodded to the old woman but said nothing.

When the door closed and the latch fell into place, the feeling of loss echoed deep in his bones.

Brenna shivered. He had been about to kiss her. She'd seen a flash of the old Garrick MacLean. Desire had flared in his eyes, making the moss-green depths glow a bright clover-green just as they'd used to before he'd kiss the very life out of her. But he'd tamped it down and said nothing but a meagre thank-you for offering up her ring rather than Ayleen's cross. They still hadn't discussed why he'd left her and had never bothered to come back or send word. Still she did not have the answers she craved and it had been days.

'Men,' she grumbled under her breath and removed her cloak.

Flora chuckled at her. 'That, my dear, will never change.'

Brenna flushed. *Had she said that out loud?*

'No doubt he'll exasperate ye till the end of yer days, that one.'

'Oh, we're not a couple, Flora.'

Not any more.

Brenna tried to will the colour to subside on her cheeks. Perhaps she could claim the cold had reddened her face.

She chuckled. 'Both of ye.' She shook her head. 'Yer

words say one thing, but yer eyes and bodies say quite another.' She grabbed a large quilt and handed it to Brenna. 'Take it from me. Do not tarry in putting those things back in harmony. Youth doesn'a last for ever.' She snapped her fingers. 'It can be all be gone in a whisper of time.'

Perhaps the old woman could be trusted, and Brenna needed to talk to someone. Garrick MacLean was making her feel addled. 'I am engaged to another,' Brenna offered. 'But there was a time when I thought *we* might be engaged.'

She tsked. 'Ah. Explains it.'

'Explains what?'

'You'll keep looking at the lad that way until ye get 'im out of yer blood.' Flora filled a cup with hot water, added some herbs and handed it to Brenna. 'Drink. It will 'elp yer body heal.'

She frowned at the horrid-smelling tea and the fact that Flora was right. Garrick was still in her blood. Even now, she couldn't stop thinking of him. What was wrong with her? He'd let her go. He'd tried to make the decision about their future for her, just like her father had. Why couldn't she just let him go as easily as he had her?

'How exactly do I do that?' Brenna asked.

'Only ye know.' She sipped from her own cup. 'But, if it were me, I'd march right back to that barn and figure it out. Regrets have a way o' lastin' for ever.'

Brenna drank her tea. She needed to confront him. Ask what she needed to know before she could let him go. But the thought of having to do it exasperated her. He needed to come to her and explain himself, not the other way around. Didn't he? She almost spilled her tea.

'Curses,' she muttered.

'Ah! Careful now. Drink up and I'll read the leaves, child. I've the gift.'

Brenna sputtered at the idea of having her future told but managed to drink the last of the tea. Flora took the cup from her and held it closer to the flames for light. Brenna clutched the folds of her dress in her hands. What would she say? What could she say? Brenna chided herself. They were leaves. She didn't believe in such things. What was she nervous about?

'Ye may not believe, but I'll tell ye what I see anyhow.'

She balked. 'How did you know I didn't…?'

'Shh.' Flora held up a weathered hand.

Brenna sat back in her chair and curled her toes in her slippers. The waiting was getting to her. *Blast.* She pressed her lips together to keep from asking how much longer it would be.

'Hmm. As I thought,' she said, placing down the cup.

'And?'

'Ye won't believe me.'

She shrugged. 'Perhaps not, but what do they say?'

'He is yer love match.'

She covered her face with her hands. 'How did I know you would say something like that? Flora, your leaves are wrong.'

'They never are, but people are.' She gifted Brenna a toothless smile, and she couldn't help but laugh.

'Well, this might be the first time. If there is one certainty, it is that Garrick and I are never getting back together.'

Chapter Eleven

Morning came early. Far too early. Brenna woke to the smell of oats, spices and Flora's humming. Cocooned in warmth, Brenna couldn't move, nor did she want to. Sunlight streamed through the solitary window in the tidy cottage. She yawned and Flora turned to her.

'Wondered when ye would wake. Your lad has already been by.' She stirred the large pot hanging over the fire that burned in the hearth.

What? How had she not heard him? She had always been a light sleeper, but she'd also never been on the run for two days before, and she'd not slept well in the cave or in the abandoned church. She scratched her head and grimaced at the tangled mess her plait had become. Then, she tucked her arm back inside the quilt and snuggled further into its folds. She didn't wish to go anywhere. Not yet.

'He bid me tell ye to ready yerself to leave within the hour.'

A knock sounded at the door.

'Which was an hour past.'

Brenna scrambled up. 'Flora!' she chided and attempted to straighten herself and her hair.

Flora chuckled, winked at her and went to the door. 'A basin of water is behind the sheet. Just ready yerself. I'll tell 'im to wait a spell.'

Brenna rushed through her ablutions and smoothed her hair as she pulled it from its plait. To keep it from unravelling again, she wrapped it into a loose knot at the nape of her neck and rushed back out into the main room. Flora gave her a small loaf of bread and some cheese wrapped in cloth and pressed a kiss to her cheek. 'The lad won't wait much longer,' she whispered. The dual meaning of her words was not lost on Brenna, but she pushed them aside. She had more important things to think upon, such as staying alive.

'Thank you, Flora.' She squeezed the woman in a hug.

'Don't forget yer cloak,' she called as Brenna went for the door. 'And yer boots.'

Brenna stilled at the sight of a pair of worn boots and the cloak she'd worn yesterday.

'I can't take them, Flora. It is too much. I—'

'Nonsense. 'Tis yers. My daughter has no need of them. Not any more. Without them, ye will suffer in the cold. Take them. Please.'

'Thank you. I hope I will be able to repay you one day for your kindness.' Brenna shrugged into the cloak and pressed a final kiss to the woman's soft cheek.

'Listening to yer heart will be payment enough.'

Tears threatened Brenna as Flora closed the door

behind her, but the sight of Garrick's annoyed scowl from atop Montgomerie banished them. Why was he always in such a foul temper?

'Ready?' he asked, studying her.

'Aye,' Brenna answered, avoiding his gaze. She accepted his offered hand, and he pulled her up easily in front of him.

He tugged her back against his chest and the solid warm presence of his body all at once sent a jolt of heat and longing in her, despite how hard she tried to ignore it. She smiled despite herself.

Damn you, Flora, and your tea leaves.

Garrick and Brenna rode out of the lost village as the sun rose against the horizon. The hot pink and orange shades were in gorgeous contrast to the light snowfall and the forest of dark greens and blacks before them. She studied the landscape in hopes of one day finding her way back to this cosy village. Despite it being a brief visit, Brenna would miss Flora. The old woman had had a way of getting under her skin even if she couldn't read tea leaves. Brenna slipped her hand in the pocket of the cloak Flora had given her and felt something cool. She pulled it from her pocket and spied the ring she had offered Flora as a trade for food and shelter.

'Flora,' Brenna muttered and shook her head.

'Aye?' Garrick asked as he turned Montgomerie into the snow-covered forest, settling into a gentle, steady rhythm as they rode. Large evergreens and naked branches of tall oaks canopied them as they went.

'Nothing,' said Brenna. 'Flora slipped the ring we

traded her back into the pocket of the cloak before she gifted it to me.'

The cool wind fluttered Garrick's hair as he turned to her and smiled, his breath coiling up in the air like smoke. 'Good people. I hope to be able to repay them one day for their kindness and generosity.'

'As do I,' Brenna agreed as she slipped the ring back onto her finger. Maybe that was the one thing she and Garrick *could* agree upon.

They rode for hours in silence, stopping every now and then to provide a rest for themselves and Montgomerie. Soon, the sun was high in the blue sky and beginning its descent. It had helped to melt away the snow, and patches of grass and leaves peeked through. She sniffed the air and her stomach rumbled.

Garrick slowed Montgomerie to a halt.

Brenna listened. At first it was nothing but the smell of something cooking. Rabbit, maybe? But then she heard talking, a low rumbling of voices. At least two men were nearby.

Garrick brought a finger to his lips and guided Montgomerie deeper into the forest. The voices stopped and Brenna held her breath. Had the men heard their approach or merely run out of things to say to one another?

Garrick cupped his hand to her ear and whispered, 'Take the reins and ride as fast as you can to the ravine below. If you can't make it there, head to the water. I will find you.'

He slid off and onto the ground without a sound and pressed the reins into her hands. He gave her hands a squeeze and then disappeared into some dense shrubbery before she could utter a word of rebuttal or question him further.

Why did he keep doing this? She shook her head in irritation and ground her teeth. Why didn't he trust her to help him? Why could they never work together as a team? He always wished to rescue her and send her away from the fray. She released a frustrated sigh and then turned down the path as quickly as she could, with the sloshy ground beneath. She spied the ravine below and headed that way.

It didn't take her long to arrive. Garrick appeared minutes later, out of breath.

'Nothing to worry over. Two brothers out hunting.'

She said nothing.

'What?' he asked, resting his hands on his waist belt. 'Why are you scowling at me?'

'Why must you *always* be the lone wolf? You send me off while you tend to whatever threat is about. Although I am not a soldier, I can be of help. Have I not already? We need to help each other to get to Oban. That can't happen if you send me off each time there is a threat. You are wounded.'

'It is not so simple.'

Suddenly, all the times she'd been set aside because she'd been seen as useless because she was a woman, and was also *Brenna*, ignited like fire in her. The dam of emotion she had been holding burst into her chest. 'Aye, it is. If I was a man, I would be asked to assist you. As a woman, I am dismissed despite being capable.'

He blinked back at her, his body still. Frozen, even.

A small slip of movement along his hands resting along his waist belt caught her eye. Then he pulled and threw a dagger in a blink of an eye. It whizzed by her ear, followed by a thud to the ground. She turned to see a dead man behind her.

Shock stifled the scream in her throat. What was happening?

Garrick grabbed Montgomerie's mane, leapt up onto the horse's back behind her and kicked the stallion's sides. The horse sped off, and Garrick covered Brenna with his body as he bent low to shield her. She couldn't breathe. They raced through the fields and up a long embankment. Hooves sounded behind them and Montgomerie took a sharp right turn. An arrow cut into the tree behind her a moment after they changed direction and she gasped.

Were there others? Had it been a trap? She clung to Montgomerie's sides inhaling the deep scent of horse-flesh and earth. Another arrow sunk into a tree near them as they continued. They were close, so close.

Please God, let us live.

'Jump,' Garrick commanded.

She opened her eyes. 'Jump?' she asked, scanning the area. It was a wide-open field. How would she be able to outrun anyone here? And how could he out-ride them?

'I'm sorry,' he said, and then grabbed her by the waist and let go. She hit the ground hard before rolling to a stop.

Sucking in a breath, she rubbed her thigh before clambering up and running into the forest. With her dark cloak, she'd have a better chance at hiding there until she could work out what was happening.

She scanned the area as she jogged along. *Thank you, Flora.* The woman's gifts of a cloak and walking boots would save her. Ducking behind a large fallen tree, she crouched down and studied the area. Dense woods to the south, open field to the north behind her and less dense woods to the east and west. Surely she should go south towards Oban? She panted for breath and closed her eyes, remembering what Garrick had told her but minutes before.

Head to the water.

She breathed in and out to slow her heart. She'd never be able to hear the water if all she could hear was her heartbeat roaring in her ears. In and out, in and out. Her breathing began to even and then slow. She could do this. Despite being a poor hunter, she had a keen sense of direction and could use what landmarks she had coupled with the sun to find her way out of this mess. But she also had to do all of that while not being killed by those hunting them down with a bow and arrow.

That was another problem altogether.

And then there was finding Garrick. Her heart thundered again. She needed him. Despite what he believed, he also needed her. Without each other, how would they ever get to Oban? Hurried and loud footfalls sounded behind her, as if someone was running towards her, and she held her breath. Crawling on the ground, she peeked out from the side of the log she was hiding behind and saw Garrick coming right towards her with two men running hard and fast behind him.

Where was Montgomerie, or the other men's horses?

Her heart sank. Had they felled Garrick's beloved horse with an arrow, or had he been snared in a trap? Rage bloomed hot and full in her chest. If they had, she would seek out her own revenge, as she'd grown terribly fond of the creature. She searched for a weapon but only found a large, long branch nearby, which was better than nothing. While she couldn't take out both of Garrick's pursuers with it, she could try to trip up one. And if they had hurt Montgomerie that was the least she could do...

Garrick ran past her with one man close behind. Once they passed, she slid out the branch and raised it just as the last man approached. His feet tangled up in it and he hit the ground hard with a groan, sliding on the wet leaves. He caught sight of her and growled. She popped up and ran in the same direction as Garrick. When she spied a tall oak, she grabbed one of the lowest branches and swung herself up. She hopped up to the next branch and then another. While she knew she couldn't outrun the bastard, she could out-climb him. He was far too large and heavy a man to be able to climb.

Don't look down. Don't look down.

That was the only weakness in her plan. She hated heights like she despised bats. She tucked herself as close to the trunk as she could, in case he was the one with the fine bow and arrow skills.

A dagger landed in the bark near her hand and vibrated from the force of the throw, and she scrabbled to keep hold of the tree. It was a near miss, but on the bright side she now had a weapon of her own. She yanked it from the bark and held it. Clinging to the bark, she dared not look below to see where the men were, or even where Garrick was. One glance would send her into a panic, so she stared out at the horizon and the hills far away from where they were now.

Way off in the distance to the south, she could see the outskirts of a small village. Was that Oban? It looked far closer than she thought it would be. If they survived this attack, they could make it there in a day if they pushed hard.

Her heart dropped. That was only if they still had Montgomerie… Her heart squeezed at the thought of losing the beautiful horse, and she wasn't certain they had.

'Ye cann'a hide up there all day, lass,' the man called up, laughing at her.

She scoffed. Little did he know that the idea of coming down this tree was even more terrifying than encountering him. She might very well be up here all night. The tree shook. Hazarding a glance down, she glimpsed the man hoisting himself up to the first branch.

Blast.

He was large and slow in his ascent, but he'd reach her in time. Now what was she to do? And where was Garrick? She'd lost sight of him and his pursuer long ago once they'd disappeared into the distance. Another blade flew up near her leg, missing it but pinning her skirts to the flesh of the tree. *Thistles.* The man had keen aim. She tried to bend over to gather the new blade, but she couldn't do it without looking down, which made her vision swirl. Leaning back against the trunk and gripping it with all her might, she sucked in slow, steady breaths. She could do this.

Useless.

She wasn't useless. She was strong. She was also a Stewart. She would work this out. She closed her eyes, leaned down and felt for the blade and, once she'd found it, she pulled it from the tree, freeing her skirts in the process. Carefully she moved back and balanced herself, taking deep breaths to steady her breathing and think clearly. She needed a plan.

Aye, I can do this.

'Prayers will na save ye now, lassie. I'm coming up.'

What?

She could hear the scraping of boots along bark and grunting as the man began his climb up, branch after branch. *Perfect.* Not only had he reached the second branch, but he was continuing up. She scanned the tree. What could she throw at him to slow his progress? She frowned. The only thing she had other than the daggers, which she might need, was her beloved walking boots. She sighed and stooped to unlace them with one hand while still clinging to the tree with the other.

Possessions won't matter if we're dead.

Garrick had been right yet again, and she muttered to herself.

She waited until the man was in view and hurled the boot at his head.

It hit him soundly on the top of his head, and he

cursed, sliding a length back down the trunk. She con-
gratulated herself on her precision.

'Ye minx. Just wait till I get a hand on ye!'

She cringed as he thrust himself back up and onto
the next branch. The man had only two more to go until
he would be able to reach up and grab her by the ankle.

She unlaced the other boot, her stockinged feet curling around the branch to steady herself. Patiently she
waited until he was in the perfect position to heave her
other boot at him. He looked up right as she threw it,
so it hit him squarely in the eyes and forehead, elicit-
ing yet another curse.

'Bitch!' He rubbed his forehead. 'Ye will wish ye
had never seen me once I get a hold of ye.'

'I fear you may feel the same about me,' Garrick
answered. He threw a blade at the man and it hit him
square in the back. He hollered and fell from the tree.
Brenna turned away to avoid seeing the impact of his
fall but winced as she heard the dull thud as the man
hit the ground.

She sighed in relief and clung to the tree. 'Sound
timing. I had run out of boots,' she called.

'You can come down now,' Garrick answered.

'Aye,' she replied shakily. 'I know that.'

'Well, come on, then. While I think this is all of
them from their scouting party, there may well be more
on the outskirts, as I'd believed there were only two of
them the first time.'

'I don't know if I can come down,' Brenna admitted, daring a glance to see where the next limb was.
She swiped her foot in the air.

How had she got up here in the first place? *Thistles*.

'Bren, we've no time for this nonsense. Climb down.'

'I am not being difficult. I'm afraid of heights, as you well know.'

He paused. 'Then how did you even get up there?'

Exasperated, she shouted back, 'I don't know. I just did. I looked up and climbed. A man was trying to kill me, if you will remember. I suppose I was more frightened of him than the height.'

Garrick uttered a curse and then the tree shifted. She stole a glance to see him climbing up one branch after another. She hated being rescued. She had to at least attempt to go down one limb just to salvage some of her withering dignity.

You can do this. You can do this.

She leaned back, let her hands slide carefully down the bark and let her back foot fall until it touched one of the branches below. She slid down and rested there. Her heart hammered in her chest, her body vibrating from the effort of descending such a short distance.

'See,' Garrick encouraged. 'You can climb down. Try another, Bren. I believe in you.'

His words stole her breath.

Did he believe in her? Why? No one else did.

'I'm only a branch below now. Step down onto the last branch and we can climb down the rest together.'

We can climb down the rest together.

Tears threatened and she bit her lip. Why did his words hit her so squarely in the chest, making it so difficult to breathe?

He wasn't talking about anything other than getting down from this tree. She was promised to another. He didn't love her. She didn't love him. Not any more.

Did they?

Yet, she felt sick to her stomach, knowing they never would be much of anything together any longer, and she didn't even know why. That was a lie. She did know why. He'd never told her why he'd disappeared and never returned. Why he'd never fought for her. Why he'd let her go without a word. He had been the centre of her belief in the world and in herself, and when he'd gone and disappeared without a trace what little hope and belief she'd had in herself had blown away in the wind.

And it made her furious.

She battled back her tears and clenched her jaw. She would get down from this blasted tree and get answers. Demand them. She deserved to know why. She deserved to be able to close that chapter of her life neatly and move on.

And knowing the truth would make her feel better.

Until then, she'd focus on her anger to get down.

She leaned back, let her leg fall out and swing until it landed on another limb below. Lowering herself down again, pride filled her chest. She had done it.

'Good.' Garrick smiled and hoisted himself onto the branch with her. He was so close, his chest pressed to her back.

She'd done it all right. *Perfect.* Crushed limb to limb against the man she hated one minute and desired the next.

'Face me,' he murmured, resting his palms on her

shoulders, the heat of him easing into her limbs like a sip of whiskey on a cold winter night. She turned in his arms, his hands sliding along her arms to steady her, leaving a trail of heat and fire. He loosened his waist belt and looped it around her before buckling it again.

'Hold on,' he whispered, synching the belt around their waists, his eyes flickering with desire. A shock went through her body at the jolt of movement that thrust them closer to each other. He guided her arms up and around his neck until his lips were flush with her forehead.

Did he just kiss her?

She had to have imagined it.

One branch and then another, and she clung to him, squeezing her eyes shut.

The ground. All she wanted was to be back on the ground.

And to never leave his arms again.

She stilled at her own thoughts. What was wrong with her? She needed to get her feet well on the ground. Being this high in the air was making her addled. The man was going to give her answers for what he'd done to her and why.

Now.

Otherwise, she would shift back and forth for ever between what had been and what could be, and that was no way to live a life or a future, especially after almost perishing up a blasted tree.

Chapter Twelve

'Better?' Garrick asked as he jumped from the last branch to the ground and settled her there alongside him. He loosened his belt from her waist, his hands lingering along her sides. His chest tightened as she stepped away from him, creating a void. His body thrummed at the loss of her. She'd always had this effect on him. Since the day they'd met, he'd felt in harmony with her on every level, and when they'd been separated he'd felt incomplete.

And everything in his life lacked colour.

How in the world could he give her over to another man, knowing how incomplete he would feel for the rest of his days?

He sighed and brushed off his hands on his trews. Because it was what was best for her. He couldn't protect her, and the idea of trying to and failing once more, of losing her as he'd lost his family, gutted him more than his desire for happiness. She mattered to him more than he mattered to himself.

Letting her go was the right thing to do. The just thing to do. She deserved a whole man to be her husband, not him. He was shattered into a thousand pieces.

'Why on earth did you toss me from Montgomerie? And where is he? Did they...?' Her face paled.

'He should be fine. I hid him by the water.'

'And you shoved me off and left me because...?'

'To keep you safe.'

'You left me alone and forced me to climb up a tree to escape when I hate heights to keep me safe?' Anger darkened her blue eyes into something close to a bluebird's wings.

He paused. He'd missed something. 'Why are you angry at me for protecting you?'

'Abandoning me, again, does not keep me safe.' She shook her head and gathered her boots, muttering to herself as she went.

He gritted his teeth. 'You are safe and alive, so I must disagree.'

'But for how much longer? If we don't start working together and staying together, we may not make it to Oban. As a soldier, you should know that.' She yanked on a boot and tied the laces.

He scoffed and rested his hands on his waist belt. 'Do you want me to keep you by my side to fight?'

'We could at least help one another. You just assume I will be of no use and cast me aside.'

'Can you throw a blade? Fight off a man twice your size?' He shook his head. 'You aren't being reasonable. Gather your other boot and let's be off.'

Unbelievable. Had *he* just called *her* unreasonable?

She couldn't let it go. He was finally talking with her, and she'd ask what she'd wanted to ask since the day he'd rescued her and been thrust back into her life. And this time he would answer it.

'Is that why you left me, abandoned me, a year ago? I was of no use to you?'

He stilled. The blood drained from his face.

'I will not leave here until you answer me. I deserve that at least.'

He rubbed the back of his neck and released a sigh. 'Because I had to.'

She shook her head, but then met his gaze, fire burning in her eyes. 'Nay. That is no answer. You are a laird. You do not have to do anything at all. The world bends to you like reeds in the wind. You could have stayed. You could have returned. You chose not to. Admit it.'

His blood hammered through his veins. Anger flashed through him. 'You know nothing of what the world has or has not given me. The world has never bent to me, Brenna, as it has to you. *I* have lost everything, not you. We're leaving.' He stalked off and down the hill in search of where he'd left Montgomerie before he lost his temper.

'By all that is holy, do not walk away from me, Garrick MacLean. You will finally explain to me why you left.' She ran to catch up with him. 'I will know the truth.'

'None of it matters. It is the past.' He watched the distance, scanning for trouble as he went, doing his best to ignore her protests and demands. 'Keeping you alive is what matters now.'

'And the only way we can stay alive is if we work together, and we cannot do that with this wedge between us. You must explain yourself. Otherwise, how can we trust one another?'

Garrick hesitated to answer. Was that the sound of horses galloping off in the distance? He cursed and hunched over to shield her as he dragged her along to a large set of boulders to their left.

'There are more,' he muttered.

'I thought Doran said this was the safer route.'

'It is.' Garrick stared out in the direction they had just come from.

He turned and eased his head up and over the boulder. *Curses*. He recognised the plaid from earlier in their journey. While the MacLeans had always been in good standing with the Camerons, the Stewarts had a rather precarious relationship with the dominant clan that butted up against their borders to their north. 'Has your father mended his issues with the Camerons?'

'Nay. He has ongoing skirmishes with quite a few clans. You know this.'

'Have the Camerons begun working with the King?'

'Nay,' she scoffed. 'They wield too much power. They have no need to. Not *that* much has changed since your departure.'

'But they are too far south. Why would they be here in these woods?'

She shrugged. 'The Camerons are everywhere. Perhaps they have eased further south. This land was abandoned by the MacDougalls after their laird passed and had a less than spectacular harvest last season. They moved in closer to the sea.'

'Why didn't you tell me?'

'You didn't ask,' she snapped. 'You were too busy throwing me off horses and keeping me safe.'

Damn. Now they had to deal with the Camerons. The soldiers on their horses approached. They'd been seen. Otherwise, they wouldn't have headed this way.

He pulled a blade from his boot and handed it to Brenna. 'Stick it up your sleeve. Be ready to throw it if need be. Perhaps you'll have fine aim twice.'

'Show yourself. You hunt on Cameron grounds.'

Garrick stood with his hands out. 'Nay. We are travelling through. We are not hunting, and upon last check these are not Cameron grounds.'

'The men with you were hunting. You cannot deny it.'

Garrick took note of the fact the man did not contest the challenge to these being Cameron grounds. 'Aye. They were hunting and tried to kill us in the process. We killed them to escape. We are travelling to Oban. We have no quarrel with you.'

'And you are?'

'Garrick MacLean, Laird of Westmoreland.'

The man stilled and studied him, narrowing his brow. 'You are dead.'

The soldier next to him pulled back his bow and arrow, ready to set it free straight into Garrick's chest at the leader's command.

'Nay. Just presumed to be. I returned to find my home and family dead. I am trying to bring this lass safely to Oban to be with her family. She was left for dead by a band of raiders along the road.'

'And the girl?' The man approached, gesturing to the boulder.

Garrick studied the man, hesitating to reveal Brenna to them. He did not know if he could be trusted. He didn't even know who he was.

'And you are?' Garrick countered.

'Rolf Cameron, son of Laird Cameron.'

Garrick smiled in relief. 'We have met, but when you were but a boy. I remember you had a fine hound. I came and hunted one summer with you and your brother, Royce, to thin the herd of deer.'

The young man studied him and recognition dawned on his face. 'Aye. That was a while ago. Ten years? But I do remember. Father scolded me for sneaking out to follow the hunt. Almost got shot by an arrow.' He nodded and the soldier next to him put down his bow and arrow and slung the pouch of quivers and bow behind his shoulder.

Garrick chuckled, relieved by the reduced threat. 'I remember. You were about the same size as the deer at the time.'

Rolf nodded. 'Aye. I was.'

'We would be grateful for safe passage through your lands. We are trying to reach the McKennas of Westmoreland.'

'Aye. We have an agreement with Laird McKenna. We will assist you.' He whistled and twenty soldiers emerged from the trees as if they had materialised out of the bark.

Garrick stilled. *Saints be.* He hadn't seen any of them. The Camerons were skilled warriors and always had been. Luck smiled down upon them. If Rory hadn't had such an agreement with them, Garrick and Brenna might have already been felled by an arrow.

'So, who is this lady you travel with?'

'Bran Stewart's youngest daughter, Brenna. You can come out now,' he called.

Slowly, she emerged from behind the boulder, her gaze fixed upon Rolf. 'We are acquainted,' she answered coolly.

'Aye.' Rolf frowned. 'We are. How is your brother?'

'Ewan is well. And your shoulder?'

Rolf shifted on his feet and rested his hands along his weapons belt. 'Healed. Although we are still awaiting repayment for the stallion lost by his carelessness.'

Deuces. Garrick commanded himself not to roll his eyes. What had Bran and Ewan done now to incite the wrath of one of the most dominant clans in the Highlands?

'I am certain the Laird of Glenhaven and his son will take care of that outstanding debt upon our safe return. Is that not right, Miss Stewart?' Garrick met her gaze, willing her to be agreeable so they might live to see Oban.

She hesitated but then nodded. 'An oversight on their behalf. My recent engagement has been a distraction.'

'Congratulations,' Rolf added. 'I had not heard.'

'Aye. It has been swift in its terms.' Garrick was thankful she did not add the bit about being engaged to an Englishman.

'Then I wish you the best upon your union.' He nodded to Garrick.

'Nay,' Brenna added. ''Tis not with Laird MacLean.'

Garrick clenched his jaw, willing her to say no more. ''Tis an Englishman.'

Rolf shook his head and muttered to himself as he turned. 'Bloody hell. Let us go before I change my mind.'

Garrick fell in step with him and waved Brenna on to join them. 'Aye. A fine idea. We are grateful for your assistance. Our journey has been challenging. I will need to stop along the stream to gather my mount.'

Rolf whistled and another man emerged from the forest, holding Montgomerie's reins. 'We have already found him. It alerted us to the situation at hand, as we have a daily sweep through this pass. It is often travelled by hunters and thieves, so we keep close watch.' His gaze slid to Brenna and then back to Garrick.

Garrick shook his head. *Of course they would.* They had the men and the means to do so. One of the few clans of the area that did. 'Aye. Thank you.'

Despite being in the hands of the Camerons, a thread of relief spooled through Garrick. They were aligned with the McKennas and would protect them because of it. No doubt it was the only reason Rolf and his men hadn't seized them already for trespass. Garrick grimaced. He was bone-weary and his wounds ached from the strain of the battle with the men they'd encountered along the way. If Brenna could keep from inciting the Camerons, they had a chance of finally reaching Oban, where Garrick could fulfil his duty of returning her safely to the fiancé waiting for her and be on his way to attempt to salvage his clan and have his revenge.

'And if we could send word to the Laird of Blackmore, so he will know of our arrival...?'

'Aye. That shall be no difficulty.'

'And Father?' Brenna asked.

Rolf's steps hitched for a beat but then he continued. 'Aye, my lady. If that is your wish.'

Garrick sent her a glare. She lifted her eyebrows at him in challenge.

He counted to ten in his head, reminding himself to be patient. He was hungry, tired and aching, and not at his best. Losing his temper would not do anyone a whit of good. Not when they were so close to reaching Blackmore safely and putting this behind them. Then, Brenna could be back on track to living the life and future she wanted, and he could begin the task of attempting to put what was left of his back together.

Even though he had no idea how to begin. How did one begin a life again without a family, clan or home to their name? His gut turned. One couldn't when there was nothing left to piece back together. Perhaps he would just return to the field as a soldier. He was good at it and the losses didn't plague him as they used to. He could even assemble a few wayward men to help eradicate the bands of reivers running rogue through the borderlands unchecked. Doran might even join him in that endeavour. He'd had losses of his own, ghosts that still haunted him as well. One of the many reasons they'd understood one another.

He thought of asking Rolf if he knew of the lost village, but if the man didn't Garrick would be exposing his new friends to being absorbed by one of the most powerful clans in the Highlands, and he couldn't risk such. He'd keep their existence to himself. He could only hope Brenna knew to do the same.

'We have a small lodging off to the south a half-day from here,' Rolf continued.

As Garrick studied the area, he realised it was familiar. He'd been here before many, many years ago as a young boy. 'Is this not MacDougall land?'

Rolf didn't answer for a moment, as if choosing his words carefully. He nodded towards two men far ahead of them. 'Aye,' he replied, his voice low. 'Their clan was overrun and the laird stripped of his title. Its members scattered and left to fend for themselves.' He paused, his jaw tightening. 'Much like yours.'

Garrick's steps faltered and he cleared his throat.

Much like yours.

So the MacLeans were not the only ones to be made an example of. He clenched his hands into fists at his sides.

'Laird McKenna and my father decided to band together and protect this area between us as best we could. There are still hunters and thieves about, but we will soon restore it to what it once was with the proper men and coin. And time, of course.'

'Aye,' Garrick answered. His throat was tight with anger and emotion. The King had no right to obliterate the clans bit by bit. One day the bastard would answer for what he'd done. Garrick only hoped it would be within his lifetime.

Rolf met his gaze. 'Father says we will have our day. And we will. But we are far from strong enough yet.'

'The day shall never be soon enough.'

'Use it to fuel you, brother,' he whispered. 'Otherwise, it will eat you alive.' The pain in his dark gaze told Garrick that he understood the words he said, as he had lived him. 'I will check on the men. Ride if you wish.' He whistled and one of the Cameron soldiers brought over Montgomerie while Rolf jogged away to catch up with the men at the front line.

Garrick took the reins and rubbed Montgomerie's nose. 'Aye, boy. Almost there.' He mounted and extended his hand to Brenna.

She hesitated.

'Whatever qualm you have with me we shall settle this eve. Until then, we ride.'

'And if I don't?'

'In case you missed the ire in Rolf's eyes, you are not revered here. I am the only ally you have until we reach Oban. Just be glad your brother-in-law is so well liked that they didn't cleave us with a dozen arrows.'

'You make a point.' She accepted his hand, and Garrick pulled her up to settle in front of him.

The rest of the afternoon was uneventful. Merely a quiet ride through what Garrick could now see was clearly a clan that had been burned out of its village, its crops torched along the way. Skeletons of cottages dusted in snow, half-fallen rock walls and the small graveyard with its markers off in the distance.

Brenna shivered against him.

'Are you cold?' Garrick asked, pulling her closer to him on instinct.

'Nay,' she whispered. 'It is eerie to travel through. So many empty remnants of the lives that were once here.'

'Aye.' He hesitated. 'Is this what became of villages below Westmoreland? Of my clan?'

Her silence was his answer. He sucked in a breath, and she placed her hand briefly upon his and squeezed it before letting go.

The gesture was almost his undoing, and he cleared his throat to keep the emotion at bay. His people had suffered this. On his watch. He faced the ruins. He would not look away at the carnage. He studied everything. The broken cookery, the scorched roof of the small house, even the burnt remnants of a plough, its iron ploughshare and beam tilted and wedged in the ground.

This would keep him focused on his mission: return Brenna and restore his clan. He didn't want to lead it any more, as he had lost such a privilege by abandoning it before, but by all that was holy he would restore his people. He would find them a home and future to live for. Somehow, he would do it, and these images would push him on until he was nothing.

The King would not win.

'Whatever you are thinking, Garrick MacLean, don't.'

Brenna's words yanked him back from his thoughts. 'You do not know me so well,' he muttered. 'To claim to know my thoughts.'

'Actually, I do, and I am reminding you that you cannot undo the past. You cannot bring any of them back.'

Her words landed like an anvil to his chest, squeezing out the temporary hope his anger brought him.

'Nay, I cannot, but I can bring the men who did this to their knees.'

Chapter Thirteen

Of course, Garrick would focus on retribution. Brenna stared out as the muted orange rays of the sun began to set over the dark, reflective mirrors of the sea that had finally come into better view. She hugged her cloak to her body. Was that not what all men did? Died for past deeds and sacrificed themselves in the name of the dead, only to unwittingly abandon the living? She was so tired of it. Bone-weary of never looking forward. All she wanted was to seize her chance, her moment of freedom and happiness, but she seemed destined to have it slip from her grasp.

Again.

First, she'd believed Garrick would be her hope for the future. That they could secure it together and build a family and something of substance on their own. When that had faded away into nothing when he'd disappeared, and after she had grieved, she'd seized upon the idea of marrying Stephen Winters, as it would bring some security to her clan. She was beginning to understand why Moira had not wished to remarry at all after her first husband's death and had wanted to live unburdened in a garden surrounded by her wee plants. For years all she had wanted was to be pretty and sought over enough to have suitors to choose from and make Father proud of her by achieving a suitable match that would enhance the clan's power in the Highlands.

She'd been such a fool.

No wonder she had been viewed as useless. A suitable match was the goal of a girl in braids, not the goal of a woman who desired independence and worth.

Maybe having Garrick leave her had been a saving grace. She'd learned to sew—not well, mind you—but she could. She had learned some healing techniques and the importance of herbs. All to prove to herself and others that she was more than pretty Brenna in lovely frocks without a care in the world or a meaningful opinion in her head. That she had worth, like her siblings.

But the moment Garrick had returned she'd realised that those goals had also been a ruse to distract herself from the truth at hand. She still had no footing, no understanding of what she truly wished to be or what mark she wanted to make in this world. She was not settled in the future, working towards her goals like her sister and brother. She was tethered to nothing and could blow away, disappearing into nothing if the right wind blew her about, and it threatened to drive her mad.

They made a final turn to what appeared to be an old barn. Its high ceilings and wide shape suggested it was little more than a structure built to break the wind and protect one from the elements. As the wind ruffled the edges of her cloak against her face, casting prickles of cool snowflakes on her cheek, she was grateful to know she would not be forced to sleep out in the cold. And even more excited by the prospect of being at Blackmore tomorrow eve. She could sleep in a warm bed, have a bath, see her sister again and not be forced to be in constant contact with Garrick, the man she still…

'Did you hear me?' Garrick asked, resting his hand on her own, sending a trill of attraction through her.

She shook her head, angry at herself for still mooning over a man who did not love her. Why could her body and heart not forget him when he had so easily forgotten her?

'You can go inside. I'll tend to the horses.' He turned to Montgomerie and Rolf came over, offering to assist her down. She accepted his hand reluctantly, but she was grateful for his strength, as she felt weak in the knees as her boots hit the snow.

'Go on in. They will have built the fire by now.'

'Aye. Thank you,' she answered gratefully. And she was. Her teeth chattered in her skull. Her belly grumbled with hunger. Her limbs ached from journeying over several days.

When she entered the structure, the warmth and size of it stunned her. There was a large set of stalls on one side for animals, an open area in the middle with a hearth and tables with benches and living quarters off to the right. She'd never seen such a place before and she stood taking it all in.

'Your brother-in-law helped us build it. A way station of sorts, for travellers as well as us when we make our sweeps of the hillside. He is generous as well as ingenious.' Rolf stood beside her.

'I would agree. He is a good man.'

'So is Garrick. Best not take advantage.'

She balked. 'What are you talking about?'

'I believe we understand each other perfectly, despite your words.' His scowl deepened as he studied her face.

Before she could challenge him further, Garrick came in and approached them. 'Quite a place you have here, Rolf. We are grateful for your generosity.'

'Thank Rory. It was his idea and coin.'

'I will, but you gave us safe passage. It will not be forgotten.' He clapped him on the shoulder.

Rolf smiled. 'Let us get you all the way to Blackmore before you give us any further praise. There are two makeshift beds on the far end. She should take the higher one.'

'Thank you.' He nodded and led Brenna to the wooden slats that acted as beds and the wool blankets covering them. 'We are lucky to have run into them and made our way to this shelter. It would have been a cold night otherwise.'

'Aye.' She avoided his gaze and shifted away from him. 'I will tend to my needs and return.' She couldn't be near him a moment longer or she'd scream.

'I'll come with you,' he offered.

Garrick followed Brenna outside. After getting her this far, he'd not abandon her now and leave her exposed. While he didn't believe those who had originally been after her were continuing their hunt, he didn't know what else or who else lurked outside in this storm.

As he followed her, she stopped and faced him, crossing her arms against her chest. 'Tell me the truth behind why you abandoned me or leave me be.'

He blinked back at her. Just when he thought he'd avoided the previous conversation, Brenna revived it once more. 'I am looking out for you. I know you are tired. We all are. Stop being so unreasonable.'

Her eyes widened and he knew he had made a misstep. 'Unreasonable? Am I really?'

'Aye,' he answered, closing the distance between them. 'What has you so riled?'

'You. You will never understand me.' She moved deeper into the evergreens as a light snow began once more, its flakes glittering along her dark cloak.

Garrick rushed after her. What was wrong with her? She couldn't run into the forest alone. Not with who knew what about. Grasping her by the arm, he forced her to stop and look at him. 'Will you…?' The rest of the sentence died on his lips. The tears he saw falling unbidden down her cheeks gutted him, and he stood transfixed.

'I hate you, Garrick MacLean. I curse the day I met y-you.' She hiccupped on the last word.

And the day I met you was the best day of my life.

He shook his head, his heart slamming in his chest. Alarm bolted him to the ground. Something was very wrong. Brenna didn't cry. The only time he'd seen her cry before was…the day he'd left.

'I am not trying to be obtuse. I am trying to return you to the life you want. The one you chose.' He gripped her by the arms.

'Why did you abandon me? Just tell me. Stop torturing me by not answering when I ask.'

'You know why,' he answered.

'Nay. I don't.'

'I left for Ayleen.'

'I know why you left, but why did you not return? Send word? Or let me go? Why keep me bound to the unknown?'

'It does not matter now. That is the past.' He edged closer.

And it didn't matter, not to him. The outcome had been the same. He'd lost her. Did they need to name how?

'It matters to me, yet you will not tell me. You torture me with your silence and stoicism, and I hate you for it.'

He let her arms go. Tortured her?

'How do I make you understand?' she pleaded.

'Just try,' Garrick rasped out. His throat tightened. If they were to both survive losing one another, they needed to move through the past and let each other go, even if it obliterated him to bits.

'For the longest time, I never felt I was enough, but with you…*you* made me realise *I* was enough. I didn't have to prove anything else to anyone. I didn't have to try to please Father, or be smart like Moira, or follow duty to the clan like Ewan. I was enough as me… Brenna.' She pressed a palm to her chest, tears streaming down her cheeks.

'But you left me and never came back, and all I could conclude was that I wasn't enough. And I hated you for it. I hated you for letting me believe that I was enough for just one moment. Because, when I realised I wasn't, I couldn't breathe. I couldn't be. I was lost.'

Her body shook. 'So that, Garrick MacLean, is why I hate you and why, now that you have come back, I hate you even more.'

By God, she was beautiful. Had she ever been more beautiful to him than now, covered in mud and dirt, her cheeks coloured with emotion? Emotion for him. All he wanted to do was crush her into an embrace, but he didn't dare move lest he startle her like a doe in the brush.

He had broken her. He'd never felt as small as he did now, knowing he had brought her to this. He also knew it was but another example of why he needed to let her go. He was clumsy with those he cared for, especially fragile bits of beauty such as her. How could he make her understand it was him, not her?

'I left you and I had planned to come back. I did. I just needed to save Ayleen, because I couldn't save my brother Lon from the fever that stole him from us too soon. You know that. You remember.' He released a shuddering breath before continuing.

'But, when I couldn't save her, I was lost. I realised I wasn't enough for you to keep you safe. Because what brother can't protect his baby sister? What brother encourages her to follow her heart and to enter the church, where she is then murdered by reivers? Who does that?'

She stared at him.

'Do you need a man like that, Brenna?' he challenged, edging closer to her. 'A man like me. Broken. A shell of a man who might have been good enough for you long ago but is no longer. Because I hate myself for not saving Ayleen. And then to return and learn that I stayed away from what was left of my family to protect them, only to find them dead anyway? That maybe I could have stopped it, but I made yet another bad decision and failed them by not being here?

'How could I ever be the man worthy of protecting you, the woman I love most in this world? How can I make you understand that? So, it wasn't me abandoning you, Brenna. I was trying to give you a better chance at happiness with someone else who was worthy and able to protect you. Not someone broken and unable like me.'

Brenna shook her head slowly and her chin trembled.

'But that was not your decision to make! You cannot simply decide for me.' She grabbed a fistful of his tunic in her hand, tugging him to her.

His body ached with the need, want and anguish that only her touch and kiss could ease, but he held himself at bay, holding his arms by his side despite how he longed to pull her into a tight embrace.

'Look at me,' she demanded.

He didn't dare.

'Garrick,' she sobbed. Her body hitched and the emotion in the sound of his name flooded his chest.

He met her gaze, unable to obey his body's command, her pale blue eyes wide and bright with emotion against her cheeks flushed pink with chill. His resolve burst and he pulled her against him, crushing her mouth with his own. He kissed her over and over again, ignoring the voice that warned him to stop. The one that said he broke everything of beauty.

She pulled him closer and he stumbled back, landing hard against the bark of a tree. Now that he had a taste of her, he could not stop. His body flared with the memories of holding her, kissing her, as they had on so many nights like this in the past.

When she had been his. She could still be his. She tugged his shirt out of his trews and slid her hands along his bare chest, sending a jolt of desire screaming through his body, and he groaned. Pulling her closer, he kissed her again and again, making him believe they could be one again. She tugged on his trews. The action thrust him back to the present, and his desire to the past.

'Bren,' he pleaded, her nickname fallen unbidden from his lips as he clutched her by the wrist, pulling her hand away. 'We must cease. You are engaged to another and I am…'

Me. Not good enough.

He didn't finish but stepped back, creating some distance between them. It didn't matter that his body quaked from the loss of her touch, and his breath came out in uneven, shattering spasms. All he really wanted to do was make love to her, but he froze and let her slip away. Just as he always had.

He cleared his throat and ran a hand down his bunched tunic. 'I shouldn't have kissed you. I'm sorry.'

'Nay. You shouldn't have.' Her eyes flashed in challenge. 'Not if you couldn't finish what you started.'

Deuces. His blood boiled. Aye, he could finish it, but he'd not fall into her bait. He rolled his shoulders and released a breath. They needed to survive, and they could only do that by trusting one another more than they were now, and by him keeping his distance.

'I need to get you back to safety in Oban with your sister and Rory. Then, we can reach out to this fiancé of yours, as well as your father, to determine what is going on and why those men were after you. Your safety is all that matters. You have a life without me already planned, remember? My purpose right now is to get you safely back to that life and I need us to work together to do that.'

And I need to keep my hands off you to do that.

Colour flushed her neck. He'd made his point.

'I had to make my own life, as you well remember!' she snipped back.

'Aye,' he answered, his gaze settling on her. 'And all I want to do is get you to that life in one piece. That will give me an inkling of purpose. Let me do that and I'll be out of your life. For good.'

'Very well,' she whispered. Her features softened, and his heart squeezed from the truth that maybe, just maybe, she had decided to let him go.

That she might give him exactly what he asked for.

Chapter Fourteen

'Time to leave,' Garrick said, shaking her arm.

She blinked her eyes open to see the high-beamed ceiling overhead and the flickering of the dim candlelight in the old barn. She turned and saw the fire was being smothered in the hearth and soldiers were busily packing up their bed rolls and saddlebags. She groaned. Her head pounded and her eyes were scratchy and dry, no doubt swollen from her emotional undoing of the night before. Garrick stared at her, awaiting her response.

'Aye,' she answered. He nodded and carried on with packing. Curse Garrick and his stoic 'nothing happened the night before' face, void of feeling this morning.

Blast. Why should she expect anything else? Garrick was steady, even and dependable. He was a soldier. He could compartmentalise his emotion and move on to the next task, the next battle, the next town without a hitch in his step. Although before he'd utilised it when he'd needed it during difficult decisions. Now, it seemed the very fabric of who he had become. He was void of extremes as well as emotion. He'd become a soldier first and a man second, not the other way around, as it had been.

She climbed down the small ladder that joined the higher makeshift bed to the floor. She smoothed her skirts and yawned. Well, at least she finally knew why he'd abandoned her, even though it didn't make a whit of sense to her. She'd never doubted his ability to protect her or whether he was a good man, but he had enough doubt for the both of them. He couldn't let go of his grief and shame, and she couldn't be with a man who hadn't chosen her and might abandon her once more. She could let him go for good now and move on towards her future to become Mrs Winters.

She sighed and stretched her back. It ached from the makeshift bed she'd slept on. While it was better than the ground, it was no feathered or hay mattress. Tonight would be bliss. Her body sung at the thought of being safe and snug at Blackmore with her sister.

A flutter of nerves bubbled up in her, and she nibbled her lower lip. It had been far too long since she'd seen Moira, and she didn't know of her upcoming nuptial with Stephen. Chances were she would congratulate Garrick and her on being the happy couple when she saw them, unless the letter or Rolf Cameron had bothered to explain such. And, knowing how little Rolf thought of her, the man most likely hadn't. He might even enjoy watching the moment Moira learned of the truth.

Brenna cringed at the awkward moment that such

a revelation would bring. The shock would be evident on her sister's face. Brenna did not look forward to that explanation. Perhaps she could just let Garrick's face do the talking. She frowned, gathered her hair back in a loose plait and shoved her boots on her feet. In half a day their journey would be over, and Garrick would have fulfilled his duty and be out of her life for good. She should be relieved, but all she felt was a dull ache in her chest at what could have been if he'd just had the nerve to fight for her, for them.

For us.

But it wasn't that simple, was it?

She collected her cloak, left the building, completed her ablutions and joined Montgomerie and Garrick.

'Did you break your fast?'

'Nay. I'm not hungry.'

''Tis a long ride,' he answered, tightening the saddlebags. He handed her a strip of dried meat. She took it, her fingertips tingling from the brief contact with his.

How would she make it several more hours riding alongside him after all she knew from yesterday? She still had so many questions as to why he'd been so quick to decide her future for her, like her father, by letting her go without a word between them. And then his kisses. They'd told a quite different story. Her body warmed at the memory of his hands and lips searing a trail of want along her body. He hadn't kissed like a man who wanted to let her go.

He'd kissed her like a man who loved her.

It would be a long last stretch to Blackmore. He pulled her up in front of him and she settled back, knowing full well that this would be their last ride together—perhaps even their last few hours, if he had his way and left immediately in search of what was left of his clan and those who had killed his mother and brother.

The morning air was crisp and cool, the latest snow having ceased during the early morning hours, leaving a pristine, fresh covering before them. A band of Cameron soldiers rode in a loose V in front of them, the only noises the sound of hooves swishing in the new snow on the ground and the slight jangle of metal on metal from saddlebags and weaponry as they travelled. Despite being pressed against Garrick's body as they rode, Brenna felt more distant from him than ever. There had been a time when she would have thought it impossible and their separation against nature itself.

What a lovesick fool she had been.

Now here she was on a last journey with him when their time together had scarce begun. Fate had other plans, it seemed, and she didn't like the detour at all. Heat rose in her chest at the memory of their kiss in the forest and how safe she had felt in his arms. How for a moment he had been the Garrick she had known long ago. But now she could see that man of before was buried in regret and shame that she could not free him from.

She willed the sadness back and focused on the dark, looming presence in the distance that was Blackmore. The expansive structure signalled safety as well as the end of her time with Garrick. She'd also have to stop putting off the inevitable: facing Father's deception about her engagement; getting clarity on what role Stephen might or might not have had in the attack on her carriage; and whether she still wished to marry the man at all. One thing was for certain: she'd get the truth and the answers she deserved before she married *any* man.

Despite Garrick's desire to slow time and make this last ride with Brenna last, the distance closed swiftly. He memorised the feel of her wisps of dark hair skimming his cheek, and the soft sway of her hips back against his own as Montgomerie galloped along the open snowy meadows, so he could conjure it up on another day when he needed to remember his purpose and what happiness had once been. This was to be the end of their time together. Never again would they be this close, riding as one along the Highlands. While he had given her up as a love match in his mind, it would be hard to let her go, and the idea of never seeing her again made him shiver against her.

Time was measured from the moment before she'd entered his life and after. Perhaps the moment she left him for good and rode off with her future husband would mark yet another. Although, he couldn't fathom being there to watch her go. Winters was not that strong or good of a man.

Garrick would ensure that whatever man it was was worthy, and at present Mr Winters wasn't that. Perhaps Rory and his uncle could make a few enquiries about the man. If he lived and worked in Oban, even if only part of the year, then he would be known. If he was innocent, which seemed doubtful, and Brenna still wished to marry him, then he would support her in such, even if it turned his stomach. He'd not be a coward and slink off at sunrise. She was best without him. As she'd said yesterday, she hated him, and he really couldn't blame her.

Most days he hated himself too.

'I will ride ahead with a few men to let Laird Mc-Kenna know to expect us,' Rolf shouted back to them.

'Aye,' Garrick answered. At least he would get to see Moira and Rory again and their wee ones. It could distract him from the inevitable: saying goodbye to Brenna. At least he'd have the chance to say goodbye to her. He'd not had that chance with many of those he had loved. He would try to do right by her and make the most of it. For once, he would be doing the right thing by someone he loved.

'Are you excited to see your sister?' he asked, extending a small olive branch of conversation. Perhaps he could help them end things as friends in the end.

'Aye,' she answered, hesitation softening her voice. 'Although I have not been to visit in a long while. I should have visited sooner.'

'It is Moira. She would never be angry with you about such. Surely you know that?'

'I do.' She shifted and toyed with the edge of her cloak. 'But that shall not stop me from shaming myself for it.'

He nodded. 'I know something about that, but do not worry. She will have only joy at seeing you. The reason for your arrival will not matter.'

'I hope you are right.'

'On this one thing, I am certain.'

Soon, the large stone drive up to the castle came into view, and bands of soldiers were at the gates. Garrick smiled at the sea of Cameron and McKenna plaids. Rory was no fool. He had his men at the main castle doors, gates and stables, ready to greet them as well as the Camerons. The Camerons might be allies, but Rory was careful to keep them in check. Garrick would have done exactly the same.

He swallowed hard. If he had a clan any more, but he did not. They were dead or scattered to the shadows of the mountains. He pulled back his shoulders and thrust the truth away for another time when he could deal with it. That time wasn't now.

As Montgomerie shifted onto the smooth stone of the drive, which was covered with deeper snow, Brenna settled back against him. He wrapped his arms about her tightly for a mere moment before letting go. One final hidden embrace. As they reached the castle doors, a young lad came up to take the reins from him.

The doors opened and Moira emerged, followed closely by another soldier. 'Brenna!' she cried out joyfully. The soldier helped her down the stairs, her belly rounded with child once more.

Garrick leaned down to Brenna's ear. 'You see? She is overjoyed at the sight of you.'

'Even if I do not truly deserve it,' Brenna whispered shakily.

He dismounted and then extended his hand. 'She has long forgotten the rift between you over her marriage with Rory. You deserve every happiness.' He cherished the warmth of her palm sliding into his and the feel of her slight weight as he helped her down from Montgomerie for the last time.

'As do you, Garrick, if you would just allow yourself to believe it.' She squeezed his hand and let go.

His heart picked up speed, pounding in his chest. Before he could respond, Moira was at their side and pulling Brenna into a tight embrace.

'I am so blessed and pleased to see you as well as Garrick.' She released Brenna and hugged Garrick. Her joy at the sight of them was contagious, and he smiled. 'We have much to catch up on but let us get you attended to. A bath and clean clothes and some food.'

She fussed over her sister like the mother she now was, and Garrick revelled in the happy turn her life had taken since he'd met her years ago. 'Garrick, Rory will be returning from the village any moment.'

'Aye,' Garrick replied. 'I will see to Montgomerie until he returns.'

'And I will steal Brenna away while I can.' She flashed a grin at Garrick and tugged Brenna along, hugging her to her side. The poor woman thought them still a love match. She would be disappointed to learn otherwise, and he was grateful not to have to be the one to provide such news.

He watched them disappear within Blackmore followed by two McKenna soldiers.

If you would allow yourself to believe it.

Brenna's words echoed in his ears, but he batted them away, even though he still couldn't loosen the tightness in his chest. *Saints be*. Words were useless things at times. They didn't change anything. Least of all his mind. Especially not when it came to her. He was doing right by her by letting her go.

Garrick followed a young lad to the large stables and took over duties for Montgomerie. The mindless task would soothe his frayed nerves and settle his spirit, as it always did. He lifted the saddlebags and plaid from Montgomerie's back and heaved it over the side of the door of the stall behind him.

Grabbing the brush to rub his stallion down after such a long ride, Garrick rolled his shoulders in an attempt to shake off his frustration and focus on the task at hand. The smooth, rhythmic strokes would help ease his mind and his temper. As the minutes passed, his heart settled into a slower cadence. As he neared the end of the task, his mind was clearer and clicking through a list of items to tend to that would ensure Brenna's safety, until they were able to get her home to Glenhaven or deliver her to Mr Winters as his bride, if she still chose to marry him.

One of the tasks included getting himself far away from here. He didn't trust himself.

'You know we have stable boys for that?'

Garrick stilled and smiled before facing his old friend, Laird Rory McKenna. He set down the brush and approached. 'I suppose I've been away too long to remember such things.' They clapped one another's shoulders in greeting before embracing.

'Glad to see you're alive. Seems we've both escaped the clutches of our supposed deaths. I have escaped a curse and you the battlefield.' Rory chuckled, a deep smile on his face.

'Perhaps the world is not yet ready to be rid of us.' Garrick smiled in return but sucked in a breath as his stitches pulled at his side.

Rory's brow furrowed and gestured to Garrick's side. 'Looks like you need tending to. I can send for a physician.'

'Nay. Just needs a good cleaning and some salve. It will heal. I'm thankful to be alive and to have got Brenna here safely.'

Rory sat down on a bale of hay and Garrick sat on one just opposite to him. He ran a hand through his hair. Exhaustion began a slow, steady advance through his body, a dull ache settling in his bones. 'How is your wife?' Garrick asked, desperate to evade any questions about Brenna.

Rory's eyes lit up as they always did when he spoke of his wife, Brenna's older sister. 'Moira is well. The twins are leading us in a merry dance, and she is expecting once more.'

Garrick chuckled, feeling Rory's joy as if it were his own. 'I am thrilled to hear it. You both deserve such blessings.'

'Thank you. Truth be told, I am blessed beyond what I deserve.'

Garrick ran his hands down his trews, his gaze dropping away.

'You are a mirror of what I once believed of myself but a few years back.'

The words cut through Garrick's fatigue, and he met his friend's gaze. 'How so?'

'I thought I had no right to love Moira or have any hope for a future. My singular goal was to sire an heir and pray that a future without me would be better for all of Clan McKenna. I was a bloody fool.'

'Your lot is not mine.' Garrick shook his head and stared at his hands. 'Everything I touch turns to ash. My entire family is dead because of me: the clan scattered about to all parts of the Highlands; my home now owned by an Englishman. All because I could not protect them. I don't want Brenna to be the next casualty in my life. I told her she is better off without me. I have nothing to offer her. Not any more.'

'You couldn't have stopped any of it,' Rory stated. 'Even if you'd been here, most likely you and Brenna would be dead now.'

'All the more reason for her to be as far from me as possible.' He scrubbed a hand down his face.

Rory chuckled. 'You and I both know that will only happen if it is what *she* wishes. Come inside. Cook will heat you a plate. Some food might help clear your head.'

'I fear it may take far more than that, but I thank you for letting us stay here until we can determine who attacked her carriage and was chasing us and why.'

'Carriage attack?' Rory's eyes widened.

'Aye. That is how I came upon Brenna. Her carriage had been attacked and she was left for dead.'

'What?'

'There is much for you to catch up on. Not all could

be relayed by messenger, as I did not know who to trust.' Garrick gave Montgomerie's nose one last rub. 'Any whiskey to pair with dinner?'

'As much as you need,' Rory answered, his brow furrowed, and questions in his narrowed gaze.

'We might need a full barrel.'

Rory chuckled. 'Let's get you tended to, bathed and meet in the study. We can talk there. Any ideas on why someone might have attacked Bran's carriage?' Rory asked as they fell in step alongside each other on the walk back to the main house.

'A few. Although it wasn't Bran's carriage that was attacked. It was that of her fiancé.'

Rory stopped in his tracks. 'Fiancé? I thought…'

'Nay, we are not promised to one another. She is engaged. And he's an Englishman to boot.'

Rory cursed and carried on. 'I cannot wait to hear how that came about.'

'As you may have guessed, it was Bran's idea.'

'And that I should have guessed.' He shook his head. 'Perhaps we should all eat before we get further into those details. Moira will be none too keen to hear it. We were both under the impression that you and Brenna were still together.'

'I am shocked she did not know. How in the world did Bran and Ewan keep such a secret from her?'

'She has been unable to travel to Glenhaven to see them, and as you well know they have always been quite reluctant to visit here at Blackmore unless they are pressed to do so.' He chuckled.

'Perhaps because her father threatened to ruin you

and your clan by claiming your elopement and marriage a sham.'

Rory shook his head. 'That and my home is a vast deal larger than Glenhaven. And, as we know, Bran is a bit competitive. He cannot even be happy for his own daughter and grandchildren to be well cared for.'

Side by side they climbed the large stone steps and entered the main hall of Blackmore. As the door closed behind them, Garrick released the first real sigh of relief afforded him in the days since he'd found Brenna unconscious in a smouldering carriage. Finally, she was protected from the men that had given them chase for days. Tomorrow would be another challenge, but for today there would be peace.

Chapter Fifteen

'May I come in?' Moira called from outside Brenna's chamber.

'Aye,' Brenna answered in a shaky breath. She was nervous to finally spill the truth she had been hiding from her sister. But it was now or never, was it not?

Her chamber door opened and Brenna faced her sister and forced a smile. Moira came to her and hugged her once more, and the tenderness of her sister's embrace brought emotion to Brenna's eyes. She squeezed her sister and pulled away, daring to hold her gaze.

'I should have tried to understand and been kinder to you when you said you wished to elope with Rory years ago,' Brenna confessed, wringing her hands. 'I didn't truly understand. Not until I was in your shoes and Father was the one trying to find *me* a match.'

Moira stilled, her eyes widening. 'What do you mean? You are promised to Garrick. You came here *with* him. You are already matched, are you not?'

She shook her head. 'Father decided I was losing my

bloom waiting for him to return. When a year passed without a word from him, I gave in to Father's suggestion to find another match, as I was certain Garrick had died. Father chose another for me, although he made me believe *I* had made such a choice, that I'd done something noble for the clan in telling him I would marry Mr Winters. That I was choosing my own path. In truth, he had made the arrangement for my hand with the man long before even mentioning him to me as a possible suitor and match.' She wiped her eyes. 'I was a fool to believe I could finally win his love and respect by doing something for the clan. That he would finally value me and see my worth.

'So, yes, I am engaged, sister—but not to Garrick.'

The colour drained from her sister's face. 'What? Who would he see as a better match?'

'An Englishman.'

Moira's mouth dropped open, and she rose from the settee. She paced the room and finally ceased and stood, staring out of the large window overlooking the cliffs and sea raging below it. She popped her hands to her hips. 'You'd think he would have learned. What a blasted fool.'

Brenna sat dumbfounded. 'Did you just call Father a fool?'

'Aye. I did. What else do you call a man who makes the same mistakes over and over and belittles his own daughters in such a way?'

Brenna chuckled. She had never heard or seen *this* Moira before. Happy. Light-hearted. Direct. Speak-

ing her mind without a wink of fear for the outcome.
Brenna rather liked her sister this way.

Moira turned and smiled at her. 'Then, we shall
just have to find you a way out of it. I refuse to let you
marry an Englishman when there is a perfect Scottish gentleman under this roof that adores you, and
you him.'

Brenna shifted on her seat, dropping her gaze. She
toyed with the edge of the ribbon on the new gown
Moira had given her to wear after her bath. The feel
of the cool fabric was soothing as she ran it through
her fingertips.

'Nay, Moira. We are not to be. He is angry. Lost. He
pushes me away at every turn. Tells me I am best without him and, now that I know he chose to stay away
and allow me to believe him dead, I agree with him.
He abandoned me without a word. He is not the same
man, Moira, no matter how it pains me to admit. Grief
has shattered him. You will see.'

Moira nodded. 'He did seem…affected when I saw
him on your arrival. I am so sorry to hear of it. I am
tempted to meddle, as I have long adored him and the
idea of a match between you, but if you do not wish
it I will bite my tongue. I will *not* be Father. You are
capable of making your own match.' She gripped her
hands. 'And you are worthy of love, respect and so
much more, sister, no matter what Father says and does.
You must believe that.'

'I am trying to.'

'Then, that is all I ask, for I know it will take time
to unwind what he has done, just as it did for me.' She

pulled Brenna into a side hug. 'And what of this Englishman? Tell me of him. Who has Father chosen for you and why?' Moira pulled back and lifted her brow.

Brenna sighed. 'Truth be told, I am not sure I will be attaching myself to him either, despite this arrangement Father has crafted. I have many questions that need to be answered before our engagement can move forward. The first of which is whether he tried to have me killed or not.'

'Sit, sister. You will tell me everything. *Now.*'

'It is a miracle you are alive,' Rory stated, shaking his head and taking a final bite of duck. He had clung onto Garrick's and Brenna's every word as they recounted the story of their chance reunion on the road to Westmoreland.

'Aye,' Brenna agreed. 'Now we must discover why the men attacked the carriage and why they continued to give chase even after the attack was over.'

'Brenna said you both believe it might be your fiancé, Mr Winters, himself. If that is the case, we cannot allow this sham of an engagement to continue. Father will just have to find some other way to gain the power he desires. And we will assist you in whatever way we can.' Moira squared her shoulders and met Rory's gaze.

'What?' Rory asked.

''Tis true,' Garrick replied. 'I just did not wish to speak out of turn. For Brenna's sake.'

Rory sat stunned. Garrick looked at Brenna. He didn't know she'd said as much to her sister and, knowing such, he felt relief at not having to sidestep his true concerns for her sake.

Colour rose in Brenna's cheeks, giving her face a soft glow in the candlelight as she met his gaze. His chest tightened. The dark blue of her gown matched the exact colour of her eyes, and her dark hair cascaded in loose waves along her shoulders and neck. She had always been beautiful, and tonight was no exception. His appreciation for her beauty just another thing his body would need to unlearn. She would never be his. Not any more.

Their separation was his choice and hers, and for the best for both of them, but that didn't mean he would hand her over to anyone less than worthy. At the moment, Mr Winters looked more than unworthy.

'You all need not worry for me,' she countered. 'Now that we have sent word to Stephen, I am certain he will come and put things in order and assist us in getting to the truth of it, however ugly it might be.'

Garrick squeezed the napkin in his hands. *Or lie through his bloody teeth, and then I will have to kill him.*

'And he does not know we are aware of his letters between him, Father and the elusive M, so I believe we are at an advantage.'

Rory nodded and rested his napkin on the table. 'It will add an element of surprise if we accuse him of treachery when he believes he is merely arriving to pick up his future wife.'

'As well as desperation,' Garrick added. 'We must

tread carefully. I do not know what kind of man he is, and desperate men make drastic choices.'

'Aye,' Rory agreed.

'Tell me of this Mr Winters, sister,' Moira added coolly.

'He is in shipping,' Brenna answered. 'Father met him at a celebration and the King supported the idea of the match between our families, or at least that is what Father told me. He told me the union would provide us some added protection, with all the political upheaval, and the King believed it would help to illustrate a show of unity between our people and his own.'

Moira narrowed her gaze on Brenna. 'Wait. Do you believe Father is involved in the attack in some way?'

Garrick held his tongue. He knew this was a question for only Brenna to answer.

They all looked at Brenna to continue. She dropped her gaze and ran her fingertips absently over the table cloth.

'I do not wish to believe so, but after all I read in those letters, and the deception he allowed to play out to gain my agreement, I no longer know.'

Garrick's heart twisted at the agony in her voice. He could hear the tears in her voice. He wished he could take the pain she felt at her father's betrayal from her, but he knew he couldn't. Only she could weather such a storm.

'I have only met Mr Winters a few times, so much of what I know of him is business-related, as he enjoys speaking of it.' Brenna cleared her throat and took a long sip of red wine as she steered the conversation back to her fiancé.

'No matter,' Rory added. 'Uncle Leo and I will send round some enquiries and get a fuller picture of the man before he arrives. That way we'll know more of him, whether he is innocent or guilty of inciting such actions against you and thereby your clan and us as your family. Whatever happens, you have our support.'

'And mine,' Garrick added before he could stop himself. He shifted on his chair. He cursed himself. He didn't have claim to worry over her any more. But, as with all things, unlearning his love and care for her would take time. Most likely the rest of his life. He pressed a flat palm on the table to anchor himself in that idea. He wasn't sure if he found it settling or terrifying.

'If anyone needs to stretch their legs, I will be going outside, as it is time to take the hounds out for some air since Uncle Leo is away this eve. They love the snow this time of year before it gets far too cold and windy.' Rory forced a smile and rose from the table.

'I think I will join you,' Garrick added, eager to remove himself from the room and release his frustration with some movement. 'After such a ride and hearty meal—which I am most grateful for, my lady—I could do with a walk.'

'I will not be joining you, husband,' Moira announced, 'As I am worn through.' Rory came over and kissed her cheek. 'Be sure to grab your bonnet,' she chided.

'Aye,' he answered. 'Do keep your sister out of trouble, Brenna,' he added, before Moira playfully swatted his arm.

'I will try,' Brenna answered, and smiled at her sister.

Once the men were all out of doors and far from the house, Rory broached the subject first. 'I shall send enquiries out tomorrow,' he offered. 'And adding more men to the watch outside is in order. Something seems…off about the whole business.'

'I am quite certain I don't have all of the pieces to the story of this union and the urgency of it, despite my enquiries of Brenna, because Bran misled her as well. What do you think?' Garrick flipped up the collar of his coat.

'If Bran is a part of it, I am sure you are right. But he is often reluctant to confide the truth in anyone, as you well know.' Rory nested his hands in his trews.

'Aye,' Garrick answered. 'So how shall we go about it without stirring up too much suspicion before our arrival?'

They walked in silence for a few moments as the three hounds bounded out in the snow, barking with pleasure as they skidded in the lush flakes and chased one another. The wind blew softly, sending an arc of snow in whatever direction they ran. The cool wind helped clear Garrick's head, and he began to think more clearly.

'The Camerons, as much as it pains me to say it,' Rory said flatly. 'If anyone can ferret out the truth, they can.'

'I believe you are right, but there is some tension between them and the Stewarts based on Rolf's reaction upon seeing Brenna yesterday.'

Rory nodded. 'An issue with a lame stallion and a delivery of goods months back. Man couldn't get all the way to the Camerons, so he stopped at Glenhaven for aid. Bran provided aid but claimed the stallion and goods as his own for his good deed.'

'Sounds about right.' Garrick shook his head.

'It's worse than you think. He is not well. I have noticed it in his rambling correspondence. I believe it is from the stroke.' Rory's brow furrowed.

'Have you spoken to Moira of it? Brenna made a brief mention of him being different, but she wasn't terribly forthcoming with details.'

'I cannot quite find the words. Bran and I never started on solid footing with one another, as you well know, so I have always been careful about sounding too harsh or doing anything to sever what tenuous connection with him we do have. He is Moira's father, after all. But, if he is ill, it may be why he was in such a rush to secure this union for Brenna without much thought to the consequences of her happiness, or really investigating the man before committing her to him.'

'But surely Ewan has some investment in this outcome and the implications of such a union? He is her brother and in line to become laird.' Garrick kicked a tuft of snow.

Rory nested his hands in the pockets of his coat. 'I believe he is trying, but he is out of his depth trying to guide Bran and the clan with all that has happened in the Highlands over the last year. Uprisings, poor crops and small bands of reivers popping up along the borderlands as well as in the middle of the Highlands. Much has changed since you have been away.'

Garrick stared out into the snowy twilight and the midnight-blue sky settled into his bones.

'We have offered aid to Ewan as well as Bran, but they rebuff us at every turn. I believe it may be due to our new alliance with the Camerons.' Rory shrugged. 'The man has the pride of his father. He is a Stewart through and through.'

'Where does that leave us, then?'

'Enquiries about Winters and a complete recounting of what happened since you discovered Brenna,' Rory answered. 'We'll meet in the study tomorrow morn and see if we can work this through after you've had a good night's sleep. Between all of us, we should be able to come to the truth of it.'

'And Brenna and Moira?'

Rory smiled. 'I am sure they're plotting as well as we speak. They are also Stewarts, as you well know. They will not sit by and let us work this out alone. Moira will come to me when she is ready with her plan.' He smiled and chuckled. 'She always does.'

An unexpected spike of jealousy rippled through Garrick. How he longed for a relationship such as Rory's and Moira's. Or at least, he used to. He was not worthy of one now. He was too broken to be able to offer much to anyone, let alone a woman such as Brenna. But it did not mean some small seed of hope within him did not still long for it, and see what Rory had as the treasure he'd once believed he might also have, and feel morose at what he had forsaken.

It is for the best. She deserves better.

And, by God, he would make sure she got the best. He would make sure this Mr Winters was not the cad his gut told him he was. If Bran had made another horrid match for his youngest daughter, Garrick would expose the truth and set Brenna free from it before it became official and binding, so she could make a better and more suitable match with another man who would secure her future. She would not suffer as Moira had from her first arranged marriage.

Garrick would die first.

Chapter Sixteen

Despite being clean with a full belly, and resting on the softest of beds, Brenna had a fitful night of sleep. She woke to sunlight streaming in her room across her feet and the dreaded feeling that she was missing something of import. She bolted up, scanned the room and then flopped back down as her stomach flipped at the realisation. She was missing someone, not something: *Garrick*.

It was the first morning she had not woken to the sight of his unshaven face above her, or the husky burr of his voice at her ear, and the absence unsettled her. 'Why can you not let him go?' she muttered to herself, shielding her eyes with her forearm. She was being a lovesick fool, and she wouldn't stand for it. They'd made their decisions to be apart for the sake of one another, hadn't they? Today needed to be the first day to her moving on with the rest of her life.

Perhaps she could marry and revel in the thrill of motherhood as Moira had. Her stomach clenched in unease. But to whom? Despite being engaged, she was uncertain of her future, as Stephen Winters' intentions were foggy at best and deadly at worst. She nibbled her lip. Could he be innocent somehow? Could the letters, coin and pursuers be some bizarre conspiracy to make him appear guilty? She rolled her eyes at her own ridiculousness.

Why on earth would anyone go to such trouble to make a man look guilty? The simple answer was that they wouldn't. Odds were Stephen was involved somehow, as some of the letters were from him, and the coin as well. Despite wanting to believe her romantic history was less horrid than her first love abandoning her and the second man, her fiancé, trying to *kill* her, she couldn't quite shake the possibility. Blast. How had her love life turned into a romantic saga? She ran her hands through her mussed hair. Maybe Ayleen had had the right idea by heading to the abbey to devote her life to something bigger than herself and away from men and their scheming.

She sighed. But Ayleen had had an even worse end, hadn't she? Brenna stared out of the large, expansive window that showcased the sea just beyond the cliffs. Its still, dark waters calmed her, and she watched until her heart slowed and her mind cleared. Her grief over losing Garrick had made her wilfully choose something just to please Father, but this was her life, and she needed to start trusting her own mind and making her own decisions, no matter the consequences. She threw back her covers and decided to take charge of what remained of her messy life. She was not married yet, was she?

She would dress, break her fast and take charge of her future. If the men were planning enquiries into Stephen's dealings anyway, she would make enquiries of her own. She'd ask Garrick to see again those letters they had found on one of their attackers, so she was prepared for her meeting with him. Now that he knew she was here, he would come for her, otherwise how would it look?

He'd look guilty without even trying. It was only a matter of when he would arrive. Today? Tomorrow? The day after? She needed to make the most of the time she had.

After breaking her fast, Brenna went to the study, where she found Garrick and Rory sitting in silence, poring over maps and correspondence.

'Good morn,' Rory offered as she crossed the threshold of his study.

The tables were filled with letters, ledgers and books, and the smell of the fire, leather and books filled her nose. She smiled. It reminded her of her father's study. 'Good morn,' she said. 'May I see those letters we found on the person of that man chasing us?' Brenna stood before them at the study door.

Garrick nodded. 'Aye. We've looked them over. Didn't see anything new of real import since we still don't know who M is.' He rose from the large chair he sat in, gathered the letters from Rory's desk and handed them to her. 'What do you hope to find?'

She avoided his gaze and took the letters near to the

hearth, so she could keep warm and be as physically far away from Garrick as she could. He smelled of clean soap and spice, and she abhorred the humming it sent along her limbs. 'I am not entirely sure, but I want to know everything I can about these letters before Mr Winters arrives. I plan to interrogate him until we arrive at the truth of what happened and why, no matter how ugly it might be.'

And ugly it might be. She prayed Father wasn't involved but a tiny whispering along her mind warned her that he might be. And, if he had been, she hoped it was not intended, but merely a consequence he had not foreseen.

'A fine idea. Enquiries have been sent out by messenger to the Camerons and some business contacts I have in Oban. I also sent word to Mr Winters as well as your father so they would be aware of what happened, as well of your safe arrival here. I also took the liberty of inviting Mr Winters to Blackmore to get better acquainted.'

A muscle worked in Garrick's jaw. 'That's one way of putting it,' he muttered.

Brenna bit her lip. While she wished to know more about Mr Winters, she was unsure of what they would find. She also worried over what Father would think of their enquiries. He never responded well to any challenge to his decisions. And despite all she still wanted him to be proud of her just once, especially if he had but little time left.

She steeled her spine and pushed away Old Brenna, or at least she attempted to. She couldn't care for her own safety *and* protect Father's feelings at the same time. It was time she put herself first in her own future, even if that meant he might never really be proud of her as she had long hoped.

'Thank you,' she replied, lifting her chin. 'I appreciate your thoroughness on the matter. I think we are all quite eager to see what those enquiries yield.'

Garrick narrowed his gaze at her, confusion written all over his furrowed brow. She smiled at him, snuggled deep into the oversized chair, flipped open the first letter and began to read, forcing the uncertainty and worry out of her mind. If she was to shed Old Brenna's insecurities, she had to be more convincing, starting now.

Garrick recognised the hesitation in Brenna's voice. It did not matter how finely she tried to mask it with her words. She was scared, nervous about trying to exert some control over her future, and he understood what an undertaking it was. Lairds were not used to being challenged and thwarted. Power bent to them and they expected their families to do the same, especially their children. 'Do not worry about your father,' he offered. 'If there is an issue, we will intervene on your behalf.'

'Perhaps I do not want you to intervene,' she stated, scanning the first letter.

'I think I shall get some more tea,' Rory said and stepped out, closing the door behind him.

Evidently, Rory knew when to abandon ship. Garrick was too stubborn to care. He was trying to help ensure a good future for Brenna and help her avoid the pitfalls he'd had with his own father. Didn't she see that?

'Why do you resist my efforts to help you at every turn?' he asked.

'Says the person who resisted my every effort to help you.'

He looked heavenward. 'We are talking of two entirely different situations, and you know it. I was helping us stay alive. I could not allow you to put your life in danger.'

'Do you not have other matters of your own to tend to?' She continued speaking with her back to him.

He frowned and approached where she sat by the hearth, reading the letters. 'Of course I do, but I cannot just leave you here without knowing who was after you and whether this Mr Winters will protect you. If he is worthy of you.'

'I will be well here with Rory, Moira and the hounds to look after me. Your task is complete, Garrick Mac-Lean. I arrived here safely. You should go.'

'Go? You must be joking. I risked my life to get you here. I will see this through.'

'Even if I do not want you to?'

Ire flared up in his gut. 'Should I have left you there in that burning carriage? Or perhaps allowed you to be killed and drowned in that stream by some English brute?' He gripped her by the arm and turned her to face him.

'As I said before. I want you to go and to never see you again.' Her eyes were bright in the firelight, too bright. Wild and uncertain, like an animal snared.

'That is not what you said to me two nights ago when you kissed the breath out of me,' he said, his words low, husky and dripping with intention. 'Have you so soon forgotten?'

Her breathing faltered and a pulse throbbed at the side of her throat. Nay. She had not forgotten. Her lips parted involuntarily.

'Nay. And if I remember, you kissed me as well,' she murmured, shifting away from the fire and out of his hold.

'Then let me make sure the man who will kiss those lips for the rest of your days is worthy of it.'

She swallowed hard. 'So be it. Do as you will, and I will do as I must.'

'I will,' he answered, taking a step away from her.

Minutes ticked by on the clock on the mantel, and Garrick willed his temper to settle and his worry over her to abate. His emotion and fear were driving his words, and such rashness wouldn't solve anything. Brenna stood staring off into the distance out of the large windows. He steadied himself. 'In order to get to the truth, we need to work together. And the only way to do that is for you to be completely honest with me. Did anyone else know you would be returning that day? Had Winters sent word to anyone else to let them know of your plans to travel?'

She didn't answer at first, and he wasn't sure if she was ignoring him or shutting him out. Then, she nodded. 'Aye. He had notified his mother, who lives in town with his sister, as well as his staff at his estate, and his business partner. But, like I said, he had planned to join us and was called away at the very last moment. If someone was waiting for him in the carriage on our way to Glenhaven, then why did they chase *us*?'

'I don't know, but the one man seemed focused on separating us and harming you.' He shook his head. 'And your father's enemies? Did any of them know?'

'His enemies are vast, as you well know. Some might have been aware of my visit, as Father was touting it about that he was doing this to please the King, and all of the extra privileges he expected to receive because of it, but I can't imagine they would have known of my early departure. Unless they were watching Stephen's residence.' Colour rose in her cheeks and she crossed her arms against her chest.

Garrick's recognised the shame burning her face and adding red blotches along her neckline. He pressed his lips together and offered what little he could: his own truth. 'You do not need to be ashamed of his scheming or your ignorance of his manipulation of your future. My father was the same. It seems they had that in common as a tactic to keep their children in line.'

Her shoulders sagged forward and she ran her fingertips along the edge of her plait. 'Moira has strong, unwavering devotion to her interests in books and botany, and Ewan is dedicated to leading the clan and learning the ways of laird. I suppose I should merely resign myself that I will never please Father, as I am neither. I have tried and tried to gain his approval, but I am always lacking. I am not witty, useful or talented enough, I suppose.' She smirked. '"Thank God, you're pretty, Bren," he used to say. "Not much else to be had."'

Garrick stilled. The words slammed against his chest with force, the intent cutting him. While he knew Bran had been a thoughtless and controlling man at times, Garrick didn't know how cruel he had been to her. So many things she'd said and done over the time he had known her made sense, the pieces of her he didn't understand clicking into place. She had been so pleasing to survive, so yielding to attempt to gain favour, and so gentle and encouraging of him because she knew what it felt like to have neither from someone she loved.

'I am just blown about with the wind,' she continued. 'I do not know what interests me other than fashion and that seems ridiculous at best. My value seems tied to whom I can marry and, when I believed I could choose a match to finally earn his respect and pride, I jumped at the chance.' She let go of the end of her plait of hair. 'Like a fool. I did not know there was no choice in it as it had already been decided for me.'

Garrick fisted his hands by his sides and chose his words with care. 'Bren, you have immense value and purpose in your own right, untethered from any man. Your worth is beyond what any man thinks of you. Not me, your father or your brother. It is within what you believe of yourself.'

While he knew all of these things to be true, he also knew how hard it was to apply it to one's own life, for he struggled to remember his own worth. He felt hypocritical to say so as he could not follow his own advice, but he had to try.

'You do not understand. You are a man. A soldier. A laird. You are respected and valued for your contributions and skills. I am…invisible.' She gazed at the tips of her shoes.

Garrick came to her and paused, hesitating at closing the remaining distance between them. Did he dare? He took one of her hands in his own, the small, fragile weight of it sliding against his flesh making him feel light-headed. The familiar friction was like tinder. He had to take care he didn't catch flame.

'Perhaps I do not fully understand,' he began. 'But I do know how words can damage a child.'

She did not move away from his hold but met his gaze instead. 'Do you?'

He nodded. 'After my brother died, my father used to tell me how he wished it had been me or Cairn that had died in Lon's place, daily for quite some time. I know it was grief, but it pained us all the same, as we were grieving too. And, despite all I tried, I could never win his approval. After a time, I gave up entirely.'

She sucked in a breath and squeezed his hand. 'I am glad it was not you that died that day, and I am so sorry you had to hear those words from your father. You did not deserve them.'

'Nor did you deserve such words from yours.'

'So, how did you overcome that sadness after your father died? Of knowing he wasn't proud of you?'

'I realised he could not love me and respect me as I wished him to. He wasn't capable of it for reasons beyond my control, and I would never understand why. I had to decide to accept the man he was for all of his frailties as my father or let him go entirely. I could never find any middle ground.'

'And what did you do?'

'Honestly? Something in between those two.'

She chuckled.

Rory came back into the room quietly, carrying a cup of tea, and Moira followed closely behind.

Brenna squeezed Garrick's hand and let go. 'Thank you for your advice. I will try,' she answered gently.

'Any progress?' Moira asked, her gaze flitting between them as she pulled her shawl tightly around her shoulders.

'Unfortunately, none. We cannot discern the purpose of the attack, nor the reason for the chase afterwards. If they were seeking Winters, he wasn't there, and Arthur, Roland and Brenna should have been spared. And if they were seeking Brenna, and she was the intended victim, then why?' said Garrick.

'We've received word from the note we sent by messenger to Winters last night,' Rory offered. His frown warned Garrick he wouldn't like the news.

'Your Mr Winters is thrilled to hear of your safe arrival and he will be here tomorrow to collect you and bring you to Oban for your nuptials.' He cleared his throat. 'Seems your father has approved a union as soon as possible due to the unsavoury events. He wishes you to be settled as quickly as possible.'

Brenna paled and sunk back in the large chair by the fire. 'Tomorrow?'

Chapter Seventeen

Brenna's heart hammered in her chest. *Tomorrow?*
She swallowed hard. For all her talk of wanting to exert
control over her life, her stomach lurched at the thought
of facing Stephen Winters. Getting to the truth of what
had happened would be ugly and dangerous. Who knew
what he might do when he realised they suspected him
of treachery?

She gripped the arm of the chair, grateful it offered
some support as her legs felt like they might buckle
from beneath her if she'd been standing. 'How shall
we go about getting to the truth?'

'Carefully,' Rory answered, handing her the letter.
'He knows of the attack and will know something is
afoot, especially if he intended…' He stopped himself.

She sighed. 'Me dead. I know.'

Moira came over and pressed a hand to her shoulder. 'We are with you. You are not alone. No harm will
come to you. You have my word.'

'Do you think Father truly agreed to moving the

wedding forward or might Stephen be making it up?'
Even after all that had happened with Father, she didn't
wish to believe he would be so eager to give her to a
man who might be wishing her dead.

Moira didn't answer but squeezed her shoulder,
which was answer enough.

Thistles. Why had she even asked?

'Your father may not have put together that Stephen
is behind the attack and thinking that you might be
safer with a husband,' Garrick offered. 'Or he may be
desperate and not thinking clearly due to his illness.'

She squirmed in the chair. The wave of uncertainty
that always accompanied her feelings of trying to
please her father washed over her, leaving her chilled
and confused. One crisis at a time, she reminded herself. She'd deal with Stephen tomorrow and then perhaps Father the next. Either way, she would be seeing
Mr Winters in less than a day and she didn't feel the
least bit prepared. Perhaps, if she focused on only getting to the truth behind the attacks, she could muster
the courage to face whatever fruits it revealed.

'What is our plan?' she asked, eager to do rather
than worry. 'If I do nothing, I will go mad before he
arrives. What can I do?'

'Perhaps you can discern a timeline of the letters.
Most are dated. It may help us see when the exchange
began and when the most recent ones were sent.' Garrick gave her a stack of the letters. 'Then we can compile some questions that may help us glean what role
he had in all of this.'

She took the letters from him. 'And the responses from your contacts? And the Camerons?'

Rory shook his head. 'I think it will be too soon to receive word back from all of them, but I hope we will have received a few prior to Mr Winters' arrival.'

She hoped so too.

'I will help you write out the timing of events,' Moira offered. After gathering a large parchment, quill and ink, she set them on the large table. After drawing out a large line, she added check marks. 'Once you organise them, tell me the start and end date and then we can plot in the exchanges as we can. Surely knowing the sequence of events shall help us glean their purpose.'

'Let us hope you are right, sister.'

Brenna set the letters out along the line one by one, moving the letters as needed when newer or later dated letters emerged. After she placed the last one, she frowned.

'What is it?' Moira asked, looking over Brenna's shoulder at the timeline now dotted with letters.

'I cannot place it, but there is something not right about this timing. There is a tight clump of letters here, then a huge gap in time without any communications, and then another bunch at the end. I believe we are missing those.' She pointed to the void on the parchment.

Moira stilled. 'Is that not when Father was ill?'

Brenna looked at the gap. 'Aye. It is. You are right!'

'But someone still managed all of his correspondence. Who was it?'

'Not Ewan,' Brenna replied. 'He detests letter writing. One of the many things he will have to overcome once he is laird.'

Garrick and Rory looked up at them both. 'So, who assisted him with that when he was ill?' Rory asked. 'It would have had to be one of his most trusted men.'

Brenna shrugged. 'They were many of the leading clansmen in and out of his chambers at all hours, and I was in such a state, I cannot say with certainty if one man had more visits with him than others. Ewan might know...but by the time we get word to him and back, it will be too late. Winters arrives tomorrow.'

'Could you compile a list?' Moira asked. 'Even if it might be incomplete?'

'Of course.' She added the names of five of Father's top leaders within the clan.

Adam
Stephens
Callum
Hamilton
Alistair

None of them had a name starting with *M*. She frowned. So much for that idea.

'Could one of them have interceded in the discourse? Could they have a batch of the letters?' Garrick asked.

'Possibly. But to what end?' Brenna asked.

'A great question,' Rory answered.

'What if Father has nothing to do with this? What if Winters has nothing to do with us?'

The three of them gifted Brenna a droll look.

'I was just being hopeful,' she murmured. 'You cannot be cross with me wishing my fiancé and Father were not part of some bizarre conspiracy to kill me.'

'Nay. None of us fault you in that. I suppose we just wish to prepare you in case they are,' Garrick added. 'What is the timeline you have?'

''Tis a year in length from November of last year to this November with a gap of about four months long between last March to July. Then, the letters begin again.' Brenna studied it. 'And the break mirrors the time of Father's illness, but other than that I do not know of its import.' She rubbed her temple. There had to be something she was missing.

When she glanced up, she caught Garrick's gaze on her. Questions registered in his eyes, and something else entirely that made her body quake from within. She swallowed hard. Perhaps he had just realised what she had.

That, despite her efforts at distance, the thing she was truly missing was him.

'I think I shall take some air. My temples throb,' Brenna stated and set aside the parchment.

Moira began to follow, but Garrick touched her arm. 'Let me go. Please.'

She smiled and nodded to him. 'I think you know where you will find her.'

'Aye,' he answered and nodded. Brenna always went to the barn when she was worried or upset. Countless times, they had spent lazy afternoons lying on bales talking...or kissing. His blood warmed and pooled at the memories. The burst of cold air on his face as he exited the castle cooled him and helped him regain his focus. When he entered the barn and saw her leaning her head against Montgomerie's, her eyes closed as she ran her fingertips along his neck and murmuring to him, he faltered.

How would he ever let her go? He swallowed hard. His mission was to put her mind at ease and to let her know all would be well. As a friend, which he desperately still wished to be, he needed to do this for her. Freeing her of his own weakness was best for her, but he had to help her to do that. He needed to let her go by explaining himself, truly explaining himself.

'I need to tell you why I never returned for you. Why I never wrote.'

Her hand stilled along Montgomerie's neck and her eyes fluttered open before she lifted her head to face him. Her brow furrowed. 'Did you not already tell me? You said it was grief after Ayleen died. You could not face returning. Was there more?'

He reached out his hand to her, and she slipped it in his own hesitantly. Garrick's heart thundered in his chest, heat flushed his body and for a moment he wasn't sure if his boots touched the ground. The only thing anchoring him to this moment was the weight of her hand in his and the warmth of it radiating up his arm.

After they sat on two bales of hay facing one another, he let go of her hand. She smoothed her skirts and cloak with her hands and then linked them together loosely in her lap. Could he do this? His throat dried and he scrubbed a hand through his hair.

When he met her gaze, he knew he had to explain so she would believe in herself, in her worth and in her value and know that she need not settle for any man. Not him, Winters, or any man lacking. She had to know she was worthy of all the world had to offer, not merely what Bran told her she was.

'You are, you were, the most beautiful gift I have ever been given, Bren.'

'Garrick—'

'Nay,' he said softly. 'Please let me say all of it. Just listen.'

She nodded, pressing her lips together in a smooth line.

'I did not write, I could not write, to you after Ayleen died…' His hands shook and he blew out a breath and held her gaze. 'Because I killed her.'

Her lips parted, her eyes searching his face. She shifted on the bale. No judgement rested in her eyes only a quest for understanding, so he continued on despite how his hands and limbs tingled and buzzed.

'I arrived in time at the abbey. It was engulfed in flames and reivers were everywhere, attacking the area and everyone within sight as they pillaged the abbey and whatever remained of the cottages nearby on the outskirts of Perth. I prayed to God to find her, and I heard this scream.' He cleared his throat as the ache of emotion tightened it.

Brenna shifted forward at the edge of the bale.

'I saw her. She saw me. The reivers were closing in. I was there in time but still could not save her because

I froze. I could have run to her and rescued her, but I did nothing, as if my legs were roots in the ground.'

A flash of heat consumed his body and illness threatened, but he swallowed it back. 'And, because I froze and did not act, she died. I saw the disappointment and disbelief in her eyes when she met my gaze and I didn't move. And, when the reiver stabbed her, the agony...' He choked back a sob. 'By the time I did finally run to her and reached her, she was dead. And *I*... I killed her.'

He looked away, staring at the barn floor as the world blurred from the emotion filling his eyes. Shame bled out of him. His fingers tingled, his heart pounded in his chest and his body heated at the acknowledgement of all his weakness had caused. He'd never admitted all that had happened with Ayleen to anyone before. Saying it out loud felt as horrid as it was freeing. At least one other person in the world knew his full shame, all of it, not just the filtered parts he had shown to her.

'And, because I failed her so completely, I could not allow myself to be your husband, Bren. I did not deserve it. The idea of failing you was more of a risk than I could take. So, I abandoned you, not because you were not worthy, but because *I* was not worthy of you and your love. I let you go...in order to save you from myself.'

'Garrick,' Brenna murmured. She sat down beside him on the bale of hay, resting her palm against the side of her face. The lovely, warm feel of comfort was his undoing, and the emotion he had fought to keep at bay burst free and he sobbed.

Ayleen. Cairn. Mother. All dead because of me.

Ack. Why did he have to be so bloody weak?

'Please look at me,' she whispered. She leaned over and clutched his face within her hands, her thumbs wiping the tears from his cheeks that he hadn't even realised were falling.

He clutched her wrists and shook his head. He couldn't meet her gaze. He didn't dare. He couldn't show her his weakness any more. He hated himself enough already. If she did, he wouldn't be able to breathe.

She let go and kneeled before him, forcing him to look into her eyes. The clear, blue depths of her eyes held no judgement or censure but...love. The way she used to look at him. As if he was the best of men. As if he could conquer the world with a flick of his wrist. He sucked in a breath. Did he scarce believe that she would forgive him for what he'd done?

'I am so sorry,' he murmured, clutching her face. 'I never meant to—'

Her gaze dropped to his lips and it was his undoing. He pulled her to him roughly, kissing her urgently, desperately, as if she was his breath that he needed to survive. Her breath caught in surprise, but she didn't pull back. She leaned into him, wrapping her legs around his waist as he pressed her tightly against him. Deepening kiss after kiss, he held her, knowing he should stop, but his body refused to obey his command. She felt like water after a drought, sun after a flood. She was all he needed, and yet nothing he felt he could still ask for.

He clutched her thigh, savouring the solid strength of her body, craving a union with her.

Ayleen.

If he didn't stop, he would compromise Brenna's very future. He pulled back, knowing full well he shouldn't have kissed her. That, even now he had finally told her the full truth of what had happened to Ayleen and why he'd chosen to abandon her, he still didn't deserve her.

Running a hand down her cheek, he pressed his forehead to her own, listening to the cadence of their uneven breaths. 'I still do not deserve you, but I wanted you to know that it was never you that was unworthy, but me. Wait for the man who deserves you, Bren. Choose your future. Do not allow any man to do it for you.'

Chapter Eighteen

Brenna shivered in Garrick's hold. His kisses, his touch, his hold affected her even more so than it always had. Her body thrummed and ached with desire. She sucked in steadying breaths and closed her eyes, breathing in his scent of soap and spice, knowing full well that she could not leave him, but knowing she had to all the same.

His telling her the truth behind his abandonment had set them both free, but it did not heal the scars of the past. They were still there alive and well, separating them. He couldn't forgive himself for what had happened to Ayleen and his family, and she didn't know if he ever could. And how could she live a life with a man who held his shame over the past closer than his hopes for the future?

She leaned in against his cheek and kissed him one last time. 'I will always love you, Garrick MacLean. You are the best of men and always will be. I hope one day you will remember that.'

She extricated herself carefully from his hold, her legs trembling as they made contact with the ground, and slipped away without a word before she changed her mind. His words had helped her realise that only she could free herself and secure her own happiness and, like her sister Moira, she would do just that.

But she'd have to hurry to set such a plan in motion as her fiancé would arrive on the morrow. As she walked back to the castle, the foundation of her plan began to shape before her. It was midday, but she would have enough time to craft her trap.

She entered the castle, went in search of her sister and found her in the massive Blackmore library and sitting room Rory had set up for his wife, poring over old ledgers.

'What are you looking for?' Brenna asked as she crossed the threshold into the room, basking in the warmth of the roaring fire and heady smell of leather and must.

Moira glanced up from the scattered books and smiled at her, attempting to rise.

'Do not get up. I will come to you. I wish to ask you a favour after all.'

Moira tilted her head, quirking her lips as she scrutinised her sister. 'What exactly are you up to? There is an unnatural twinkle in your eyes.'

'I am merely taking a page from my eldest sister's doings and seizing my right to make my own match.' She gleamed, and Moira clapped her hands together.

'You and Garrick have mended your rift and your engagement to Winters is off! I am so relieved.'

Brenna sat at the table with her. 'Nay, sister. Although we have mended many of our differences, we are not engaged. Nor have I ended my arrangement with Mr Winters. But I do wish to enlist your help in preparing for my meeting with him tomorrow. Can you help?'

Moira's smile fell. 'Aye. Of course, you can count on me. What can I do?'

'I will need you to craft a letter in Father's hand and secure a seal to it to make it look as if it is from Father. As you did when you planned your elopement with Rory.'

'First of all, I did not forge a letter from Father, but merely the seal to escape detection when Rory and I were scheming my escape.' She lifted her nose a touch to emphasise her point.

Brenna rolled her eyes. 'Either way, can you do this for me? I will draft what I would like you to put in it. Then, if you will copy it and seal it.' She shifted on the seat. 'And then if you could ask Rory to present it to him as if it is from Father.' She smiled.

'He will only do so if you tell him why.'

'I wish to attempt to make Winters reveal more of his hand if he is involved in this plot to harm me and our family. If he is innocent, he will be nonplussed by the letter from Father.'

'You mean the fake letter from Father?'

'Aye, the fake letter from Father.' She gifted her sister a full smile. 'So, will you do it?'

'Aye,' she answered, grasping Brenna's hand in her own. 'Draft what you wish me to write and I shall begin.'

* * *

Garrick rubbed his eyes. 'The words are beginning to swim upon the page,' he complained, and glanced over to Rory, who was also immersed in correspondence.

'At least we have heard back from some of our queries,' Rory replied.

'Too bad most of it contradicts one another.'

'It is odd. I have never seen such opposing views of a man. Some of Uncle's contacts claim he is a fine businessman while others that he is a debtor and just short of a criminal.' Rory set the pages down and leaned back in his chair.

Garrick stood to stretch and then walked over to the large window. 'Looks like rain.'

'Most likely it will be snow. Temperature is falling.'

'Aye.' He stared out at the rolling sea, the smooth waves reminding him of the feel of Brenna against him. His body began a dull hum and his palms ached to hold her.

'Do you plan to just let her go tomorrow?' Rory asked. The words cut through the air like an arrow and Garrick's heart sputtered as if it had hit its mark.

He sighed aloud and let his head flop forward momentarily before he looked back up. 'Aye. I do not wish to, but I am not the man she deserves. I want her to choose the best man and future for herself. That is not me. I am broken, and I literally have nothing to offer her. Not even a roof over her head or a bed to sleep in.' He released a bitter laugh. 'I am laird over a clan that

no longer exists, and a man without a home or castle.'
He rested his hands on his waist.

'If I am any example, Stewart women like their men
a wee bit broken. Look at me. I was cursed and dying
when Moira chose me and agreed to become my wife.
I did not deserve her in the least, but she is the best gift
I have ever been given. Because of her, I have a life, a
family and a future. She fought for my life and well-
being when I had stopped fighting for it myself. Seizing the chance you gifted me was the best decision I
have ever made, even though I was certain I had made
a fatal error at the time.'

'You and Moira are different. 'Tis not the same with
Bren and me.'

'No? Seems exactly the same to me, but you are a
mite bit more stubborn than I am.' Rory chuckled at
his own joke and set back to reading his correspondence. 'Have you located anyone who might be the M
from the letters?'

Garrick shook his head. 'Unfortunately, no.' He
glanced back at the two letters that remained unopened
on the table. 'But I have two more to read. Let us hope
one of them is the hidden piece of the puzzle we seek.'
He set aside his longings for Brenna and went back
to read the remaining letters. 'While there is no mention of who M might be, these two letters speak of the
suspicion that Winters has been earning favour from
both sides of the coin. Perhaps that is why some speak
favourably while others do not. They suggest he is in
league with the King while also trying to show alle-
giance to a few of the southern clans.'

Rory whistled.

'What?' Garrick asked, eager to know what his friend was thinking.

'Think upon it,' Rory urged, sitting forward in his chair, his palms pressed flat to his desk. 'If that is true, then he very well may be the fiend we believe he is. It might also explain why he might be eager to create a rift between the two sides. And what better way to do that than to murder the daughter of a laird that was set upon marrying an Englishman? Everyone would be engulfed in anger and no one would win. All sides would be at odds.'

'That would set England and Scotland at odds with one another. And you are right, everyone would be enraged. The Scots for the death of a laird's daughter and the English for a man losing his betrothed.'

The hall clock chimed six. 'Let us meet to dine at seven and tell Moira and Brenna our theory. From there, we can determine the best way to ensnare Mr Winters for the rat we believe him to be.'

Garrick nodded, but he balked at the idea of how they might go about it. He couldn't think of a way of entrapping the man without using Brenna as bait, and he was none too keen to do so. Desperate men were dangerous creatures, especially if they were as cunning as Mr Winters seemed to be. Not just anyone could fool both sides into believing in his loyalty. Only a man gifted in deceit could weave a bevy of lies into a tapestry, and he feared Winters might be capable of such treachery.

Chapter Nineteen

Brenna took a steadying breath and pulled back her shoulders before rounding the corner and entering the long main hallway of Blackmore. Each step along the stone corridor was a reminder of who she walked towards and why. This was her chance to get the answers she needed, and she would get them no matter what. Her smile fell away when she saw the man before her.

'Where is Stephen… Mr Winters?' she asked, befuddled to see a man other than her betrothed at the door, handing off his coat and gloves to the young maid who had greeted him.

'Do not worry, darling,' Stephen called as he entered through the expansive doors of the castle. 'I am here. I am relieved to see you looking so well.' Stephen came to her, gathered her hands in his own and smiled, pressing a kiss to her knuckles.

What had come over him? While this *looked* like the Stephen Winters she had meet in Oban during her visits, he had never been this attentive and affectionate before. Maybe he did care for her, but he had been more reserved before their betrothal had been made official. Had almost losing her thrust him into being a more doting fiancé?

Did it matter?

Brenna hesitated before gifting him a full smile. 'I have Laird MacLean to thank.' She gestured to Garrick, who frowned at Stephen. She nodded to him, her eyes pleading for him to be kind. Their ruse would not work if he was too sceptical of the man.

'I am indebted to you, my laird.' He nodded to Garrick. 'I hope to one day be able to repay you for your bravery in rescuing my bride-to-be.'

Garrick cleared his throat and stood in a soldier's stance with his feet apart and his hands linked behind his back. 'You can start by explaining why you did not send her with more protection.'

Brenna's throat dried. So much for subtleties.

He shrugged. 'Ignorance of the ways of these lands. I did not think it would be such a risk, and with my plans changing at the last minute I could not find more men to send with them. I was trying to please her by getting her back home that night, as she wished. It is a mistake I will not repeat, I assure you.' He pulled Brenna to his side and kissed the top of her head. 'I am so grateful you came along when you did.'

Garrick shifted on his feet. 'As am I.'

The meaning of his words was not lost on her, and she blushed.

'Welcome to Blackmore, Mr Winters,' Moira said. 'Please come in. We would love you to stay for dinner, if you can. We would like to get to know our future brother-in-law.'

'Such a generous offer, my lady. I wish we could stay. I would like to get us home and settled by dark to avoid any further danger to Miss Stewart. With our nuptials only a handful of days away, we cannot tarry, even if we wish to. But I would not shy away from a refreshment before we depart. Perhaps tea?'

'Of course. I'll see to it. I am glad you can stay for a visit, even if it is a brief one.'

Brenna exhaled in relief as they moved into the main hall. So far, so good.

'Thank you for welcoming me into your home, Laird McKenna, and for your correspondence about Miss Stewart. I was sick with worry when we heard the carriage had not arrived at Glenhaven as planned.'

'As were we, Mr Winters. Correspondence from Laird Stewart arrived for you as well.' He handed him the note.

'Ah, thank you,' he answered. A slight hesitation in his reply was his only flicker of uncertainty. He tucked the letter in his jacket pocket.

'Do you not wish to read it now?' Brenna asked, hoping she didn't sound as eager as she felt. He needed to read the note for her to know whether he was involved in the plot against her. 'It could be about our nuptials and whether Father will be well enough to join us.'

He smiled at her. 'Quite right. I will scan it to see if there is anything to be shared.' He opened the seal and read. His smile flattened out before settling back into place.

Brenna pulled at the sleeve of her gown. Surely the man could hear the sound of her heart pounding wildly in the cage of her chest, awaiting his answer? He glanced up to see Garrick staring at her, uncertainty flashing briefly before he sent her a lift of an eyebrow.

'Any news?' she asked.

'Nay. Sadly, he will not be able to join us for the wedding. His health is still poor, but he promises to host us for a visit after our trip.' He patted her arm and goose flesh rose along it.

That was not even close to what was written in that letter. She should know. She'd drafted the very words themselves, and Moira had written it out in as close to Father's hand as she could, using the letters they had brought with them for reference.

Brenna fidgeted with the end of her plait. 'That is disappointing,' she replied, trepidation filling her voice. It was not difficult to muster. Most likely she was standing next to a killer. Or perhaps merely one who ordered others to kill. Either way, she didn't wish to stay near him a moment longer, but if their plan was to work she had to play her part.

'Do not fret, my love. I have a wonderful surprise for you to distract you from such disappointing news.'

Brenna bet he did.

'Shall we sit?' Moira offered, gesturing them to follow on through the corridor.

They all went through the main hall with its large

banquet table into the sitting area, ladies first followed by the men. Garrick caught Rory's gaze and fisted his hands by his side. While Mr Winters was very English and bit too groomed for his liking, he did not seem the villain Garrick thought, or rather hoped, he might be, which made him even more dangerous. He was quite the wolf in sheep's clothing.

The tall, thin man with his dark pristine trousers, shockingly white tunic and vibrant maroon waist coat sat on the edge of the settee and ran a hand through his dark hair. He had a ring on his little finger with a family crest, and boots that reflected the sunlight. He looked exactly like what Garrick had expected: he looked like a bloody Englishman.

'Have you been able to make arrangements to bring Arthur and his son back to Oban, for their family's sake?' Brenna asked the moment they had all been seated. The dreaded Mr Winters placed a hand over hers and nodded.

'Of course, my darling. I've sent a man to see to it. Such a shame that you were attacked by thieves. Barbarians.'

'I don't believe the attack was random, but planned, and not by thieves. The men we encountered had training. They were quick, efficient and tracked incredibly well. They were also much better dressed than the average thief in these parts,' Garrick stated.

They also had your coin on their person.

He left that part out, eager to see what information he could gain without it. Playing the part of the serious soldier and protective suitor was quite easy. Too easy.

He reminded himself that Brenna was still to marry another, even if it would no longer be this scoundrel.

Mr Winters balked. 'Why would anyone be after Miss Stewart?'

'We believe they may have been after you, sir. You were supposed to be with Miss Stewart except you were called away at the last minute based on what Bren— Erm, Miss Stewart told us.'

A flicker of unease skittered across the man's brow before he rubbed his chin and answered. 'It was a last-minute decision. One that I regret now. To know that you were alone, left for dead. That you had to witness such an attack.'

'I am fortunate not to remember most of it,' Brenna murmured. 'And that Laird MacLean found me when he did.' She sent him a smile.

'Aye. It is quite the miracle,' Moira added.

'So, you do not believe that you could have been the target, sir?' Garrick slipped in another question.

He shrugged. 'I cannot imagine why. I don't have enemies and my business dealings are sound.'

Garrick sat back, knowing full well the man was now lying through his perfect white teeth. 'Anyone jealous of your pending marriage?'

Other than me.

He smiled. 'Most likely, but no one would harm her because of it.'

'It makes little sense. They came after her, then after us, to ensure she was dead. It seemed quite personal.' Garrick locked gazes with the man to see if he'd flinch.

'Like she was being hunted?' he asked, his gaze

zeroing in on Garrick. A flash of warning entered his eyes. His suppressed anger towards Garrick was unmistakable. Their ruse was working.

'Just like,' Garrick answered coolly, without missing a step in their verbal dance.

He dropped his gaze and gripped Brenna's hand. 'My dear, I—' His words broke off. 'I am so sorry. I don't understand how or why anyone would wish to harm you.' He tucked a lock of her hair behind her ear. She shifted on the settee, the colour draining from her face. He stilled, noting the change in her. 'We did have a break in the afternoon of your departure. They took the coin your father had brought along with some correspondence. Perhaps they believed you had more coin with you after they read the letters. Word of our pending nuptials is the talk of Oban.'

'Was anyone hurt?' Brenna asked, unable to hold her gaze.

'No. I was out handling business and the staff was out tending to duties to prepare for our nuptials.'

'I am glad to hear of it.' She met Garrick's gaze. 'Perhaps the answer is as simple as that. A robbery and then an attempt to steal more?'

'Perhaps.' His answer sounded as flat and dry as he'd hoped.

Garrick frowned. Mr Winters was a fine actor meant for the stage.

'Although your father is too ill to attend our wedding in Oban, perhaps your family and friends here could come? I would like you to all meet my family as well. They will love you all, of course.'

'There is no cause for the rush, Stephen. We could wait until Father is well enough to attend, or even marry in Glenhaven.' Brenna stated, shifting away from him.

Careful, Bren.

Winters noted the shift in her demeanour and moved closer to her, clasping her hand in his. 'I had hoped to surprise you, but a friend has helped me organise a journey for us to see all of Europe, but we must be on the boat by Thursday to depart on time. That is why I wished to hasten our union.'

Brenna gasped, her surprise genuine. 'Oh, my! That is...unexpected. I know not what to say.'

'Why? When we have children, we will not have such freedoms, but now is the perfect time for you to see the world with me.' He clutched her hands in his.

'I am merely surprised, that is all,' she replied.

'That is fine news,' Garrick added to try to help Brenna along.

Garrick mustered what strength he could and smiled at her. This was taking a toll on her, and now he had second thoughts. 'We would not miss attending your union for the world.'

'Then, it is settled. Brenna and I shall depart tonight, and you all shall join us in a few days' time to celebrate our nuptials. Perhaps we should not delay after all, but head back now. You look absolutely pale, my love.'

'She won't be travelling anywhere with you, Winters,' Garrick stated, rising from his chair and moving in closer to the man as he spoke.

He laughed. 'Why is that? We are engaged to be married, and I have come here to collect her by the laird's invitation. You have no stake in her future, MacLean. I know full well you are laird of...nothing these days.' His eyes flashed a warning, a hint that the darkness in him would be bubbling to the surface soon.

'Because you are a cheat and a liar. What are you scheming at? We know you were involved in the attack on Brenna's carriage.' Garrick continued his approach and Rory began to move in to block Moira from the man's reach.

'And you are as daft as they come, MacLean.' Winters pulled a blade from his boot and had it at Brenna's throat before Garrick could reach him. 'I would hate to cut this pretty flesh,' he warned. 'Stay back. And order your men to clear a path, McKenna. I know you must have some ridiculous scheme to trap me, but she is my key to a safe passage.'

Brenna whimpered and leaned away from the blade, but Winters only increased his hold on her. It would take only a flick of the man's wrist to cut her throat.

Garrick's feet tingled and his ears buzzed. *Damn.* It couldn't happen again. *Not now. Not now.* He sucked in air through his mouth. His legs felt heavy, his body as if it belonged to someone else.

He couldn't fail her. Not now when she needed him most.

'While I do appreciate your offer of tea, Lady McKenna, I find I have worn out my welcome, so I'll be going...with my bride to be, of course. We have much to accomplish before we reach Oban.'

'I cannot say I will be sorry to see you leave, but you will unhand my sister,' Moira answered.

Rory edged closer and Winters tightened his hold, pricking Brenna's neck. A small thread of blood glided down her throat.

'Ah-ah, McKenna. One more step, and I might lose my grip.'

A tear slid down Brenna's cheek and Garrick held her gaze. 'Stay calm,' he told her. 'We will find you. You have my word.'

'Oh, I would not hold much promise in a rescue from him, my dear. He has had a rather poor record as of late. I believe your entire family is dead, isn't that right?' The man's dark eyes glistened in the light.

Everything around Garrick went silent. Rage coursed through his veins, and he commanded himself not to charge him. If he did, Brenna was as good as dead. 'You will die, Winters. That is a promise.'

The man laughed. 'Not by you,' he spat. 'Nor any of your men, McKenna. They had best provide me a clear path to my carriage where my driver awaits. I would hate my bride to have an accident before our nuptials.'

Chapter Twenty

Stephen shoved Brenna into the carriage, and she tumbled hard into the side of the squabs and onto the floor, scrambling up into the far corner of the seat in the darkness of the small space. The curtains were drawn and it had a remarkable likeness to a tomb: perhaps her own. She shivered and waited for her eyes to adjust to the darkness. If she could only find a weapon. If she could defend herself for a moment, she might be able to free herself and jump from the carriage. Heaven knew that whatever was outside would be better than being with him within. She hurriedly felt around the seat and the floor but found nothing.

Curses.

Winters entered, slammed the door shut and locked it before tapping his cane on the roof to signal for the carriage to be off. The carriage lurched off with a sudden start, sending her backwards into the seat, and her head hit the back of it.

'Careful, pet,' Winters snarled.

'As if you care,' she snapped.

She watched him. Perhaps if she challenged him, he would make a mistake and she could free herself. 'It must be quite tiring to hide your madness. You genuinely had me fooled. I just believed you to be an arrogant dullard.'

'Are you trying to make me kill you?' he asked, peeling the gloves from his hands. 'It will not work. Too much is at stake.'

She frowned. Another tactic would be necessary, but what?

'How is your father?' he asked.

She narrowed her eyes at him, unsure of his change in topic. 'The same. He is ailing, as you well know.'

'Near death, I do hope,' he answered. His cold, dark eyes met her own.

She gasped. 'What have you done?'

'Nothing yet, but I have men in place in case they are needed. My hope is that your death will cause him to succumb to his illness. The death of a youngest child, a daughter as pretty as you, will come at some cost. But, if not, there are other means.'

'Sorry to disappoint, but I do not plan to die any time soon.' She gripped the bottom of her carriage seat.

'We shall see. This whole business is very tiresome, but it will be over soon. By my estimates, I will be settled at home this eve free of a future wife and father-in-law, but full of the coin from your coffers and those from the King for having set such chaos in motion.' He set his full gaze upon her and the cruelty within its depths chilled her. 'All part of a greater plan. One far more important than just you and I. Your sacrifice is needed for England's future.'

'Sacrifice?' Her stomach pitted.

'Yes. When we met your father and realised his level of desperation to secure more power and safety for the future of the Stewarts, your clan was the perfect mark. Enlist the laird's help in helping to ease tensions between England and Scotland, while promising him protection as well as a gainful marriage for his daughter. And the sot asked few questions. I can only assume it was because he cared little about the truth. He just needed you settled before he died.' He smiled at her. 'And you will be. Just a bit further under the ground than you may have planned.'

'It is too late for you, Winters. We knew of your plan and have already sent word to my family, as well as the Camerons. Everyone will already know of your scheme. Marrying me will secure you nothing.'

He studied her and tilted his head. 'Hmm. Well, I had planned for the interference from McKenna and your own family, but I did forget that blasted alliance your brother-in-law has with the Camerons.' He smiled. 'But I am sure I can concoct a way to shift the blame to them. From what I hear, the Camerons have many enemies, as they are so large and powerful. Perhaps I can pool the other clans against them.' He nodded. 'Yes, yes, I shall do that. It may delay things a day or two, but in the end it will make the chaos in the Highlands even more extensive.'

She gaped at him. 'You truly are mad. You cannot merely turn clans against one another on a whim. It is not a chess game. Thousands of lives are at stake.' She leaned forward in her seat.

He pulled an extravagant pocket watch from his coat pocket and opened it. 'Your family at Blackmore should be dispatched within the next hour or two by my men. And, now that I think upon it, I am rather sure our vicar can produce a marriage licence with or without your blessing.'

He returned it to his pocket and pulled a small roped cord out in its place. 'So, I best be on with it. You must all be dead by nightfall for my plan to stay on its new course.'

He frowned, winding the rope around one of his hands. 'Although, it is a pity. You are quite pretty in your own way, even if you won't stop yapping about.' He lunged forward with the rope.

Brenna scrabbled away from him to the other end of the bench seat, her limbs flailing against him. Her mind whirled as she kicked and screamed to free herself from him. She had to save herself so she could warn her family at Blackmore and Glenhaven to protect them from whatever horrors Winters and his men had sent their way, but how? She landed a blow to his shin, and he cursed. She prayed it wasn't already too late.

As soon as Winters' carriage roared out of the drive, Rory shouted orders to his most trusted and valued manservant, Angus. 'Add more men to the watch, alert the Camerons and lock down Blackmore. No one goes in and out except for me and Laird MacLean.'

'Aye, my laird,' Angus answered and disappeared down the front steps.

'And I will go after Brenna,' Garrick stated. 'If I hurry, I may be able to catch up with her carriage before it is too late.' His gut tightened and every fibre of his body seized in agony over the idea that he might be. All because he had frozen up. Again.

'You will, my friend. You will.'

Garrick prayed to God that his friend was right.

He jogged to the barn, saddled up Montgomerie and rode him at neck-breaking speed out of the slick grounds of Blackmore and along the road that paralleled the cliffs overlooking the Firth of Lorn. As the only road wide enough to allow for a carriage, it would have been the only route possible for Winters and Brenna to have taken. Now it was only a matter of whether he could intercept them soon enough.

Dirt and snow kicked up behind him as he rode low against Montgomerie's lean form. After several minutes, Garrick saw the carriage, sunset glistening off the black lacquer sheen as it roared far too quickly down the road. The man was not only mad but reckless. At any moment, one of the horses could lose their footing or a wheel hit a rut, sending the carriage out of control. Regardless of the danger, relief sang through Garrick's body at the knowledge that he could save her. He eased up on Montgomerie's reins to steady his approach along the narrowing pass. Just then, the carriage jerked wildly to the left and then the right, skittering dangerously close to the cliff's edge and the water below.

'Stop!' Garrick called to the driver.

The man turned, saw him and clapped the reins along the horses' sides to drive them on faster.

Saints be. The fool of a man would get them all killed. He sped up and travelled along a parallel track above them, as he'd run out of space along the road to ride alongside. His idea was foolish and reckless, perhaps even more so than the driver's. He hesitated. The side door of the carriage flew open and Brenna screamed as she slid partly out of the moving carriage. Her arms clung to the small handle and she pulled herself back in. The door swung back open and clapped along the side of the carriage as it continued on.

Garrick's heart dropped. His legs tingled. He had to jump now, no matter what happened. Brenna was running out of time and soon he would be at the edge of his own path and unable to follow any longer. He had to jump and stop that carriage. He yanked Montgomerie to a halt, dismounted, ran along the hillside until there was no more earth beneath him and leapt with all his might.

Brenna screamed as her upper body felt the rush of cold air around her and saw the drop to the loch below.

Stephen laughed, before yanking her back inside the carriage. The door clapped against the side as they barrelled down the slushy road, the wheels spraying up wet snow as they went.

'Sir?' the driver called down to him, swerving again. 'Shall I stop?'

'Keep on, Edward!' Stephen growled. 'Go faster.

My fiancée and I are coming to an agreement about the role she shall play in my life. Give us but a moment to sort it out.'

He shoved her out again, for longer this time, before yanking her back in.

Brenna paled as she clutched his forearm. She panted for breath and shivered at the knowledge she was going to die at the hands of a madman.

'What shall you do now?' He snickered.

When she didn't answer, he shrugged. 'Just as I told my mother before you left. You are nothing. A vapid space covered in beauty. Other than a good poke, you are useless. Bloody useless.'

Useless?

Rage erupted from her and she lifted her hand to slap him, digging her nails into his fine pasty cheek. 'I am not useless!'

'You bitch!' he exclaimed, clutching her neck by the throat. 'Beauty can be so easily replaced. I hope you can swim. If you survive the drop, that is. It matters not to me.'

He grinned and she gasped for air, clawing at his hand and wrist to release its hold on her neck. He growled as she dug her nails into his flesh, drawing blood along his hand.

He cursed again and squeezed harder.

'Stop! Stop the carriage!' a voice boomed from above them.

Garrick. Thank God.

Distracted, Stephen loosened his hold momentarily, and Brenna freed herself. She sucked in greedy breaths and coughed as she struggled to get air back into her lungs and scoot away from him.

'Sir?' the driver called back. 'Shall I stop?'

'Nay, fool. Go faster,' Stephen shouted.

He returned his wrath to Brenna, sliding over to her as the carriage jostled them around as it picked up speed. 'You must be dead for me to fulfil my orders to the King. The Stewarts must be ended one by one, and the clan erased from the Highlands.'

'Erased?' She coughed, clutching her throat and watching his approach. 'You cannot erase thousands of people. You are mad.'

'Perhaps I am mad, but it can be done. Isn't that what happened to your Laird MacLean?' He snickered again. 'Some of my finest work, my dear.'

Her blood chilled. 'You did that?' she asked. How could one man end a people?

'Yes. How else was I to bring down your own clan? We could not have you two marrying. That would have only strengthened the Highlands.'

'You will pay for what you have done,' Brenna promised. And he would. She just needed to survive this first.

A thud sounded atop the carriage, and it lurched hard to the right towards the cliffs, sending them both sliding towards the open carriage door, which still clapped against the sides as they raced down the hill. She glanced out, saw the loch far below and regretted it. A wave of dizziness washed over her. Why couldn't they have been driving on a flat stretch of road by a stream instead? She cringed.

He lunged for her, and she slid deftly out of his reach as the carriage pitched to the side again. 'You were never quite so urgent for my attentions when we met,' she chided, trying to focus on something other than the perilous drop below if she got much closer to the open door.

'I'm quite eager to be rid of you before we run out of cliff, so I can enjoy the money from your father and the King. I also do not like being a fiancé. I prefer my freedom.' He held onto the handle of the other, still-closed carriage door and stretched out as far as he could. He grabbed for her. Unable to move any further away without falling out of the open door, she was caught in the vice of his hold on her forearm. He wrenched her arm and she cried out as her arm burned from the force of his hold. If she could hang on a bit longer, they'd be out of danger, as the turn in road away from the cliffs was just ahead.

'Hang on, Bren! Slow the carriage!' Garrick shouted from the bench seat.

The driver cried out and then flew from the bench seat of the moving carriage onto the road to their left. He crashed to the ground.

'Looks like you will be in need of a new driver,' she murmured.

'He is as replaceable as you are,' Winters sneered, yanking her away from the seat and closer to the open door.

She screamed, scrambling for a hold on the door, but lost her grip. She pitched to the side and clawed into his arm for purchase. He attempted to kick her away, but the carriage swerved as Garrick pulled the horses' reins to slow them, sending Stephen in the opposite direction towards her and the door that clapped precariously against the side of the carriage.

She wrapped one arm around the seat to hold herself as Stephen slid past her and partially out of the open door. He clung to her arm. Her eyes watered at the strain of his weight pulling against her shoulder and her grip on the seat.

'Pull me up,' he commanded as his torso dragged along the cliffside and he attempted to get his footing as the carriage slowed.

She cried out in agony as her fingers slid from the seat. Stephen's weight was too much for her to counter. As they bumped along, his hold on her arm loosened.

Just hold on a minute longer.

He yanked on her arm. 'If I go, you go!' He laughed.

She cried out as her fingers lost their hold on the seat and she fell through the open carriage door.

She hit the ground hard, even though the carriage wasn't moving as fast as it had been, and felt the air along her legs as her body pitched over the side of the cliff. Stephen's hand slid off her forearm and she heard his yell as he cascaded down into the waters below. Her flailing hands closed around the flat edge of a boulder as her legs swung in the air. She sighed in relief.

She wasn't dead. Yet.

The waters of the loch crashed against the shoreline below as she stared up at the sky. She screamed, but it sounded hollow and empty. Had Garrick even heard her? How long could she hold on?

Carefully, she pulled herself up slowly until she was hugging the boulder to her chest, her arms shaking from the effort to hold on. Her teeth chattered from the wind and cold.

'Bren? Bren?' Garrick called from above.

'I am here,' she cried out.

He ran to her and skidded to the ground, extending his arm over the side. He couldn't quite reach her. Her stomach bottomed out.

He met her gaze. 'Take my hand,' he said.

What?

She shook her head, her body vibrating from fear. She'd been too high for too long. 'I can't… I can't let go.'

'You have to. Trust me.'

She shook her head. 'I'm slipping. If I let go, I'll drop into the loch.'

Thinking of the loch, how far up she was and how far it was below made her dizzy, and she squeezed her eyes shut.

'Bren,' Garrick murmured, his tone softened. 'Trust me.'

The insides of her floated, light as air. Did she dare? Would she fall if she did? She knew she would die if she didn't. She opened her eyes and met his gaze, his green eyes steady and certain, and nodded.

Then, with one big breath, she let go of her right hand and reached up while still holding on with her left, and as soon as she did he grabbed her by the arm. Instead of plummeting to her death, she was pulled up until she was close enough for him to reach her with both arms.

When she was entirely on the ground, she flopped back, eager to feel the weight of firm land and solid earth beneath her torso.

Garrick leaned over her, his eyes bright, his breath coming out in uneven pants. He brushed back the hair from her face and cupped her cheek with his palm. The warm, strong feel of him made her eyes close in relief. 'Are you hurt?'

'Nay,' she panted, covering his hand with her own, letting her heart slow as she settled into the knowledge that he was there, and they were safe. 'But you must get us back to Blackmore. Mr Winters has much more ruin planned.'

'I will. Catch your breath first. You almost died.' The husky hitch in his voice made her open her eyes. The pad of his thumb rubbed gently on her cheek.

'Thank you,' she whispered, reaching up to him.

'For what?' he asked, leaning into her touch as her fingertips skimmed his neck.

'For saving me…again.'

He pulled her into an embrace, hugging her fiercely, whispering into her hair. 'Always, Bren. I will always move heaven and earth for you.'

As she clutched him to her, she wished he could be hers, that he could let the past go, but she knew deep in her soul that he still held his pain and shame as close to his heart as he held her to him now.

Chapter Twenty-One

'It is a miracle you are both alive,' Moira said. She'd fussed over Brenna and Garrick since they had returned to Blackmore. Each had been tucked in tartans, given copious amounts of tea and sat huddled on the settees in front of the burning hearth in the main hall. Brenna feared her sister might dissolve with worry.

'Moira, please sit down and rest.' Brenna reached for her sister's hand as she walked by her.

'How can I possibly sit?' She paced in front of the hearth. 'You were almost killed, we have no idea if Ewan and Father are well and who knows how many more of these men are set on destroying us? Sit? Ridiculous.' She shook her head.

Rory walked up behind her and wrapped his arms around her waist. 'No one is being ridiculous. There is nothing we can do as of this very moment. We have sent word to everyone we can, and have added extra soldiers to guard Blackmore, as well as the border between us and the Camerons. They also are on high alert.

If there is anyone in this scheme left to be found, we will find them.'

'I find your certainty appalling,' Moira answered, her lip quirking up.

'As do I,' Garrick agreed.

Fatigue pressed in on Brenna. Now that the rush of energy and fear of almost being killed and needing to get word to Glenhaven about what they'd learned from Stephen had run its course, it felt as if her bones had turned to oats. She yawned into her hand.

Escaping death was tiresome.

'Tomorrow I will leave for Glenhaven,' Garrick announced.

Brenna blinked and sat up. 'Why?'

'To ensure your family is well.'

She shook her head. 'Garrick, there is a strong possibility you would be killed along your journey. Stephen alluded to this being a large-scale scheme with who knows how many men involved. Men may be looking for you even now. And you have not even healed from your initial injuries from before. Rescuing me has ripped out your stitches. You are oozing blood even now.' She gestured to his wound.

'Would you prefer I stand by and do nothing?'

She quirked her lips. 'You have not exactly been standing by and doing nothing.'

'Perhaps not, but I have failed you in letting you almost marry that man, and my own clan and family by not being there to protect them. But I can help your family now. You must let me.' The desperation in his green eyes and the strained pitch of his voice stilled her.

The agony he felt matched her own. She had also been part of this horrid scheme. She had agreed to marry a man she did not know to please her father, even though she didn't wish to, and she'd never asked for details.

It was high time she also gained her footing in this world and sought her own place in it with purpose. And speaking with Father was the first step in doing that.

'We go together.'

'What? You just proclaimed it was not safe.' He frowned at her.

'It isn't, but I need to return home. And there is no one else I trust more with my safety...than you.'

The air between them stilled and his eyes softened, the longing in them telling her all she needed to know. He loved her as she did him, despite all they'd endured. But she also knew that too much needed to be settled to reclaim any of that love or passion between them just yet. And, without that, they'd never survive the future, no matter how much they cared for one another. Love could not exist in a space without trust and one full of fear. Letting go of the past would take work from both of them, but she knew she was willing to do it. She just needed to see if he was.

'Aye,' he answered. 'Then, we will go together.'

'Now I shall never be able to sit again,' Moira quipped.

'Well, then, we shall just stand together until they return,' Rory teased.

Angus hurried into the hall. 'Sir, y'er needed.'

'What is it?' Rory asked, his body stiffening in alarm.

'A man's been found at the edge of the grounds. Sean found him.'

'Take us to him.' Rory commanded. He fell into step with Angus, and Garrick wasn't far behind.

As they reached the barn, Sean waved to them from far off in the meadow. He stood at the break between meadows and deep forest. They jogged to him and, once they arrived, Garrick's stomach dropped.

'This is the other man who was in the party searching for us when we fled Loch Linnhe.'

'Are you sure?' Rory asked.

'The scars on his face are unmistakable. It is him.'

'Why would he be dead here?' Rory asked.

'Have you searched him?' Garrick stooped to get a closer look at the man who appeared to have been felled by a large blade to the gut.

Sean shook his head, his face pale.

Garrick searched the man's coat pockets and found nothing. He then searched the man's trews to see if he'd hidden anything further on his person. He pulled two letters from him. He cursed.

'One of these is addressed to you, Rory.' The other had no identifying information on the outside of it.

Rory took the letter addressed to him and opened it. 'This was the letter from the Camerons that we had been expecting. They have nothing good to report on Winters.'

'Evidently Winters knew that and intercepted the letter somehow.'

'How would they even know we sent such an enquiry?'

'Perhaps he has allies, as we do, and used them to prevent this information from getting to Brenna in time.'

'And it might have worked, had you not intercepted the other letters, and we received word from Uncle's other contacts in Oban regarding some of his questionable business dealings.' Rory rested his hands on his waist.

Garrick opened the other letter and scanned it. 'This is a map.'

Rory read over his shoulder. 'Of the Highlands.'

'Aye.' His heart raced and then dropped into his stomach, stealing his breath. There in bold lettering was a map of all the clan borders in the Highlands. Of great interest were the four to the north of Blackmore: MacLean, Stewart, Cameron, MacDougall. MacLean and MacDougall had an X through them.

'They are destroying us one by one, just as Brenna said Winters was boasting of. And, by the looks of this, the Stewarts are definitely next.'

'We cannot wait until the morrow. I must go at once before it is too late.' Garrick sprinted out to the barn. Rory ran alongside him.

'They cannot destroy Bran and the Stewarts,' Rory challenged as they reached Montgomerie's stall.

'And I did not think they could bring down the Mac-Dougalls, or my own people either. But our clans and lands have been splintered and scattered in a handful of months. By continuing to destroy us one by one, the

King will get his wish of a complete elimination of our people, won't he?'

Rory balked. He shook his head. 'I cannot fathom it.'

'This union with the Stewarts was no union but a means of bringing down the entire clan.'

Rory gripped Garrick's shoulder. 'All the more reason for you to have a plan before you ride off into the night. We will meet with my men, send out new missives by messengers to ensure their safety before your arrival and you and Brenna will rest before you collapse where you stand.'

'I hate it when you are right.' Garrick frowned.

Rory smirked. 'I know.'

The return journey to Glenhaven was an uneventful and quick one, as they had a carriage and fresh horses changed out along the way, so they did not have to pause along their journey. They slept soundly in the carriage, with soldiers riding alongside them as they went, and the days it would have taken due to the snow hampering their journey were reduced. They arrived at Glenhaven two days later without incident.

As the carriage rolled to a stop, Garrick's chest tightened. Although all seemed as it should, with soldiers posted outside the castle walls and main doors, he wouldn't feel any relief until the soldiers that rode alongside them checked the area and returned with a report that all was indeed well at Glenhaven.

'I do not know what I shall do if anything has happened to them,' Brenna whispered. She studied the castle doors.

He took her chilled hand in his and squeezed it briefly before letting go. 'Whatever has come to pass, we will face it together.'

'Aye.'

The castle doors opened and Ewan Stewart, Brenna's older brother, emerged.

'Ewan!' Brenna's hand flew to her mouth and her eyes filled with tears. The soldier waved to them that all was secure, and Brenna rushed from the carriage and into her brother's arms.

Garrick watched from a distance, not wishing to crowd their moment. A deep ache filled his chest. He would never have such a moment with his siblings again, and the agony of it seized him anew. He swallowed the emotion. Knowing he could give this to Brenna lightened some of his loss, so he clung to her joy as if it were his own.

When she turned to him and waved for him to come in, he smiled, eased from the carriage and remembered this could still be his, but he had to choose it. And, in order to choose it freely, he had to be whole again and the man he used to be. Taking a deep breath, he approached. Each step towards her was a step away from the safe, dark place of isolation and shame and into the light of uncertainty tinged with hope.

'Ewan.' He nodded to Brenna's brother as he approached. He'd aged since he'd last seen him, and an edge of wariness pulled down the corners of his eyes.

'Garrick.' He clapped him on the shoulder. 'Thank you for all you have done for Brenna and for us. We owe you a great debt. We have secured Glenhaven and sent word to our people. We are on watch for any further threats from Winters and his men because of your warning. I believe many lives have been spared.'

Garrick nodded, feeling awkward and uncertain under such praise.

'I am glad all is well. I was fearful the warnings would not reach you in time. How is Father?' Brenna asked as they followed Ewan inside.

'He will be better knowing you are both here, alive and well.'

Garrick did not miss the forced pitch in the man's voice. Brenna's smile fell. Evidently, she noticed it as well.

'May I see him now?'

'Of course. I will take you to him.'

Garrick's steps faltered. 'I will allow you some privacy,' he offered.

Ewan turned. 'He wishes to see you too, Garrick. Join us.'

Garrick hesitated. Did he wish to see Bran? The man who had believed him dead and almost married off his daughter to a murderer, all to gain favour with the King? Not really. But, when Brenna's expectant gaze met his, he nodded. 'Certainly.'

As they entered Bran Stewart's chamber, the smell of sickness and the horrid stench of ointments and other cures assailed Garrick. He sucked in a breath to steady himself. He was shocked to see that the once strong, dominant man full of bluster was now a small, diminished figure propped up in his bed on a sea of pillows, his features sunken and flat. At the sight of Brenna, light came back into the man's eyes, and he struggled to straighten up.

Garrick's heart squeezed for Brenna as she forced a smile and rushed to his bedside.

Thank God they'd come when they had. It did not take a doctor to know this man had not long left in this world. It pained him to know Moira had not come as well.

'Daughter.' Bran spoke and hugged her to him. 'The sight of you warms me.' She pressed a kiss to his cheek.

'Garrick,' he called, reaching out a shaky hand to him.

Steady.

He came to the other side of his bed, and the sight of him so ill cut Garrick to the bone. Red puffy eyes rested amongst the shadows beneath and pale pallor of his face. Had he lost so much weight since he'd last seen him? Garrick's stomach curdled as he took the man's once fierce grip into his own, hardly feeling the pressure of his hold on his flesh as he greeted him.

He set his warrior mask in place, so Brenna would not read the emotion gurgling beneath. He needed to be strong for her, and he would be.

'I am for ever in your debt for rescuing Brenna, not once but twice.' His gaze dropped. 'Especially when I am to blame.'

The man's words shook him. Had Bran just acknowledged a failing? Garrick glanced at Ewan, who nodded to him. This must be the new Bran, the one attempting to right his wrongs before it was too late, and Garrick would not deny him that, no matter the past. No matter what he had said and done to his daughter and the slight he had given Garrick by refusing him as son-in-law.

'No one could have known the plan they had in place, Bran. We were lucky to have had such great support from the Camerons and the McKennas. Without them, we would not be here.'

He nodded. 'Please give them my thanks.'

Brenna's lip quivered. 'You will get well and tell them yourself, Father. You cannot just give up. The physicians said you could improve.'

'I will leave you two to speak,' Garrick offered, knowing he needed to give Brenna this time with him.

'Thank you, my son. Thank you for what you have done for both of my daughters.'

Garrick pressed a hand to the man's shoulder. 'I will always protect them. You have my word.'

'If you need me, Bren, I'll just be outside the chamber door.'

'And I've work to attend to Father. I will leave you.' Ewan stepped out of the room.

Brenna kissed her brother's cheek and then met Garrick's gaze, her eyes bright blue pools of sorrow, and he couldn't breathe. As she nodded to him, a tear slid down her cheek.

Chapter Twenty-Two

Bran Stewart was a shell of the domineering, controlling man he'd always been. As Brenna stared at him, she wondered what she had ever been afraid of. Her father was like everyone else: he was human, he had frailties and he was not guaranteed to live for ever.

But he'd also lied to her, manipulated her and almost got her killed. And, sick or not, he would answer for those decisions. She needed to know before he died why he had been so cruel and why she could never earn his praise and affections.

She wiped her eyes, pulled back her shoulders and said what she'd rehearsed in her head over the last two days before she lost her nerve. 'Why did you lie to me, Father? You made me believe I was choosing to marry Mr Winters to please you and gain your favour, but you had already promised me to him. It was no choice at all.'

'Daughter,' he said, the gruff tightness she was long used to back in his voice. 'You cannot understand the duties and responsibilities of a laird. But Ewan will soon.'

'That is exactly what I mean,' Brenna answered, frustration boiling beneath her skin. 'I almost died trying to earn your favour and yet you still will not tell me the truth because I am not Ewan or Moira. I can understand your responsibilities, Father. I am not obtuse or addled.'

'You will not speak to me as such!' he boomed.

'It is time I did,' she countered. 'I deserve your respect and truth.'

He stared at her. 'Do you?'

She shivered and her voice quavered. 'I do,' she replied, crossing her arms against her chest. 'And I do not understand why you have always viewed me as less than I am. I am more than a mere decoration in this household.'

She faltered after the words had escaped her lips. They had always ignored their issues and failings. Speaking of them seemed unnatural and awkward, and somehow a betrayal to him. Even with all of his unkind words and horrid decisions, he was still her father, and he always would be. What if these were the last words they shared with one another? Her throat dried. But at least she would have asked. She would have tried to understand. She would have finally stood up for herself.

He stared off, anger furrowing his brow.

She tried once more. 'Tell me why you see me as so useless to you, Father. I deserve to know that, after all that has happened. Do not deny me the truth.'

He shifted on his bed. 'Why can you not let it be?'

'Leaving things *be* almost killed me. You and I both know you are sick. We may not get another chance. Why can you not just be honest with me?'

He cursed under his breath and sighed, pressing deeper into the folds of the pillows. He looked heavenward. 'I never tried with you as I did with Moira and Ewan. You reminded me too much of your mother.'

Her eyes filled with emotion. 'Did I?'

'Aye. After she died, I could scarce stand to be in the room with you, you reminded me of her so, and my grief consumed me. The older you became, the more you were a mirror of her. Under all of the trappings of fashion and gowns and beauty, you had a kindness and light that others responded to just like she did. *You* bring people back together, add peace to a person's heart just by looking at them. You held us together, our little family, after your mother passed, didn't you? Always in the thick of it with your brother and sister, and fussing over me and keeping me well, even when I was not grateful and batted you away like a fly. And the things I have said to you over the years, lass…'

Were those tears she saw in his eyes?

'Come here,' he commanded.

She hesitated but approached him and walked into his embrace. He hugged her close to him and kissed her head. 'I am sorry, so sorry. They were the opposite of the truth. And I want you to live the rest of your days knowing that. Promise me you'll remember this and not the past.'

'Aye. I will.'

'Good. That is all I ask.'

She turned and met his gaze. 'Is it?'

'For now.' He winked at her.

'Now, that is the father I know.' She sniffed and wiped her eyes, grateful to be set free by knowing the truth behind his cruelties at last.

The squeak of Bran's chamber door opened, giving Garrick a start. It was merely a maid bringing in fresh linens and a basin of water. He glanced at the clock. It was midday, and he would need to leave soon to reach Westmoreland by nightfall. Of course, he hadn't told Brenna of his plan, and now that he'd seen the state of Bran he was reluctant to leave her.

He also knew he was desperately trying to find reasons to avoid the truth that such a journey would bring and the agony an acknowledgment of what he had lost would cost him.

Ewan approached. 'Brenna still in there?'

'Aye.'

Ewan sat down on the bench next to him outside the chamber door. 'I stepped out a while ago to give them some privacy. I have an update on Winters and his scheme.'

'Oh?' Garrick lifted his brow. 'What have you learned?'

'Word of the man's planned destruction of the clans has been relayed to all of the lairds and chiefs and spread like wildfire through the villages. As we speak, the traitors are being rooted out one by one. We are united even more tightly now that the threat from the King and his men has been brought to light. I believe in time the Highlands will be safer and stronger than ever.' Ewan smiled.

'That is an unexpected miracle.'

'My thoughts exactly. You and Brenna may have saved us all.'

Garrick nodded at the irony. *If only we could save each other and our future together.* But he didn't know how to do that. Not yet, anyway.

'How are you?' Ewan asked.

How did one begin to answer such a question?

'Alive.'

Ewan leaned forward, resting his elbows on his knees. 'Sorry for the believing you were dead part. I should have known better.' He smiled up at Garrick.

'Aye. Seems I'm indestructible in most ways. Even if I don't wish to be.'

Ewan shook his head. 'Give yourself some time. It has to be quite a shock to return with everything so… changed.'

'That's a polite way to put it.'

Ewan shook his head. 'If we had known what was happening, we would have interceded. It was a horrid to know what had been done. It sent Father reeling. All he could think of was preventing that from…' He paused as he caught what he was about to say.

'Happening to you? From being as unlucky as us?' Garrick tilted his head. 'Who could blame him?'

'There wasn't much we could do afterwards, but we gathered volunteers to go with us to Westmoreland and the surrounding lands to bury the dead.'

Garrick gripped the seat of the bench, steeling himself from the raw emotion tightening his chest. 'That is a great kindness to me and my people. Thank you.'

Ewan hesitated, his Adam's apple bobbing in his throat. 'I know you would have done the same for us without question.'

He nodded. He would have.

'Your mother and brother were brought to the family plot. We placed them next to your father and brother.'

He nodded, blinking rapidly to keep the flood of emotion at bay. 'Aye. That is where they would have wanted to be.'

What was he doing here? Why wasn't he there already? Putting off the past wouldn't change it.

He bolted up, unable to sit a moment longer. 'May I borrow a horse?'

'Of course.'

'Tell Brenna I left for Westmoreland and will return on the morrow. There is something that I cannot put off a moment longer.'

'Garrick...' Ewan called after him. 'I am sorry. Sorry beyond words.'

As am I. As am I.

Once the cool fresh air of the outdoors hit his face, Garrick sighed. Soon, the tingling in his limbs subsided. He couldn't stay inside the castle a moment longer. The tide of sorrow had pressed in on him heavy and thick, and he couldn't breathe. Once his heart stopped hammering in his ears, he headed to the stables. While he couldn't take Montgomerie after such a long ride the last few days to reach Glenhaven, he would borrow a stallion and head to Westmoreland.

He could set aside his grief and duty no longer. Even if he was a laird of nothing and no one, he still held the title of Laird Garrick MacLean of Westmoreland. He would see to the end of it, no matter how broken it made him. If he truly wanted to attempt a new beginning with Brenna, he had to face the past and his part in it, wherever it might lead. It was the only way to know if they had a whisper of a chance of a future.

He mounted his borrowed steed and headed out without looking back. Soon the distance melted away and he brought his horse to a halt, as he had but a week prior at the base of the hillside, looking up at the haunting profile of Westmoreland in the moonlight. He'd half hoped to see the MacLean crest whipping in the wind at the highest turret, but it wasn't there among the dusky night sky. He frowned. In fact, no flag flew in the air, and no torches glowed in the distance within or about the castle save one small flickering light in the old grounds keep, due east of the castle.

He was in no mood for surprises, and without reinforcements, but he couldn't turn back or he'd never return. He wasn't strong enough to make this journey a third time, knowing what he did about what he would discover upon his arrival. He was too broken.

He rode in as far as he dared before dismounting and walking the rest of the way to the keep. While Westmoreland was supposed to have been captured and taken over by an English duke for a residence, it seemed unoccupied. Overgrowth that had since died back in the cold clogged the paths, and the drive was not smooth but scarred with pits and holes that could injure a horse or break a carriage wheel. No duke would be living here. Not like this. A branch snapped ahead outside the small keep, and Garrick silently drew his blade from his waist belt.

While he didn't wish to battle anyone, if he had to down a man to get to the truth of what had happened to his home and his family and find peace, he would. The smell of wood smoke and stew filled the air and Garrick's stomach rumbled. He grimaced. Perfect timing. He hadn't eaten since he'd broken his fast that morn, and his body reminded him of his poor choice at the most inopportune time.

Taking one step and then another, he silently reached the window of the keep. A fire burned in the hearth and a small pot bubbled over the fire. The keep was cosy and tended to. *Occupied.* Someone was living there and had been for some time. Had the duke left the castle in the care of a single man? None of it made any sense.

'Dinn'a take another step,' a man warned.

Garrick froze. 'And if I do?' he challenged.

'My laird?' The old man stepped into the light.

'Phineas!' Garrick rushed to the man and pulled him into an embrace.

'I knew ye would return,' the old man said. 'Let me look at ye.' Phineas wiped a tear from his eye as he pulled back to take the sight of Garrick in.

'It does me well to see you,' Garrick said. 'I thought to never see any MacLeans again.' He pressed his hand to his chest where his heart soared with hope. The old man had been the groundskeeper for as long as Garrick could remember. His long, wavy grey hair was even whiter than he remembered, but his pale blue eyes were the same. Soft, kind and full of wisdom.

'Come, come.' He waved Garrick in. 'I've just started some stew. Join me.'

'I would love to,' Garrick answered and followed him into the keep. The small space was neat, tidy and cared for, unlike the rest of Westmoreland. The Mac-Lean tartan draped over the end of the man's meagre bed made Garrick's heart soar with pride.

The clan was not erased yet. A few of them remained.

'So, where have ye been?' the man asked, stirring the stew as he stood over the fire.

'Not here, unfortunately.'

'And Ayleen?' he asked.

'Nay. She is gone. I could not save her.' The truth made his mouth ache. Somehow telling him seemed easier than saying it to himself.

'Ack.' He shook his head. 'I am sorry to hear. Sweet lass she was.'

He nodded. 'Aye. A great loss...to everyone.'

'The MacLeans have had many losses as of late. I assume ye come from hearing the news of what has come to pass?'

Heat flushed his body and he shifted on his feet. 'Aye.'

Phineas stood and went to a small table with two chairs. 'Sit. It needs to simmer. I've something for ye.'

Garrick settled into one of the two chairs and rested his hands on the table. He slid his fingertips over the rippled grain in the wood, the slight friction soothing as he awaited the man's return. Phineas sat opposite him and placed a small wooden box on the table.

The sight of it made his eyes well. His mother's jewellery box. He blinked back the emotion, but it thrust forward, and he wiped a tear from his eye.

'She never believed ye had died. Said she would have known. Would have felt the sorrow in her bones. Asked me to save it for ye for when ye returned.'

Garrick wiped a hand over his mouth and then reached over to open the lid. His mother's wedding ring and locket lay next to the laird's ring with the MacLean family crest on it. Garrick had left it for Cairn to wear in his absence. His baby brother had been so proud to be acting laird. His eyes welled as his thumb skimmed the cool silver surface. He'd been far too young to die. And far too good. Unlike him.

'He wanted ye to wear it again,' Phineas added. 'Said ye were too bloody stubborn to die.'

Garrick laughed, choking on the sob of grief sitting in the back of his throat. 'I think God was just too busy to get to me.'

'Nay,' Phineas answered, his blue eyes meeting his gaze. ''Tis not yer time.'

Garrick wasn't so sure.

'The duke up and abandoned the place after a few months. Too isolated, and the wife didn'a like it. Too cold and lonely.' He rolled his eyes. 'Feckless the lot of them. Glad to see them leave. Wish I could have driven them out meself, but I am not the young man I once was.'

'As do I.'

A letter with his name on it rested beneath the jewellery and, although Garrick wanted to read it, he didn't know if he dared. Was he ready? He closed the lid. He wasn't.

Phineas nodded. 'Should be ready. Hungry?'

'Aye,' Garrick replied, wiping his eyes. Some food would definitely help. He knew he had to face the past, but he didn't have to do it all at once or on an empty stomach.

Phineas filled two bowls, returned with spoons and then brought them each a tankard of ale.

'Is it just you out here? Alone?' Garrick blew on the hot stew even though he longed to devour it.

'Aye. I stayed on when the duke came. I wanted to be here when you returned. I promised your mother. I kept my word.'

The first spoonful went down hard on the knowing that Phineas had stayed because of him and out of devotion to his family. Phineas was a far better man than Garrick could ever be, and yet here he was in this tiny keep.

'Everyone else?' he dared ask.

'Many were lost in the uprising. They tried to stop what was happening. Protect your mother and Cairn. Protect Westmoreland and the lands. But the more we resisted, the more brutal the retaliation from the King's men became. In the end, Cairn commanded them to cease their fighting and leave, so they scattered to other parts of the Highlands and were accepted into other clans. His command saved us in the end.'

'Cairn,' Garrick muttered, clenching his jaw.

Phineas smiled. 'Ye would have been proud of him. Brave. Acted like the man ye knew he could be when ye left him in charge.'

'I am proud, so proud.' Nausea made his stomach clench around the little food he had eaten. 'But I am also sick with grief.' He pounded the table with his fist and the bowls and spoons clattered from the force. 'I killed them by not being here. I did that. I killed them all.' The dam of emotion burst within him, and Garrick sobbed, so loudly and for so long that he did not know if it would ever cease.

The old man reached over and gripped his forearm when the torrent of emotion finally subsided. 'Nay, son. Ye did not kill them. Ye know that. The King and his men did. Because ye left and have now returned, the MacLeans may yet survive. Ye can bring them back here, begin anew, raise havoc with the King and show him we will not be disappeared.'

Garrick stared at him in disbelief.

'Ye will help us survive, my laird.'

'What are you talking about? We cannot claim what has been seized. I am no longer laird of anything.'

'Westmoreland has been abandoned, has it not?'

Garrick met his gaze. 'Aye. It has.'

A mustard seed of hope bloomed in his chest. Could the old man be right? Could he begin again?

Aye. He could.

Chapter Twenty-Three

'Where is he?' Brenna asked, staring out of a window buffeting the front doors of Glenhaven.

'Sister, he gave no indication of when he would return, only that he *planned* to return today. It is hardly mid-morn. Even if he left at sunrise, he would not be here by now.' Ewan shrugged into his coat and grabbed a pair of gloves.

'Where are you going?'

'To check on Montgomerie. Garrick will have my head if a piece of that stallion's mane is out of place.'

'Let me join you.' She rushed over to gather her own cloak and gloves, and they descended the castle stairs together. She slipped her arm through his and hugged him. 'I have missed you, brother.'

'Where is all of this softness and affection coming from? If I'd known all you needed was to be tossed about in a carriage and chased down to near death to make you kinder to me, I would have done it long ago.' He winked at her, and she swatted his arm.

'Hush, now. None of that is the least bit funny.'

His smile flattened. 'I know. But to make light of it makes me better able to manage it. You are my baby sister, and I adore you. The thought of losing you was unbearable. And seeing you again has brought all of us joy, especially Father. He even asked to dine with us this eve.'

'That is wonderful! You see, he will improve.'

'Bren,' Ewan started. 'He will enjoy what time he has left. I do not wish you to get your hopes up. The doctor said he is nearing the end.'

She sniffed and wiped at her eyes that were misting in the cold weather. 'Aye. I know.'

'But, for now, let us fuss over Montgomerie so the boy is in fine spirits when Garrick returns.'

'May we invite Garrick to stay? He is alone.' She began to brush Montgomerie's haunches while Ewan brought him fresh hay.

Ewan shrugged. 'Of course, but he may not wish to. I would not get your hopes up. I have never seen him in such a state, and he may feel worse after his visit to Westmoreland.'

'You are right. I just wish so many things had turned out differently between us.' She leaned into Montgomerie's side, and he nuzzled her back.

'Who says it is too late?' Ewan answered, spreading out the hay.

'He does. He cannot forgive himself for what has happened to his family.'

Ewan shook his head. 'Never stopped you before.'

She lobbed a stable cloth at him. He dodged the

towel successfully, as he always did. He threw a few rogue pieces of hay at her, and they stuck to her cloak, as they always did. She made a face at him, and he laughed.

'Up to the same old mischief, I see.'

Brenna's heart jumped at the sound of Garrick's voice behind her as he galloped up the drive.

'Glad to see you returned,' Ewan offered. 'Just taking care of your stallion, as promised.'

'Thank you.' His eyes settled on Brenna.

'I'm sure Father needs me, so...' Ewan clapped Garrick on the shoulder and disappeared, leaving Brenna standing staring up at Garrick, all words having fled her mind.

'How was your visit?' she asked, and then cringed. 'Sorry. I am certain it was horrible and yet I asked you anyway.' She plucked some of the hay from her cloak and then gave up.

'Better than I anticipated.' He dismounted and stepped closer to her. The sheer heat of him made her breath catch in her throat. The harder she tried to ignore her body's response to him, the more her body reacted.

She held her ground. 'Oh?' she asked.

'I will tell you everything,' he said, his voice dropping. 'But for now...' He took another step, and his body was a sigh away from her own. She rested her hands on his chest to steady herself. The back of his fingers slid slowly down her cheek and his eyes flared a mossy green. The man was going to kiss her. Her stomach pooled with heat in anticipation. Her palms tingled against his chest, and her heart picked up speed. What was she doing? What were they doing? This was no way to go about moving on from one another.

'Garrick, I...' She began but, before she could utter another word, he seized her lips with his own. The intensity and urgency of his kiss as his arms wound around her with purpose and ferocity nearly knocked her out of her slippers.

She sighed against his lips and kissed him back with all she had and the repressed longing and love for him poured out of her. She had missed him more than mere words. He pulled her closer, deepening his kisses, and she savoured the feel of him pressed against the length of her body. A bucket dropped behind them, and Garrick pulled away. He glanced out to the main entrance of the stable and chuckled.

'I think we may have given that poor lad more than he bargained for,' he teased.

She looked past his shoulder. The boy must have run from the place at the sight of them, as a wooden bucket sat abandoned on its side in the doorway of the barn, water still trickling onto the ground. 'Aye. Good thing he interrupted us when he did, or it might have been quite unseemly.'

Garrick smiled against her hair, and she snuggled against him. His warm, solid frame comforted her, as did the relaxed quiet between them.

'Will you stay through Hogmanay?' she asked, her words light and airy despite the uncertainty she felt about what his answer might be.

'Aye,' he answered. 'I would like that.'

She pressed a kiss to his cheek. 'Then, we shall have a wonderful time.'

His agreement was just one of the many miracles that had happened since they had returned to Glenhaven.

He pulled back and ran a hand down her hair. 'I have much to attend to this morn, and correspondence that needs to be sent out as soon as possible, but I wish to speak with you when the time is right.'

'Then, go,' she answered. 'I have some correspondence and duties of my own to complete. Father wishes to dine with us this eve. Join us if you can.'

'I wouldn't miss it.' He pressed a kiss to her cheek and jogged back to the main house, a lightness in his movements.

This was the Garrick she had known, the man she had fallen in love with. Something about his trip to Westmoreland had freed him. Just as her conversation with Father had set loose her shame and sadness. She hoped one day they would be whole enough to come back to each other again. This moment was the first step in doing that. Now she just needed to get on with the second one: working out what would make her happy so they could begin their future together as two whole people, not the fractured parts of each other they had once been.

Garrick hadn't anticipated the hum of energy he would feel in his bones after visiting Westmoreland. Seeing his mother and brother's graves and speaking with Phineas had loosened his grief. While he was a long way from having healed from their losses, the heavy ache in his chest was lighter. He still hadn't read his mother's letter, but he had the box on the chest in his guest chambers at Glenhaven. He would read it when he was ready, but he had many other tasks to tackle until then.

One of them was sending out enquiries to the nearby clans to enlist their support in rebuilding his own. Perhaps it was a risk, and not all would comply, but even if half of them supported his cause he would feel accomplished.

Phineas had agreed to continue on at Westmoreland as caretaker of the keep as well as whatever else he could manage. Garrick owed him more coin than he might ever have, but the man had agreed without hesitation. When the MacLeans were able to reclaim their home and lands, Phineas would be repaid in full, and more besides. Because of him, Garrick had hope for the future, and because of Brenna he still wanted to live it.

The hard part was beginning again. He'd never been good at dealing with failure, but he had to learn how to. He couldn't allow loss and grief to consume him as it had for so long. His family wouldn't have wanted it and nor did he. After awakening from a dormant sleep in his grief, he wished to live life with the sun on his face and with Brenna by his side.

Hours passed quickly, and before he knew it the sun began to descend in the afternoon sky. A stack of correspondence ready to be sent out by messenger teetered on the desk, and Garrick was pleased in all he'd accomplished. They would be en route to the clan lairds and elders on the morrow, and he would be ready for the next step in his plan: to learn all he could about how to reclaim his land and castle. He'd start with the books in this very library, and then with Bran himself if he was up to it. The man had a wealth of knowledge and might even know how to shorten the time it would take for Garrick to re-establish his clan.

He closed the book on the desk and ran his hand over the supple leather. If he couldn't reclaim Westmoreland and his clan, he would begin anew, perhaps even join the lost village or settle in the old MacDougall lands nestled between the Camerons and the McKennas. He would not give up on the life that had been spared in him.

Phineas had reminded him of that. So had Brenna, but he'd been too bull-headed to accept it at the time.

'This was always Moira's favourite part of the castle.' Brenna stood in the half-open doorway of the library.

He rose from his chair, stretching the ache from his back from sitting for so long. 'It is peaceful.'

'Aye.' She came into the room. 'Dinner will be within the hour. You look to have accomplished a great deal.' Her fingers skimmed over the letters and the stamped crest in the wax seals securing each of them. She smiled. 'I see you have your ring back.'

He looked down at the ring on his finger and nodded. 'When I went to Westmoreland yesterday, I saw Phineas. He gave me a box from Mother. This was within it.'

Her hand stilled and she met his gaze.

'The old groundskeeper? He is alive?'

He chuckled. 'He is. Stayed on when the duke took over, and even after when the place had been abandoned.'

She sat in the chair opposite him, her eyes wide. 'Abandoned?'

'Aye. Westmoreland sits dark and empty. He lives in the small keep and cares for the grounds as best he can. He even helped to bury the dead with your brother, father and the other soldiers they sent.' His eyes welled. 'Their kindness in giving them peace, my family peace when I could not, shall not be forgotten.'

She reached out and took his hand in her own, rubbing her thumb over his palm. 'I am so sorry. I wish I could...' She faltered 'Spare you this grief, take it from you.'

'I think I have given you enough grief from my own actions in the past, and I am grateful you still care for me at all.'

'I more than care for you, you know that.' Her eyes welled.

He squeezed her hand. 'I do. And I more than care for you, Bren. I do not wish to muck it all up as I did before. I need to find my way back to who I was before I can try to claim you as my own. I want to be the man you deserve.'

'You already are, you fool.'

He rose and pulled her to him, brushing a lock of hair from her forehead. 'I am not, but I adore you for believing so in me when I did not believe in myself.'

'I always will. I always have.'

'I did not understand it then, but I do now. I am grateful for it.'

'Are you finished with your work this eve?' she asked.

He stared at the box before him. 'There is one more thing I must do today. Will you help me with it? I am dreading it.'

Her eyes narrowed on him. 'Of course. What is it? Surely it cannot be worse than all we have been through, you and I?'

It would be for him, but perhaps if they forged it together he would survive reading the last words his mother would ever say to him.

He lifted the lid off the box and handed her the letter. When she looked at it, she frowned. 'I do not understand. It is addressed to you, not me.'

'Phineas gave it to me. It is from my mother. Her last letter. I need to read it, but I cannot bear to. Not alone.'

'Oh, Garrick.' She released a breath and ran a hand along his cheek. 'Of course I will stay with you while you read it.'

'Dare I ask you to read it to me? I do not think—' His throat tightened with emotion.

She squeezed his hand in her own and let go. 'Aye. I will read it to you.'

They settled on the settee before the fire together. She opened the letter and looked at him. 'Are you ready?' she asked, her voice far steadier and more certain than he felt.

He nodded, as he could not form any words.

She held the letter in one hand and gripped his hand fiercely in the other.

He released a breath and closed his eyes, steeling himself from the agony his mother's last words would surely bring. Silence pressed in on him and all he could hear was the mild crackling of wood in the fire and his heart thudding in his chest in anticipation.

My darling Garrick,
By now you know what has become of us and Westmoreland, and I am sorry beyond words that I could not tell you one final time how proud I am of who you are, and the glorious, steadfast man you have become. You were always the best of us, despite what you believed of yourself, and to know that you will return and breathe life back into our clan and this land once more gives me great peace.

And I know that you will see all of us in heaven, even Ayleen. I felt her pass and, whatever happened then and now, you cannot blame yourself for it. You must be the strong, good man you have always been and carry on with hope in your heart. Knowing you and raising you has been one of the most blessed gifts a mother could have ever received.
With much love,
Mother

Garrick covered his face with his hands. Heat flushed his body and emotion shook him from within.

Mother. Her last words were as eloquent and beautiful as she had always been. He sobbed into his hands. To never hear her voice again. To never see her smile again. So many moments she would miss, and so would he. All because of what—land? Money? Power?

He hated the King and all he had brought down upon his people and him. He hated himself for not having been there for his siblings and her when they'd needed him most. But, most of all, he hated how much time he had lost agonising over all of the things he could not change, and by hiding from the truth of what had.

Brenna rested her hand on his thigh and then kissed his cheek before she rose to leave.

'Thank you,' he murmured as he wiped his eyes, reaching out to touch her arm.

She paused and faced him. 'I will always be here for you,' she whispered, leaving him in the solace of his thoughts.

Chapter Twenty-Four

The days leading up to the new year passed quickly and Brenna loved the normality of it all. Father's health continued to improve despite everyone's expectations, and Glenhaven had a new whirr of life humming beneath its bones. While Moira and Rory decided not to travel to visit for Hogmanay, they promised to join them within the month to celebrate the coming year of 1744, and to bring the twins for a long overdue visit. Soon, there would be yet another McKenna to welcome to the world, and Brenna secretly hoped it would be a girl.

Garrick had made quick work of finding many of those MacLeans scattered about the Highlands and was scheming to secure a way to officially reclaim his home at Westmoreland and his lands, so his people could return and rebuild what had once been lost. Phineas had continued to care for the grounds, and Garrick had enlisted men who needed work to help set the inside of Westmoreland back to its former glory.

Rory's and Father's contacts had also hurried along

many of Garrick's requests regarding his clan's future. With the chaos of Stephen Winters' attempt to create an uprising along the Highlands still fresh in everyone's minds, the clans set aside their past differences and feuds to protect their united future. They vowed never to allow what had happened to the MacLeans and MacDougalls to happen again, no matter the cost. No other clan would perish without a fight, and thanks to Garrick the lost village would not become any larger than it already was.

Ewan had even helped Brenna in seeing to and coordinating the proper return and burial of Arthur and Roland to Oban, so their family could have the peace and finality they deserved. Her brother had even begun the tedious task of finding a wife. Although his attempts were half-hearted, he was at least trying rather than avoiding it altogether. Little by little he let the memory of his first love, Emogene, go.

The scandal with Stephen Winters had finally started to diminish as well. Moira's lengthy letters only confirmed that Brenna had made the right decision in returning to Glenhaven with Garrick weeks ago. If she'd stayed in Oban, she would have been harassed beyond reason. With every article, it seemed there were new details to be had about the complex ploy that had almost been a success in overthrowing the balance of power in the Highlands.

Once word of what had transpired with Mr Winters and the King's men—who turned out to be the mysterious M referenced in the correspondence they had discovered—had reached the streets of Oban, the story of corruption, foul play and the innocent deaths of Arthur and Roland were on the tongues of the gossips in town for weeks. More than once, McKenna and Cameron soldiers had found strangers lurking in their meadows, attempting to gain access to Blackmore to spy upon poor Moira and Rory to see how they'd fared after almost losing their sister and sister-in-law to a murderer set on creating dissent in Britain. Uncle Leo's hounds had been set upon them each time, chasing them all good naturedly from the grounds. The thought of it made Brenna laugh out loud once more.

She'd even assisted in cleaning the castle prior to the holiday and had enjoyed rustling through old closets and trunks, discovering treasures old and new. She was eager to set Glenhaven to rights, release the dirt and air out the old of the year to make room for the joy and hope of the new one to come. Moira would have balked at the sight of Brenna wearing an old gown and apron with cobwebs strewn through her hair.

Brenna smiled. She'd discovered there were many things she liked over these last few weeks, such as cleaning, that she had never tried before. She'd also realised she was good at a great deal of things as well, and one of them was throwing a blade. The man she had downed near Westmoreland had not been a fluke. She had keen aim. Slowly but surely, she would find her footing and purpose. Her worth belonged to her alone, and it seemed her father finally understood that about his daughters.

'Is this what you plan to wear to our fine dinner this

eve?' Garrick asked, pulling on one of her loose apron strings from behind. 'I do not mind it.' He winked at her.

She twirled around and playfully batted his hand away. 'Nay. I am finishing up before I get ready. I am eager to be rid of 1743 and to charge headlong into 1744, and the best way to do that is to sweep and clean out the old dirt and air before you let in the new.'

His smiled faltered. 'I am equally eager for this new year, although this year has not been all bad. I have found my way back to you.'

She slid into his arms. 'And I you.'

He peeked down the hallway and then tugged her against him, pressing an intoxicating and achingly gentle kiss to her lips.

As a maid rounded the corner, Brenna pulled away. 'Perhaps the hallway is not the best place to show me your affections.'

'When you decide where,' he whispered. 'Let me know. I'll be there.'

She laughed as he left her to continue on his way to the library, where he spent most of his days poring over books on law and property. The man she had loved had found his way back to life and to joy. His plan to re-establish the MacLeans had given him renewed purpose and hope, rather than sorrow, and she prayed that he would be rewarded for his efforts.

Garrick stood staring out at the fine spread of food, wine and family in the long banquet hall of Glenhaven. A young lass played the harp by the glowing hearth, and evergreen scented the room. All the colours of the season graced every nook of the castle, and Brenna's skill at decorating shone in all the fine details nestled in each room. Even Garrick's own chambers had been given a seasonal flare, and he could not begrudge her efforts.

He never could have imagined he would be here, dressed in his best and preparing to welcome in the new year a few months ago. Yet here he was, preparing to bring in the new year with the woman he had loved and lost and the family that had given him up for dead. While his chest ached at not being with his own family at Westmoreland, he knew how lucky he was to be here with Brenna and hers.

Phineas came over to him. 'Kind of ye to invite me, my laird.'

'You are my family. Why ever would I not? It wouldn't be the same without you here. I am glad you came.' He clapped the man on the shoulder in greeting.

Phineas dropped his voice. 'The lady was very insistent. I didn'a think to dare *not* come.'

Garrick laughed. 'You are a wise man. Miss Stewart can be quite persuasive once she sets her mind to something.'

'Aye.' The older man sipped from his tankard of ale and shifted on his feet. 'Not the same without them, sir.'

'Nay. It isn't. But there are times when I feel them with me.'

'Always.' Phineas pressed his hand to his heart.

Garrick stilled at the sheer beauty of Brenna when he spied her descending the staircase across the crowded room. Her long green gown spilled out like a liquid emerald to the floor, and her Stewart tartan was wrapped skilfully over it, accentuating every one of her curves. Her long, dark plait swung loosely down her back as she turned to chat with the other guests and her blue eyes sparkled with joy and amusement. She wove through the sea of guests, donned her cloak and headed outside.

He swore to all of the heavens that she had never been more beautiful than she was this eve. His heart thudded in his chest. It was now or never, and he wouldn't freeze this time. Not any more. He would act.

'Excuse me, Phineas,' he apologised. 'I must see to something.'

Phineas turned and chuckled as he followed Garrick's gaze to Brenna. 'Best ye do that, sir.'

Garrick cut across the room, intent on his mission.

This eve he would secure a wife.

He was the lost laird no longer, as his heart and his hope had been found.

It was almost midnight, and a new year would soon begin, yet Brenna could not shake the feeling that she'd left something from the past year undone. Perhaps it was that she should have been a wife by now. She shuddered at the thought of almost becoming Mrs Stephen Winters, and the fact that he'd almost killed her in his endeavour to upset the fragile balance in the Highlands. She started at the crunch of snow behind her and turned to find Garrick approaching, looking devastatingly handsome in his royal blue frock coat and kilt in honour of the event.

'Are you missing the days of being out in the cold huddled in a cave, Miss Stewart?'

She shook her head at him. 'Very funny.' She accepted the arm he offered. 'Care for a stroll to see the lights dancing off the meadow? You can see the villagers below heralding in the new year.' They walked along in silence and then paused, staring down at the winking lights and revelry below.

'It is beautiful, is it not?' she said.

'Aye. It is…as are you.'

She rested her head against his arm, and they watched the sights and sounds of the village below as they welcomed in 1744. The sight filled her heart with purpose and hope for the year that was to come. All because she had not given up on him, and he had not given up on her. By some miracle, they had found their way back to one another. All was right with the world and with this moment. There was nowhere else she wished to be.

'I've something for you,' he said.

Brenna faced Garrick. He held a small wooden box in his hand. Its lopsided red bow captured her attention and she smiled.

'What's this?' she asked, tilting her head to him. 'I did not bring your gift with me. It is inside.'

'It is but a small token for Hogmanay Day. I could not wait.'

'Garrick—'

'Because of you, I have hope, which I have not had in a while. I leave on the morrow to meet with Doran in the lost village to see what can be salvaged of Clan

MacLean and Westmoreland. Seems he knows a thing or two about land claim and taxes. There are also some MacLean clan members there. I hope to find a way to bring them home for good.'

Her heart skittered in her chest. 'Leaving?' She couldn't keep the sorrow from her voice. She had just got him back.

'Aye. But this time I am headed *to* a future rather than fleeing the past. You have taught me the difference.'

Why did he have to say such lovely things to her? Her limbs felt tingly and weak. He took her hands in his own and placed the box in them.

'And I hope you will come with me,' he said, his voice husky and deep. 'To begin the new year together.'

She hesitated.

'Open it.'

She untied the ribbon with shaking fingers and opened the box. Inside were two simple silver bands. A small one and a larger one.

Confused, she met his gaze.

He smiled. 'Your father has a gifted blacksmith. He was able to melt down Ayleen's cross and fashion it into two rings. While I know it is not common, I asked him to make one for you and the other for me. If you will choose me, that is.'

He knelt in the snow and took one of her hands in his own. 'I know I have made mistake after mistake and pushed you away when I should have run to you. I know I do not deserve you, but each day I will endeavour to be that man. To be the husband you deserve.'

She stared into his eyes as hot tears blurred her vision.

'Will you be my wife? Will you marry me, Brenna Stewart?'

'Aye, Garrick MacLean. I will. And I will endeavour to be the wife you deserve as well.'

He stood and recited part of her favourite Alexander Montgomerie poem, his Scottish burr rolling deep and strong:

The dew as diamonds did hing
Upon the tender twistis ying,
Our-twinkling all the trees;
And ay where flouris did flourish fair.

'Are you trying to seduce me, my laird?'

He nodded and brushed a lock of hair from her face. He leaned in close to her cheek. 'Aye. Is it working?' he asked, his breath skimming her ear and sending goose flesh along her skin.

'I'll let you know,' she murmured, meeting his lips halfway for a kiss as the snow began to fall.

* * * * *

CONVENIENTLY WED
TO THE LAIRD

To the Englert, Ambrose, Tarlton, West and
Williams families:

Thank you for welcoming me into your homes and
hearts when I married Brian so many years ago.
Your unconditional love, encouragement and kindness
has always overwhelmed me in the best of ways.
I am so grateful to have you as family.

And to Brent:

I always wonder what conversations we might have
had and about all the things the world has missed out
on without you in it. Your time on this earth was far
too short. We miss you, always.

Chapter One

Edinburgh, Scotland, June 1744

'Is that all of it, then?' asked Ewan Stewart, Laird of Glenhaven, staring out of the carriage window and summoning the last thread of his patience. This *brief* holiday to Edinburgh to aid his sister in her wedding preparations had become anything but. He'd be lucky to be home by week's end. The sun was high in the early afternoon sky.

'I've only one last errand to the milliner's shop, brother.' Brenna patted his hand as if he were but a child and not her older brother and laird of the clan. '*You* insisted on joining me on this journey. I could have been escorted by your men instead.'

He scoffed and moved away from the window and deeper into the plush squabs. 'Aye. You could have, but after being attack by mercenaries during your unchaperoned carriage ride through Loch Linnhe last fall, your fiancé and I agreed this was necessary to ensure your safety. We cannot risk losing you again.'

'Brother, none of that was my fault or yours. No one could have foreseen such events,' she complained.

He lifted his brow at her.

'Not even you,' she said.

'I am not as certain. Father should have suspected such foul play from Mr Winters due to the man's eagerness to secure a match with you. We will be far more vigilant about who moves within our inner ranks from now on.'

Knowing whom to trust in the Highlands was not as easy as it used to be. After Brenna's brush with death at the hands of brigands trying to destroy their clan from within last winter, her fiancé Garrick and Ewan had vowed to keep close watch over her. Neither of them could bear another loss. The last year had been rife with them.

'As you wish. Perhaps you could turn your attentions to finding a bride, brother, rather than my affairs. There seem many eligible ladies about.' She smiled innocently.

Ewan frowned at her well-placed barb. He was less than eager to find a wife after almost sacrificing everything to be with a woman who cast him aside like a worn-down horseshoe when a better prospect came along. After his experience with Emogene, he no longer trusted his judgement about women or love, and his sister knew it. 'I hope all of the hats are too small for your head,' he said, mirroring the same feigned sweetness in his reply as she had in her own.

'You shall not snare a bride with a forked tongue like that.' She waited for the carriage to come to a rocking stop, her face softening in concern as she studied him.

'Do try to enjoy what remains of our visit if you can. You have been so dour as of late, and who knows when we shall return.' She pressed a light kiss to his cheek. The door opened, and their driver assisted her exit onto the bustling streets of Edinburgh.

He muttered a response and watched her enter the milliner's shop. Resting back against the seat, he sighed. At least the trip had not been an entire waste of time. He had met with a few businesses regarding investments for the clan yesterday after they had arrived. He had also called on the solicitor earlier this morn during Brenna's dress fitting to apprise himself of the pending taxes and the clan's current financial situation. While the clan was in good standing for now, changes would have to be made for it to remain that way.

Changes some would oppose. There were more than a few leaders within the clan who would be rankled by his suggestions to bring the mining and farming techniques up to modern standards. But he also knew that if things didn't change, tradition would put a stranglehold on their growth and advancement. They'd be overpowered and absorbed by other clans or worse, the British. He'd need to earn their trust. They held great power and sway over the village. Without their support, Ewan had a slim chance of making the changes that would help their clan survive. The problem was that they didn't trust him, and they had good reason not to.

Ewan had almost brought the clan to its knees years ago when he'd gone against his father's orders and courted Emogene despite the arranged marriage set up with the Robertson clan prior to Ewan's birth. By not marrying the laird's daughter, Ewan had severed the Stewarts' alliance and fractured his relationship with his father: all for love, for her. And then Emogene had tossed him aside as if he were rubbish to secret herself away and marry a Sutherland. She'd left him for a man with more power and larger purse strings.

And even though they never married, the damage had already been done, and the alliance between the Stewarts and the Robertsons fractured to bits. His face heated with the shame he still felt over what he'd done. He'd not be that foolish over a woman ever again.

Ewan scoffed and turned the gold signet ring on his third finger. He'd not survive another misstep such as that, so making decisions about the clan exhausted and oft-times overwhelmed him. So many people he loved and cared about depended on him making sound decisions. Unfortunately, finances were but one of the clan's many issues that Father should have warned him of before he died, but Ewan wasn't terribly surprised by the omissions. Father wasn't one for addressing any weaknesses, within himself or the clan, and abhorred the idea of lingering too long on any problems he couldn't immediately glean a solution to. Being laird didn't have quite the shine to it Ewan had expected, but he'd keep at it. Surely it would get easier, and finding his place in this world would as well.

He tugged at his cravat. Restless, he emerged from the carriage and stretched, scanning the busy streets. Perhaps Brenna was right about one thing: he should try to enjoy their visit. Who knew when they would have the time to travel to and from the city again? The

Grassmarket was within sight down the hill, and he watched lads handing out penny broadsides shouting bawdy headlines and men peddling their wares of livestock, trinkets, and the occasional oddity in the warm early afternoon sun.

Ewan walked a few steps, studying the area teeming with life and excitement below, a far cry from the rather subdued Highland markets. He itched to explore the sights and soak up something new and interesting. But leaving Brenna was a risk. The lass attracted chaos like his other sister attracted order. And he attracted... well, he wasn't quite sure yet. The three of them were quite an odd trio, but they were family. And he was bound by duty and his promise to his father to protect them at all costs.

'You must keep the family together and this clan thriving after I am gone,' Father had pleaded before his heart gave out. *'Promise me.'*

Like a fool, Ewan had agreed and made such a promise. Months later, he found the task daunting as his spirited sisters set out on their own pursuits. His sister Moira was with her husband, Laird Rory McKenna, in Oban, and soon Brenna would be wed to her fiancé, Laird Garrick MacLean, and reside in Loch Linnhe. That meant he would be all alone as Laird of Glenhaven, attempting to keep the Stewart clan and its legacy afloat. At almost eight and twenty, he knew he *should* take a wife, but the thought of choosing one woman to spend the rest of his days with made his chest tighten and his body shudder.

What if he chose wrong again like he had with Emogene? He was laird, and any mistakes he made in love or otherwise would cost him and his clan dearly. And with times as difficult as they were now, mistakes could end the Stewarts.

Forever.

He'd seen clans disappear from existence, as if they had walked into the Highland mist, never to return.

'I can keep watch on her, my laird.'

Ewan shook off his melancholy and glanced up to the driving box of the carriage and then back at the milliner's store. Brenna was never one to decide quickly upon anything, so he had some time. Perhaps some air and the renewed flow of blood through his limbs would restore his humour and distract him from his fears. 'Aye, thank you, Aaron. I'll just stretch my legs.'

His driver nodded to him, and Ewan rolled his neck. He tucked his hands into the pockets of his trews and settled into the feel of the cobblestones beneath his boots. The hard, firm, unrelenting pressure was a reminder that not all was lost. Not yet. The Stewarts were bedrock. As such, they would endure. As would he. The tension abated with each step as if the yoke of responsibility loosened, slipping away the farther he was from the carriage with its Stewart coat of arms. The June sun warmed his cheeks. The sights and smells of cooked meats, leather, and coal from the market swallowed him as he approached. A lad pressed a broadside into his hand, and Ewan gave him a penny.

Ewan scanned the sheet and frowned. *A wife for sale?* What a farce. One couldn't buy a wife, not in Scotland, at least. And why would one want to? He shuddered. He tucked the sheet into his coat pocket and carried on his way. He'd take another minute to look about the wares and return to the carriage.

'Wife for sale! One guinea!' a man shouted.

Ewan turned. A small crowd formed around a stout older man as he yanked a young woman behind him. She wore a leather halter like one used for livestock, and her hands were bound in front of her. Ewan froze, shocked and angered by the sight of a woman being treated thus. He fisted his hands by his sides. Surely this was some ill-humoured jest.

She was a person, not a mule. If this was what happened at the Grassmarket, he'd missed nothing.

But on it continued. 'I be 'er husband. She be foulmouthed, prone to laziness, and disobedient, despite me best efforts to make her so. I'll be pleased to be rid of 'er. Once ye purchase 'er, she is divorced from me and bound to ye by marriage. So, take heed with yer coin! Yer purchase is final. No returns for this lass.' He released a bawdy laugh.

Ewan studied the pale, thin woman clad in dirty, worn clothes, her long hair falling loose from its light auburn plait and shielding part of her face like a veil. He wondered what would become of her. A flare of protectiveness flashed through him. Surely this wasn't legal. He tugged the crumpled broadside from his pocket and scanned it. He balked.

According to this, it was. The single exchange of coin nullified the first union and verified the new marriage. He could scarcely imagine such a concept. Several men approached to gaze more closely at her, their interest evident in their stances and overt ogling. One tugged at her skirts, attempting to peek beneath, and she kicked the sot in the head. He staggered back and cursed at her.

Ewan scrubbed a hand through his hair, and his pulse picked up speed. This was someone's daughter. Someone's sister. But where were they? His gaze swept through the growing crowd that jeered and spat at her. It appeared there was no one to speak out on her behalf. She was alone. Defenceless.

Just like Moira.

He felt the familiar anguish and tightening in his chest with the memory of his eldest sister's abuse at the hands of her first husband. Ewan's awareness and rage sharpened to a fine point. If he'd known what was happening to her, he would have stopped it, but he'd not found out until it was too late. And he'd never forgive himself for that. But this? What about all these people? How could they merely watch this woman's suffering and not intervene on her behalf?

'Ye see 'er disobedience!' the husband shouted as another keen buyer came too close and the woman elbowed the man in the gut. 'I am eager to be rid of this bony, cold, ungrateful lass and find another, more willing woman to warm my bed. One guinea! Step right up and claim 'er if ye dare.'

'I'll take her for half that,' a man called off in the distance. The crowd opened for him, and when Ewan saw the man's face, he cursed.

Dallan MacGregor.

A cheat and a brute, among other things.

Ewan clenched his jaw. He'd known the bampot since

childhood, and MacGregor had only become crueller with age. Rumours still abounded around his involvement in the death of a young woman at last year's royal ball in Perth, even though he was never charged with the crime. There was a reason no father allowed his daughter to marry MacGregor, despite his coin. Perhaps that was why he was attempting to buy a wife now. Although Ewan couldn't imagine she would survive long under the bastard's care.

'Any other bidders?' the husband called to the crowd.

Silence answered.

Dallan grinned, grabbed the lass's wrist, and yanked her to him. 'Seems a bit thin to warm my bed, but I will make use of her. She will learn to obey me.'

She pushed him and tried to stomp on his foot. He grabbed her by the hair to subdue her, and she cried out in protest.

'Kneel,' he commanded, yanking on her hair again.

She whimpered and fell to her knees.

'You see, we are already coming to an understanding.' He laughed, fishing for coin in his pocket. A few other men in the crowd cheered him on.

Ewan's heart thudded in his chest, and his ears buzzed. The lass would be dead by week's end if MacGregor had his way with her, and who would know or care?

He would.

Ewan cursed aloud. He knew what he had to do. It was the lesser of two evils.

'I'll buy her for the full,' he called out, his voice booming across the market.

Dallan stilled, and upon catching Ewan's gaze through the crowd, he smirked. 'Stewart,' he said. He shoved the lass away. She stumbled and skidded to the ground from the force.

Ewan clenched his jaw. His gaze slid to the woman, who, although startled, seemed unhurt, and then back to Dallan. 'I see you haven't changed, MacGregor,' he stated, squaring his shoulders upon approach.

'Neither have you.' Dallan spat at the ground and ran a hand through his hair. 'Still as soft a heart as ever. Do you plan to save this whore as well as your dwindling clan from ruin now that your father is gone? Not likely. Enjoy your wench and your brief reign as laird. I'll save my half a guinea.' He laughed and sauntered off with two of his men in tow.

'Bring her here,' Ewan commanded, rage lacing his words. The crowd turned to him.

The lass's eyes widened as her husband yanked her up from the ground. She clambered after him, holding the rope of the harness fitted to her torso as she was tugged along.

'Unbind her hands and remove that ungodly harness from her. *Now*,' Ewan ordered. 'She is no animal.'

'Ye might think differently after ye get her home.' The man winked at him. 'I'll leave 'er be. Otherwise she'll run.'

Ewan scowled at him and shoved a guinea into the man's open palm, even though he wished to punch him in the face instead.

'Pleasure doin' business with ye.' The man grinned

and pressed the guinea to his lips. 'I shall celebrate my freedom this eve!'

Ewan shook his head in disgust as the man walked away. He faced the lass. 'Are you hurt?'

'Nay,' she answered, slowly lifting her gaze to him.

Her large amber eyes arrested his attention. He'd never seen such a shade before.

He cleared his throat. 'Come with me,' he told the woman. He turned and began the walk back to the carriage, his body vibrating with anger.

'What shall you do with me, sir?' the woman asked, walking a step behind him. He slowed his pace to ensure she didn't drift far from him, his gaze sliding behind him at regular intervals. Dallan was not a man to lose at anything well, and Ewan wouldn't allow the woman to be harmed further.

'I'm not sure yet, but you'll not stay here.' He didn't dare spare her another glance but kept a quick pace up the road to the carriage. He'd had enough of his brief visit to the Grassmarket. He'd had enough of a great deal of things.

A bell chimed ahead of them as Brenna emerged from the milliner's shop door and handed off her parcels to Aaron. When she turned and saw their approach, she froze, her mouth falling open.

'Aaron, get my sister inside,' Ewan ordered as he reached the carriage. 'I also need a larger blade than my sgian dubh. *Now.*'

'Aye, my laird.' His driver's gaze landed upon the lass for a moment before flitting away. 'Miss?' He opened the door for Brenna, who still stood gobsmacked.

'Brother, I leave you for one moment,' she muttered, shading her eyes from the sun as her dark hair fluttered in the wind. 'What has happened?'

'In the carriage, Brenna. We are leaving,' Ewan commanded.

'Brother?' she faltered, still staring upon the woman.

'The carriage,' he answered, the edge in his voice as sharp as any dirk. Her eyes widened at his harsh tone, and she clamped her mouth shut and did as he instructed.

Once she was safely within, Aaron retrieved a large dagger from beneath his driver's seat and handed it to Ewan.

'Your wrists,' he stated, his tone harsher than he intended.

The woman hesitated and then lifted them to him, keeping her head down.

He took her left hand, then paused at the sight of the numerous scars along her knuckles and calluses on her fingers. His thumb skimmed the soft inside of her wrist as he severed the rope. Her tremble at his touch passed through his arm, and he let go.

The lass had been poorly treated. For how long, he didn't know. Nor did it matter. That would end today.

'Turn,' he said, his voice softening. The last thing he wished to do was frighten her further.

She hesitated, turning slowly as if she half expected a shove or slap. He stared at the bindings of the worn leather harness criss-crossed along her back. How could a woman live such a life, and why? He shuddered to think how long she might have lived this way. He shook away the thought and brought himself back to the present.

He swallowed hard and slid his hand between the rope and her tattered walking dress, her body flinching at his touch. She possessed a small, muscular, thin frame, and he tugged the rope away from her body as gently as he could. The harness was so tight, he struggled to do so with care. *Blast.* He didn't wish to harm her.

'Go on,' she murmured. 'It doesn't hurt. Not any more.'

His touch faltered at her words, and he held back the tyranny of curses bubbling up in his throat. *What kind of a man...?* He answered his own question. He knew exactly the type. Ewan severed the taunt harness bindings. When they fell away from her body, the woman sighed, her body sagging forward. He wished to beat her former husband senseless, but he needed to get out of here. Far from here before he did just that and brought shame and ruin to his clan. He was laird. He needed to focus on his clan and his family, not this stranger who was now in his care, or her brute of a husband. He stilled.

Now *he* was her husband.

Shock roiled through him. What had he done?

What he'd had to.

To do nothing would have haunted him the rest of his days. He only hoped this decision wouldn't as well.

'Step inside, miss,' he said, gesturing at the still-open carriage door.

She nodded and stepped within, settling in neatly next to his sister.

Brenna looked at her and then to Ewan without a

word, although her wide eyes held the thousand questions he knew she wished to ask.

'Well, sister,' he offered, as Aaron set the carriage in motion towards Glasgow. 'You told me to find a bride, so I did.'

Chapter Two

'What?' the woman asked, crinkling her nose. 'One cannot find a wife in the time it takes me to purchase a hat.' She rolled her eyes at the man and straightened her light blue cloak over her gown as the carriage lurched forward. Her fine gloved hands fluttered like a dove's wings before settling in her lap.

Catriona Gordon bit her lip and hid her own bare, dirty hands in the folds of her skirts.

'You heard me,' the man answered, an edge of irritation lacing his tone.

The woman stilled and studied him. 'I do not believe you, brother.' Her voice dropped lower. 'Father was after you for years to marry, and you committed in an instant? To a woman you do not know, but met in the Grassmarket?' She scoffed. 'Doubtful. This is one of your ruses, and I will not fall for it.'

Catriona lifted her eyes and met the woman's light blue stare. When the woman said nothing, Catriona flushed and looked away.

Dash it all.

They spoke about her as if she weren't there or like she was a child, and they her parents.

Should she say something on her own behalf? But what exactly could she say? She frowned. Nothing that would make the situation any less ridiculous, and getting in between their sibling squabble seemed a poor idea. She had enough problems.

The dispute faded into silence as the carriage settled into a steady advance, moving in and out of the way as other carriages and merchants passed along the narrow-cobbled lanes of Edinburgh.

Catriona leaned against the cool wooden frame of the small window and stared out through the spotless glass. She'd never been in such a fine carriage, with its plush seats and dark stained interior. There was a heavenly hint of rose water, no doubt from the woman seated beside her. While she'd never been much affected by wealth or power, she had also never been so close to it. According to the exchange in the market, this man who had bought her was a laird. He'd spent a whole guinea on her. She'd never even seen a guinea in real life until today.

The man had means. Great means. If she hadn't been so terrified of the unknown, she might have allowed herself to sink further into the soft, voluminous seat and rest her eyes. But she needed to be alert and aware until she had more of an idea who this man was and what his plans for her were. She didn't dare meet the man's gaze despite the flood of questions assailing her mind.

What a fine mess Thomas had landed her in. Shame and anger heated her skin. To trade her away as if she was a mare without use, too old and weak to keep on because she had rebuffed his attentions this morn? Did she not have the right to choose what happened to her body despite his claims as her husband? Evidently not. Why could he not have merely abandoned her as everyone else that no longer wanted her had in the past? But this, being sold off to another man in the market square, was a new low in a long line of humiliations she had endured. Yet she would survive it as she had all the others before. She squared her shoulders and took in a breath. One day she would be free of all of this, just like Nettie always said.

Nettie.

Catriona missed the sweet old woman who had raised her in the small cottage off the coast of Lismore since she'd been lost at sea as a child with her parents never to be found. If only the dear woman had lived longer. Since Nettie's passing several years ago, when Catriona was only thirteen, she had worked as a servant on the island to the Chisholm family. When she turned nineteen, Thomas had come to her 'rescue', offered for her, and brought her to the city of Edinburgh.

Unfortunately, it turned out not to be a rescue after all, but servitude more than a marriage. Despite how she'd come to be in this carriage with this strange man and his sister, Catriona was grateful to at least be out of harm's way. This man didn't appear to be cruel. Although she'd thought that before with Thomas, hadn't she? She released a shuddering breath.

She rubbed her toe on the singular coin in her slipper to calm herself. A trick Nettie had shown her when she was a wee girl and afraid of everything. The cool feel of the worn threepence in the lining of her shoe was a reminder that she had been through worse and that she would survive this new development, no matter what was to be born of it.

'*Child, ye canna go through the world afraid of yer wee shadow,*' said Nettie as she ran her hands over Catriona's damp hair.

She sat curled in the woman's lap as she rocked back and forth in the fine carved chair her late husband had crafted from one of the trees from the glen. The fire crackled before them as the sun set off in the distance, bringing a glow to the small, cosy room.

'*But Nettie, all I have in the world is you.*'

'*Aye. For now. But I will teach ye how to conquer yer fears and how to care for yerself, so when I am gone, ye will be strong and brave.*'

'*Will I learn to be fearless like you?*' she asked, snuggling deeper into the wool folds of the blanket wrapped around her.

'*Aye,*' she whispered, pressing a kiss to her forehead. '*Ye will be braver than all of us. Ye survived a storm, remember? Any other lass would have drowned in those waters, but not ye. Ye washed up on my shore, strong and certain as if ye were meant to be there. Ye are a fine weathered stone capable of enduring anything, and don't ye forget it. The sun will shine on ye one day, and ye will be free and have all that was meant for ye.*'

But today would not be that day.

Catriona's body swayed with the carriage as it turned onto a lane taking them through the outskirts of the city.

Soon the tall, sharp edges of the buildings in the marketplace disappeared, and they headed through the heart
of Edinburgh, away from the familiar sights, sounds,
and smells of the city. Edinburgh castle loomed off in
the distance. Its dark towers were a reminder of how
small and insignificant she was.

It seemed she had escaped the clutches of one horrid man only to be placed into the hands of another.
She pursed her lips. This man hadn't looked *too* horrid
at first glance in the Grassmarket, but one could never
tell, could they? Appearances were only that. What lay
hidden beneath was what mattered.

She slid her eyes up to peer at the man through the
curtain of loose hair shading her face, so she could
study him without him knowing. He had short, straight,
black hair, as dark as a raven's wing, and blue-green
eyes the shade of a piece of sea glass she'd found once
along the pebbled coast when she was but a child. His
features were strong, but not sharp, and his form was
pleasing enough. His dark fitted trews revealed his muscular legs, and the matching jacket with its fine silver
buttons at the cuffs showcased his prominent shoulders as well as his wealth. She quirked her lips. He *was*
quite an improvement from the smelly, flabby sot of a
husband she'd woken up to this morn, but he was *still* a
husband. As if she wanted or needed another husband,
especially not one in such finery as this. No doubt he
would be hard to please.

Despite being a laird—according to the man who'd
almost bought her—he didn't have the arrogance of one.
If anything, he'd been strangely kind, taking great pains

to be gentle in removing the harness that Thomas had bound her in. Almost as if the laird was up to something. She narrowed her eyes as he sat stoic as one of the Standing Stones she'd seen once upon a journey with Thomas. Minutes of aching silence passed, and she wondered if they'd forgotten she was even there. She shifted closer to the door.

Perhaps they had.

They weren't moving terribly fast yet. If she acted now, she *could* jump from the carriage without much injury and disappear into one of the side streets. She was fleet of foot and always had been. Resting her hand on the door handle, she began calculating where they were, the best place to jump, and how fast she could run into hiding.

'I wouldn't if I were you,' the man stated.

Drat.

She released her hold on the handle, settled her hands back in her lap, and met the man's gaze: her new husband's gaze. His eyes didn't miss much, which would prove an added complication. She'd only share what was required of her until she had a better idea of just how quick-witted he was. Thomas was thick as a stump, which had been one of his attributes. One of the few.

'I am Ewan Stewart, Laird of Glenhaven,' the man offered. The tone of his voice rolled in smooth, deep waves, like the sea. 'This is my younger sister, Miss Brenna Stewart.'

She nodded. 'I am Mrs Catriona Gordon.'

'Mrs?' Miss Stewart asked the laird. 'I thought you said you found a wife.'

''Tis a bit complicated, sister. For now, you only need know that she will be our guest along our journey and at Glenhaven until our transaction can be sorted.'

'Transaction?' The woman's eyes widened more. 'What happened while I was in the milliner's store? I was not gone *that* long searching for a new hat, was I?'

Catriona pressed her lips together to smother a smile. If only she could speak so freely. All such direct talk had earned her in the past was a swift rebuke or an even swifter smack across the cheek.

This laird did neither. He was either a weak man she could walk all over or...kind. She wasn't entirely sure which was more unsettling. Time would tell as it always did, but she had plans to not be under his thumb for long, husband or not. It was high time she had her independence. Despite the longing she felt for Nettie and the family she had lost as a child, Catriona now yearned to be alone and free from the shackles of another's expectations and control. She wanted to live a life of her own choosing, and to finally ask herself what *she* wanted out of this world and have the quiet long enough to hear the answer.

'Where are we going, my laird?' she asked. Since he'd not answered his sister's enquiry, perhaps he might answer hers, since it required a much simpler answer. The sooner she knew their destination, the sooner she could begin crafting her escape.

He lifted his gaze to her once more. 'To our home in Argyll in the Highlands. We will stop at an inn in Glasgow tonight to rest, as the journey will take two days by carriage. We will arrive by nightfall on the morrow.' He muttered a curse. 'My apologies. Do you need to gather anything from your home? We can turn about and fetch your belongings before we travel further.'

'Nay,' she answered without a beat of hesitation.

He studied her, his brow furrowing. 'You have nothing you wish to retrieve?'

'What I care about I wear on my person. All else is replaceable.'

Miss Stewart smiled, her pale blue eyes as clear as the sky. 'We seem about the same size, Mrs Gordon. I am happy to provide you some gowns and such until the seamstress can make something to your liking.'

Catriona rubbed her hands together and swallowed uneasily. 'Thank you, Miss Stewart. That is very kind.' The offer was unexpected, so much so that she did not understand it or trust it, especially from a woman so pretty. She'd never found pretty women to be kind. If anything, they were cruel. But this woman seemed different, or perhaps just better at disguising her true self, much like Catriona was doing.

She stared out of the window and watched the city disappear into rolling hills and pastures. If she remembered correctly, Argyll was far north of here on the west coast.

'Have you any family we need send word to upon your arrival?' Laird Stewart asked.

Talk of family always turned her stomach. It would be far easier to lie, but she told him the truth instead, as it often brought any further questions to an abrupt end. 'Nay, my laird. I have been on my own since I was thirteen.'

'Is that how you came to be in such a position?' Miss Stewart asked.

'Sister,' Laird Stewart warned.

''Tis a fair question,' Catriona answered. She appreciated the woman's directness. 'Aye, it was. A woman without a dowry is not much use in the world, it seems.'

Although the woman didn't answer, the sympathy in her gaze stilled Catriona. Could she somehow understand her woes? She couldn't possibly. A woman of her looks and wealth? But as the woman's gaze fell away and her grip tightened on the reticule in her lap, Catriona wondered if being a woman of wealth and means was as limiting as being a woman of nothing.

Her stomach clenched, as she didn't wish to know the answer. Not now, as she travelled cross-country with a stranger who was now her husband to a place she had never been.

'When we arrive in Argyll, I will send word to our solicitor,' Laird Stewart began, staring down at a broadside in his hand. He paused. 'I am not familiar with the terms of our...arrangement. I want to have a better understanding of what your Mr Gordon was about this morning in the market. Never seen anything like it, to be honest. I still cannot fathom it is legal to buy a wife.' He folded the paper in half and tucked it within the pocket on the inside of his jacket.

She nodded. What did one say to that?

His sister balked. 'You bought her? You cannot *buy* a wife, brother.' She scoffed and shook her head.

'See for yourself,' he answered, handing her the broadside.

Miss Stewart read the paper. As she finished, her face paled to a stark, unnatural shade of white, and her mouth gaped open a bit. When she finally faced Catriona, her eyes were bright with unshed tears. 'I am sorry. I cannot fathom it.' She swallowed hard and reached out her gloved hand to gently take Catriona's filthy bare one. 'I am glad you are here with us. That Ewan saw fit to step in on your behalf.' She squeezed her hand briefly, and let it go before turning her gaze upon her brother. 'You are a good man, Ewan. Mother would be proud of you.'

He smiled back at her.

The affection between them made Catriona's gut twist. Such warmth thrust a distant memory of her own back to the surface. One of the few from her childhood. The laughter always came first.

'You must hurry... The waves come even now to crash upon the shore. We must chase them!' her eldest brother called to her and her siblings.

She laughed and ran after them, charging down the sandy shore deep into the dark waters, the coolness biting along her ankles and then her thighs. Soon she passed her sister and then her brothers. The water met her waist and then her chest, but she pushed on.

Her brother called out to her, and as she tried to turn to him, a roaring wave crashed over her head, swallowing her into silence. She fought against the waves as best she could, but the sea pulled her along as if she were a petal in the wind. Kicking her legs and flailing her arms, she tried to reach the surface for air, but the sea pulled her deeper and farther into its depths until there was only darkness.

'Mrs Gordon?'

Catriona looked up and met the Laird's gaze. 'Hmm?'

'Are you unwell?' he asked, his brow furrowing.

'Nay. I am fine, sir.' She lied.

He paused before nodding to her, a sliver of disbelief resting in his gaze. 'If you have need of anything along our journey let me, my sister, or our driver Aaron know. You are safe now.'

'Thank you,' she answered, knowing full well what could have happened if the other man had purchased her from Thomas. 'I am grateful for you stepping in when you did. The other man did not seem…as kind as you. I do not know what would have befallen me.'

A muscle flexed in his jaw. 'Nay. I wouldn't wish my worst enemy to the likes of MacGregor.' He shifted in his seat. 'And it gave me some sense of…relief to know that I had been able to help you when I wasn't able to do so before for someone I loved.'

Something heavy rested in his words. Perhaps a regret he wore close to his heart? A part of her softened at the sight of it. She gifted him a nod of understanding. She had a keen knowledge of regrets and what they did to a person.

Catriona stared back out the window, knowing full well she would not be there to hear the answers to any queries the laird sent out to his solicitors or any dressmakers' suggestions for new gowns. She would be gone as soon as she had some coin. It was just a matter of figuring out how to escape, where she would go once she did, and what new identity she would create. The possibilities seemed endless, and her stomach flipped with hope, a feeling she hadn't had in a long time.

This was her chance.

A life of freedom awaited her, and she would seize it. Nothing and no one would stand in her way. Not even a handsome and wealthy laird who might well be her new husband.

Chapter Three

Curses.

Ewan tugged at the cravat around his neck. Why had he not left it alone? Most likely Mrs Gordon could have cared for her own affairs. He could have done nothing, returned to his carriage, and been on with his day.

His gut twisted.

Nay. He couldn't have. Not when he had an idea of what would have happened to this woman if she'd fallen into the hands of MacGregor or some other unseemly character. While he'd not known about his older sister Moira's suffering at the time of her marriage and been able to prevent it, this woman was a different story. He had seen the abuse and danger she was in with his own eyes in the square. And he'd promised himself he'd step in if he ever saw another woman in such danger, just as he wished someone would have stepped in on Moira's behalf and saved her.

He'd done what he'd had to, but now what could be born of it? He needed a wife like he needed a swarm of locusts over his fields, especially when he didn't know if she was even his wife at all.

Yet again his emotion had ruled his mind and actions with rather dire consequences. His jaw tightened. Father was right. The Stewarts needed to be feared or else they might be conquered. If Ewan didn't begin to harness his feelings and emotions, all his 'care' for others would run the clan and his family's future adrift into the firth.

Perhaps he already had.

He glanced across the seat at Mrs Gordon with regret.

What fool bought a wife at market?

Evidently, he did.

The carriage was beginning to feel as snug as a coffin, and he couldn't escape the unease settling on him like a stone on his chest. Shifting further in the seats, he bumped the woman's knee as she sat across from him. 'My apologies, Mrs Gordon,' he murmured and shifted his leg away.

Her eyes flashed up to meet his briefly, and those amber irises arrested him once more, just as they had in the market. Such an unusual shade intrigued him. Hell, all of her did. He had never met a woman so at ease with the oddity of her situation. Most likely her nerves could withstand a battlefield. Her face was a mask, void of emotion. The only flicker of feeling he'd spied upon her face was in the brief moment before she'd admitted to having no family and having been on her own since she was in her teens. A glimmer of sadness had registered in her eyes before being hidden away under a cool nod as she had answered his enquiry and stared back outside the window.

Blazes. He ran a hand down his face. What would he do with her now?

The last woman he had spent any extent of time with alone whom he wasn't related to was Emogene. *Emogene.* He cracked his knuckles, and his throat tightened. Best he not think of her right now or he'd jump from this bloody carriage himself. He glanced up and met Mrs Gordon's assessing gaze. She was studying him for some reason. Could he blame her? She probably wondered if he would ravage her or throw her to the hounds upon their arrival at the inn. Of course, he would do neither, but she didn't know that. She didn't know him.

Just as he didn't know her.

'We will arrive in Glasgow at nightfall and secure rooms as well as food so that you are comfortable and cared for. And when we reach our home at Glenhaven,' he offered to put her at ease, 'I will ask our housekeeper, Mrs Stevens, to get you settled in one of our many guest chambers. She can also assign you a lady's maid to tend to your, erm…needs.' He tugged at the cuff of one of his coat sleeves. He was bumbling this miserably. 'And as my sister mentioned, she will find you some gowns you can borrow until a proper seamstress can be sent for to make you a wardrobe of your own. In due course, we will find out the legality of this marriage of ours and discuss the future.'

'Thank you,' Mrs Gordon answered, releasing a breath that caused her bosom to rise and fall against her rather drab and worn brown dress. The small silver chain of a necklace winked at him as it caught the sunlight. It led down her neckline but disappeared into her bosom, tucked away and hidden from view. He wondered what resided at the end of that chain, and why she took pains to hide it there.

When he glanced back up at her face, he was horrified to find she had noted the fall of his gaze. Pink flushed the apples of her cheeks and along her neck as she glanced away. *Blast*. And now he was an impertinent cad. He glanced outside at the rise in the terrain and spied the familiar outline of the city in the distance. At least they were not far from Glasgow. His lungs burned for fresh air, and his legs desired a reprieve from the cramped carriage. This simple trip to town for a few errands for his sister's upcoming nuptials had turned into quite the opposite.

He would return home with a bride.

The evening meal at the Black Lion Inn had been the usual hearty, but rather bland, fare of stew with bread and cheese often served at travelling inns such as these, but Ewan would not complain. Being out of the carriage with a full belly and a bed awaiting him one floor above was enough to make his heart sing. It had been a day he'd rather forget.

Mrs Gordon had quietly eaten, quietly talked, and quietly listened. Ewan wasn't sure what to do with her, but Brenna held the woman's subdued demeanour in stride by filling most of the silence with a running discourse of her own. To his surprise, Mrs Gordon seemed content to listen and smile and add in a quip or two.

After freshening up and draping one of Brenna's cloaks over her tattered and torn dress, Mrs Gordon blended in with them quite well. All in all, to an outsider the scene might look to be a small family gathering or a meeting of friends, not a woman who had just been bought for a guinea sitting with her new 'husband' and sister-in-law, if that's what they even were. Ewan blanched.

It sounded as bad as he thought it might in his head.

How in the world would he explain this to the leaders of the clan? To Moira? To Mrs Stevens? To the entire clan? His stomach churned with doubt.

Not well.

'How did you come to be in Edinburgh with Mr Gordon?' Brenna asked.

His sister's question piqued his interest. Mrs Gordon's answer might very well help him in explaining away the awkwardness to those who enquired.

Mrs Gordon set down her wine and cleared her throat before settling her hands in her lap. 'It is an odd story, really. I was raised by an older woman named Nettie on the island of Lismore from the time that I was six until she passed just after I turned thirteen. After that, I lived with the Arrans for a short time. Then, I worked as a servant to the Chisholm family. I truly believed that Thomas, Mr Gordon, was rescuing me from a rather squalid fate when he came to our small island on a fishing excursion and offered for me. I had no dowry and did not have any expectations for my future.' She bit her lip, and her gaze dropped away.

'May I ask what happened prior to staying with Nettie?' Ewan asked, his own curiosity getting the better of him.

'Nettie found me unconscious on the shore when she was out walking one morn, and brought me to her cottage to care for me. Said I slept for a full week before I woke, and could remember nothing of who I was or my family. I could not even remember my name or age, so she gave me the name Catriona and age of six, her guess as to how old I was.' She shrugged. 'Now I can remember that I had a family—parents and siblings—prior to living with her but no real details of who they were or my life before washing up on the shore.'

'Saints be. So, you had a family?' Brenna asked, her eyes wide in surprise. 'But you cannot locate them?'

'Aye. Nettie sent word out about finding me, but no one ever replied, and my parents never came for me. Over time, Nettie told me she believed they most likely drowned after our boat must have capsized at sea and that I was lucky to have survived.'

Her eyes told him there was far more to her history, but he'd not push her. They'd only just met, and she'd had quite the trying day, as they all had. He checked the wall clock and fought a yawn. 'May I escort you ladies up to your rooms? We have an early departure in the morn, so that we can reach Glenhaven by dark. Best we get some much-needed rest.'

'Thank you for the meal, my laird.'

'Of course, Mrs Gordon. 'Tis the least I can do after all you have been through today.'

And as he followed them up the stairs, he wondered

just how much more she had suffered and whether he wished to know the truth of it at all.

Catriona stared out her room window. She'd been up for quite some time after snatching a few hours of fitful sleep despite the soft bed and tidy accommodations the inn offered. It was dark, quiet, and perhaps the perfect time to escape. She looked at her empty room and felt around in her threadbare pockets. Perhaps not. How far would she get with no coin and no plan for supporting herself? She had no money except the threepence in her shoe and only the clothes on her back.

But…what if she waited until she reached Glenhaven to flee? The Highlands were more remote, with so many places to hide. She frowned. *If* you weren't found by the wrong person, that is. But she could manage that. Over the years, she had become adept at reading people's intentions, so she merely needed to trust her gut. She could make this work and be free at last. With some money, clean clothes, and some rest, she might just make a go of it.

She'd just have to keep her nerves and her wits about her until she had those things in her possession. The laird and his sister were kind, but they were not fools. They might expect her attempt to run. It was a good thing she had a day-long carriage ride to plan out her escape. She could close her eyes, feign sleep, and figure out all the details that she could. The laird and his sister had also told her a great deal about Glenhaven and the people and places within it, and most likely she'd learn more on the ride today. She could craft the layout of the castle and the list of what she would need in her head. Once they arrived, she could get clean clothes, eat, figure out where she could secure some extra coin and food, and be on her way. She could disappear into the Highlands, maybe even this eve, if all went to plan.

After an indecently long journey, Catriona woke with a start as she was jostled into Miss Stewart. 'Apologies, miss,' she mumbled, looking around her. The carriage lurched again as the horses pulled and began a steep ascent along a narrowing road. She glanced out of the window at the lush greenery and setting sun.

Blast. How long had she been sleeping? They were far from any city.

'We have almost arrived, Mrs Gordon,' said Laird Stewart as he met her fuzzy gaze. 'Only a few more minutes now and we will be at Glenhaven. I hope you will find your stay with us a comfortable one. As I mentioned before, Mrs Stevens will show you to your room and assign a maid to assist you.'

Before she could respond, the carriage rounded a turn, and a castle came into view, its tall sandy grey towers climbing high into the dusky sky and its arms spreading out far in the horizon.

Lord above.

So much for having already mapped the castle out in her head. She could never have imagined a place as great and looming as this. She'd never seen a castle so large. Well, except for Edinburgh Castle itself.

'Welcome to Glenhaven, Mrs Gordon,' he offered.

She blinked at this 'Glenhaven', unable to look away.

She commanded herself to at least close her gaping mouth, so she wouldn't look like a hooked fish pulled from the water, even if it was exactly how she felt arriving here after being plucked from the streets of Edinburgh. The fine estate rested atop vibrant green rolling hills and fields as far as she could see. Off in the distance there was what appeared to be a village to the south, the whitewashed cottages dotting the valley at intervals and disappearing down to what was most likely the banks of a river. She spied a large barn to the west, and several smaller workhouses, mills, and drying sheds to the east. *This* was her new life?

Perhaps Thomas wasn't such a bastard after all by gifting her this new life, even if he had sold her off like cattle.

A flicker of temptation to stay here as the laird's new wife snuck up on Catriona, but she batted it away quickly, fiercely. *Stay? Why ever would I stay when I could run and have a future of my own choosing at last?* Having independence and freedom would be worth far more than any luxury, wouldn't it? And she didn't even know this man. Nor did she know if this marriage was legal. He could be a horridly cruel master or a liar and a cheat. She met his half smile.

She furrowed her brow. Or maybe he was as kind as he appeared? *Dash it all.* What did one even do with a kind man? She had no idea. It would be easier if he were a brute. At least she knew what to do: stay out of the man's reach and tend to her own affairs. Mayhap it was the same with dealing with a kind man? Take care not to fall under the spell of false security, for happiness couldn't be trusted as it never lasted…or at least, it had never lasted for her. All those she loved she had lost somehow. By age, by nature, or by cruelty. She'd not fall for the idea of security again.

She was not born to the privilege of such certainty.

The carriage slowed to a stop in the drive, and Catriona's heart threatened to beat out of her chest. While she had been quite eager and ready to jump from the rolling carriage yesterday, now she was rather hesitant to leave its familiar confines. How did one even behave in such a place?

The driver jumped down from his box seat and opened the carriage door. 'Mrs Gordon?' he offered, extending a hand to assist her.

She swallowed hard, settled a mask of indifference on her face, squared her shoulders, and accepted his hand. What other option was there? She couldn't stay in the carriage with the hope of being forgotten. It was a trifle late for that.

As both of her feet settled onto the cobbled drive, she let go of his hand and breathed in the air of Argyll. A breeze ruffled her hair and kissed along her cheeks. Despite everything, she sighed aloud, enjoying the fresh air full of the crisp scent of new growth, as if one could smell the green of the grass. Not that one could. But she'd not smelled such fresh air in such a long time that her lungs savoured it.

The laird approached and offered his arm to her. 'Shall we?'

She pressed her lips together, uncertain of what exactly he had in mind, but she nodded and slid her hand into the crook of his elbow, acutely aware of the feel of his muscles beneath her touch.

They followed his sister inside, where they were greeted by a maid who offered to take their coats. Another servant gathered the parcels from the driver as he arrived behind them in the entryway.

'My laird, I trust ye had a successful outing.' An older woman greeted them as Catriona handed off her tattered shawl to a young maid, feeling nervous and exposed. The lass wore finer clothes than she. Catriona fiddled with the end of her torn dress sleeve as she awaited an introduction. No doubt she looked a mess and out of place despite her best efforts to hide her past. Her chest tightened. The memory of first being brought to a new home after Nettie died pressed upon her, and the same shame of such uncertainty made her fingertips tingle.

'Aye, we did. Thank you.' He straightened his cravat and faced the woman. 'Mrs Catriona Gordon shall be staying on with us awhile, Mrs Stevens. Could you provide her a lady's maid and whatever additional comforts she requires? My sister will be loaning her some gowns until a seamstress can be sent for, but before then, I would appreciate your assistance in seeing to her needs.'

The older woman nodded, only a small widening of her light grey eyes giving away her curiosity. To her credit, she asked no questions, but greeted Catriona with a warm smile and small curtsy. 'Welcome, Mrs Gordon. As the Laird stated, I am here to provide ye with whatever ye require.' The woman's soft smile put Catriona at ease, and she released a breath.

'Mrs Gordon,' the laird began. 'I will leave you to get settled in and rest before dinner. Does eight suit you?'

Did it suit her?

Catriona cleared her throat. 'Aye, my laird,' was all she could sputter out.

'Until then,' he replied and disappeared down a corridor with his sister not far behind.

'I'll send in one of our girls in shortly to assist ye, Mrs Gordon, but until then, let me take ye to yer room. I think the Goldenrod Room shall suit ye just fine.'

Catriona nodded and fell into step behind her, doing her best to slow their pace so she could take in the opulence and beauty of the castle. Rich, colourful tapestries hung from the walls amidst landscape paintings offset by the dark mouldings framing the walls and stone floors. The place was so large that their footfalls echoed with each step, and Catriona pressed her lips together to smother a bit of a giddy smile.

She was being ridiculous, of course. It was merely a castle, and she wasn't meeting the king or any such royalty. All the same, a flicker of joy filled her chest as they slowed and the maid... Catriona paused.

Was she a maid? Housekeeper? What did one call her?

Before she could land on one term of address, Mrs Stevens opened a door wide for effect. 'Yer chambers during yer stay here, Mrs Gordon.'

Catriona stood in awe. If she thought the hallways were glorious, this bedchamber, *her bedchamber*, was heaven itself. The room glowed in soft yellow hues. Not a loud noisy colour, but a light yellow like a buttercream set off with whites and subtle greens. In essence, she felt as if she were staring into a garden lush with blooms.

'I hope it is to yer liking?' she asked.

'It will more than do. It is beautiful.' Catriona couldn't tear her eyes away.

'Glad to hear it.' She paused. 'Do ye have any belongings ye wish to be brought in?'

Her words yanked Catriona back from her reverie, and she faced the older woman. 'Nay.' The single word sounded as final as it did tragic, especially surrounded by such opulence.

The woman's eyes softened. 'Aye. I'll send Betsy along with some fresh clothes for ye. Would ye like a bath drawn for ye to wash away yer journey?'

Did she?

Aye. More than she dared admit. She smothered a sigh at the thought of a warm bath. How long had it been since she had experienced such a luxury? She couldn't remember. 'That would be lovely. Thank you.'

'I'll see to it, Mrs Gordon.'

'Thank you.' Catriona fought the urge to grab the woman's hands and squeeze them within her own like she used to with Nettie when she was young and full of excitement. She clutched the folds of her skirts instead.

As the woman left, securing the door closed behind her, Catriona walked deeper into the large room and took it all in. There was a large, beautiful bed covered with plush, soft yellow bedding, a sizable wardrobe and matching dresser for clothes, a pale green sitting couch, and a small but tidy writing desk with a chair facing the outdoors. Sunshine beamed in through three small windows, the light bouncing off the bedding and the long flowing white drapes. A small potted plant with vibrant purple flowers bloomed in the corner of one window and winked at her from afar. While she had no idea of its origin, it was the perfect fit for the space with its double bloom dangling down the side of the clay pot.

She blinked. A harsher contrast to the living quarters she had shared with Thomas could not be possible. This room was spotless, full of light, quiet, and…peaceful. She sucked in a deep, greedy breath and closed her eyes, taking in the clean, crisp smell of laundered bedding, the faint remnants of polish, and the subtle sweetness of the blooms of the unknown plant in the room. Her room.

She opened her eyes. Even if she didn't stay long, she would revel in the peace this space offered her and pretend she was worthy of it. Their arrangement as his possible wife would be brief as she had plans to flee, but even a few hours of being the lady of the castle would be blissful. She'd never been the lady of anything. She'd never truly had anything except for the clothes on her back, the locket around her neck, the threepence in her shoe, and the thoughts in her head. All of this was quite overwhelming.

Realising she had at least a few minutes before the maid would arrive with her bath and clothes, she bit her lip, glanced back at the closed door, stripped off her tattered dress, stockings, and shoes, and gave in to the childish wish in her heart. She rushed over to the bed, dove onto its lush bedding with only her undergarments on, sank into the downy folds of material, and sighed.

Chapter Four

'Mrs Gordon?'

Catriona opened her eyes slowly, and then sat up with a start, her heart racing in her chest. She blinked and scanned the room. *Blazes*. Where was she?

The next thing she knew, a young maid was standing over her, a look of worry woven into her brow. 'Mrs Gordon?' she asked. 'Would ye like to take yer bath now, or shall I return with the water later?'

The girl appeared to be but a few years younger than Catriona. Her clear brown eyes blinked down at her in uncertainty. 'My apologies. I knocked, but when ye did not answer, I came in. I feared ye were unwell. Please do not be angry with me.'

'Nay,' Catriona answered, smiling at the girl. 'I merely fell asleep.'

Catriona hugged her arms to her chest as she realised she only wore her shift and had left a heap of dirty clothes on the floor. A blush heated her cheeks. 'My apologies, miss. I did not wish to soil the beautiful bedding.' She scrambled off the bed and onto the floor to gather the items she had so hastily discarded.

The girl rushed to her and began to take the items from her. 'I will get them for ye, Mrs Gordon. That is my job.'

Catriona stilled and pressed her lips together. 'I am sorry. I...' She faltered and let go of the soiled items and one of her worn boots as the girl gathered them from her and set them aside near the door.

The maid returned, no doubt as confused by Catriona's actions as she was. Catriona's shoulders slumped, and she risked the truth. 'I am not accustomed to being tended to.'

The girl smiled, revealing a dimple in each cheek. 'Then we shall get on well, Mrs Gordon. My name is Betsy. I have just started here as maid, so I am not used to how exactly to best serve ye.' She blushed and released a tentative laugh.

'Yes, we will be quite the pair. A lady unused to being tended to, and a maid unsure of how to tend.' Catriona could not resist joining in and allowed the first laugh to escape her body in quite some time. The release of the pressure of hardship, even if it was only for a few moments, felt almost as blissful as the downy bedding.

Almost.

'Shall I bring in the water for yer bath?' Betsy asked, her smile full and relaxed.

'Aye, Betsy,' Catriona answered. 'That would be lovely.'

She nodded. 'I shall be right back in. The tub is behind the wooden screen. Perhaps ye would like to select a soap?'

Before Catriona could enquire further, the slip of a girl was gone from the room. Select a soap? There was more than one? She approached the tall, decorative screen used for privacy for the bath. Walking on the smooth, clean wooden plank floor cooled the soles of her feet, and she paused for a moment. She could not remember when she had last dared to walk barefoot inside. One didn't walk about unprotected on dirty floors covered with refuse and vermin. She forced herself to remember she was safe here in this beautifully clean room and that she was awake. This was no dream. She shook her head, stepped around the screen, and spied a simple tub large enough for a soak. There was also a small table covered with soaps and bottles of what she could only assume were fragrant tinctures and mixtures for bathing. Again, she had little experience with such excess. She'd grown quite used to having one singular bar of soap, a cloth, and a basin to clean herself once a day if she were lucky. Baths were for the wealthy, not for the everyday person. Such water to waste was a luxury she'd never been accustomed to.

And you shouldn't get used to it.

For she wouldn't be here long. Not if she wished to claim her independence as she had always dreamed of. But it didn't mean she couldn't enjoy this one bath, so she would. Five shaped bars were laid out in an array before her on a small cloth. Lifting one to her nose, she breathed in deeply. Her toes curled and uncurled as the pull of soft lavender and sage filled her nostrils. Setting it down and lifting the next one to her nose, she smiled as the mixture of rose and dew greeted her. She

smelled it again and sighed. The third bar smelled of
sweet goat's milk and a summery floral scent, but she
couldn't place the flower.

The door opened and closed. She set the soap back
down and peeked around the screen, the thin strap of
her shift sliding down her shoulder as she gripped the
edge of the wood. Betsy walked slowly, the strain of
lifting the large wooden bucket evident in her laboured
gait. Catriona hurried around the screen and grabbed
the handle to assist her.

'I may be new, but I am quite certain ye should not
be helping me to make yer bath,' Betsy offered, even
though she did not resist Catriona's help.

'Since I am unused to such pampering, I'm happy to
assist you. I cannot remember the last time I had a hot
bath.' She leaned her face over the steam rising from
the contents of the barrel, basking in the bliss of warmth
hitting her cheeks.

'I can say I have never met anyone like ye, Mrs Gordon, and we have only just met.' Betsy smiled, and together they carefully poured in the water.

'Nor I you,' Catriona answered, smiling back.

'There is another bucket outside.'

Another full bucket of hot water? Catriona could
scarce believe it, but soon enough Betsy returned with
another steaming barrel identical to the first and set it
on the floor. She closed the chamber door and lifted the
bucket. Catriona rushed over once more to help, and
they giggled as they carried it over to the bath. They
poured the contents in.

'Feel free to step in, my lady, and I will set this outside for the footmen to retrieve.'

Catriona removed her necklace carefully, setting it on the small writing desk. Then she walked back to the tub, cast her threadbare shift off to the side, eased her foot into the perfectly heated water, and sighed. Guiding her legs in one after another, she stood in the tub as the water warmed her, and then slowly sat, the water sluicing over her limbs, the heat so luscious she moaned aloud.

Betsy chuckled and appeared behind her. 'Is the bath to yer liking?'

'Aye,' she murmured as she closed her eyes and rested her arms on the sides of the small tub.

'I am glad of it. Have ye selected yer soap?'

She hadn't even finished smelling all of them, but on instinct, she chose the one that had stirred a flicker of interest in her as it was unknown. 'There was one that smelled of sweet goat's milk and some other flower I could not name. What is that one?'

Betsy smiled. ''Tis elderflower. A summer bloom. Ye may have seen them along the road. They have beautiful white sprays of blossoms. Quite delicate little things, but they smell divine.'

'Aye. Let us use that one.'

Catriona plugged her nose, dunked her head in the water, and emerged to hear Betsy's chuckle.

'I could have wet yer hair with the pitcher of water, my lady.'

'No need, Betsy,' she answered, wiping the water from her eyes. 'That was heavenly.'

'Hair first?'

'Aye.'

Betsy knelt beside her on the floor, scooped up her soaked hair, and began to work the soap into it until a lather formed. The feel of the girl's hands kneading Catriona's scalp felt blissful as the warm water relaxed her muscles and the sweet floral scent of the soap filled her nostrils.

Soon, Betsy set aside the soap. 'If ye'll sit forward and tilt yer head back, I'll rinse yer hair.'

Catriona did as the girl asked, and water cascaded down her hair and back once and then twice. Betsy squeezed the remaining water from Catriona's long hair and brought the heavy tresses forward to rest around her neck and down her chest. 'Ye have lovely hair, my lady. I have ne'er seen such a shade of—' Her words faltered, and a hitch sounded in the lass's throat.

Catriona moved further forward. 'Is that better?'

When Betsy didn't answer, Catriona turned to find the girl staring horrified at her bare back. Catriona flushed in embarrassment.

'I—I'm sorry, miss. I should not have noticed. I just—' She stammered out the apology but hesitated with the bar in her hand as she met Catriona's gaze. 'I do not wish to hurt ye.'

Catriona turned away. 'You need not worry, Betsy. Those scars have long since healed.'

On the outside anyway.

She shivered and pulled her legs up to her chest, wrapping her arms around them as she leaned forward.

Betsy tentatively rested the soap along the ugly

raised scars Catriona knew resided there and gently washed her back. It had been years since she had bothered to look upon them, and she had no wish to. The man who had put them there, Mr Arran, was the head of the first family that had taken her in after Nettie died. Although kind at times, when he drank, the man was prone to lose his temper.

As the eldest child in the household at thirteen, she had put herself in his path to protect the younger ones from his horsewhip. When she told a neighbour what he had done, the woman helped her secure work in the neighbouring village as a servant for a wealthy family, the Chisholms, where she stayed until she met Thomas. While Catriona was freed of his abuse, she often worried about the other children and the man's wife. She wished she had been able to save them, but as a lass struggling to survive herself, she had nothing to offer except some of the wages she sent back to them each month to help put food on their table and repay the kindness of taking her in after Nettie's death.

She could remember the feel of the lashings against her skin and the man's cruel words. *'Ye be nothin', lass. That's why yer parents never claimed ye.'* She closed her eyes to wish the memory away. It was a good thing she was leaving, and the laird would never have to cast his eyes upon them. No doubt he would be even more shocked and repulsed than Betsy.

Water cascaded down her back in two waves. 'I am sorry for whatever brought ye such, my lady. Ye seem kind to me. I am sure ye did not deserve it.'

'As you well know, Betsy, deserving is not always a qualification for such treatment from men.'

The girl paused. 'I do not know much about the ways of men other than my father and brothers. They are stern, but fair. Never once set a hand to me.'

The smooth soap slid down Catriona's arms, and the sweet smell and slight pressure loosened the discomfort in her chest. She stilled Betsy's hand with her own and met her gaze. 'Then you'd best keep it that way, you hear me?'

Betsy nodded. 'Aye, my lady.'

Soon, Catriona's hair was towel-dried and brushed, the gleaming light auburn locks almost unrecognisable as her own in the hand mirror. She shook her hair, gliding her fingers through the wavy, silky threads. Had she ever been this clean before? Every part of her skin seemed to shine and glisten as the sun set behind her. At a quarter 'til eight, Betsy entered the room with two gowns spilling from her arms. When she saw Catriona, the maid stopped short.

'My lady, ye are beautiful even without such finery,' she said as she gestured to the gowns she spread out on the bed.

Catriona shook her head. 'I do not recognise myself. I believe you have washed layers of dirt from me that I did not know I had, or perhaps there is magic in that goat's milk and elderflower soap.'

'Nay. Even I know there are no such magical soaps. Ye are a natural beauty.' She dropped her voice. 'I believe the men in this castle may trip over their own boots at the sight of ye.'

Catriona's throat dried. Beauty was not always an advantage, as it brought unwanted attentions. She had learned that from her first position as a young servant. *'Never be alone in a room with a man ye are not betrothed to,'* the older maids warned. And they'd been right. One of her fellow maids had been dismissed when she was found to be with child after being compromised by a young footman. It was one of the reasons Catriona had married young. She thought a husband would protect her and bring her respect in the world. Little did she know she would eventually need protection from him. She gripped the chair and placed the hand mirror face down on the dresser.

'I have two gowns from Miss Stewart. She picked them out with yer colouring in mind. What do ye think of them? Shall we try both?'

Catriona's stomach twisted as if she'd drunk goat's milk rather than bathed in it. She had no idea how to act at a fancy dinner such as this. She wrung her hands.

It is only one night. She could handle anything for one night, could she not?

'My lady?' Betsy asked.

'Both,' she sputtered out and rose, pasting a smile upon her face.

One night, one night, one night.

Then she would be free and on her own, travelling to a place of her choosing for the first time in her life. The thought sent a ripple of calm through her, and the nausea subsided. She finally looked upon the gowns Betsy had brought in, truly looked at them, and as her eyes settled on one, she could not deny her desire to wear it. 'The gold gown. There is no need to try on the other.'

She had never seen such a gorgeous gown in all her life, and if this were to be her only night to pretend to be a lady, a true lady, in a castle, then by all that was holy, she would enjoy it.

Betsy clapped her hands in glee. 'I had hoped ye would choose that one. I know just what to do with yer hair. Let us begin.'

Chapter Five

Ewan's stomach growled, and the mild irritation he'd felt at Mrs Gordon being a mere ten minutes late to their intended dining time was fast transforming into, well, something far worse. He sighed and shifted in his chair.

'Brother, you will not perish by waiting a few more minutes,' Brenna stated, trailing her fingers across the tines of her fork. 'Mrs Gordon has had quite a trying couple of days. Allow her some grace. I shall not bother to remind you how much of my life I have spent in the wings waiting for you or Father to come to some decision or another.' She smiled at him with the *you know I am right, so do not bother to refute me* look and head tilt that drove him mad. Then she settled her cloth napkin back in her lap.

The echoes of heeled footfalls sounded in the hallway, indicating Mrs Gordon's approach. 'Finally,' Ewan muttered and stood, sending a glare to his sister, who sent him a quelling look in return before giving a genuine smile to the woman who entered the room.

A woman Ewan did not wholly recognise.

Brenna warmly greeted Mrs Gordon and gathered her hands in her own, pointing out where she was to join her across the table. Ewan stood like an oaf struck dumb.

Blazes. By all that was holy, she was stunning, gorgeous even. A far cry from the tattered, broken woman he'd rescued.

She shone like a topaz, a fabled gemstone he had only seen in drawings. The gold gown, one of Brenna's, for he recognised it, looked joined with her flesh in a way he could never have imagined, and her pale skin glowed. Long, lush waves of her auburn hair cascaded down her back along with a crown of braids and a few loose strands that framed her face. His throat dried as the rest of his body tensed.

'My laird,' she greeted him as she rounded the table to her seat beside him.

He met her gaze and those familiar amber eyes. Then he regained his composure and half bowed to her before taking his seat. If her eyes had not been identical to those he'd seen before, he would not have believed this woman to be the one he met in the Grassmarket days ago. 'Mrs Gordon. You look lovely.'

'Thank you, my laird. I am grateful for your sister's kindness. Otherwise I would have had little to wear this eve.'

While her words were harmless on their own, Ewan shifted in his seat. The thought of her wearing 'little' sent his thoughts to rather devilish places.

She looked more than lovely. His words were a hollow attempt to remark upon her beauty, but his mouth seemed incapable of uttering a syllable more the longer he gazed upon her. Annoyed by his own weakness, he focused all his attentions on his napkin and the fine cutlery near his plate.

Deuces.

This was the absolute last thing he needed. Attraction led to nothing good, so it was best he smothered it entire. As their steak pies were set before them, he realised the appetite that had raged in his belly but moments ago had disappeared into nothingness while his utter awareness of her had surged in its place.

'And thank you for allowing me to stay here until I get my own affairs...tended to, my laird.' She cleared her throat, the meaning of her words not lost on him. The woman did not intend to stay, nor did he intend to ask her to. He had enough of his own affairs to sort out as the new laird. A fresh batch of correspondence as well as complaints from several of the clan leaders had arrived while he had been away.

'You may stay as long as you need, Mrs Gordon.' His words spilled from him before he realised what a terribly poor idea it was.

She nodded and released a breath. The relief registering in her eyes was unmistakable, and he felt like a cad. Perhaps the poor woman thought him as cruel as Dallan. Lairds did not possess the best of reputations for good reason, but he was not Dallan, nor was he the previous Laird of Glenhaven. He was trying desperately to be a good laird, one without regrets or distractions, and one who didn't rule by brute force or intimidation. But he also didn't want his emotions or attraction to this woman to cloud his judgement and cause a mistake like the one he'd blindly made with Emogene. A mistake that could cost the clan its future.

'Then, you are not married after all?' Brenna asked, her eyebrows arching towards her hairline.

Ewan rested his fork on the edge of his plate. While he adored his sister, at times she was as subtle as a rooster at dawn. He placed a mask of patience on his face. 'I am sure of little other than my uncertainty on the matter. I will send word to the solicitor in the morn to see what we can glean on the lawfulness of such an agreement. Until then, I cannot say one way or the other.'

'But you did buy her did you not? Is she not at least free from this Mr Gordon?' Brenna countered.

'Aye,' Catriona replied as colour filled her cheeks. 'He did, and I am grateful for it. I am hopeful I might buy my freedom from him or perhaps work off such a debt.'

'There is no need to discuss what we do not know. Let us simply enjoy the meal.' Ewan's words were tight and a touch too loud, but his message had been received.

Brenna smirked at him and set her sights on a new topic of conversation. 'Well, I am grateful you are here,' she told Mrs Gordon. 'It is far too serious in the house with just my brother and me here. Perhaps you can help brighten up this place.'

Ewan sighed and tried to remember to enjoy his food and not let his little sister's words prick him too much. Soon she too would be a bride and far from here, married to Garrick. And he would be all alone, which he didn't like to dwell upon at all.

* * *

Catriona thought not once, but twice about running her finger along the edge of her plate and bringing it to her lips to lap up every bit of the savoury sauce that remained. Had she ever eaten such a fine meal, and had her belly been so full? Nay. Did they eat this way each evening? She couldn't fathom it.

She gripped the napkin in her lap and commanded herself to keep her hands exactly where they were as her plate was cleared away. Soon a dainty little dessert was placed before her, and she almost squealed in delight like a child. It was a lovely cake covered in cream and berries. Her mouth watered despite her belly being full. The promise of sweetness the concoction offered threatened to consume all her reason.

Miss Stewart and Laird Stewart lifted their spoons, and Catriona did the same. When she raised the bite to her mouth, she closed her eyes as the sweet cream, cake, and berries burst into a perfect harmony of flavour. The next bite was exactly the same. Catriona listened contentedly as the siblings spoke of Miss Stewart's upcoming wedding without a care in the world, a feeling that was new and bewitching to her. She would savour their easy conversation like this dessert: for as long as it lasted.

Which, knowing her luck, wouldn't be for much longer.

She tried to push aside her worries and the knowledge that this was not a place she could or should stay for long. The laird might seem kind now, but she did not know him.

Had she ever really known anyone? Other than Nettie, not really. She'd moved too often or been too scared to tell people she met the truth about her past. Even Thomas hadn't known all of it.

She shoved away that thought too and scraped as much as she could from the bowl without drawing attention to herself.

'Do you know where your family was from, Mrs Gordon?' Miss Stewart asked.

Catriona stilled. It was a simple enough question, but she dreaded answering it every time it was asked. 'Nay. I am not certain. I cannot remember much of my childhood before being with Nettie.'

Too bad all the years after Nettie had died cut deep and sharp in her memories. Time had not dulled them.

'I am sorry to hear such,' Miss Stewart offered.

The laird sat silently. When she discovered him staring upon her scarred knuckles, she glanced away and tucked her hands in her lap. The familiar heat of embarrassment crawled up her neck and into her cheeks.

But she realised it was a bit late to hide the truth from him. He'd seen her shackled like an ox. Would anything shock him? For once, she'd not shy from it. She pulled back her shoulders and met his gaze while answering. 'I try to not focus on what I am sorry for, but what I have learned from all of those experiences.'

'Is that not but a way to deny it ever happened?' Laird Stewart asked. To her surprise, no challenge rested in his blue-green eyes, but a twinge of desperation to know the answer, as if he too had much invested in her next words.

So she chose them carefully. 'It could be, but I use what I have learned, despite how those lessons may have come about. Over the years, what I have realised from those many experiences has kept me alive.'

'Such as?'

'Such as me seeing you are desperate to know how I have survived thus far, but you are unwilling to ask me directly. Someone made you believe it was rude to be direct, but it isn't. Being rude is lying about one's intentions.'

He pointed to his chest. 'You mean me?'

'Do you think I do?'

He balked. '*I* have no ill intent. If anything, I saved you from peril with no thought to my own person or how this may further complicate my plans as laird.' He was flustered, so she nudged once more.

'Your eyes speak other words, my laird.'

He said nothing, and she had her truth.

And she'd gained the very answer she had wanted: the man had no bloody idea what to do with her. That was why he sat vexed and frustrated without finishing the food on his plate. He'd bought a bride he did not want and seemed altogether overwhelmed by his new role as laird. She almost felt sorry for the man.

But she didn't.

It was hard to feel sorry for a man who had inherited such power and wealth and yet had little idea of what to do with it. If *she* was in charge, she would have lists of ideas she'd attempt, and she would make no apologies for their successes or failings. She'd yield to no one... for once in her life.

'If you will excuse me, I have much to catch up on after being away for so many days.' Laird Stewart rose from the table, his gaze narrowing on her for a beat too long. Perhaps she'd overstepped a touch. She was his guest, after all.

She wrinkled her nose and brought herself back to reality.

She'd do well to remember her place. She was no laird, had no power, and never would. Well, not unless she seized it. She toyed with the napkin on her lap as she watched him walk away. But how did one do that with no money, no rights, and no hope for the future?

Simply answered: one didn't.

Unless the person was her.

This was her chance. She would not allow her one opportunity to seize the life she wanted to pass her by.

Chapter Six

'Where exactly do you plan to go, *wife*?'

Catriona froze at the threshold. Her hand grasped the door handle, a satchel stolen from the kitchen strapped to her back. Never mind the coin and food she had also 'borrowed' from the cook's coffers tucked inside it. There was no mistaking her purpose. She was fleeing in secret in the dead of night. It was as clear as the hard, chiding edge in the man's tone on the word *wife*.

Her hesitation was her downfall. If she'd but thrust the door open, she might have gained a start upon him and had a chance to disappear into the lush forest that whispered freedom across the edge of the large, empty fields. But now, with that beat of waiting, she had lost the option. Laird Ewan Stewart melted out of the shadows of the room. A slant of moonlight hit his blue-green eyes, and that flash of iris the colour of sea glass she'd noted on their first meeting sent a jolt of awareness and heat through her once more.

How did a man even learn to look upon someone that

way? She felt exposed and held all in the same moment. She shivered. It was wholly unnatural.

She leaned against the door, turning the handle slightly, and he ceased his advance, lifting an open palm in supplication.

'I mean you no harm,' he began, his voice softening to a rolling wave over her as if he was placating a small foal unknown to human touch. 'But I do wish for us to have one last conversation before you decide to leave.'

She turned the handle a degree more.

'Deuces. Just listen. I believe we may be able to help one another.'

Help one another? She almost snorted aloud.

What a farce. Or perhaps this was a finely veiled trap? She was a poor woman with nothing and no family to her name. He was a wealthy laird with power. While *he* could help himself to her, which is what one might expect from a man in his position, there was little she could offer him.

But even so, her curiosity at his play of words intrigued her, and he could have already lunged and pinned her to the ground if he'd wished to. He was no small man, and he had quick eyes. He didn't seem to miss much, which was becoming quite the nuisance. Dim-witted men suited her far better. This one was, well…quite peculiar. She couldn't sort him out at all.

She held his gaze, studying him. He was a puzzle amongst men.

No deception rested in his eyes, and she knew people. It was one of the things that had kept her alive for so very long. Being able to read them and foresee their intentions had spared her life on more than one occasion.

She let go of the door handle. Her instincts had kept her alive this long, so she'd trust them again now. 'Go on,' she replied, ever watchful for any unexpected movements.

'What is it you want, Mrs Gordon?' he asked.

What do I want?

She balked and narrowed her eyes. 'What?' she asked, shifting on her feet.

'You heard me.' His voice was steady, clear, and certain. The very opposite of how she felt at this moment.

It had been so long since anyone had asked her what she wanted that she was flummoxed to think of an answer. She sputtered out the first word that formed in her heart, 'Freedom.'

He lifted a brow and nodded. 'Not exactly what I thought you might say.' He crossed his arms against his chest. 'But I still believe we may be able to help one another.'

'Why should I help you with anything?' She bristled. 'I can still run from here.'

'Aye,' he answered, his gaze sweeping across her form with approval. 'You seem strong and capable enough. I believe you could survive...for a time. But for how long would a woman such as yourself be able to travel alone through these parts safely?'

He had a point, and it plagued her to concede it, so she refused to. 'I could make it.' She lifted her chin and squared her shoulders to rally her full height, no matter how meagre it was.

A smile tugged up the corner of his lips. 'I have no doubt as to your will. It is the will of others I would not trust. As you well know, not all men are kind.' His smile fell into a flat line.

A shiver scurried up her spine.

'And what are you, then?' she asked quietly.

He paused. 'What do you believe I am?'

'I believe you are like most men. It depends on how you need to be. You can be kind, but also cruel.'

To her surprise, he didn't become angry, but nodded in agreement.

'Aye. Quite right. I possess the duality of most men, but I believe my actions at the Grassmarket might earn me at least a listen.' He came closer, his steps measured and precise like a man trying not to startle a grouse in the brush. He paused an arm's length from her. 'But first, I would have you set down your satchel, or shall I say the cook's satchel, so I know you will stay long enough to hear out my proposal.'

She blushed. 'I would have returned it...someday.'

'No doubt. I have her to thank. She noted it was missing along with a few coins meant for the deliveries arriving tomorrow.'

Blast. Catriona's shoulders slumped. No wonder she'd been caught.

He reached out an open hand to her slowly and paused before touching her, staring into her eyes while awaiting her approval. She gave a nod, and he slid his hand under the worn leather strap of the bag, the heat from his fingertips seeping into her shawl, igniting a small trail of awareness along her shoulder and arm as he slid it away from her to rest at her feet.

She swallowed the nerves fluttering in her throat. He was close. Too close. She could see the fine shape of his jawline and the soft shadow of stubble on his cheeks. His slight scent of mint tickled her nose.

Her heart picked up speed. He swallowed, his Adam's apple bobbing in his throat, as if he were not entirely sure of his words even as he began to speak them. 'If we are not legally married by this transaction of ours, stay and be my wife. I know it seems an unusual request since we know so little of one another. But I think such a union could benefit us both. I need to solidify my new standing as laird, but I have no desire to go through the manoeuvrings of the clan leaders to find a bride. And in return, I could grant you security, protection, and immense freedom to pursue your interests as you desire. I saw the way your face softened at the sight of the clarsach and pianoforte in the salon. Whether your interests lie in music or art, it makes no matter to me. And once enough time had passed and you felt comfortable, er, with me...we could begin the task of begetting an heir.'

She blinked back at him. 'What?'

He chuckled, a deep smile brightening his features. A hidden dimple emerged and winked at her. Her heart skittered in her chest.

'You heard me.'

'But you own me already, my laird. You could just seize me now. I am at *your* bidding.'

He shook his head and took a step closer.

'Nay. I know you do not know me, Mrs Gordon, but

I am not that man.' He lifted one of her hands in his, running the callused pad of his thumb so gently over the small scars that covered her knuckles that she almost gasped aloud. 'I do not pretend to know what has befallen you.' He let go of her hand once his thumb reached her fingertips, and her breath hitched in her chest. 'But I will not add to it.'

She stared into his face, looking for deceit, but only truth shone back at her.

'So, you would just let me leave?' Surely she had misunderstood.

He shrugged. 'Aye. If you so wish it.'

'Why?'

'Because I do not own you despite this foolishness of the guinea at the Grassmarket. I just wished to save you from further injury and acted impulsively. I had not a thought past that moment of liberating you from your husband and MacGregor.' He ran a hand through his hair. 'And, I have no desire to own you. My offer to you now is one of partnership that would benefit us both. You could be safe, settled, and have all you require to live a good life here at Glenhaven, and you would assist me in being my wife to help solidify my standing as the new laird. Things are quite precarious at the moment.'

'Why not merely marry one of the many lasses who no doubt fall like petals at your feet? As laird, the men of the clan must have their daughters fawning about you and clamouring for your hand.'

'Aye, but that is the problem. I have no time or talent to manage such manoeuvrings, and I am uncertain of whom to trust, especially with the balance of power so in flux amongst my late father's friends. I believe some of them wish I were not laird, and some of them might well wish me dead, if I am to be entirely truthful. You would come to me with no ulterior motives and no expectations.'

She lifted her brow.

He shrugged. 'Aye, perhaps *fewer* expectations.'

'And your expectations of me?'

'As I said, assist me in solidifying my position as laird, help me root out any men with unsavoury intentions within the clan, and take part in begetting an heir, when the time is right. Oh, and our marriage will be an arrangement free of the entanglements of romantic love and that nonsense. I need no further complications in *that* area of my life. This would be a marriage of convenience for the both of us. Nothing more.'

A muscle worked in his jaw, and a coldness came into his eyes, darkening his features. The sudden change in him was stark and unsettling. *Dash it all.* A woman had hurt him. And deeply. That much was clear to see, but it made no matter to her. She was fine without love. She'd never experienced it, so why worry over it now? And she found him attractive. Much more so than Thomas. It might not even be a trial to endure his attentions in the siring of that heir of his.

But she'd not give in just yet, not when she clearly had the advantage for once in her life. 'And my allowance?'

He smiled. 'What is the monthly sum you require?'

'Five shillings.'

He pressed his lips together and sighed as if deciding whether he could agree to such an exorbitant amount.

'Done.' He extended his hand to her. 'We have an agreement, Mrs Gordon.'

She smiled and clutched her hand in his. 'Aye. Perhaps we could address one another by our given names now, since we are to be husband and wife after all.'

He drew his hand away slowly, and his smile faltered on his lips. 'Aye. Catriona, we can.'

Her name on his lips sounded forbidden, and her pulse increased. She longed to hear it again. A skitter of uncertainty clogged her throat. Had she just made an agreement with a saint or the devil?

Only time would tell, as it always did.

'May I escort you back to your room?' he asked.

'No need. I won't flee, but I'd like to sit and enjoy the view for awhile.'

He nodded. 'It is gorgeous.'

'Aye.'

'Until tomorrow then,' he said.

She faced the rolling hills, the moonlight glistening off the dark grasses bending in the breeze.

'And, by the way,' he called back to her.

She glanced around her shoulder and met his playful smirk and rogue dimple.

'I would have given you ten,' he said.

She shook her head as he continued, disappearing around the corner until she was left with only the small satchel, which she'd need to return to the cook with a hefty apology, and the view of a place that would now be her home.

While she'd woken up with plans to flee to seize her freedom, she was going to bed tonight in Glenhaven as the wife of a laird with the promise of more freedom, security, and protection than she'd had all her life.

Chapter Seven

Deuces.

By all that was holy, what had he just done?

Ewan scrubbed a hand through his hair and blew out a breath before he closed the door to his chamber. Had he made the best or worst decision of his life by making such a proposal?

His hands trembled as he leaned back against the solid wood of the door, the firm pressure a reminder he was alive and what he'd just done had not been an imagining. Mrs Gordon, Catriona, had agreed to stay and be his wife. And despite the utter panic he felt now, his desperation at the sight of her perched at the door ready to flee had been a thousand times more potent. His limbs tingled from the memory. All he knew was that he couldn't let her go.

Had he acted on instinct and done what he needed to do to keep her safe, just as he had at the Grassmarket, for fear of what might happen to her if she charged off into the Highlands alone at night? It felt like something more had sent him into such a state, but he cared not to acknowledge it. Perhaps it was just lust or attraction that had propelled him on so fiercely and with such certainty. He'd just reacted. He'd thought of nothing else but keeping her from leaving him…but why? He hardly knew the lass. But what he knew of her, he was drawn to, intrigued by, and it had been a long time since any such interest had flickered in him since Emogene.

And as much as he didn't want to say it, he was overwhelmed by the prospect of being alone at Glenhaven after Brenna married, and tackling the sea of decisions being a laird entailed. If only Father had told him how difficult it would be to fill his shoes.

Pushing off the door, Ewan rolled his neck and walked over to the bank of windows that overlooked the glen. He could see as far off as the moon and mountains would allow. The sharp and subtle bends of grey and black amongst the moonlight were as familiar and clear as the lines on his palms.

'That is Stewart land.'

Laird Bran Stewart rested his hands along Ewan's shoulders, and Ewan stood on his tiptoes to spy over the lower window frame.

'How far does it go, Father?'

'As far as you can see, son, and in time it will all be yours. Yours to care for, lead, and bring to greater prosperity.'

'It will?'

'Aye. Once I am gone, it will be your responsibility to care for our people, our land, and the fruits of it, for one day you will be laird.'

'How will I know how to be the laird?'

Laird Stewart released a deep laugh. 'Because I will teach you. The rest of it was sewn in your bones the day you were born to this world.'

'What if I don't want it sewn in my bones?'

'What you want doesn't matter, son. Your duty to the clan is above all else. Do you understand?' His father's voice was stern and unyielding.

'Aye, Father.'

But in truth, Ewan hadn't understood. He never had. His bones hadn't been filled with the duty and knowing of a laird, but with uncertainty laced with doubt. He shifted on his feet. But there was only one way through his choices now, and that was forward. He'd not go back on his word to Mrs Gordon. To Catriona. He swallowed hard and ran his hand through his hair. He knew far too well what the consequences could be from breaking one's promises. When Ewan had broken his promise to marry Robertson's eldest daughter in order to marry Emogene, an alliance was lost, his relationship with his father and clan fractured, and when Emogene left him in the end, Ewan's heart and belief in love were shattered. He'd sacrificed all for nothing.

He clenched his fists by his sides, let out a steadying breath, and headed over to his desk. Brooding was a waste of time. Perhaps one of the few things he and Father had ever agreed upon. Lighting a candle from one of the winking wall sconces, he settled into his worn desk chair. He found fresh parchment and his ink pot and quill. Enquiries would have to be made to find out the legal manoeuvrings of his agreement with Mr Gordon over Catriona. Best to know what would need to be done to ensure she was truly legally free of her husband before Ewan attempted to claim her as his wife in public.

As he ended the first word with a flourish of his quill, he settled into the rhythm of action, and some of the uncertainty from earlier melted out of the ink and onto the parchment. Action always soothed him far more than worry ever did.

A small knock sounded on his door.

Saints be.

Could he not have more than a handful of minutes of peace?

'Brother?'

Apparently not.

'Come in, Bren,' he called, knowing full well he'd not latched his door. He never did. Perhaps he should.

He set the quill back it its pot and rose as his sister entered the room. Worry creased her usually perfect brow. He prepared himself. Bad news had been the norm.

She settled into the chair near the window, tucking her legs under her and fidgeting with the tail of the tie of her cream dressing gown.

'Has something happened? 'Tis quite late.' he said. He was reluctant to sit. He preferred to stand for bad news.

'Nay, but I cannot sleep. When I saw the candlelight beneath the door, I decided to just come ask you about my worries.'

'Worries?'

'What are you to do…with Mrs Gordon? Surely

you will not send her away after all she has suffered.'
Brenna met his gaze, her eyes flashing with concern.

'Of course not. I said as much at dinner, did I not?'
He widened his stance and crossed his arms against
his chest.

She shifted and rolled her eyes heavenward. 'Aye.
I know what you *said*, but is that what you will do?'

'Is there oft a difference?'

She lowered her gaze. 'Aye. Sometimes there is.
Your...opinions—' she paused '—are not always fixed.'
She straightened her robe around her slippers.

'What does that mean?'

Silence.

'Bren?'

She huffed, but finally answered. 'You are often in-
fluenced by Father's friends and trying to be the perfect laird since Father passed, as if there is even such a
thing, and I wondered what you might do if they said
they disapproved of her staying on until she found
another...opportunity.' She locked on his gaze.

'I am in the midst of drafting enquiries as to her
situation to see what legal grounds there are for ensur-
ing she is legally free from her husband. I assure you,
I will not merely toss her out into the glen.' He set his
hands to his waist and walked to the window. His pulse
picked up speed. 'That way I will know when I can
marry her properly.'

There. He'd said it aloud and to Bren. There was no
taking it back now. It might as well be etched in stone.

When she said nothing, he turned to face her. Her
piercing blue eyes searched his as they often did when

she wished to assess his sincerity. She stood and walked to him. 'You are serious?'

'Aye. I would not joke on the matter of marriage, as you well know.'

'Do you love her?'

'Of course not. I barely *know* her, Bren. I met her in the Grassmarket a mere few moments before you did,' he scoffed and shook his head.

'Then, why on earth would you be wanting to marry her?' His skin heated under her scrutiny. 'She is not to be trifled with, brother. The woman has been through enough.' She frowned at him, crossing her arms against her chest.

He lifted his palms in supplication. 'I am not trifling with her. I proposed to her, you fool.'

She froze. 'Why?' she asked in a raised voice.

'*Because* I do not love her, and she comes to me with few expectations, unlike everyone else in my life. I will not have to endure the endless manoeuvrings of the elders and Father's most dear friends as they thrust their beloved available daughters upon me. And I will be free of your scrutiny as well as Moira's, for I will have finally taken a bride.'

Her pained expression told him his words had hit their mark, even though he hadn't meant to be quite so forceful in making his point. As she studied him further, her expression softened.

'Do you mean our care and concern for you?' she asked. 'For that is what it is, brother, not scrutiny. We have been worried for you since Father's passing. You put so much pressure upon yourself to solve all the problems of this clan. You hardly sleep, from what I can tell. You overwhelm yourself and think all must be resolved, but there will be new issues to address. That is the way it always was and will be.' She approached him and took his hands in her own cool, petite ones. He commanded himself not to pull away, despite the discomfort in his chest and emotion clogging his throat.

'The confidence and joy you once had seems to have been buried with Father, and neither of us know why. He is not here judging you, nor are we. We are your family. We care for you and wish you every happiness. And choosing Mrs Gordon as a wife because you do not know or love her seems a poor choice.' She squeezed his hands, and after a beat he pulled away and turned away from her.

Anger simmered in his blood. 'You do not know what is best for me. No one does. I am laird, and I will make the decisions for this clan and for myself.' He turned to face her.

She held her ground. 'So we should merely stand by and allow you to make yourself more and more miserable?'

'I am not making myself miserable.'

'Oh, no?' She popped her hands to her hips. 'You rarely laugh or have fun anymore, Ewan. You have become some serious facsimile of Father.'

'Nay. I have not.'

She scoffed. 'Then I will leave you to it, my laird. But do not come to me in a month's time asking for advice on how to undo the tangled web you have woven. By then, it will be far too late.'

'Do not fear it, sister. I won't.'

And with that, she glared at him and left the room, closing the door rather loudly behind her.

He cursed and scrubbed a hand through his hair. Why was everything so difficult? Couldn't one thing be easy? He thought of Catriona. Aye, having her as a bride might be just that—easy. She seemed an intelligent, sensible woman who was not afraid of hard work or difficulty. But first, he had to ensure she was legally free from her first husband, and Ewan could only do that by finishing the enquiry letter to his solicitor that he had intended to finish a half hour ago. He cursed once more and set down to task, his quill striking the parchment with a violent flourish, snapping the fine tip in half.

Chapter Eight

Catriona awoke in a plush armchair. She squinted against the striking rays of dawn streaming into a set of sizeable windows overlooking the glen. A light fog hovered over it, and the sunrise burned an orange pink in the distance. Unsure of where she was, she started, and half fell out of the plush cushions but recovered before she ended up on her backside on the floor. Her heart raced as she studied her surroundings, sitting on the edge of the chair, gripping the solid, steady arms of it fiercely. Finally, the memory of where she was clicked into place, and she sighed.

She was safe. She was at Glenhaven.

She froze.

She was also engaged to the laird even though she might be still married to Thomas. She groaned aloud and flopped back into the chair. She didn't know what anything meant any more. The only thing certain was that the days would climb on one way or another. The sun would always rise, the sun would set, and day and night would rest in between. It always had, and it always would. What she did with those days was the uncertainty.

Although being married to a laird might bring her more security and safety than she had ever had before, the freedom he promised was more of a question mark. She had never known a man who encouraged a wife to have freedoms.

Only time will tell, I suppose.

'Mrs Gordon?'

Catriona bolted to standing and whirled around, her arms high to protect herself.

Betsy, her lady's maid from the night before, stood wide-eyed like a deer surprised in the wood by a foe.

Catriona relaxed and dropped her arms to her sides. 'My apologies, Betsy. You gave me a fine start.'

'I am sorry, Mrs Gordon. I came to yer rooms with yer morning basin of water, and when ye weren't there, I started to worry for ye. I went looking to see if ye had need of me. Did ye sleep out here all night?'

'Aye,' Catriona answered. 'I was watching the stars and...' She shrugged.

'Fell asleep?'

'It appears that way. I am sorry you keep finding me asleep in the oddest places.' She covered her mouth as she yawned.

Betsy smiled. 'Ye had quite a journey the last few days, so I'm not surprised. Would you care to freshen up and dress? I can even bring ye a tray to break yer fast if ye wish.'

She smiled and released a breath. 'Aye to everything.'

Catriona completed her ablutions and dressed quickly with Betsy's help. With her stomach now full, she wondered what to do with her day. She couldn't remember the last time she had not a task or a chore to complete. Betsy had chided her more than once to stop doing her work, but being pampered was an odd, foreign feeling, and restlessness bubbled in Catriona. What did a woman do if she had no chores? She worried her hands. What did she *want* to do?

It had been a long time since she had asked such a question of herself, let alone answered it. She quirked her lips and wandered through the castle, nodding to the many servants as she passed, until she found herself near the salon the laird had shown her the night before. She peeked into the room with its muted hues and gentle floral accents that offset the dark, rich wooden flooring and decorative rugs. It was an invitingly feminine room, and she risked one step and then another across the threshold.

Once inside, she smiled as she scanned the room. Off in the corner sat a glorious wooden clarsach on a rose-coloured fabric-covered stool, and her fingers itched to play it, despite having no idea how. Just the thought of hearing music soothed her as it always had. Nettie had a lovely singing voice and often sang her back to sleep when she had nightmares. And more than once she had stood at the edge of the ballroom, watching the musicians play and tapping her toes to the music between serving wine and food to those who attended the seasonal balls at the Chisholms', where she had worked as a servant.

Perhaps she could sneak in just for a moment. It was early yet, so she'd need to be quiet. She closed the door behind her and prayed she wouldn't wake anyone else in the household as she didn't know if she was even allowed to roam so freely.

Thankfully the sound of her footfalls was swallowed up by the large rug that covered most of the floor. Her fingers tingled in anticipation as she approached the small harp, and once she reached it, she stopped, admiring the delicate floral carvings that curled along the triangular-shaped wooden frame and fine strings beneath. She picked it up and settled onto the stool, resting the clarsach on her lap. She ran her index finger along three of the strings, and they sang in delight as if they were also longing to be touched. She smiled at the sweet sound and did it once more but included five strings along the run. It sounded even more glorious. She bit her lip and dared run her fingertip along all the strings, and it sounded like a sunset in her ears.

'Do you play?'

Catriona stilled. *Laird Stewart.* While she'd only known the man a few days, she knew that voice. Too bad she didn't know him well enough to judge his tone. She wasn't sure if he was angry or intrigued to find her in the salon.

She turned to face him, stunned by the difference in his appearance from yesterday. He stood in sandy trews with high boots and a freshly starched cravat, but no jacket. He appeared more relaxed and at ease, even though he looked just as formidable as always as his form filled the doorway. She met his gaze and risked a light tone. 'Nay, but I would like to one day learn.'

'Does today suit?' He smiled and tucked his hands in his trouser pockets.

She balked, surprised by such an offer. 'Today? As in this minute?'

He shrugged. 'Why not? My sister is convinced I am too serious and having no fun as of late. 'Tis early. I am not needed yet.'

She studied him. 'You play?'

'I do.'

His simple answer threatened to bring her flat to the floor. A laird who played the clarsach? It sounded near impossible, but the last few days had been nothing but one impossibility after another, had they not? Why should today be any different?

'I will take your surprise as agreement to begin your first lesson.'

She nodded.

'May I?' he asked as he approached.

She started to get up from her seat, but he shook his head. 'No need. I can guide you from where you are sitting.' He pulled up another stool and settled in beside her, his knee lightly bumping her own, sending a tiny current through her thigh.

'We shall start with something simple,' he said. His muscular frame filled the space between them as did his familiar scent of tallow, mint and something she couldn't quite name.

She watched him in awe as his large hand made the harp sing sweetly in what appeared to be an effortless rhythmic stroke of his fingertips across the first, third, and then fourth strings in a repeated refrain.

'That was lovely,' she told him.

'Now you try.' He handed her the small harp, and

she settled it in her lap. A flash of his rogue dimple appeared and disappeared just as quickly as if it was flirting with her.

Confidently, she sat up straight and did exactly as he did, but it sounded horrid. She cringed.

'May I?' he asked, reaching for her hand.

She hesitated but finally agreed with a nod.

He cupped her hand in one of his own and guided her fingers near the instrument. 'Try keeping your thumb pointed up to the ceiling and using just the pad of each of your first three fingers here to pluck the strings,' he said, tracing the plump part of her fingertips with the thumb of his other hand. Shivers scurried along her skin from the heat and intimacy of his touch, and a dull ache pooled in her core.

'Try again,' he said, undeterred, as if that hadn't been the most unpleasant music he had ever heard.

She swallowed the tightness in her throat and nodded. Taking a breath, she floated her fingertips along the strings again, and...it sounded even worse. *Ack.* Heat filled her cheeks. 'You make it appear quite easy when it is not.' She tucked a loose lock behind her ear and bit her lip.

'*That* is the first lesson of the clarsach,' he said lightly. 'Playing the harp is *never* as easy as it looks.'

She laughed aloud. 'Perhaps. Who taught you to play so well?'

His smile faltered. 'My mother. She was an incredibly talented woman. Her music and laughter used to fill these halls, especially this room. She could play the clarsach, the pianoforte, and even sing while playing and not miss a note.'

Catriona scanned the room imagining just that. A woman playing while the laird, Ewan, and his siblings danced with a fire blazing in the hearth. Her eyes paused on a large portrait of a fair-haired woman with rather delicate features across the room.

'Aye.' He nodded, reading her thoughts. 'That is her.'

'I like her smirk,' Catriona added.

Ewan chuckled. 'She had a glorious sense of humour, but she could also quell us all into silence with a single lift of her eyebrow, even my father.'

'Sounds like a magnificent woman, to be sure.'

'She was, and we were shocked when she died suddenly. In this very room, actually,' he added without her enquiry. 'Her heart just gave out. I have not been in here in far too long.'

'Why not?'

He shrugged and looked about. 'Too painful, I think. It was as if she took all the laughter and light with her that day. Being in here was a reminder of that. We plodded along as best we could, but it was never the same. I always thought it affected Moira the most, but now I realise it was Bren who suffered deeply. Turned herself inside out to be loved and pleasing, especially with Father.'

'And what of you?'

'Me?' he asked. 'I just miss her and the way it used to be. Of what could have been if she were still here. The conversations we might have had.' He gazed down at his hands. 'It is hard to think she has been gone over ten years.'

She could imagine him now, not as the strong, vibrant laird he was now, but as a younger, dark-haired lad sitting in this very room, having lost his mother, staring upon her portrait in silence. 'I am sorry. That must have been difficult.'

'It was, but it was perhaps a far cry from your own difficulties.' He ran his hands along his thighs and studied her face again with those deep, penetrating blue-green eyes that made her feel cared for and exposed all at once.

She looked down and toyed with the chain around her neck. 'It is hard to miss what one cannot remember. Not truly remember, anyway.'

'I doubt that.'

The truth of his words stung her, and her breath caught. She glanced up to find him assessing her once more.

The clock chimed, revealing the turn of the hour.

'Ah, the morn is getting away from me already. I will leave you to practice,' he said, rising from the stool. 'Just keep running your fingers along those first few strings to get the feel of it. Once you have mastered that, I will show you another note.' He nodded to her. 'I will be meeting with some of the clan leaders this morn, but I will try to find you later to give you the grand tour of the place. If you have need of anything, let Mrs Stevens know.'

'Aye,' she answered, unable to utter anything else.

Then he was gone.

Dash it all. She felt entirely unnerved and intrigued by the man all at the same time. She scrunched up her face. *How odd.* Men usually didn't make her feel much of…anything. She shrugged off her wonderings and looked upon the small harp in her lap.

Her fingers drifted across the strings just as his had, and she cringed. It still sounded horrid. Staring down at her hands, she wondered how a man such as him, a laird of a clan, had made the strings of this clarsach sing so pleasantly under his touch?

Probably the same way he had made her skin sing. Frowning, she set aside the harp on the other stool, then shivered and rubbed her arms. Best she remain watchful and alert, and keep her distance until she figured this man out. There was no need to care more for him more than she needed to. While she might have agreed to become his wife, she intended to enjoy her freedom for the first time in her life. She also needed to keep her part of their bargain: there would be *no* romantic complications.

Chapter Nine

'What has you smiling this morn, brother?'

Brenna's question yanked Ewan from his thoughts as he walked down the main hall to his study, where three of the clan leaders would soon be joining him. Immediately he frowned and squared his shoulders, preparing for whatever his sister dared say next, which could be anything.

'What do you mean?' he countered.

She fell in step with him, matching his stride. 'I saw you. You were smiling as you were walking down this hallway.' She glanced behind them, curiosity evident in her tone. 'From whence did you come?'

He rolled his eyes and ignored her, unwilling to give away any of his thoughts regarding why he might be smiling, if he was at all, because of their talk the night before. Her doubt as to his intentions with Catriona still stung. 'Do you not have more pressing matters today to attend to? A fitting? Correspondence perhaps?'

'Ugh. Aye to all the above.' She poked him playfully in the arm. 'You are positively no fun, brother, but do not think I have forgotten what I just saw with my own eyes. You. Were. Smiling.'

'I think not. Perhaps you were imagining things.'

'I also have additional plans for the day. I am sorting through my chamber and deciding what shall stay and what I shall bring to my new home. Garrick will also be joining us for dinner this eve. Do not forget.' She dropped her voice to a whisper. 'How shall I introduce him to Mrs Gordon?'

He stopped short, and she paused alongside him.

Blast. 'I'd forgotten that was tonight,' he said. 'Leave the introductions to me. I will speak with her before our dinner, so she is somewhat…prepared.'

'Shall I warn Garrick?' Brenna asked.

'And tell him what? That I have bought a bride?' He scoffed at her, his voice in a hushed whisper.

She pressed her lips together and shrugged. 'Maybe?'

He scrubbed a hand through his hair. 'He would think me mad. Tell him nothing. I shall explain to him when he arrives. I will think upon it until then.'

'He will understand, brother.'

'Brenna, how can he understand what even I cannot fathom?' He shook his head. 'I must go,' he grumbled. 'I must be prepared for when the elders arrive.'

'What is it you must speak with them about so early this morn?'

'Ironically, we were scheduled to discuss when I would be expected to take a wife.'

To his relief, she said nothing and let him walk away unscathed.

He stalked down the hallway, entered his study, and

closed the door loudly behind him. He rested his hands on his waist and paced the room. What exactly *would* he tell them?

I have bought a bride.

Nay.

I found a bride.

Nay.

I no longer need help in selecting a bride.

Maybe.

I have chosen a bride.

Better.

A knock on the door sounded.

'Aye,' he answered.

'They have arrived, my laird,' Mrs Stevens called. 'Shall I send them in?'

I have chosen a bride, it is.

'Aye. Send them in. You can leave the door open. Thank you, Mrs Stevens.'

Ewan reminded himself that he was laird, not them, as their heavy footfalls warned of their approach. He was leader of the clan, not they. Niven, the oldest and most difficult of them all, paused in the doorway, his dark, brooding countenance and large build like the weather itself. He was known to have the power to darken any room, and he was Ewan's father's oldest friend.

Niven nodded. 'My laird.'

Ewan nodded in kind. 'Good morn, Niven. Come in.'

Harris and Broden followed him, each offering a greeting and nod of respect before they settled into the chairs at the large table before them. How many times over the last century had terms been agreed to by his forefathers over this bruised wooden table? Ewan settled in last and pressed his palms flat to the wood, saying a prayer to be guided by patience and humility rather than arrogance, as he knew the men would test him. While he liked all three of them individually, together they created a trio of discord to be rivalled by even the most challenging of men. Ewan scarcely ever left one of their gatherings without either a megrim or a need to spar with his best soldier for a good hour to release the frustration and anger the men could stir within him.

Niven raised his coal-black eyes to Ewan's and set the tone of their gathering with a single phrase: 'Have you decided?'

While Ewan knew full well what he was enquiring about, he sought a delay in clarifying. 'Upon?' he asked.

Niven slammed the table with his open palm, and temper coloured his cheeks. 'You know full well what I am referring to. You need to select a bride *and* decide on what we shall do with the border we share with the MacGregors. Any further delays only put us at more risk. Times are growing increasingly uncertain in these parts with the uprisings against the king and so many alliances in question.'

'Aye. I do, and I have,' Ewan said. He narrowed his gaze at the veiled reference to their fractured alliance with the Robertsons caused by his disobedience. As if he needed any reminders of how his decision had negatively impacted the clan.

They all stared back at him, awaiting more information. 'And?' Harris chimed in.

'It will be announced.'

'When?' Broden asked, leaning closer. 'When I am dead, my laird?'

The other two men chuckled at that. Ewan avoided the bait and quoted one of his father's most irritating and effective replies. 'When I am ready. I am laird, after all.'

Their laughter dwindled to nothing, and they were back to the awkward silence of moments ago.

Ewan offered them a scrap. 'But I will approve the repairs to the stone wall and add soldiers along the northern border with the MacGregors. We'll not lose one more head of livestock to them, nor will we allow them to cross into our lands to get to the loch after all that has happened. They have taken advantage of our kindness long enough. If they don't like our new arrangement, then MacGregor can come to me straight away, and we can form some more permanent understanding. Go ahead and speak with your men about it this eve, and have the plan set in motion on the morrow.'

Niven sat back in his chair, studying him. 'And the marriage?'

'As I said, when I am ready, all will be revealed, as the terms of the arrangement are still being settled.' Ewan should have known that a scrap would not be enough for the old man. He wanted all when he wanted it. Not a moment sooner or later. It was one of the reasons why Niven and Ewan's father got on so well: they understood each other.

Niven pushed once more. 'By end of summer?'

Ewan didn't dignify the man's overt challenge to his authority by answering.

'Perhaps we should move on to our next order of business,' Broden offered, attempting to guide them along. No doubt he noted the precarious territory they were meandering into and hoped to pull them from it before the men came to verbal blows.

'What business is that?' Ewan enquired, not aware of any additional matters to be addressed this morn.

Harris glanced over to Broden and shrugged. 'Might as well tell him. Ye brought it up.'

'There's talk of whether we'll be overrun. Driven out by the British. Or absorbed by another clan. The villagers are nervous. They think we don't have enough weapons or men to protect us from either.'

Ewan leaned forward, resting his elbows on the table. 'Well, is there any truth to their concerns? Do we have enough arms and soldiers to fend off an attack, if needed?'

Harris and Broden looked down at the table. When neither answered, Niven said, 'Nay, my laird, we don't.'

'Why not? Where has the money usually spent for such a purpose gone to?' Ewan asked. 'I've seen the ledgers. There is money still set aside for just that purpose, and there has been for years.'

''Tis not enough, and we have but two blacksmiths who are skilled enough to make such goods. The rest have not the experience as they are not far enough along in their training.'

'Well, send out word, quietly, about taking on more skilled blacksmiths to forge for us. We must have weapons.'

'And the soldiers?'

He hesitated. 'I'll not take on men for hire. 'Tis too great a risk. They have little to no loyalty to anything or anyone other than coin.'

For once, the men nodded with him in agreement. 'An alliance, perhaps?' Broden offered.

'That is an idea. I will think upon our options over the coming week.'

'Do not think upon it too long, my laird. This is not the Scotland of your childhood. We are more vulnerable than we've been in quite some time. All of us who wear a kilt are. The British are pressing in on us. 'Tis only a matter of time before they attempt to take all of it from us.'

As the new laird, Ewan was as vulnerable as the clan, and the older men knew it. 'I'll expect an update on the rock wall and the men who will be on guard in the coming days,' Ewan stated as he stood, the signal that their meeting was at an end whether they had additional issues to discuss or not. He needed to escape what he knew would turn into a fruitless debate over the old and new Scotland if the conversation continued any longer.

The other two stood, with Niven being the last to rise, his face brimming with the words his lips no doubt wanted to say. But to Ewan's surprise, he nodded and followed the other men out without protest. Perhaps the meeting had gone better than Ewan had thought.

As Niven had almost cleared the door, he paused and faced Ewan. 'We both know your father would not have hesitated at the thought of seeking out an alliance to protect us. I hope you know what you're doing, my laird. Our livelihood and lives depend upon it.'

Before Ewan could censure the man for his disrespect and challenge to his authority, he was gone. Ewan slammed his fist on the table and cursed. Before he did anything rash, he pushed his way through the side door that led to the glen. He closed his eyes and sucked in one greedy breath after another and assured himself as he often did that he could be laird. He didn't have to be his father. He could be his own man. No matter how treacherous the path was.

And by all that was holy, he would be his own man without driving the clan into chaos and ruin.

'How did your meeting go, my laird?'

Ewan opened his eyes to find Catriona standing almost next to him without having heard her approach at all. 'Blazes. You could give a man a start with such a stealthy approach. If you'd meant to kill me, I'd be dead.' He scratched the back of his neck and shook his head.

The wind ruffled her skirts and the rogue locks of hair escaping her plait, and she smiled. 'Stealth is one of my many talents. You learn to be quiet to avoid being found or being hurt.' Her eyes dropped away from his gaze and settled on the glen and the loch far beyond them.

His stomach knotted at all that remained hidden within her words.

Before he could reply, Rufus gave a rowdy bark below and charged up the hill. Ewan smiled. His favourite wolfhound must have spied him and decided it was time for a game of fetch. The large, grey, wiry hound barrelled into him and would have knocked Ewan flat if he hadn't bent his leg to brace for impact. The hound was still as playful as a pup despite being almost four years of age. Ewan scratched him behind his left ear, and Rufus's left leg thumped on the ground.

'This is Rufus, and this is his favourite spot to be scratched,' Ewan said to Catriona, who stared down at the hound in awe.

'I've never had a dog before.'

'He won't bite. Just put your closed hand down for him to sniff.'

She did just that, and Rufus answered her interest in him with a slobbery kiss on her hand. She laughed and squatted beside him. Rufus abandoned Ewan and leaned heavily on Catriona before swiping a kiss to her cheek. Her laughter trilled out in the air, and Ewan stilled. She was even more beautiful when she was happy.

His chest tightened. Had he made a mistake in bringing her here? What if he made her miserable? What if he couldn't protect her? What if—

He caught sight of the scars across so many of her knuckles and chided himself.

You saved her. You can protect her. You might even make her happy. She might even make you happy.

That last thought cooled his blood. He didn't know if he feared that the most. Happiness never seemed to last in the Highlands. And wasn't not having it better than having it and losing it like he had with Emogene?

'Pence for your thoughts,' she called as Rufus landed another rogue kiss to her cheek.

He cleared his throat. 'Just my meeting.' He *had* been thinking upon it earlier, so perhaps it wasn't a complete lie.

Yes, it was. He tucked his hands in the pockets of his trews.

'Perhaps a walk in this fresh air will clear your head,' she offered as she stood. 'You can tell me about this place, you, and how I can help you, since I am to…stay awhile.' She paused, and he noticed she had failed to say she would be 'staying awhile' as his wife.

As he wondered upon the reasoning, she interrupted his thoughts and asked, 'Unless you have changed your mind?'

He faltered. Had he changed his mind? Was this doubt over his decision seeping in, and she was offering him a gentleman's way out of their hasty arrangement? He met her steady, unwavering gaze, her eyes amber pools flecked with gold and tiny hints of moss green. How he wished he had such certainty, such sense of self. No matter his answer, she appeared accepting of whatever came her way. Could she teach him such?

'Nay,' he answered. 'I have not changed my mind. Have you?'

Doubt flashed in her eyes before she answered. 'I have not, but I am acutely aware of what I lack here. Thrice now Betsy has chided me for doing her work. I find I do not know what to do with myself without chores and tasks to do every moment, and I have been here a day.'

She shrugged and laughed. Her ease was contagious, and he found himself relaxing as they walked along the meadow.

'Perhaps you can busy yourself with learning the clarsach,' he teased.

She shivered. 'You and I both know that will take some time, and it may drive your servants running from Glenhaven.'

'Then, you can help me in securing my position here. You said you are a keen judge of people. Perhaps you can help me get somewhere with my most challenging and peevish of clansmen: the elders. That was who I just met with.'

'I'd be happy to try on all accounts. It shall keep me from enduring Betsy's chiding.' Rufus nudged her leg with a stick he'd clearly fetched from somewhere. She took it from him, ruffled his ears, and threw the stick a vast distance down the glen.

'Or perhaps I shall enter you in the Tournament of Champions and have you put the best of the eligible lairds to shame come fall,' he said. 'That was quite some throw.'

'Oh?' She lifted her eyebrows and shrugged. 'Just gave it a toss, that's all.'

So she was strong, hardworking, and humble. He'd add them to the list of mysteries he was set on solving about her.

'Tell me of these leaders, these elders, although I would love to meet them. Seeing them in person would tell me a great deal. Perhaps they could come to dine?'

Ack. 'Dinner. Aye. A fine idea. I can invite them later in the week, but before I forget, Brenna's fiancé, Laird Garrick MacLean, is coming to dine with us this eve. Bren reminded me of it this morn. How shall I introduce you?'

She stopped, quirked her lips, and crossed her arms against her chest. 'Do you know him well?'

'Aye.'

'And you like him and trust him?'

'Aye. He is the best of men.'

'Then just tell him the truth. It shall be easiest until all is sorted.'

'You will not be…embarrassed by me speaking such truths to him about what happened in the market?'

'The truth has never bothered me. It is the lies I cannot keep up with,' she offered. 'I look forward to meeting him.' And with that, he watched her set off once more. Little unsettled her, while nearly everything unsettled him. How did one get to be so at ease with oneself and the world?

She paused. 'Coming?' she asked, turning to him.

'Aye,' he answered and jogged to catch up with her, distinctly aware of the irony of him being laird and certain of little while she had nothing and was quite certain of everything. There was something about her calm that settled him almost as much as her beauty unsettled him. It was an odd, heady mix to be sure, and he didn't quite know what to do with it.

Rufus charged off and then looped back around them as they travelled along the glen side by side. The tall green grass leaned to and fro in the breeze, and off in the distance, men worked in their fields while children played in front of their cottages with their mothers not far away. The scene was idyllic in every sense. He soaked it in. *This* was what he was working so hard for, wasn't it? Perhaps he needed to remember that the meetings and manoeuvrings were for a better and greater purpose far more important than him and his happiness. Thousands of people depended on him.

'Tell me of your meeting this morn with the clan leaders.'

Her enquiry caught him off guard. 'Do you truly wish to know?'

'Aye. How else can I help you with knowing who your greatest supporters and challengers are to your position?'

He couldn't remember a time when Mother had asked Father of anything regarding his meetings with the clan or the elders, but perhaps she asked in private, far away from the ears of their children. What did he have to lose? They were to be married, were they not? A partnership was born of trust, not secrets. Life had taught him that lesson well.

'They wished to speak with me about two main issues. The first was my marriage, for they are eager for me to claim a wife and secure my footing as the new laird within the Highlands by establishing an heir. The second was about the border with the MacGregors.'

She paused and smiled, plucking a small purple nettle from the grass. 'Well, hopefully you were able to solve at least one of them.' She tucked it behind her ear, a simple action that reminded him of a time when Emogene had done just that very thing before she'd left him heartbroken for another man, never to be seen again.

Her smile faltered. 'What is it? You've gone as pale as a ghost.'

'I must go,' he said hurriedly. 'I just remembered there is somewhere else I need to be.'

'I understand. Go on then. I'll be fine.' Her brow furrowed as she shielded the sun from her eyes with her hand.

His heart raced, and he turned to leave. He had to get away. He couldn't breathe. He couldn't see anything other than his history of losing the things he'd cared for and loved. Losing his mother, losing Emogene... Was he beginning to care for Catriona too? What if he loved her and lost her?

He couldn't and he wouldn't. It was as simple as that.

Chapter Ten

'That was odd,' Catriona muttered to Rufus. She knelt in the grass to pet his floppy ears and wiry hair.

One thing was for certain. She *knew* people, but Catriona couldn't understand this Laird Stewart at all. One moment he was sincere and attentive, and the next he flitted off like a startled thrush. 'Shall we walk on, you handsome devil?' she asked the pup, and he yipped in agreement. She climbed and then descended into the lower valley, tempted to walk into the village to meet more of the clan and knowing full well what a horrid idea that was. How exactly would she introduce herself?

My name is Mrs Catriona Gordon. The Laird bought me at the market to be his wife.

She cringed and retraced her steps to return to the castle. Veering a little further to the forest, she spied what appeared to be a small graveyard, even though there was no chapel in sight. She climbed the remaining distance and edged over to the headstones. Most were quite old and slightly overgrown with moss and a smattering of wildflowers, but there was one that seemed recent, with a wide area of disturbed ground. She knew whose it was before she even looked upon the carved letters.

His father.

And beside him was his wife, Ewan's mother.

Catriona ran her fingertips over the curling script of the chiselled stone. They had spared no expense in the monument to the laird and his wife. The headstones were of the finest polished slate. Under Laird Stewart's name was the family crest, and beneath Lady Stewart's name was a beautifully engraved cross and harp. Catriona smiled. It warmed her heart to know that Ewan had been loved by such a woman, even if their time together had been cut short. Now Catriona's fingers trailed along her necklace, and she tugged the worn silver locket from her bosom. It was the one thing she had from her past. Although she could not place from whence she'd got it, she'd always had it, and it gave her great comfort each time she touched it. The design on the locket was worn away in some places from her own touch over the years. She'd used it as a worry stone and comfort when she had been frightened, alone, or desperate. She had felt that way quite often over the years since she'd been found along the shoreline by Nettie, with no memory of who she was or where she was from. She'd protected the necklace with her life and felt as connected to it as the air in the sky and the soil beneath her feet.

She tucked it back in her bodice and lifted her skirts as she began the walk back to the castle. Rufus had long since abandoned her on her journey. Far too many furry temptations abounded. Betsy waved to her as Catriona approached, and the young lass smiled until she spied the bottom of her dress. Following her gaze, Catriona looked down. Her beautiful dress was stained all along the hemline from her exploits through the meadow, as were her walking boots.

She cringed. 'I will help you set them to rights,' Catriona offered. 'I should have been more careful. I'm not used to having to worry upon ruining my clothes. There wasn't much to ruin in the past.' Her cheeks warmed.

'No harm done,' Betsy replied. 'I have mended far worse than this. Let us get ye back inside and changed before the laird sees ye.'

Catriona stiffened. 'Why? Will he be angry?'

The man hadn't seemed the type to be concerned with such trifles, but she didn't know him. Not really.

Betsy paused, studying her. 'Nay. I did not mean to alarm ye. He is a good man and not prone to fits of temper like his father was.'

Catriona still didn't move. 'You are sure? I don't wish you to be in trouble either.'

Betsy grasped her forearm. 'Nay,' she assured her. 'There is no cause for alarm. Let us get ye inside and changed.'

Catriona nodded and followed the maid, her heart still thrumming in her chest. It would be hard to unlearn the fear that could spike within her at the slightest hint of displeasing whatever authority loomed over her. It mattered not if it was an employer or a husband. The fear of being hit or chided as she had been in the past brought out the wee lass in her, and once she was out, it was quite hard to settle her down.

Pulling in a breath, she reminded herself that she was safe with a man who seemed kind and in a place that could offer her more than she had ever dreamed possible. While not free, she would have more freedoms than before and experience new things each day. Chores would not fill all her waking hours. The exploration of interests would mark her days. She might even discover other facets of herself never allowed to emerge. She could be one of the butterflies she was always so intrigued by and emerge from a cocoon into something spectacular.

Her boot sank into a glob of mud.

Or things might be the same.

But one thing was for certain. She'd never find out if she didn't go inside and change.

She'd also never know the truth about the laird's past if she didn't enquire. She fell into stride next to Betsy as they climbed the final hill to the castle door.

'Has the laird been married before?' Catriona asked.

Betsy's pace hitched for a mere moment, and then she continued on. 'Nay, my lady.'

She quirked her lips. He sure acted like a man spurned. 'A broken engagement, perhaps?'

Betsy walked a step closer and opened the door. 'Not here,' she whispered. 'May I take your shoes?' she asked in a normal voice as a footman passed. Catriona bent down to assist her in removing them.

The servant turned the corner. 'Is it a secret?' she asked.

The worry in the young maid's eyes sent Catriona's heart aflutter. The lass shook her head. Catriona's heart dropped. Had something scandalous happened? Was the laird cruel after all?

Betsy grabbed Catriona's shoes and continued. Catriona followed her in her stocking feet. By the time they reached her chamber and sealed the door shut behind them, Catriona had crafted a story in her mind of Laird Stewart as a murderer and a cheat.

'And?' Catriona asked.

'Let us get ye out of this first,' Betsy began to undo the column of buttons down Catriona's back.

'Betsy, by all that is holy, you must tell me. I need know the man I am to marry before I commit to him.'

Betsy froze. 'Are ye not already married, Mrs Gordon?'

Catriona cringed. *Blast.* Silence ticked by, and then she sighed. 'You must tell no one, you promise me?' she pleaded and faced her maid.

Betsy nodded with her hands still mid-air. 'Aye.'

'The laird purchased me at the Grassmarket. My husband sold me to him.'

'What?' she asked. 'A man cannot sell or buy a wife. 'Tis not legal,' she argued, crossing her arms against her chest. She seemed full of outrage and disbelief, much like Catriona had felt.

'That is what we are trying to find out. Until then, I will remain here.' She left out the part about them marrying in hopes Betsy might conveniently forget that piece of information.

The maid narrowed her eyes at her. 'But ye just said, "But I need to know the man I am to marry *before* I commit to him." One cannot marry a man if ye are already married…can ye?'

'Ugh…' Catriona groaned and hid her face in her hands. 'Nay. One cannot marry again if one is still married, but we do not know if this transaction in the marketplace was even legal. I had planned to run last night to free myself and him from this conundrum, but he asked me to stay. Proposed to me, even. I need to know why. Why would a laird such as him propose to me? It makes little sense. He is handsome, young, and seems quite normal by all accounts. Don't you agree?'

Betsy seemed struck dumb and said nothing for a few moments. She then closed her gaping mouth and sputtered out a reply. 'I agree. It makes no sense to me, my lady. The fathers have been all but parading their daughters by him, and the laird has been tasked with accepting one of them by the end of the month. He has many options other than…'

Thank goodness the lass stopped short of adding *you* on the end of the sentence, to spare Catriona some of her pride.

'So that is why I must know what has happened to him that would make him choose me: a woman he does not know, with no family, money, or title. What would make him do such?'

'Loss.'

Her answer was simple and landed heavily on Catriona's heart.

'Loss? What kind of loss? His mother? He told me of that.'

Betsy returned to unbuttoning Catriona's dress and

continued. 'It all happened about six years ago when I was a teen and living with my parents in the village. The laird was engaged to the most beautiful lass in the clan: Emogene.'

Catriona held her breath.

'But the engagement came at a great cost. Ewan was supposed to marry Laird Robertson's daughter. When Ewan went against the arrangement and his father's orders by becoming engaged to Emogene, it fractured the alliance between our two clans, and Ewan was close to blows with his father. It brought great shame upon him, the family, and the clan. Then, weeks before Ewan and Emogene were set to marry, she ran off and married a Sutherland who had greater wealth and power.'

Catriona gasped. 'So he was left with no wife and with the knowledge that he had harmed his clan's future?'

'Aye. It was horrible.'

'What happened to Ewan?' Catriona's chest ached.

'When he realised what she'd done, he didn't speak for days, and then disappeared for several weeks. When he returned, he never spoke of her again and raged at anyone who dared say her name. She became a ghost after that. Many say so did he.'

'He doesn't seem a ghost now.'

She shrugged. 'Perhaps not, but is he really living either? I've heard the stories of him swearing off love and attachments.'

The lass's words hit Catriona like an arrow hitting its mark. 'Aye. That is true. It is one of the reasons he said we'd make such a fine match.'

'Oh?' Betsy asked. 'Why is that?'

'Because he does not know me or care for me at all. And he wishes to keep it that way.'

Chapter Eleven

'Mrs Gordon is quite lovely and an unexpected surprise this eve,' Garrick offered as he approached Ewan, who stood near the mantel of the large, empty fireplace off the dining room.

Ewan sipped from his tankard, uncertain.

Garrick nodded towards the two women. 'Even Bren seems taken with her, which is quite a feat, as you well know.' His friend chuckled, as Bren was known to be devilishly hard on other women and took on new female friends like oil took on water, which was rarely.

'Aye,' Ewan dared. The two ladies sat on the settee chatting, which was really Bren rattling on about her wedding and Catriona listening attentively.

'Care to tell me what the devil is going on?'

It was Ewan's turn to laugh. His friend's directness was as sharp as a dirk, but well intended. The man wasn't capable of cruelty, just as Ewan seemed incapable of certainty. He risked taking Catriona's advice and telling him the truth.

'The day before yesterday, when I took Bren into

Edinburgh for a dress fitting and to visit her favourite milliner, I bought Mrs Gordon in the Grassmarket.'

Garrick stared at him.

'It is a fine situation that leaves you speechless, MacLean.'

Garrick shook his head and stuttered out a reply. 'Sorry, did you say bought?'

His face heated. 'It was the better of two horrid options.' He shifted on his feet and gestured for Garrick to follow him outside. His friend sent a glance back in the ladies' direction and then followed him out of doors.

'I was wandering about the market looking upon the wares when I heard a man calling out that he was selling his wife. There were even handing out broadsides with the announcement, if you can believe it.'

'Just when I thought I'd heard all things,' Garrick replied, pinching the bridge of his nose.

'At first, I thought it a farce, but then when I walked through the crowd and saw her there—' his throat tightened '—bound in a harness like some bloody animal, I couldn't think straight. And then, when Dallan MacGregor chimed in to buy her for even less than her arse of a husband was offering, I just reacted. I offered to buy her for the full price, to save her. All I could think of was... Moira.'

'Ewan,' Garrick began, his eyes softening in sympathy, 'you cannot blame yourself.'

'Actually, I can,' he answered. 'If I'd paid more attention and been less distracted by my own affairs, I might have noticed what was happening to her. But since I didn't, and because I cannot unwind the past, when I saw Mrs Gordon in such distress and knowing worse could happen to her if MacGregor got a hold of her, I couldn't let it be. I gave her husband a guinea and hustled her out of there before the sot could change his mind.'

'You bought her for a guinea?' Garrick asked in disbelief.

'Aye. I'd like to think I merely freed her for a guinea. And it seemed her husband, Mr Gordon, would have taken less.'

'Lord above,' Garrick murmured.

'Aye.'

'And your plan now?' Garrick asked before taking a drink from his cup.

'I sent word to my solicitor to enquire over whether any of it was legal, as the broadside stated that by buying her she would instantly become my wife, which I cannot imagine to be true. Receiving the answer will take time. She will stay here until that is sorted.' He hesitated.

'And?'

'And I asked her to marry me when we know for certain that she is free of Mr Gordon.'

Garrick coughed, almost spitting out his wine. 'What?'

'You heard me. I mean to take her as my wife.' An unspoken challenge rested in the sharp edge of his voice even though it wasn't what he intended.

Garrick held up his hands. 'She is beautiful and quite charming, but you do not *know* her. You do not even know if what you did was legal or if she can even divorce this Mr Gordon.' He stepped closer and dropped his voice. 'And selecting a wife outside of the clan is sure to cause you more harm than good.'

Ewan dragged a palm down his face. 'Of course. I *know* that,' he replied, 'but I also know I'll make enemies with any bride I choose within the clan. Even now they jostle for power, biding their time while hoping for my failure.' He drank the last of his tankard. 'What would you do?'

Garrick chuckled. 'You mean if I still had a clan to rule?'

Deuces. Ewan cringed. 'You know that isn't what I meant. And you and I both know you will have your clan assembled once more and Westmoreland returned to rights. It will merely take time and patience.'

Garrick smiled good-naturedly. 'Aye. I do know. And I have plenty of both these days. But why do you not take your own advice and be patient with yourself as you get settled in as the new laird? You cannot expect it to fall into place in only a few months.'

'Time is not something I can afford to waste. All the Highland lairds as well as the leaders within our clan are watching my every move, and the MacGregors continue to breach our borders and steal from our herds. The elders complain that I do not make decisions fast enough, and I worry that I will make them too quickly and make a costly misstep. Why did no one tell me being a laird is an impossible task? No one is ever happy.'

'Were you expecting to be adored?' Garrick asked.

'Aye.' Ewan chuckled. 'I was hoping to be.'

'So, now that you really know what it is like to be laird, what is your plan?' Garrick asked. 'You cannot mean to take this woman to be your wife when you do not know her. She could be a criminal for all you know.'

'A criminal?' Ewan asked, frowning at his friend and gesturing towards Catriona, who was cooing to Rufus and ruffling the hound's ears. The woman had convinced him to let the dog in after they dined. 'Perhaps a touch persuasive, but that is no crime.'

Garrick's gaze followed Ewan's to the ladies.

'You think that woman is a mastermind trying to overthrow the clan with subterfuge and intrigue? Is her crime spoiling my hound?'

Garrick conceded. 'Perhaps not, but what do you know of her? You don't even know if she will be *able* to marry you legally. All I'm suggesting is not to rush into a betrothal. Why don't you at least have a trial of time together before either of you commits to each other for the rest of your lives? Those seem the fairest terms for both of you, especially if her past marriage has been as difficult as it appears.'

Hmm... 'Like a trial marriage?' His gaze skimmed over Catriona's petite features as her head tilted back with laughter at something Brenna had said.

'Of sorts.'

Ewan paused. His friend might very well be onto a fine suggestion. 'That's not the most ridiculous idea I've ever heard. Perhaps we could see how it goes, and if I don't find that I wish to become her husband and she my wife, say in a fortnight's time or until we hear back from the solicitor, we will dissolve our agreement and be free of one another.'

'And if you do decide you want her to be your wife?' Garrick asked with a smirk.

'Then perhaps I will become a married man before you are, Garrick MacLean.'

'Remember, she would have to choose you willingly as well.'

'In that case, you may well beat me to the altar after all.'

Chapter Twelve

Catriona hummed as she walked down the hallway to her chambers, her belly rather full of another lovely dinner. She glanced behind and, noting the hallway was empty, she tugged off her slippers and stockings. When her bare feet touched the cool, clean floor, she sighed, rolling the balls of her feet and her toes. She felt so carefree and happy, just like that girl on the beach laughing with the sun warming her face and the sand between her toes.

She twirled once and then twice down the hallway, her skirts flying freely and lifting in the air, exposing her ankles. She chuckled aloud and hummed one of her favourite tunes as if she were dancing in a ball with a handsome laird.

'Mrs Gordon?'

Blazes.

She stumbled to a stop and turned, hiding her shoes and stockings behind her back. 'Aye, my laird?' She blew an errant lock of hair from her eyes. Blasted useless hairpins.

Ewan cleared his throat, his gaze wandering over her face and then drifting down to her bare feet. She flushed. He wasn't immediately able to continue, his gaze lingering on her toes so long that she looked down to ensure her feet hadn't turned into flippers.

'My laird?' she asked again, feeling awkward and self-conscious.

He shifted on his feet, her words yanking him back from wherever he'd gone. 'I wish to have a word with you about what we discussed last night. Discuss some new terms of our arrangement. Do you have a moment?'

Her pulse thrummed. There was something in the way he said the words that made worry skitter along her spine. He'd changed his mind about something. Perhaps it was about her? Had his friend, Laird MacLean, told him how unreasonable and ridiculous it was to marry her? Did he finally see the fault in such a scheme? Would he cast her out this eve? Despite having wished to escape the night before, worry about doing just that bubbled up in her now.

Why?

If he offered her freedom, wasn't that exactly what she had wanted? Why would she not wish to leave now? Before she could answer that, she felt herself nodding her head as if she were no longer attached to or controlling her body. Instinct was setting in, a survival tool she had harnessed well over the years. While part of her was present, the other part was scheming and seeking out a way to escape. It was a facet of her she couldn't turn off, not yet at least.

'Would you like to put your shoes back on? I thought

we'd step outside since the weather is so fine this eve and you enjoy the stars.'

'Or you could take your shoes off as well, my laird? It is such fine weather, as you have just stated.' Her voice held defiance. What had come over her? The words had tumbled from her mouth unbidden, as if they had escaped of their own free will. She was in no position to defy him about anything, yet here she was, doing just that. Disbelief registered in his eyes.

When his lip quirked up and his rogue dimple winked at her in answer, she almost giggled aloud. 'Is that a challenge, Mrs Gordon?'

She pressed her lips together to hold back her laughter once more. 'Aye, my laird, it is. What say you?' She tilted her head, brought her shoes from behind her back and clacked the heels together.

He chuffed off one boot, then another, followed by his own stockings. The sight of his muscular calves and large bare feet sent a thrill of attraction through her. He was such a handsome creature. The light sparkled off his eyes as he lifted his boots and clacked the heels together in answer. 'I say you have a deal, Mrs Gordon.'

She couldn't have been more enthralled by a man as she was in that very moment. She had cast a test, and he'd answered in kind. Her pulse increased, and she smiled.

'Care to expand it to a wager?' he asked.

She stepped closer, and then dared another step, her gaze slipping down to his glorious legs and feet once more. 'Aye. First one to the grass gets a wish from the other.'

'You're on,' he answered. 'I'll even give you a head start.'

'I shan't need it, my laird,' she chided, but then darted off.

He counted to five and gave chase. The man was fleet of foot and quickly gained on her as they rushed along the main corridor. She banked right and then a final left. She could see the doors to the outside, just as she could hear the slapping of the soles of his bare feet along the floor behind her as they passed the last lit torch before the outdoors. As she slowed to reach the handle and open the door, he reached her, and together they flew out through the doors at the same time. Unable to slow her speed, she tumbled down part of the hill. She skidded to a stop on her backside and laughed aloud with glee. A laugh so pure and full that her stomach ached. She had not laughed so hard in ages.

Ewan slid down the grass and stopped next to her, a smile on his face. 'Are you harmed?' he asked, out of breath. He brushed the hair from her eyes, and his fingertips lingered along her cheek. His expression held the slightest uncertainty, a veiled concern for her safety.

She grasped his hand and squeezed. 'I am fine. However, Betsy may become apoplectic when she sees I have stained yet another lovely gown today.' She cringed.

''Tis no matter,' he answered, sitting down beside her in the cool, lush grass.

She flopped back into the lawn, revelling in the cool, crisp smell of the field, the dark sky with its perfect stars, and feeling so free. Freer than she had ever felt. While she knew she was still bound to another man, the realisation of it did not sting her, for this man made her *feel* free.

Ewan stared down at her in silence, his gaze holding an answer and a question all at once, which seemed to be the way of him.

'What?' she asked.

'You are definitely not the woman I expected when I first saw you.'

'Did you even see me?' she challenged.

He shook his head. 'Not really. Nay. I didn't. I couldn't see anything. I just reacted.'

'Why?' she countered, wanting to know the truth. 'Why risk getting involved? You saw how many men walked by and did nothing. Why did you step in as you did?' She propped herself up on her elbow. She'd wanted to know the answer for days.

He hesitated. His eyes beat back and forth, searching hers, but for what? Acceptance? The truth? Certainty?

'Because of what happened to my eldest sister, Moira,' he said. He looked away and stared back up at the sky. 'Her first husband was cruel. He hurt her...' He paused, a muscle flexing in his jaw. 'And we did not know what was happening, how he abused her, until he was dead. I've always wished I'd paid more attention, known what was happening, so I could have stopped it as a brother should. I promised myself that if I ever saw anything like that occur again, I would step in.'

He faced her then, studying her, assessing her response.

'I am so very sorry that happened to her. Is she cared for now?' she asked, her throat tight.

He smiled. 'Aye. She is remarried to a kind, good man who cares for her and protects her and their children.' His smile deepened. 'You would like one another; I am sure of it.'

'I'm sure we would.'

His brow creased. 'May I ask… How did you end up with him, your husband, I mean?'

She cleared her throat and released a breath preparing to tell him of her past, since he had just shared about his sister.

'Well, Nettie cared for me for several years after she found me along the shore, but she died when I was thirteen, and I had no one to care for me. A family took me in on Lismore, and at first, all was well. I helped care for their children, did chores, and I thought about how lucky I was to find another kind family to care for me.' She paused. 'But then one night, the father had far too much to drink and lost his temper, hitting his wife and then one of his children. After that, I used to bait him when he was angry, so that if he was to lash anyone, than it would be me rather than them. I did not want to see the children hurt. They were so small.'

He reached out and took her hand, squeezing it briefly before letting go. 'I am so sorry, Catriona. That was an incredibly brave thing to do, especially for a young girl.'

She shrugged. 'Like you, I did not think about it, but merely reacted. When I told a neighbour what was happening, she helped to secure me a position with a wealthy family, the Chisholms, in a neighbouring village. I worked as a servant, and there I learned to read and write. Although I often sent back money to that family to help them, I always worried about what was happening there. The neighbour promised to look after them, but… And one day I met Thomas at the market while I was picking up the Chisholm children's new clothes. I thought he was my chance to have a family and be happy, but I was wrong.'

'I am glad you are here now,' he replied.

'I am grateful that you brought me here.' And she was. Attraction was buzzing through her.

'What do I get as my prize, since I did win our foot race?' She grinned at him.

He flopped back in the grass. 'It was a tie.'

'How on earth could that possibly be a tie, when I touched the doorknob first?'

He propped himself back up on his elbow to answer. 'Because without me turning the handle and pushing it open, we would have slammed into the door stacked upon each other in a quite unceremonious way.'

She blushed at the thought of how intimate such a scene might have been. A small part of her wished just that very thing had happened, and she chided herself. *Fool.* She needed to focus on the purpose of their talk: to discuss the terms of their agreement. Not to get caught up in a fairy tale of falling in love with a laird, especially when love was never to be part of their arrangement, if indeed there was still one. Perhaps his whole point of speaking with her was to cast aside their agreement all together?

He brushed aside his hair from his face, the subtle

action making her wish it was she who'd had such a familiar touch along his forehead.

Blazes. Get hold of yourself, Catriona.

She needed to stop looking upon him. Letting herself fall back in the grass, she sighed and closed her eyes. That was much better.

'Catriona?' he asked, leaning over her, his handsome face even closer than before, his brow stitched with concern. 'Are you unwell?'

She sucked in a breath. 'Nay. I am fine. Merely looking upon the stars, which you are now blocking.'

His face slipped back into its familiar mask, and he moved, settling into the grass beside her.

She cringed. She hadn't meant to sound so harsh, but she needed to get him away from her somehow. Her fingers itched to touch him, which was altogether ridiculous. She hardly knew him.

Deuces.

Ewan frowned, interlocking his fingers behind his head to prop it up. He could not remember when he'd last lain in the grass like this and felt so free and alive. And with a woman as beautiful and glorious as Catriona? *Never.*

He could not imagine a woman who would be so at ease lying in a field at night next to an unfamiliar man. And he'd mucked it up. Badly. That look on her face spoke far more than her words ever could.

What had he done to cause such a shift in her mood?

Perhaps he'd moved too close or asked too many prying questions. He would need to be far more careful in

the future if he intended to make her his bride, which
he did. The more unplanned moments he spent with her,
the more he craved to know every part of her. When
he'd heard her laugh earlier, it felt like air spilling into
his lungs and as if the ground was shaking under his
feet. A sickness roiled through his stomach, warning
him of the danger ahead.

Ack. He had to be careful.

This was a truly ridiculous feeling that he had to
keep at bay. He was treading in a field of thistles barefoot and hoping not to get barbed.

Nay. He would not fall in love with her; it was a ruin
he had scarce survived once with Emogene, and he had
promised himself never to swim into such deadly waters again. Loving and losing Emogene had broken him,
and he wasn't sure if he'd ever been put together rightly
since then. His heart was jagged edges and pock marks.

But it didn't mean that he couldn't enjoy Catriona's
company. He could care for her as any good man would
care for a wife. Without giving over his heart, he could
revel in the long dormant passion and desire that she
had awakened in him. But first, he needed to seal their
new terms. For as much as he did believe she was right
for him, he needed to be sure. And he also wanted her
to have the option to choose him as well. This trial marriage, if one could call it that, would protect them both,
and from what he had just learned about her past, the
woman deserved protecting.

Being a laird's wife was about as precarious as being
the laird himself. Not only would she have to manage
him and all his foibles, but also the ever-shifting po-

litical ground beneath their feet, all while raising their children. The woman also deserved to make the choice for herself, a far greater gift than his sisters had ever had when Father had secured their dreadful first matches. Both had been disastrous, with his sisters scarcely surviving with their lives. Ewan wanted his marriage to benefit him and his bride.

'Shall we talk of your new terms, my laird?' she asked, her words snatching him back from his own thoughts and to the matter at hand. Despite being beside him, she sounded far away, her voice small and brittle, as if she stood in the valley below, calling up to the hillside.

'Aye. Laird MacLean had a great suggestion that I think will benefit us both.'

'Oh? I am surprised he did not disapprove entirely of our plan.' A touch of mirth entered her voice, and he smiled.

'Nay. Garrick is a good and thoughtful man with the sound, steady reason of a soldier seasoned by battle and loss.'

'Hmm. That makes sense to me now. There is loss in his eyes when he thinks no one is watching.'

Catriona's words cut Ewan to the quick, and he held his breath for a beat, gathering himself before answering. '*That* is the type of awareness that cannot be taught. It is such that I wish for you to teach me as my wife.'

'Do you not have men who advise you? Men you trust who serve you and your best interests first and foremost?' She propped up on her elbow once more, and he dared to do the same.

Did he?

'I have men who were loyal to my father who now serve me, but I do not believe that is the same.'

'Then why have you not pulled men you trust into your ranks and replaced the others? You are laird. You can do anything you wish, can you not?' Her brow furrowed. She studied him and shrugged. 'Or perhaps it is not so simple?'

'Aye. It is and isn't.' He plucked a wildflower from the grass and handed it to her. The bloom was closed for the eve but would open full in the morn. Just as he hoped she would open up to him over time.

She chuckled. 'You sound like a laird, but what do *you*, Ewan Stewart, mean by such an answer?'

What did he mean?

His heart beat feverishly in his chest. *This* was what he didn't want her to know: his weakness. He didn't know how to be laird. He didn't even know how to express his own opinion. For so long he'd been under the thumb of his father. How could he learn to trust his own mind, especially when he'd made such bad decisions before?

'Ewan?'

'I do not wish to change too much too quickly. Especially when there is such discord in the ranks after Father's passing.'

'Discord?' she asked. 'They cannot challenge you, for you are the son of the laird. Why would there be discord?'

'Aye. Only some of the conflict comes from my rule. Edinburgh has not been touched by the hand of the

British in the unrest as we have been in the Highlands. Clans have been absorbed and disappeared. Driven from their homes. Murdered for their lands. I must protect us from being absorbed by more powerful clans and attempt to keep my people happy. What I wish is not always part of that.'

'I suppose that makes sense.' She studied him, her eyes glinting in the moonlight. Her face as soft, smooth, and brilliant as the flower she held and twirled in her fingers.

He cleared his throat. It was now or never. 'So, my revised proposal would be that we allow each other a fortnight or until we hear from the solicitor, whichever comes first, to get to know each other and see if a marriage between us could suit us or not. During that time, you could see how comfortable you felt about the idea of being my wife. You could observe my duties and what it would mean for you to be the wife of a laird. You could also observe and report back to me your thoughts on the men and women of the clan and whom you think I should bring into my inner circle to keep our clan safe, prosperous, and thriving with me at the helm of it. You could teach me how to know and understand the motives, happiness, and dissatisfaction of those around me better than I do now. Many of them are as well-versed in deception as you are in observation and knowing people.'

'And you wish to be as well?'

'Nay. Not in being deceptive, but in being able to recognise it in others.'

'That is your new term?'

'Nay, just part of it. The other is that if we decide we do not wish to become husband and wife, then we will part and move on with our own lives without any additional explanation needed.'

Her eyes widened. 'And if I decided to leave? You would not be angry with me?' Doubt rested in her eyes as if she herself did not believe the words he said.

He nodded. 'I will send you on to the destination of your choice in my own carriage with your allowance as well as any personal items you wish to keep from your stay. You could start your own life, and I would not stop you.'

There was a small hitch in his voice, which surprised him, but he cleared his throat and continued. 'By then, we should also know if your marriage to Mr Gordon or my…agreement with him in purchasing you as a wife is legally binding or not.'

'And what shall you tell everyone, my laird? Surely it would seem odd to have a woman here for such an extended stay without reason?'

She made a solid point. 'Perhaps you are a cousin?' he said. 'Or a friend of an acquaintance?'

'A dead one, I hope. Otherwise, how will I answer all their questions about why I'm unchaperoned?'

'Perhaps I could enlist Laird MacLean to claim you as a distant cousin, since he is in on our ruse anyway.'

She tilted her head back and forth, seeming to ponder such a possibility. 'That could work. Do you think he would agree to it?'

'Aye. I think he would. He is to be my brother-in-law,

after all. We will be keeping each other's secrets from here on out for the rest of our lives.'

'But do you think he will keep mine, even if I choose to leave?'

The idea of her leaving sent an odd current of alarm through his limbs, but he ignored it. 'As I said before, you cannot find a better man. He would keep your secret to protect your honour and your future.'

'Then, I believe, Laird Stewart, we have a renewed agreement.' She sat up and narrowed her gaze at him. 'But there are still the terms of the wager I won earlier to be settled.'

He laughed and sat up as well. 'Terms?'

'You said the winner could have one thing they wished.'

'And here I thought we had agreed that we had both won.'

'I still claim victory. Do you call me a liar? Shall this be our first disagreement as pretend husband and wife?' She crossed her arms against her chest and gave him a playful glare of disapproval.

'Perhaps. For I claim we could never have reached the outside without me helping you open the door.'

She held his gaze undeterred. Her fire and resolve to claim her prize only fanned the flames of his budding interest and attraction to her. 'Then we may be at an impasse, my laird.'

'May I suggest a truce?' he said. 'What if we both claim victory and both are allowed a prize? Would that suit you?'

'While I would prefer to claim the victory as my own,

I could be persuaded to allow a joint victory this one time. What is it you wish to claim, my laird?'

You.

The answer hit him hot and full in his gut. The desire for her seared through him as if he had touched a blacksmith's iron without a glove. He swallowed that answer away, but not before his gaze fell and lingered upon her lips.

Her eyes widened, but she recovered from her alarm, squaring her shoulders and schooling her features. She was no fool as to what he wanted, so he decided not to attempt to disguise it. He risked the truth—well, at least part of it. 'A kiss,' he stated.

She shifted on the grass and nodded. 'All right, then.'

Her ready agreement shocked him, but he recovered. 'And yours? What is it you require of me for your prize?'

'A secret.'

He watched her, awaiting more.

'Tell me of the woman who broke your heart. Tell me of Emogene.' Her eyes held his, unflinching and powerful in their demand.

He clenched his fists by his sides. How dare she ask something so impossible, so personal, and so infuriating?

'What you ask I cannot give you.' He stood and brushed off his trews. 'I shall take my leave.' He began to walk away, but she called to him.

'And that, my laird, is what shall cost you in the end. You cannot allow anyone to know your weaknesses.'

'Oh? Does it not work both ways, Mrs Gordon? For you have also just shown me yours.'

* * *

'What?' she asked, but he continued walking without answering. She stood and rushed after him, a bud of anger tightening in her chest. 'I have revealed nothing to you. I merely challenged your past.'

He whipped around, his figure towering over her. His eyes were heated and wild in a way she had never seen, and his hair ruffled in the breeze. 'Nay. You have done far more than that. You have taken your finger and stuck it into an open wound on purpose. Why?' He took a step, and even though they weren't touching, she could feel the heat of his body. 'Because you don't wish for me to kiss you?'

She fought the urge to take one more step and set her hands upon his chest, curious to feel what was sure to be rippling muscle beneath. For as much as she was loath to admit it, she feared his touch. Not that he might hurt her, but that she might like it far too much. 'Aye,' she answered in reply.

'Why?' he asked. 'You came willingly with me out of doors in the night, and I have done nothing to make you fear me. I am not the sort of man to take advantage. If I was, I would have already. You insult me by suggesting as much, especially after all I have confessed to you about my sister.' Hurt registered in his features, which intrigued her. It was as if being feared as a danger to women was more of an insult than being inept as laird.

'Because I do not trust myself,' she answered, taking another step and resting her palm against his chest, savouring the warmth beneath his thin tunic.

He sucked in a breath. 'Do you tease me, Mrs Gordon? I fear I do not understand you. You do not wish for me to kiss you because you do not trust yourself, not because you fear me?'

'Aye. That is exactly why.'

'Then perhaps you should take your hand off my chest and stop looking at me that way. Otherwise, I *will* have to kiss you.'

'Then maybe you should.'

'Which is more reason why I shouldn't, for I cannot fulfil my end of the bargain by answering your enquiry, can I? And the last thing I wish is to appear an untrustworthy mate,' he quipped, the harsh snap to his words reflective of his anger. He stepped back, and her hand fell away. 'Until tomorrow, Mrs Gordon.'

He turned and left her in the field, his dark form disappearing into the backdrop of the sky. What she had hoped might give her an upper hand in their arrangement had just set her back twofold. For now, she did not know if he could ever get over his hurt regarding Emogene. Also, he knew she found him attractive. He could use both as a weapon to bring her to her knees.

She smiled. But perhaps so could she.

Chapter Thirteen

The next morning, Catriona found herself practicing the clarsach with little success. Her irritation over her current failings with the instrument and frustrations from her encounter the night before with Ewan threatened to drive her mad. The man seemed determined to avoid her this morn, having broken his fast well before dawn, according to Mrs Stevens. Brenna had yet to rise, so Catriona had eaten alone. The day was spinning into one irritation after another. She plucked another series of strings and cringed. Perhaps she should just leave the estate and the laird while she could before the two weeks were out. She wasn't meant to be idle. Nettie had taught her at a young age how the mundane routine of physical labour and chores could be used to ease worry from her body. Catriona's body and mind were used to such work through her servitude at the Chisholms' home and years of marriage. Despite how she had long wished to have time to explore other interests, now she wasn't sure, especially with so much restless energy churning through her body. A handful of days into her so called new life and 'freedom', and she was almost bored to tears.

'Mrs Gordon, the laird has need of ye,' Betsy called from the doorway of the salon as if she were an angel sent from the heavens to spare Catriona from her struggles.

And the idea of Ewan summoning her in any way made Catriona smile. Perhaps he was not as angry with her after their encounter last night as she had feared. At least, she hoped that was the reason for such a request. She'd find out soon enough, wouldn't she?

'Thank you, Betsy. You have saved me from further frustration.' Catriona rose and followed the maid through the castle. When they passed the laird's study and continued down another corridor unknown to her, uncertainty surfaced. 'Where am I meeting the laird?' Catriona whispered. 'I have never been this way before. What is down here?'

When Betsy said nothing but quickened her pace, Catriona picked up her skirts and hustled up to the maid's side. 'Where are we going?' she whispered to the lass.

Betsy glanced over to her. 'The laird bade me bring ye out this side of the castle. He did not say why.'

'And as the maid, you did not ask.'

'Aye. It is never my business to question his orders, my lady.'

Betsy stopped at the last door on the hallway. 'He said ye were to leave through this door and follow the tunnel to the end, and that I was not to accompany ye.'

'Did you say a tunnel was connected to the castle?'

'Aye. On this one portion. Built as an escape when needed.'

Was it needed today? And if so, why? Questions spooled in her mind, but she dared not ask. No doubt, the more questions the young maid answered, the more questions Catriona would have.

'Thank you, Betsy. I will see you later this afternoon to dress for dinner.'

She hoped.

'Aye. Enjoy your journey.'

Journey?

Before Catriona could gather some clarification on what 'journey' Betsy referenced, the maid curtseyed and left Catriona in the corridor. There were no windows near the doorway, so she wasn't sure exactly where she was or where this supposed tunnel would lead. Unease sidled up to her as she nudged the door open a sliver. But what choice did she have? She had no idea where she was, and Betsy was gone.

Blast.

She pushed the door completely open. It was a tunnel as promised and a dark one at that. If not for the wall torches burning brightly at regular intervals, she would not have been able to travel more than a step at a time for fear of tripping over her own feet. The door closed behind her, and she grabbed for the handle. She tugged, but it didn't budge.

Drat.

Forward it was, then. It was lucky she wasn't scared of the dark or confined spaces. Otherwise, she might have screamed. She started her journey, slowly and with caution. Despite being so hidden, the tunnel appeared carved from rock or part of a mountain. It was also quite wide. Two people could walk side by side as they travelled. Perhaps Ewan hadn't sent her to an early demise after all. Knowing that helped her relax. She studied the tunnel as she walked, running her hand down the cool, hard walls, carved with care and worn from use. The soles of her boots gripped the sloping ground as she travelled deeper before making a slow rise back up. Soon an opening appeared in the distance. The glow of light became brighter and brighter as the tunnel sloped downward once more. At the end of it, she squinted. Her eyes adjusted, and she stood stunned. She was at the mouth of a cave. Before her was a lush green valley and running further along was a stream. She stepped out and stared around her, shifting her attention high atop the meadow that rose to her east. Glenhaven stood tall and proud before her in the distance, and the valley she had spied yesterday stood just beyond her below. Animals roamed and grazed the hillside in the distance, and small cottages dotted the landscape. It was breathtaking.

'I see you made it.'

Ewan.

Catriona whipped around and saw Laird Stewart standing behind her. 'Where did you come from?' she asked, scanning the area.

He pointed to an outcropping. 'Just beyond the rocks. Since I missed giving you a tour yesterday, I thought we'd go for a ride today, so I can show you the lands under my care. I thought it might help you to see what a laird does and therefore what his wife might also be responsible for.'

Ack.

She hesitated and pulled at her fingertips. While she expected it would come up at some point, she did not know it would be today. 'I do not ride, my laird.'

He balked, his eyes widening. 'You do not like to ride?' he asked, disbelief in his tone.

'Nay. Well, I do not know if I like to ride or not. I never learned.' Heat warmed her cheeks and neck. She smoothed her skirts to attempt to soften her embarrassment. Not knowing how to ride was akin to poverty.

'Oh,' he answered.

'There was no need for me to learn. I have never had a horse or known anyone who could afford their own. Well, except for the Chisholms, and they never allowed staff to ride their horses.'

'Do you wish to learn?'

She shrugged. 'Perhaps,' she said, trying to shake off the uncertainty filling her from her toes to her hair. 'Where did you wish to ride to?'

He pointed above and behind her. 'Up through the valley and along the borders. As much as I can show you of our lands in the time we have today.'

Her stomach lurched. *Blast.* How would she manage a horse on her own throughout these sections of rock and inclines? And what of the descents? She balked.

She wouldn't.

'Or I can have the stable hand return your mount to the barn, and we can ride together?' Ewan offered.

''Tis your choice, but is too far to walk, and I do wish you to see the land.'

She hesitated and then gave in. 'I will ride with you, then.'

He smiled. 'I will let the lad know and return with our mount. Wait here.'

As if there was anywhere else she would go.

This is a new adventure. Take a deep breath. You can do this. He will be just like a carriage horse.

Ewan returned, leading the largest horse she had ever seen in all her days. *Curses.* This dark, looming stallion was no carriage horse. It was an impressive creature that could toss her from its back at its whim or crush her beneath its sizable hooves in a heartbeat. Catriona took a step back as Ewan brought the horse to where she was standing.

'This is Wee Bit,' he stated, rubbing the horse's nose, which was as dark as black tar.

She scoffed. 'You named him *Wee Bit*?'

He smiled. 'Nay. I didn't, but the stableman's son did. The lad has a keen sense of humour.'

'I can see that,' she murmured, not that she found any humour in it now.

'Come. Don't be afraid. Give him a pat so he can smell you. It will put you both at ease.'

'And if he doesn't take to me?'

'We'll find that out rather quickly,' he said with a wink, brushing his hair off his forehead.

She rolled her eyes at him. 'Just the words to give me courage.' She stepped forward and approached the large beast, focusing on slow and steady movements that wouldn't scare the horse or her. Then she put her splayed palm out to the horse's snout. Ewan reached out and quickly squeezed her fingers together. 'You want to cup your palm with your fingers close together, so he won't accidentally bite one off.'

'Blazes,' she murmured, her heart hammering in her chest.

He chuckled at her curse. 'Just trust him...and me.' He met her gaze and held it. She nodded and released a breath. Then Wee Bit nuzzled her hand.

Ewan pulled a piece of apple from his coat pocket and placed it in her palm, the faint skim of the coarse pads of his fingertips against her skin igniting a trail of awareness. The horse gobbled up the apple slice from her hand a second later. The tickle of hair from its whiskers and sweep of its tongue on her palm made her laugh. Ewan smiled. 'See?'

She reached up and dared pet its snout. The stallion leaned into her hand, and she savoured his sweet acceptance, as it was a mirror of Ewan's own. 'He's gentle,' she whispered.

'Aye. He may look like a beast, but he is a gentle giant.'

'Like you?'

'I suppose,' he answered, looking away.

'It isn't a flaw to be kind, my laird.'

'In these parts, it might as well be. The people are used to my father.' He ran a hand absent-mindedly down the neck of Wee Bit. 'Bran Stewart was a hard, demanding, and unyielding laird, and they respected him for it. But I cannot be that man, for I am not him. And when

I attempt to be, well, I just look like an arse *trying* to be a laird, not actually a laird at all.'

'Then don't be your father. Be yourself.'

He stilled and met her gaze. His Adam's apple bobbed in his throat as he swallowed. 'You believe the people would accept me if I were myself and not like my father?' The urgency of his question revealed his desperation to her, and her heart squeezed at the realisation of it. Even a laird such as Ewan struggled to find his way in the world. It wasn't just her, and that knowing brought her a sense of peace. Maybe she didn't have to know everything right now. She didn't have to be keen on an escape from this place and from him just yet. She could stay her two weeks and try to figure out what she wanted. For once, she could embrace the time she was given and enjoy it without fear.

She risked the truth. 'Aye. I think it's possible. I can't predict how they would react, but from what I know about men, you seem a good one, and that should count for something. Should it not?'

Bollocks.

Ewan squeezed the reins in his hands, feeling the leather tattoo his skin, but he held fast. It was the only thing keeping him from kissing the life out of her. If the woman didn't stop saying things like that, things that made him feel seen, things that made him want to be a better man, to be the man she believed he was, he wouldn't be able to walk away from her. Worse yet, he wouldn't be able to stop himself from loving her. The longer she set her beautiful amber eyes upon him, so full of expectation and belief, the more alive he felt, and the more drawn to her he was. But part of him knew that he was the moth to her flame, and that opening himself up to her would be allowing himself to be consumed entire. He'd scarce survived losing Emogene. He wouldn't survive a loss as heavy as that a second time.

'I wish goodness mattered here in the Highlands,' he replied, cutting his eyes away from her, 'but I don't think kindness will keep you alive. Only exerting power and control will.'

Hurt flashed in her eyes before she glanced away, and he knew he'd done what he'd needed to: kept his distance. If they married, they would be happier without the vice of love to squeeze the very life out of them. The sooner she knew that, the better off they could be. He pulled up on his mount and settled back in the saddle.

'Care to join me?' he asked, reaching out an open hand to her, attempting to lighten the mood he had just squashed to bits.

She lifted her gaze and bit her lip, a tell of her nerves he was beginning to recognise. 'How do I?' She gestured to him and the saddle.

'Put your shoe in the stirrup, grab my hand, and I'll hoist you up in front of me.'

Her gaze went from the stirrup to his hand to the horse, and she stepped back, shaking her head. 'I don't think...'

'Is it that you do not trust me, or the horse?'

When she didn't answer, he knew what she was thinking: both.

'I promise I won't let you fall.'

She closed her eyes and let out a deep breath. Then she shoved her boot in the stirrup and grabbed his extended hand, and he pulled her up. She was so light that she almost flew right back off the saddle after she landed in front of him, but he gripped her waist in time to bring her back to centre.

She clutched his thigh to steady herself, and he stifled a groan. Perhaps this wasn't the best of ideas. She smelled of something light and floral that he couldn't name, and the wisps of hair escaping her plait ran like silk threads against his cheek. This ride would drive him mad, and yet he craved the madness it would stir within him, just like that moth and its flame. The warmer she felt against him, the closer he wanted her, even though he knew in some deeper, faraway place that it would never be close enough.

'Ready?' he asked, his voice far huskier than he intended.

She released his thigh and clutched the horn of the saddle so tightly he feared it might be crushed to dust. 'Aye,' she said, even though it sounded more like a question than an answer.

With a click of his tongue and his heel, they were off at a slow trot along the valley. After travelling several minutes in silence, she finally relaxed against him.

'This is the valley where we used to play as children.' He couldn't keep the mirth from his voice. 'Even though it would start as a game of hide and find, Moira always allowed herself to be found first so she could sit among the flowers. She always loved botany and would bore me to tears with her explanations of what plants could be used for and where they grew best. Strange how I miss such talks now.'

The sun was climbing high in the sky, its rays chasing away the chill of the morn as they continued. He paused at the crest of the hill and pointed out to the horizon. 'Do you see our men far off in the distance working along the stone wall?'

She leaned forward. 'Aye.'

'Our lands run up until the wall we share with the MacGregors. If you follow that wall, it wraps along the edges of the borders we share with the Camerons as well.'

'It is impressive.'

'And thousands of men, women, and children depend on us keeping it that way.'

'Surely you don't place that burden solely on your own shoulders? One man cannot keep a clan thriving and in order. It is the responsibility of all to maintain such things.' She spoke with a certainty that made him smile.

'If only all had such a belief.' He clicked his tongue, and Wee Bit carried on to the south end, slowing as they descended a section of rocks and small boulders. Catriona slid forward in the saddle and gasped in alarm.

'Steady,' he murmured. He wrapped one arm around her waist as he gripped the reins with the other. He was startled by the slightness of her form. To know she was so fearful of riding was an odd contrast to all that she had endured and the strength he knew she possessed. The land levelled out, and she relaxed in his hold. He loosened his arm around her all too soon.

As they roamed, he pointed out the cottages clustered about the various farming, mining, sheering, livestock, and herbal centres of the clan. Many of the men and women stopped their work to greet them, while others watched with suspicion, wondering no doubt about why he travelled with a woman who was a stranger to them.

Little did they know the importance of it. Mrs Catriona Gordon might very well become his wife.

Chapter Fourteen

'Tis a glorious thing to have my feet settled back on the ground,' Catriona stated. Her sides tingled from where Ewan had just released his hold about her waist after helping her dismount from Wee Bit. She stroked the large horse's nose. 'And *you* were quite gentle, kind sir, as your master promised.'

'You see, you did not perish during your ride.' Ewan smiled as he passed the reins off to the stable boy. 'Take good care of him, Reed,' he told the young lad. 'Extra oats for him this eve,' he added with a wink.

'Aye, me laird,' the boy answered with a smile and nod. 'My lady,' he offered with a small bow before he led the horse off to be brushed down.

'You are right,' Catriona answered. 'I indeed did not perish, although I did imagine myself toppling off the horse and careening down a few of the hillsides as we travelled.'

'I would never let any harm come to you,' he said. And the way he spoke the words made her heart twist and turn, as if it too wished to believe his words but didn't quite trust them.

She pressed her lips together.

He nodded. 'Slow to trust?'

'Perhaps.'

'Then, we are a well-matched pair,' he jested as he brushed dirt from his trews.

It was now or never.

She squared her shoulders. 'I gathered that from last night. I am sorry I pushed you. It was not my place to enquire about something so personal, especially when we really do not know one another.' The apology fell stiffly from her lips, but she meant it.

He stilled and met her gaze. 'And I am sorry as well. I should not have acted like an arse with my answer.' He shrugged and sighed. 'I have not spoken about her to anyone in a long time.'

'I understand. There is much pain from my past that I choose to keep close to me rather than share, which makes me an arse for expecting you to share your own so freely.'

He chuckled. 'I was angry, but only due to the feeling it brought up for me. Shame more than anything. I went against my clan, my father, and an alliance, all for her, because I believed she loved me.'

She waited for him to continue.

'We were to marry, but in the end, she married a Sutherland. All because he had more power, more coin. It was a hard lesson for me to learn.'

'What lesson was that?'

'That love is not always enough.'

'Ah. So that was the reason for your no-love clause in your proposal to me? To prevent such misfortune again?'

'Aye. It is to protect us both.'

'Thank you for telling me, so that I could understand.'

He shrugged. 'If we are to wed, then you should know what you're getting into,' he said with a smirk.

'I suppose you are right.'

'I thought you might like to walk down to the loch. Are you up to it?' he asked.

'Aye. It sounds glorious. I'll have a chance to stretch my legs after the ride and remind myself of what it feels like to have my feet fully anchored to the ground.'

He laughed. 'The riding will become easier. And the first time you let your horse free across an open field, you will love it. I know you will.'

'You do?' Did he claim to know her already? Her pulse increased.

He nodded. 'Aye. I do. You have spirit, Mrs Gordon, and didn't you say you crave freedom?'

'Aye.'

'Well, there is not much that compares to the freedom you feel riding full out on your own mount across an open field with the sun beaming on your face and the wind whipping through your hair. I hope I get to see that moment. That will be a sight to behold.'

She sucked in an unsteady breath. The way he looked at her, as if he knew things about her that she did not even know about herself, sent every fibre of her being aflame. It also made her long to know what would set him free as well.

'And you, my laird, what is it that would set your spirit free?' She walked alongside him, her fingertips accidentally skimming the back of his hand for the briefest of touches.

He paused.

'Honestly?' he asked, stepping closer.

'Aye,' she whispered.

'Kissing you.'

Her breath hitched in her throat, and she swallowed hard. 'Then why don't you?'

He stared devilishly at her lips as if they were water itself before meeting her gaze. 'Well, we do not know if you are still married to Mr Gordon or not. And you have already told me that you do not trust yourself around me, so if *I* do not hold the line on our attraction to one another, we will be in dire shape, will we not? And I know I couldn't stop myself at one kiss.'

His gaze held images of such abandon, and she released a breath. 'Then I am grateful for your restraint,' she answered, leaning forward until her breath blew across his cheek. 'Let us see how long it holds for both of us.'

She stepped back and began to walk down the hillside towards the loch below, its waters dark and rippling. This playful banter between them was something she'd never had before, and she found she liked it far more than she wished to admit. She also knew she was playing with fire. One false move and they might both be consumed.

Deuces.

Ewan rubbed the back of his neck and ruffled his hair. If anyone had told him a week ago that he would find a woman to become his wife and burn with attraction for her as well, Ewan would have laughed aloud at them and sent for the doctor to have them checked for fever. But it was true. He'd felt more alive with Mrs Gordon in these last few days than he had felt in years. His steps faltered.

More alive than he had felt since losing Emogene.

While he knew he should be tending to his duties as laird this afternoon, all he wanted was to spend more time with Mrs Gordon. To learn what made her laugh, to know the secrets of her heart, the pain that had shaped her into who she was today. All in all, he was acting like a lovesick fool, and despite the terror that elicited in him, there was a small seed of wonder growing in his gut.

Could he have love like Moira and Brenna had and not be consumed by it? Was he doomed to a life of plodding along one foot in front of the other as laird, or could he also have happiness? Hell, could Catriona help him become a better man, be the laird he wished to be? She had a way of pushing him and challenging him that he admired, and yet she also possessed a directness that relaxed him.

He followed her down the hillside, watching her take those first steps onto the craggy shore. A smile played on her lips as she turned to him, her hair whipping in the breeze, the sun setting her face aglow. And wasn't she turning into some other woman each day she stayed here? She was far from the tattered lass who didn't dare make eye contact with him at the start of their journey in the carriage from Edinburgh to Glasgow. Each day, more light came into her eyes and her spirit, as if she too had been hidden from the world and perhaps from herself.

Together, they seemed to be finding one another. And it was equally compelling and terrifying.

He reached the shore and stood alongside her on the grey rocks that filled the coastline. For minutes they just looked out at the loch in silence, water rolling in along the shoals, the rhythmic ebb and flow of the small tide and smell of the water filling his senses.

'It is incredibly peaceful here,' she said.

'Aye.'

'I have few memories of my childhood,' she offered, staring out into the dark waters. 'But the strongest one is of being on a beach. I can smell the sea, feel the warm sand between my toes and the sun heating my arms and face. I remember laughing with my siblings, being teased by one of my brothers, and then chasing him and the waves along the shore.'

'That is all you remember?'

'And being swallowed by the waves, desperately trying to reach the surface for air, and failing.' She shivered. 'I also remember snippets of things.' She bent to pick up a small pebble, freckled with minerals but smoothed by the sea. 'I remember finding a piece of sea glass that day, a vibrant blue-green. Your eyes reminded me of it when we first met.'

He tucked his hands in his pockets to keep from touching her. 'What happened to it?'

'I don't have any idea. I remember finding it and showing it to my brother.'

'Do you ever wonder what happened to them? Your siblings. Your parents. Why they did not come to find you, claim you?' His questions tumbled out before he could think better of it. After all, it wasn't his business, was it?

'Every day,' she answered without pause as she threw the pebble far out into the loch.

He understood the anguish in her voice and the pull of insanity such a daily thought was. It was how he thought upon the death of his mother and the betrayal of Emogene, even though the losses were dissimilar. They still caused pain as open wounds that couldn't be healed, much like her own.

'Now, who is poking their finger into an open wound and expecting a bloody answer?' Her words hit him like tiny barbs lancing his skin. She faced him. Her features were pinched, pained even, and he wished he hadn't asked, that he could gather his words back and hide them away, but he couldn't.

'I did not mean…' he murmured, uncertain how to continue.

'You did not mean to ask me the truth? No doubt, you did.'

He nodded. 'You are right. I am sorry.'

'I believe I've had my fill of fresh air,' she replied.

'I'll escort you back,' he offered.

'I can find my own way, my laird,' she answered, lifting her skirts and starting up the incline. He watched her go, knowing that he had placed a wedge between them after all the connection they had just built, and he couldn't help but wonder if he'd done it intentionally to keep her at bay.

For the prospect of loving anyone was a scary venture, especially the thought of daring to care for a woman as enchanting and mesmerising as Mrs Catriona Gordon.

Chapter Fifteen

The man was working her temper into a fine boil. Catriona climbed the hillside and drew in long breaths to calm the anger brewing. His simple questions shouldn't create so much ire in her, but they did. Most likely because she also wanted answers to them, and she had for years. Why hadn't her parents come for her? Did they not love her enough to search for her? Had they given up so easily? Why?

Perhaps she wasn't good enough.

Mr Arran's cruel words echoed in her head. *'Ye be nothin', lass. That's why yer parents never claimed ye.'*

The familiar shame at the thought of it being true emerged, and her chest constricted. She could not hold the feeling for long before she wished to simply scream.

Blast.

The man could drive a sane woman to the asylum.

She huffed out a breath, picking up speed as she climbed. The burn of exertion to her legs and body felt delicious because she hadn't been working as hard as her body was used to doing for days now. She'd have to discover some outlet for all her excess energy, or she might just murder the man over the coming weeks until her departure.

Departure?

She faltered. Did she truly want to leave?

At this moment she did, but what of later when her anger cooled? In the last few days, she had been cared for, laughed, met kind people, and explored more new facets of herself and the world than she had in the last decade.

But she could also be free. The wind whipped up around her, and she snuggled deeper in her shawl. A storm was blowing in, and soon there would be a downpour. She hustled up the remaining distance to the castle and entered through the side door. Soon Betsy intercepted her.

'Did ye enjoy yer time with the laird?' she asked, falling into step with Catriona.

She paused. 'Aye. I enjoyed the tour of the lands. I could have done without the enquiry that came along with it,' she huffed. There was no use in keeping her anger hidden. Betsy was no fool.

To Catriona's surprise, Betsy smirked. 'Is that so?' she asked.

'Aye. 'Tis so.' She dropped her voice. 'The man could drive a nun to murder, I tell you.'

Betsy smothered a laugh. 'Let us get ye changed. The elders will be joining ye for dinner.'

'They are?'

Betsy shifted on her feet. 'The laird said he would

mention it to ye, but perhaps with all that has happened...' her words trailed off.

Catriona frowned.

'Best ye work through that temper before they arrive. Perhaps a hot bath would do the trick?' Betsy offered with a smile.

Catriona sighed aloud. 'Aye. That sounds heavenly.'

'Say no more. I will let the other servants know, so they can begin heating the water, and then I'll return shortly to help ye out of yer gown.'

She gave Betsy's arm a quick squeeze. 'Thank you.'

With her spirit lifted at the thought of yet another hot bath, Catriona hurried along the corridor to her chambers. As she reached her door and set her hand on the knob to open it, she stopped cold at the sound of a footman speaking with Mrs Stevens down the hallway.

'Correspondence from the solicitor has arrived,' he said. 'Instructions were that I was to hand it directly to the laird and only the laird.'

'Hmm. Ye may be in for a long wait, lad. He's not returned yet from his travels along the borders with Mrs Gordon.'

'Should I leave it in his study then? I've many a chore to do before dinner with the elders this eve.'

'Aye. Head on. I'll leave it on his desk in the study. No one should bother it. I'll send him in to look upon it as soon as he arrives.'

'Aye, ma'am.'

Following the sound of footfalls and a door opening and closing, Catriona stood still, deciding on what to do. She *could* sneak in and peek at that letter, or she could leave it be. He would tell her the contents one way or the other, wouldn't he? But if she opened it, he might know what she'd done.

Or she could reseal it and he would never know. Well, he might not know.

Or she might break his trust entirely.

Would it matter?

Ack.

The thoughts in her mind were akin to a game of keep away. Why could she not decide whether she wished to stay or go, or care for the man or despise him? And why could he also not decide whether he cared for or despised her?

Before she could think longer upon any of those things, she needed to decide if she would sneak into his study and look upon the letter or not. Betsy would return soon, and then her option would evaporate. She gave in to the devil upon her shoulder and snuck down the hallway, careful to see if anyone was coming her way. Even though she was the laird's guest, her snooping about in the study alone would not be well received. So far, the corridor was empty. No doubt many of the servants were busy preparing the meal and dining room for the arrival of the elders which the laird had failed to mention to her.

She grumbled under her breath and set her handle upon the study door. She turned the knob, and it easily gave way. The door hadn't even been locked. *Blazes.* What had she even been worried about?

'Mrs Gordon,' the laird said behind her, his tone

smooth and curious. 'Were you looking for me so soon after our outing? I must say I am surprised.'

Catriona stilled, clenched her jaw, and cursed under her breath. What was he doing back already, and how on earth had she not heard his approach? She let go of the handle, set a tight smile to her face, and turned to him. When she saw his feet were clad only in his stockings, she knew exactly how she hadn't heard him. The man had no shoes on.

She lifted her brow as she looked upon his soiled stockings.

He shrugged. 'Stepped in a large mud hole near the barn when I went to see Wee Bit. Mrs Stevens kindly asked me to leave them on the steps out of doors.'

'Aye,' she answered. 'I thought you would be some time still.'

'Oh? Did you have need of me already? Here I was thinking you were angry at me.' He flashed a rogue smile at her as if he were all too pleased with himself and her visit.

She wanted to crown the man, but she decided to seize her advantage instead. The best defence was to have a strong attack, so she pulled from what little she had in her arsenal. She crossed her arms against her chest. 'Aye. Betsy informed me that we were dining with the elders tonight. Was there a point in time that you were going to let me know that, so I could prepare? How are you even going to introduce me?'

His smile faltered, and he cringed. 'Aye. I did forget to tell you. I did not think upon it as we were out this morn.' He ran a hand through his hair. 'Come in. Let us speak of it now.' He pushed the door open for her and followed her inside.

'Betsy will be bringing along water for a hot bath for me shortly, so...' She lingered near the door.

He studied her. 'Are you still angry?' he asked.

'Aye, my laird. I am.'

He sighed and sank down in the chair before his desk. 'I did not intend harm in my question. I wanted to know so that I could understand, not shame you.' He lifted the letter on his desk and scanned the writing, momentarily distracted by it before he set it aside. No doubt it was *the* letter she was desperate to know the contents of, yet he seemed to have little interest in it. *Odd.*

'Understand what?' she countered. 'There is no mystery in how you found me. Isn't that all you need to know of my past?' A flush heated her cheeks. Now that she had set some of her anger and frustration free, it was quite hard to wrestle it down. Her pulse increased, and she couldn't slow her breathing.

'I asked so I could be better at...' He paused searching for the right word before he gave up. 'Better at being your husband if it comes to that, and understanding what might be hard for you to adjust to here as my wife. There was no malice in my enquiry, despite what you may believe.' He met her gaze.

'Even though I may decide to leave you?'

He frowned. 'Aye. Even then.' He interlocked his fingers and sat back in his chair. 'As you may have guessed, I am not used to opening up to people. My attempts have been clumsy, but there is no ill intent.'

She wiggled her toes in her slippers. What did one say to that?

'Oh,' she replied and pressed her lips together in a fine line of regret.

'As for our dinner this eve,' he began, ploughing on to a new topic before this one had been anywhere near resolved, 'you will meet the elders. What do you wish to know about them before they arrive, so you can be ready?'

'Now that I think on it, it may be best that you tell me nothing, so I can have a clear and untainted view of them and their intentions. However, I do need to know what story you shall give them about me.'

'As we discussed as a possibility before, I will tell them you are Garrick's long-lost cousin who is staying with us while his own castle is under repairs, which is true, so that you can be comfortable, but also have time to get to know his new wife-to-be, my sister, of course.'

'And Laird MacLean and Brenna have agreed to this?'

'Aye. They have.'

'Then, I look forward to our dinner and observing what exactly these men are up to.'

'I will see you at eight then,' he said.

She walked towards the door, and as her foot hit the threshold, he called to her.

'And Mrs Gordon, if you ever want to know what is in my library, you can always just ask.' He winked at her and then turned away before she could answer.

Blast. The man had known what she was up to from the start. If only she knew exactly what *he* was up to.

* * *

'You made quite the impression this eve, Mrs Gordon,' said Ewan as he returned to the dining room, having escorted the elders out for the evening. She had quite affected him as well. The woman surprised him every moment she spent with him, and those surprises spoke to his soul in a way he didn't wish to acknowledge as he became more and more attracted to her.

Even in profile, she was astounding, and he shored himself up against it as best he could, which wasn't very well at all. 'Were you as interested as you seemed in our discussions?' he asked, attempting to keep their conversation on neutral ground.

Catriona turned away from the windows and faced him, the candlelight catching the shadows and light across her face. 'Almost,' she replied.

'As I suspected.' He scanned the room. 'Where did Brenna go?'

'She retired. Something about being bored for so long that she might as well go to bed.' She chuckled, and the small locket at her throat winked at him in the glow of the wall sconces.

'I cannot say I blame her,' he added. 'Once Niven begins, it is quite hard for him to end.'

'However, he could be your greatest asset,' she stated, lifting her brow at him. Her words stopped him in his tracks.

'Are we speaking of the same man?'

'Aye. The eldest of them. The one who appears to be the hardest on you wants you dearly to succeed. I can see it in the way he looks at you. But Broden...he is quite a different story. Envy shines in his eyes when you speak. He wishes to have everything you possess. *He* is the one I would watch out for. He is an opportunist, and he is waiting for a chance to unseat you to arise.'

'That does not surprise me. He was angry when I did not give him rein over the soldiers for I did not believe him skilled enough to train them. And Harris?' Ewan asked, unable to wait a moment longer for her thoughts on him.

She shrugged. 'Perhaps a nuisance, but he is no threat. I believe he will take the path of least resistance, whatever that may be. He seemed to shift allegiances as the conversation went on. No doubt that is his plan moving forward. He may be an ally or a foe.'

'You decided all of this from one eve with them over one meal?' Ewan frowned at her. 'How can you be certain?'

Her fingertips trailed over the rim of her wine glass until it sang under her touch. A sweet high-pitched tone that filled the room. Once she ceased and it faded away, she met his gaze and held it. 'Because in my experience, making a mistake in the judgement of a man can cost you your life. So, aye, I am sure. And in exchange for this help I have provided you, I would like to know what was in the letter today that you went to great pains to make me believe held little or no significance despite its importance to me…and to you.'

He smirked. 'Interesting. You mean from my solicitor?'

She nodded.

He tilted his head. 'And you would know that he sent

me a letter, how? You do not know his script. Even that is beyond your skill set, I believe.'

'Aye, it is. I do not know his penmanship, but I over-heard your footman bring it in, and upon being unable to find you, Mrs Stevens bid him leave it on your desk. He was quite reluctant to do so as that went against the messenger's orders, but he did it anyway. Mrs Stevens can be quite persuasive.'

'Ahh. So now I know why you were attempting to enter my study.'

She did not confirm or deny his assertion, which was an affirmation of her intentions if there ever was one, the little minx. He should have been angry but found himself intrigued by her boldness and ingenuity instead.

'I have not opened it,' he offered. He sipped from his wine glass and set it aside on the mantel.

She approached him, narrowing her eyes. 'I do not know if I believe you.'

'You cannot read me after all our time together? That I find interesting, especially after your speech about the importance of being able to read people to protect oneself.' He walked closer to her. 'Do you not see the answer in my eyes?'

She stood in silent assessment of him, her gaze slowly scanning his face, the light catching those gold and moss specks in her amber irises and her shoulders rising and falling delicately with each breath. The lavender gown she wore this eve was quite devastating against her pale skin, and her hair was swept artfully into a low knot at the nape of her neck. How he would kiss that neck if he could.

She smirked just then as if she could read his thoughts, and heat flushed along his neck. *Deuces.* He hoped she wasn't *that* good at reading people.

'I believe you. Let us open it now, then, so I can know my fate. It is important to know which husband you are married to, is it not?' She laughed and set her glass down before boldly clasping his hand in hers and tugging him along to follow.

The feel of her hand in his sent a bolt of fire through his body, and he held on fiercely. He caught up and then challenged her to match his pace as they jogged down the corridor to his study. Her laughter filled his ears as he let go of her hand at the doorway and went in. As he strode to the desk, he realised how desperately he wanted to be her husband. How much he craved to claim her as his own.

And how much he feared all he felt for her, as she could leave him even now. The realisation soured his throat. She had power over him. He hesitated, but then took the letter in hand.

'Well, go on then. Do not leave me wondering. Am I still Mrs Gordon, or am I now Lady Stewart?'

He set his mask in place as he popped open the heavy wax seal of the letter from his solicitor. He scanned its contents and then set it on the desk before slumping down in the chair and releasing a curse.

'You are disappointed I am your bride?' she teased.

'I do not know anything for certain, nor do you. See for yourself.' He tossed the letter across the table and set his boots up on the corner of the desk, crossing them at the ankles.

Why could nothing be easy?

She picked it up and read it before setting it back down and sitting in the seat across from him. 'What exactly does *more time* mean, do you think? A day, a week, a month?'

'A good question. It seems he will let us know the moment he hears something more official, but until then, he is unsure whether what happened in the Grass-market was a legal contract or not and whether you are my wife or not. He cannot be certain until he completes more enquiries of his own.'

'That's rather grey, isn't it?'

'Aye,' he said, resting his head against the back of the chair, 'it is.'

'So now what do we do, merely wait?'

'Do you have other ideas?' he asked.

'Nay, my laird. But what if the answer takes longer than our two-week trial? What will we do then?'

'Perhaps we should just take it a day at a time. Then, once we reach the end of our two weeks, we can decide.'

She shrugged. 'I suppose that is as good of an idea as any…as is going to bed.' She stood and stretched her arms over her head, looking every bit like a cat stretching her sleek limbs high in the air. He swallowed hard. Too bad her latest statement had not been an invitation. He would have accepted it in an instant.

'Thank you for your help with the elders this eve. I would never have deduced their intentions in such a way. I hope you will teach me your methods.'

'Much of it cannot be taught, my laird. You must

learn to trust your instincts, your gut, that small voice in the back of your head that tells you the truth.'

He sat up, settling his feet back on the floor. 'I am not sure I know what you mean.'

'Then perhaps that shall be my lesson for you tomorrow. After you finish your meetings in the morn, meet me at the stables.'

'The stables?'

She nodded.

'I will see you there.'

'I bid you a good eve and good sleep, my laird.'

'And to you, Mrs Gordon.'

'And be sure to wear something you don't mind getting a bit dirty tomorrow morn for our lessons,' she said. She smiled, and the twinkle of playful mischief was back in her eyes. He found he could scarce wait to see what plans she had in store for him. Each day with this lass was an adventure. He felt more alive than he had in ages, and it scared the blazes out of him.

Chapter Sixteen

'I am here as requested,' Ewan stated.

Catriona turned to face the barn door and smiled. 'I am pleased to see you eager for your lesson today, my laird.' She glanced at his worn tunic and trews. 'And that you came prepared to get a bit dirty.'

Anticipation raced through him. While he found he wasn't always one to enjoy surprises, he did enjoy hers. He lifted his brows. 'Eager may be an overstatement. I am more curious as to how you will teach me the ways of men in the stables, of all places.' And how he would manage to focus on her lessons. She wore a plain brown dress rather than one of Brenna's frocks and found the simplicity of the cut quite flattering. Her hair was also pulled back in a long singular plait, which showcased the beauty of her face.

'You look quite lovely this morn,' he said.

She paused her work and blushed. 'Thank you. Betsy was kind enough to loan me a day dress so I would not soil another one of Brenna's gowns.' She lifted a bale of hay and plopped it near the barn door. 'Have a seat,' she said, patting the bale with her hand.

He came over to the bale and sat as requested. 'Now, close your eyes,' she said.

He frowned. 'Why?'

'Because it is the first part of my lesson for you this morn. Eyes. Closed.'

'Hopefully it will not be my last,' he muttered and then closed his eyes.

'I am blindfolding you for this first part.'

'Isn't the whole point for me to learn how to read cues from people based on what I see? How can I do that if I am blindfolded?'

'Seeing is only one part of understanding someone and their intentions.' She cinched the scrap of cloth around his eyes tightly. 'Shush.'

He captured one of her hands in his own and kissed the tips of her fingers. 'In case this is my last chance to kiss you,' he chuckled.

She wriggled her fingertips away. 'You will not perish unless you continue to complain.'

He smothered a smile.

'Now, I want you to sit quietly and tell me everything you hear.'

'What?'

'Please just try it.'

He took a deep breath and released it. Then, he listened. 'I hear some rustling in the barn, most likely from the animals, mixed with some of your impatience with me.'

'I am quite sure you can do better than that,' she called, some distance from him now.

'Aye.' He listened again, taking pains to truly try. 'I hear the leaves in the breeze. Also, an animal drinking water, perhaps a goat or dog. And now I hear footsteps approaching me, most likely you.'

'That is better. Now tell me what you smell.'

He wrinkled his nose. 'Definitely hay, manure, dirt, and perhaps a tinge of a sweet-smelling soap from you.'

'Now extend your hands, and tell me what you feel.'

He smiled at the feel of fur beneath his touch. 'A goat, but I could have deduced that by its scent.'

He heard her walk away and then back to him.

'Good. And what about now?'

A slobbering kiss lathered his hand and he laughed. 'Rufus.'

'Aye. Perhaps too easy. Now, imagine what you already know about the layout of the barn and walk to my voice. Careful though. I may have placed some obstacles in your path.'

He stood and frowned. 'How on earth is any of this helping me to read people?'

'Tsk tsk, my laird. Just try.'

'How shall I ever reach you if you are moving?'

'Ah! Very good. You see, you are improving already. You can tell I am moving from you and not in a fixed spot. Keep walking to me. But take care to mind your steps.'

'Why do I feel this is a trial of humiliation rather than a lesson in deciphering behaviour?' He reached out his arms and felt around him but didn't touch anything. Then he stumbled over an object beneath his feet. Though he saved himself from falling, it was not without a curse.

'Keep going, my laird.'

After an additional stagger over what may or may not have been a broom handle, he slowed his steps, walking carefully. He listened for hints of where he was, imagined the interior of the barn he had been in thousands of times, and sniffed occasionally to see if he was moving further away from her or closer to her. That sweet floral scent of hers was intoxicating. He kicked over a bucket with a thud and paused. Finally, he took another step, reached out his hand, and touched Catriona's arm.

'Well done. You may remove your blindfold,' she said.

Ewan released his hold on her forearm and tugged off the blindfold. He glanced back to see he had travelled across a large section of the barn floor that had been scattered with objects. He counted himself lucky not to have stepped on the trio of eggs on the ground. He frowned. 'So, what was the point of such an exercise?'

'To be in the moment, use your senses, and to trust yourself and your instincts more. For example, you began to stop, listen, and gauge your steps more carefully. You were present to your surroundings, assessing where you were, where I was, and how to reach me safely.'

'I was?'

'Aye. My hope is this will serve as a reminder for you to trust your instincts. Everyone has them. You seem to always doubt yours, except for that day in the market. You set aside your doubts and acted on pure instinct.

You rescued me and trusted me enough to ride for two days in a carriage with me.'

'I believe that was more madness.'

'Was it? Or were you allowing your heart, your gut, your instincts to drive you into action to save me? And if you had not done that, I might very well be dead.'

He swallowed hard. Imagining her dead, not here with him, made his heart thunder in his chest and the blood in his body constrict.

She took both of his hands in hers. 'Let yourself feel. Listening to the part of you that gives you instinct will also give you insight, but you have to allow it to come to the surface. Your emotion, your kindness, your care, your love…that is what you must harness to be able to read the motivations of others better. You cannot know those things about others if you do not know them of yourself. I believe you are best when you listen to yourself, follow that heart of yours you seem so keen to set aside, and trust your instincts about people. What you believe to be a special skill I possess is merely self-reliance. Everyone has it, even you. But you must allow yourself to feel it, even when it is uncomfortable.'

He held her gaze, and something shifted deep inside him, as if her words played a song in his heart that he had waited his whole life to hear. This woman felt he was enough as he was. He was not lacking. He did not need extra skill, but more self-belief.

He needed to believe in himself like she did.

He swallowed hard, emotion and confusion clouding his mind. He narrowed his gaze at her. 'Are you telling me you believe I could have deciphered what you did about the elders at our dinner by paying more attention and trusting my instincts?'

'Aye. I believe you could decipher more about everyone if you did those things.'

He shook his head. 'I don't think so.'

'Why not? You have such skills with animals. I have seen you ride Wee Bit. You two communicate with each other and trust each other. That is based on you using your senses to know what you can and cannot do together as horse and rider. If you applied that same confidence and belief in yourself when you met with the clan leaders and elders, you would know who you could count on and trust as part of your inner circle and who you couldn't.'

A knock sounded on the frame of the barn door. 'Are you ready for your ride today, Mrs Gordon?' Hewe asked. The clan's most skilled horse trainer and rider glanced around at the random items all over the barn floor.

Catriona let go of Ewan's hands, and a sweet flush rose into her neck. 'I did not realise the time. I am sure the laird is ready to be done with my mischief.' She smiled. 'I will clean up and join you shortly.'

'Aye, Mrs Gordon. I'll ready yer mount.' Hewe headed out.

Catriona picked up a few of the scattered items and returned them to their shelves and racks. Ewan silently assisted her until they were done. Although he desperately wished to talk, he couldn't. He didn't know what exactly to say. He had so many questions, and so many uncertainties.

'Can it be so simple?' he asked, placing the trio of eggs in the small bowl she held.

'Aye, my laird. It can.' Her eyes were steady and clear.

'Your certainty is something I wish dearly I possessed.'

She shrugged. 'Then choose it, Ewan. There is no secret in it. Trust yourself. I do.'

And with that, she handed him the bowl of eggs, pressed a kiss to his cheek, and left the barn humming the clarsach melody.

Ewan stood frozen, wondering what had just happened and why everything that seemed so impossible without Catriona seemed so bloody possible with her.

Chapter Seventeen

'A letter from the solicitor has arrived.'

Catriona glanced up from the settee to see Ewan leaning on the door frame of her chamber. She smiled at the sight of him. He looked devilishly handsome with his mussed black hair, rolled shirt sleeves, and loosened cravat, all signs that he had been hard at work poring over maps or the account books for the clan when the letter arrived.

She put the pressed flower he'd given her from one of her first nights here on the page of the book she was reading to keep her place and closed it gently. The adventures of Cecilia and William would have to wait for another day, it seemed. She sat up, tucked her stocking feet under herself, and stifled a yawn. The afternoon sun had almost lulled her into a nap, a luxury she would have scarcely thought possible weeks ago. 'I am surprised to hear he has posted a new development to us so soon.'

He lifted his brow at her as he came into the room.

'It has been over a week. I was surprised he had not had news sent to us earlier.'

A week? She quirked her lips.

'Has it already been a week since his last missive?' she asked. Days were tumbling one over another since she had arrived, and she and Ewan had fallen into a soft, gentle rhythm with one another. They spent time each day together and other times apart working on their own pursuits and activities. He settled in beside her, and the settee sank as it gave in to his weight. At first, she might have shuddered and been afraid of the man's proximity, but no more. She had grown to care for the ease he made her feel. He accepted her, and the kindness that she had viewed as weakness upon their first meeting, she now saw as the greatest strength a man could possess.

Butterflies whirled in her stomach as he smiled at her, his dimple flashing its usual warning that she needed to keep her feelings in check. Who knew what that letter held? Who knew what would happen at the end of their fortnight together? And heaven only knew how she would recover if he chose to move on without her.

'Care to do the honours, my lady?' he asked, extending the letter to her.

'Of course,' she answered with a bravado and confidence she did not feel. As she slid her finger under the wax seal, she prayed the news would be what she wanted. Too bad she didn't exactly know what she wanted that news to be.

While she knew she no longer wished to be Mrs Gordon, did she want to already be Lady Stewart? Did she want her freedom after all? Was she beginning to care far too much for this man she was not contractually allowed to love even if they did marry?

Her mind whirled with these questions, but she clamped them down as she flipped open the folded pages. She cleared her throat and read the correspondence aloud:

Laird Stewart,
After much exploration into the legality of your arrangement with Mr Gordon, and following up with the local laws, I have found that the exchange of money—your guinea—for Mr Gordon's property or goods—his wife—was legal, but that Mr Gordon was still viewed by the court of law as her husband.

After learning this, I attempted to locate Mr Gordon to speak with him about the terms of a legal divorce. After several days of seeking him and being unsuccessful, I visited the morgue on the suggestion of a local shopkeeper. Unfortunately, Mr Gordon was there. He had been brought in dead two days prior. Evidently he was killed by the husband of a woman he was found with. The man is now in custody and awaiting a hearing.

Due to Mr Gordon's unfortunate demise, Mrs Gordon is now a widow. The law does not recognize you as married to her based on your single agreement/transaction with Mr Gordon in the market. If you do wish to marry, you will have to apply for a licence as one normally would.

If you have any further enquiries on the matter, do let me know. This has been a very compelling and unique case that has intrigued me. I appreciate, as always, your trust in me as your solicitor.

Sincerely,
James R. Sullivan

Dead?
Saints be.

Catriona put down the letter and sat silently, taking in the reality of what she had just read. She was free. But free because Thomas was dead. Odd emotions welled up in her. Happiness at her freedom, but also sadness as to his gruesome murder, even if he had been a horrid man and husband.

But as of this very moment, she was no one's wife and under no one's thumb. No more Thomas Gordon harming her and blustering her about. No more harm would come to her person, for she'd never allow it again. The woman who had left Edinburgh was dead along with Thomas. She was no longer his wife, nor would she ever be. She choked on a sob as the emotion and knowing of that shook her to her core.

She covered her mouth as she sobbed once more, her eyes welling with tears, betraying her efforts to keep her emotion at bay.

'I am sorry about Thomas,' Ewan offered. 'I know he was your husband, despite—' he paused '—all he did.

I understand if this comes as a shock. Perhaps I should have read it on my own first.'

'Nay. I am sad for his brutal death, but these are tears of happiness and relief, for I am his wife no longer.'

Ewan cupped her face in his hand and gave a tentative smile. 'So, you are happy?'

'As horrible as it sounds to hear of another man's death. Aye. I am. I am free.'

'You *are* finally free. And you are safe.'

'Thank you,' she choked out, pressing a hand over his. As he wiped away one of her tears, she pulled him into a tight hug, unable to keep her happiness and gratitude at bay. 'You said you would save me, and you did. Thank you. Thank you for keeping your word to me. No one else other than Nettie ever has.'

Blazes.

He sucked in a breath. His whole body shuddered as she pressed against him. How long had he wished to hold her like this? She was warm and soft, and she smelled of summer. He sighed as he held her, closed his eyes, and stroked her hair as she wept on his shoulder. How much she had endured, he didn't know, and the imaginings of what such could have been clogged his throat. To know that she no longer hurt and was free from Mr Gordon filled Ewan's heart with hope even as it filled with dread. He could lose her now. Her decision to stay was in her hands as he had wanted it to be, but he'd never thought or dared imagine he would grow to care for her as much as he did now. He knew he wanted her here as Lady Stewart, even if he risked his heart by falling in love with her. Hell, whom was he fooling? Despite his best efforts, he already was falling for her slowly over the tiny little moments with her that breached his barriers each day.

She hiccupped against his neck, her lips skimming along his flesh there by accident and sending a thrill of alarm through him. He was a gentleman and disciplined in his affections, but if she continued to be so unintentionally alluring, it would be a struggle for him to remain so. Finally she leaned away from him and sat back against the cushion of the settee, wiping her eyes. Her whole face was as swollen and pink as a newborn baby squalling for milk, and yet she was gorgeous. He smiled at her.

'I am sorry, my laird.' She hiccupped again, still attempting to control her emotion. 'I had not realised how much I desired to be free of him and how bound up I was about what would come of that letter from your solicitor until I read it.' She shook her head. 'I am free.'

'Aye,' he answered in a croak of emotion. 'You are. And as we are nearly at the end of our fortnight arrangement with one another, you are free to make your choice. You may stay and be my wife, or you may leave to pursue your own future.'

Her eyes widened. 'You would not go back on your word?'

He scoffed. 'Nay. I made you a promise.' He reached out and took her hand between his own. 'While I would love for you to stay and be my wife as I think we suit one another well, I will set you free if that is your desire.'

Even if it breaks me in two.

'I thought you might change your mind now that the solicitor has sent his findings on to us.'

'If there is one thing I have learned through my own mistakes with Emogene as well as my father's mistakes in his attempts to arrange marriages for my sisters, it is that I want my wife to choose me as much as I choose her, and I do not want any woman to marry a man out of duty or desperation. No good came from those situations, and I will not repeat them.'

She said nothing but pulled her hand from his. 'I fear your touch clouds my judgement.' She smirked at him.

He laughed. 'You always surprise me, Catriona. It is one of the things I like best about you.'

'And I you.'

'So, what do you wish to do the rest of the afternoon before dinner?'

Her eyes lit like fire before she smiled and said, 'Ride.'

'You think you are ready to ride on your own? 'Tis only been over a week that you have worked with Hewe.'

'Aye. Hewe says I have a natural feel for riding, and I have already ridden alone. I just did not tell you.'

He grinned. 'Why am I not surprised? So, you are sure?'

She locked onto his gaze. 'I've never felt more ready for anything in all my life. I am finally free.'

Ewan couldn't believe the skill and nerve that Catriona had acquired over the week she had been working with the stable hands and Hewe to gain confidence in her horsemanship skills. She smiled with glee as Reed brought her preferred horse, a mare named Starlight, of all things. The first day she had ridden atop her, it had been a match, and Ewan wasn't surprised to see that Catriona had asked for them to saddle the beautiful brown mare with white markings along her nose.

'Ready?' he asked.

'Aye,' she answered. She mounted with ease and smiled at him. 'Race you to the large rowan tree at the end of the meadow,' she challenged him.

'What are we racing for?'

'Whatever it is you wish, my laird, although it doesn't matter. I shall win.' She urged her mare on with a click of her tongue and her boot.

Ewan laughed, and he and Wee Bit gave chase through the meadow. The horses galloped abreast, trimming the distance between the barn and designated rowan tree with speed. Catriona shouted and laughed as she rode, a joy he had never witnessed emanating from her. She was alive and happy, and all at once, Ewan realised he felt the same way. A wave of hope washed over him along with a desperate longing that she would choose him and Glenhaven and be a part of their lives forever.

The horses cut through the meadow, their hooves thundering along the grass, kicking up dirt. The ride and the sweet smell of the field filled his senses. There was nothing like galloping full out with the sun kissing your face and wind hitting your cheeks, washing away every care. So he gave in to the moment and forgot about all his worries as he revelled in Catriona's beauty, in being alive, and in being here as Laird of Glenhaven.

There was nowhere else he wished to be and no one else he wished to be with. He was content in who he was with her right now. The rowan tree became larger as they approached, and the two of them raced past its mighty limbs side by side. They pulled up to a slow cantor, and then into a walk, their horses breathing as heavily as they were.

'Seems another tie, my lady,' Ewan offered.

She laughed. 'Is there any other way for us to compete? Perhaps we do not wish the other to win but also do not wish to lose.'

'I think you may be on to something,' he added. He dismounted and led Wee Bit over to the shade of the tree where the horse could graze. He tossed the reins loosely over the lowest branch and walked over to assist Catriona with her dismount.

She accepted his hand and was easily guided down to the ground. His breath hitched at the sight of her. Colour was high in her cheeks from the exertion, her hair loose from its plait from the wind. The relaxed ease of her face made him literally weak in the knees, and his fingers tingled.

'You were right,' she murmured. 'Riding like that gives me a glorious sense of freedom. I am glad you encouraged me to get over my worries and try riding. I can with certainty tell you that I do indeed like it... as I do you.'

He stepped closer. 'You do?'

She batted his arm. 'As you well know.'

'Aye, I do know. And I have developed...affection for you...as you well know.' He was careful to not say *love*, for love was still forbidden to him. But affection and desire were allowed, and both burned brightly in him. He stepped closer to her, as close as possible without touching her. He'd been disciplined at keeping himself at bay as she was still officially married, but now...now that he knew she was no longer the wife of Mr Gordon, he found it even harder to stay the course.

She let her fingertips trail along the side of his face, and he summoned all the strength he had left not to react.

'So, what are we to do about it? 'Tis your decision as to whether you stay or go. All the cards of the future are in your hands to choose from. What say you?' he asked.

He held his breath for her answer.

'I cannot make such a decision without knowing one thing.'

'And what is that?'

'What it feels like for you to kiss me,' she murmured, moving closer.

He closed the space between them with one step and clutched her face, seizing her lips with the hunger and desire he had kept smouldering for so long. She matched the intensity of his kiss, which only heightened his pleasure. She wound her fingertips around the nape of his neck, and he deepened the kiss over and over. If he kissed her much longer, he'd be unable to pull away. The woman had asked for a kiss, not a ravishing, so he commanded himself to stop. With reluctance, he did just that.

As he stared into her eyes, her lips swollen and parted, the desire he saw there reflected his own. They were more than compatible, it seemed, on all accounts. It was up to her as to whether they had a life together, and for once he hated his own gallantry. Why had he offered her such an out?

Because he would not be like all the others in her life. He would not control her but give her a choice and voice in her future.

He clenched his jaw.

'You provide a persuasive argument, my laird. Those lips could bring a woman to swoon.'

He ran a thumb across her lips, his hunger for her still coursing through him.

She stilled his hand with her own. 'My answer is yes.'

Time stood still.

'Yes? Yes, to being my wife?'

'Aye, my laird. Despite my ability to choose freedom, I choose you, for you have taught me that I can have both.'

He seized her lips again and kissed her over and over and over.

Chapter Eighteen

'I cannot help but think upon the fact that meeting you was a miracle. All because I needed to go to the milliner's store. What are the odds?' Brenna said as she held up one square of fabric after another next to Catriona's cheek, while standing near the bank of windows in Catriona's room. 'Nay,' Brenna muttered, making a sour face. 'This one has a yellow undertone, which makes your beautifully creamy skin look quite ghastly.'

Catriona laughed. 'I have never received a finer compliment. Thank you, my lady,' she mocked, bobbing a faux curtsey at her soon-to-be sister-in-law. 'Are you sure they are not all the same shade? They all seem... blue.'

Brenna frowned. 'They are not all merely blue. Some have yellow undertones and others green. There are times when you sound just like Moira. My eldest sister will adore you.' She grinned. 'But only half as much as I do.'

'How can you adore me? You have only known me for two and a half weeks,' Catriona challenged her, part in jest but also part in truth. Why this family had accepted her so readily, she didn't understand. She'd not had a family for so long that she didn't trust the idea of having one again, despite how much love she felt for them already. More than she could ever have asked for. Although she'd have to be careful about her 'love' for Ewan. He was still bent on them not getting too caught up in feelings for one another.

Brenna set aside the squares of fabric and gripped Catriona by the shoulders. 'You are one of the most interesting women I have ever met. You are strong, have your own mind, and you...' Her eyes grew glassy with unshed tears, and she cleared her throat before continuing. 'And you have made my brother happy, which was something I did not dare dream possible.'

To her surprise, Catriona's own eyes filled with emotion. 'I hope I do not disappoint you,' she murmured before pulling Brenna into a hug.

'Never, sister. Never.'

'Never?'

Brenna stepped back. 'Not unless you do choose that ghastly blue fabric for your gown at our celebration ball next week to announce your engagement to Ewan.'

Catriona laughed. 'Speaking of the ball, what are my chances of the clan accepting me as Ewan's wife? I am a poor widow and not from the Highlands.'

'To be honest, they will all be against you from the start, but you will win them over just like you did us. You are a gem amongst women, Catriona. *We* are the ones lucky to have *you* in our lives. Now stay still as

I have a few more possibilities.' She held up another square and then tossed it aside with a flourish.

Catriona worried her hands, and her stomach flipped. She hoped dearly her future sister-in-law was right. Otherwise, this engagement of theirs might be very, very brief indeed.

Music from the main hall echoed throughout the walls of the salon at Glenhaven despite having the door closed. The evening of the ball had arrived in a blink, and here Catriona was about to be announced as the future Lady Stewart. She stared upon the portrait of the last Lady of Glenhaven and swallowed hard. Is this how she had felt upon the announcement of her marriage to Ewan's father? She doubted it. Self-confidence emanated from the woman's keen, unflinching gaze and subtle smirk.

'I wish you would tell me your secrets, my lady. I am in dire need of them.'

Catriona rubbed her arms from the chill of expectation and paced up and down the length of the room once more. She knew it was almost time for Ewan to fetch her for the announcement.

Was it too late to run?

She stilled. *Fool.* She didn't wish to run. She wanted to stay. The life she could have with Ewan and his family was more than she had ever dreamed possible for herself and her future, but nagging fear raced through her. What if they rejected her? Shamed her for having such a murky past? She'd already endured enough shame and hate for a lifetime and didn't wish to have any more rebukes thrust upon her, especially by those who didn't know her.

The door squeaked open, and Catriona turned from where she stood in the shadows of the room.

'You could not look more lovely,' Ewan murmured, his voice husky and deep as he closed the door behind him.

Appreciation glowed in his gaze as his eyes swept over her. Warmth and happiness loosened the knot in her chest. No man had ever looked at her with such reverence as if she were beauty itself and he a mere pauper allowed to gaze upon her. She fidgeted with the locket around her neck. It hung at her throat on a matching blue ribbon from Brenna. That way she could wear it nestled around her neck rather than hidden deep in her bodice.

Catriona sighed at the sight of him upon approach. 'And *you*, Laird Stewart, will make every woman at this ball weak in the knees at the sight of you.' She meant it. Even now, a quiver ran up her arm as he stood before her with his blue-green eyes piercing into her and dressed in his regal red Stewart plaid, which revealed his muscular knees and calves. He wore his finest white tunic and cravat, and a black dress coat. Even his dark hair had been styled with care, not a single strand out of place.

He looked every bit a laird.

And she was a no one.

She swallowed hard as doubt thrust itself between the two of them.

He pressed a kiss to her cheek and meandered towards her lips, eventually capturing them for a heated and full kiss, which melted all her doubt and reason away.

'You make thinking clearly quite a challenge, my laird,' she murmured after he pulled back. He smelled of tallow and mint, and she breathed him in as he ran both his hands down her bare arms, sending her senses ablaze.

'Are you ready for the wrath that shall consume you upon your announcement?' she asked, unable to keep her fears at bay after all. Her nerves were frayed and taut at the knowing that the excitement over their news would most likely send the clan and its leaders into uncertainty and chaos.

'The elders loved you when they came to dine,' he offered.

'Aye. They loved Mrs Gordon, cousin to Laird MacLean, who had no intention of staying. When they learn the truth about my past and that I will be part of the clan and their future as Lady Stewart, I believe their love of me shall morph into something quite different. Something more akin to hate.'

She was relieved to have at least said it aloud, so she did not have to hold all her worries upon her heart alone. That was what marriage would be, would it not? A sharing of concerns and bearing the weight of burdens equally, as well as events that gave cause for celebration?

He leaned his forehead against hers. 'They may be upset or even angry, but that will not deter me or my decision. I hope it will not change yours.'

'Not a chance,' she said with as much courage as she could muster. Truth be told, she wasn't sure. She was nervous and had a pit of worry settled deep in her stomach, where her doubts lingered and multiplied. Over the years, she'd learned not to trust the possibility of good things.

She also wanted to be able to tell the man she loved the truth, that she was indeed falling for him and longed for their marriage to be allowed the complication of love, but the man didn't wish to be loved, did he? So she shoved it down deep with her doubt about being accepted and gifted the laird a smile instead.

'Shall we go?' he asked. 'While the music and spirits are high? Mrs Stevens tells me everyone has arrived, even the elders.'

'I suppose I cannot hide out in here all night. The clarsach and I have not quite come to an understanding yet, as you well know.'

He offered his arm to her, which she readily accepted. 'There will be time enough for more lessons, Mrs Gordon. I plan to teach you them all.'

She smiled.

He whispered in her ear. 'And many of those lessons will have nothing to do with music.'

His devilish smirk made her laugh, and before she knew it, she was within the hall by his side. The room glowed with candlelight and wealth. Ladies were adorned with jewels and the finest gowns, and the men wore their best plaid, jackets, and broaches. Shoes shone from a recent polish, and the air was alive with the smells of cooked meats, sweet cakes, and wine. A more glorious celebration she could not have imagined. She met Brenna's gaze across the room and smiled. Her future sister-in-law nodded back, her face full of determination and happiness.

A hush filled the room at the sight of Ewan and Catriona together, and she lifted her chin and steadied herself. If nothing else, she needed to look like a lady even if she didn't entirely feel like one in her bones. But she knew if she looked weak or uncertain about herself, people would crush her to the ground. So she smiled, squared her shoulders, and remembered that he had chosen her, he had saved her, and she owed him more than she could ever repay. She'd not embarrass him or herself. She would act like Lady Stewart, and anyone who besmirched her also besmirched him. And she'd not let that happen. He had given her an opportunity for a new life, a different life far beyond what she could have ever dreamed possible for herself. She'd not let anyone seize it from her now that she had also chosen it.

'Ladies and gentlemen,' Ewan began, his voice booming across the crowd of guests, 'thank you for coming this eve to celebrate my upcoming nuptials with my bride, whom I will introduce to you now: Catriona Gordon from Edinburgh.'

Since she couldn't claim a home to be from, they had decided upon Edinburgh. Anyone who dug much further into it would know quickly that she had been raised in Lismore and had no living relatives. She held her smile as all of this raced through her mind and a silence fell over the crowd. When the quiet extended to one beat and then another, Laird MacLean raised his tankard. 'Slainte!'

Despite a bit of an awkward pause, the crowd echoed

his cheers to them and drank from their cups. Then, thankfully the music started up again. Ewan kissed her cheek, grabbed her hand, and guided them through the throngs of people to Laird MacLean and Brenna. Slowly the noise in the room picked up as the guests returned to dancing, chatting, and feasting.

'Saving the day as always. Thank you, brother,' said Ewan, clapping Laird MacLean on the shoulder.

'Just helping out a fellow laird,' he joked. 'Congratulations to the happy couple-to-be,' he said.

'Thank you,' Catriona answered. 'For allowing me to claim you as family, and for bringing that rather awkward silence to an end.'

'You will be family soon, and I am grateful for such an honour,' he replied. 'Now, just be yourself, and they will adore you.'

His kindness helped to calm the worry racing through her. She would do just as he said and circulate about the crowd to meet as many people as she could; she would not cower and hide as if she should be ashamed. Her past was just that and nothing she could control. Her future as Lady Stewart started now.

'Perhaps I will do just that, my laird,' she replied, lifting a brow at him.

'Not alone you won't,' Brenna added. 'Allow me to help you weave through the lion's and lioness's dens.' She flashed Catriona an impish smile and wove her arm through hers, and off into the crowd they went.

They greeted several of what Brenna described as the more powerful women of the clan, as their husbands had been advisors to her late father. Some of them were kind, while others endured an exchange of pleasantries but little more.

'I cannot help but notice the elders have made their way to Ewan. Shall we rescue him?' Catriona asked as she watched halfway across the room.

Brenna studied him and shook her head. 'Nay. He is handling his own. Garrick is also with him. Despite his innate kindness, he can cut a man down to the quick if need be.' She leaned closer. 'Besides, you must meet Susanna Cameron, whose brother is laird. The Camerons are the most powerful clan in the Highlands, especially since the fall of the Campbells, who had quite a battle with their long-time rivals, the MacDonalds. Rumour has it that it was Susanna and her men who helped Laird Campbell rescue his now wife and child from being murdered at the hands of her own father.'

'What?' Catriona asked stopping in her tracks. 'Can you explain that again?'

'No matter for now.' She waved her hand. 'Come. You will adore her, I promise. Her glare can slay a man, I tell you.' She sighed. 'If only I had such powers.'

Catriona smiled and followed behind Brenna as the men and women were packed in tightly on this side of the banquet hall.

'Why are there so many soldiers over here?' Catriona muttered as she passed by dozens of them chatting with their tankards of ale and wine. One almost sloshed his drink on her as she squeezed by. 'And some appear rather deep in their cups,' she added, glancing back at a soldier who almost fell over his own boots.

'No need to worry. The Camerons always travel with soldiers, many soldiers.'

'All of these soldiers are watching over this one woman?' she asked.

'Aye. Her brothers were unable to attend, so these men are also her escorts to ensure her safety.'

When she reached Brenna's side, Catriona paused and met the gaze of a woman whose eyes seemed capable of cutting through stone. They were a light ice blue in stark contrast to her pitch-black hair and pale, pearly skin. Despite being indoors, she was partially hidden by the hood of her dark cloak, and Brenna could only imagine how shockingly beautiful she might be without hiding part of herself from the world.

'Susanna,' Brenna began, 'this is Catriona Gordon, my future sister-in-law. And Catriona, this is Susanna Cameron, sister of Laird Cameron. We share a border with her people.'

'Lovely to meet you, Miss Cameron,' Catriona offered up, unable to look away from the woman's compelling gaze.

Susanna paused and stepped closer. 'Have we met before, Miss Gordon?' she asked, her gaze falling to the locket around Catriona's neck.

She fought the urge to take a step back and commanded herself to hold her ground. According to Brenna, this woman and her clan were important, and Catriona needed to make a good impression on her. 'Nay, my lady. Prior to a few weeks ago, I did not often travel up to the Highlands from Edinburgh.'

She commended herself on how calm she sounded as

she wove an answer that resembled truth even though one couldn't say it was completely true. Brenna glanced over at her and cleared her throat.

'You are sure?'

Catriona searched her memory, and nothing came up. 'If you do not mind me saying, Miss Cameron, I do not believe I would have forgotten such a meeting. You have a very distinctive face and compelling presence about you.'

The woman's gaze shifted to Catriona's face, and she smiled and nodded. 'You are correct in that not many people forget me. But you also have a remarkable face, and your eyes, such an unusual shade of gold and brown.'

'Thank you,' Catriona answered. A small seed of uncertainty budded within her. Just as she had always been able to sense when Thomas was in a foul temper, Catriona could feel something was in the air with Miss Cameron. Catriona's throat tightened as she prepared for whatever verbal lashing the woman was about to give her.

'And where did you come by that locket?'

Catriona's pulse increased, her heart pounding in her chest as if she were riding in the fields on Starlight's back. 'I do not know, but I have always had it. For as long as I can remember,' she answered, her throat suddenly dry.

'Oh?' Susanna asked taking another half step towards her. 'You have no recollection at all?' Her tone was sharp and unyielding. She gripped Catriona's upper arm.

'I don't understand what I've said to upset you, Miss

Cameron. I honestly do not know who gave me the locket.'

The woman tightened her grip, and a wildness came into her blue eyes. A few soldiers noted her distress and closed ranks around them. Brenna chimed in as she was pressed close to Catriona. 'Susanna? What is this all about? Tell your men to stand down.'

'I will do no such thing until this woman tells me who she is and how she came by this locket.' Susanna glared at her, pain flashing bright in her eyes.

'I am Catriona Gordon from Edinburgh.'

'I know what you have said, but I doubt the truth of your words,' she hissed in frustration. 'Who gave you this locket?' She yanked Catriona close to her face.

Alarmed, Catriona tried to pull back from her, but it was too late. The circle around them was too tight, and Susanna's grip far too strong. There was nowhere to go. Against her better judgement, she stated the truth. 'I do not know. I cannot remember much before I was around six years old.'

'And why not?'

'Because I lost my family at sea. I woke on the shoreline with no memory of who I was or where I was from. I was lucky to have survived and been found by Nettie, a woman who then raised me.'

'You believe yourself to be an orphan?' The woman gasped.

'Aye, my lady,' she said, shame heating her cheeks. 'I don't just believe it. I am one. I have no family.'

Chapter Nineteen

Susanna let go of Catriona's arm as if the words she spoke slapped her. Catriona rubbed her upper arm where the woman had gripped her so fiercely.

'That's not possible...' Susanna began, but paused, noting that a crowd had gathered and that many of the conversations around them had ceased as others watched their exchange. 'Not here,' she commanded and clutched Catriona by the wrist.

Frightened and confused by the woman's bizarre behaviour, Catriona freed herself. 'Nay,' she said as calmly as she could without creating a greater scene. 'I'll not go anywhere with you, Miss Cameron, until I know what this is about.'

Susanna dropped her voice low. 'Trust me in that you do not want this conversation aired about in here for everyone to hear.' Her eyes flashed with a warning Catriona decided to heed.

'Then I will find Laird Stewart and meet you and your men in the salon, but I will not be dragged from here by force.' She'd been treated so before, but she'd promised herself never again. And that meant today. It didn't matter if Miss Cameron was from the most influential clan in the Highlands. She only hoped Ewan would understand and that she didn't muck up too much by standing up for herself.

Susanna nodded, which seemed the closest Catriona would get to a verbal agreement, so she began scanning the room for Ewan. Brenna was at her side as she carved a path through the crowd.

'What happened?' Brenna asked. 'I've never seen her like that before. She's usually as composed and cool as a frozen loch, but not today.'

'I don't know. None of it made any sense, but she seemed quite undone by my locket. Why?' she mused. 'It is a rather crude piece of jewellery worn by time and age. I only cherish it as it is from my childhood. I do not even know who gifted it to me. Nettie said I had it on me the day she found me.'

'That is odd. Why would Susanna care a whit about your locket or who gave it to you?'

'That is exactly what we must find out, but I need Ewan to be there in case things go poorly. If she is as important as you say, this situation between us could have a devastating effect on the clan, and I don't wish for that at all. Will you help me find him?'

'Aye,' Brenna murmured. 'Him and Garrick.'

Catriona and Brenna continued, struggling to see over the heads of tall soldiers and around the billowing gowns of the ladies in attendance, as they made their way through the crowd.

'Ah!' Brenna cried out. 'I see them. Their backs were

to us, which is why they did not see the exchange and come to intercede. I will let them know what has happened. We will meet you in the salon.'

She paused. What if she went in there and he didn't come? What if he saw it as a sign that she had failed in her duties as Lady Stewart before she had even begun?

Trust him.

If she wanted to marry this man, which she did, she had to start trusting him. Right now. Not when it was easy, but when it was hard. She snaked through the crowd as quickly as she dared without drawing any more undue attention to herself and made her way into the salon. She closed the door behind her and stared up at the portrait of Lady Stewart.

Why did I ever think I could do this? I've already upset the most prominent clan in the Highlands as well as the elders, and my engagement to your son has only just been announced. What do I do now?

She would do what she always did.

She sucked in a deep breath and released it, not once but twice. Then she squared her shoulders, lifted her chin, and carried on.

The door opened behind her. Ewan and Brenna rushed in with Garrick not far behind.

'What is this Brenna tells me about Susanna Cameron?' Ewan asked, his brow furrowed. He reached Catriona and took her hands in his own.

She met his gaze, her nerves settled by his words and his touch. There was no anger, only concern for her in his tone. Why had she been so worried? Her stomach fluttered in relief. 'She was certain we had met before, but I told her we hadn't. Then she carried on about this locket, which has no value to anyone but me.'

'Your locket?' he asked.

'Aye.'

'Why?'

'I don't know, but when I could not answer who gifted it to me, she became more upset. Finally she asked for us to speak outside of the hall, to not draw any further attention to our conversation. She was becoming quite…impassioned by it all, and people were starting to notice. There were more than a few gazes set upon us as we spoke.' She gripped Ewan's hand, steadied by the warm, firm pressure of his hold. 'I fear I may have embarrassed you already. I confessed to her I was an orphan to try to convince her and calm her that she was mistaken in her thoughts as to who I was.' She searched his gaze seeing if this would be what drove him off, but he kissed her hand instead.

'You could never embarrass me. I'm glad you told her the truth. Now people will know just how strong you are, like I do.'

Her breath caught in her throat. Before she could reply, the door opened. Susanna Cameron strode in with her long, dark cloak trailing behind her, along with three of her men. She nodded, and they closed the door and stood guarding it, providing them the privacy and perhaps the barricade she asked for.

'My laird,' she said as she saw Ewan. 'Thank you for joining us.'

Ewan let go of Catriona's hands and stepped between her and Susanna. 'You seem to have made a scene, Miss

Cameron. Care to explain why you are harassing my betrothed on the night of our celebration? Surely your enquiry can wait.' His words held a chastisement to her behaviour that couldn't be missed. He sounded like a laird setting a member of his community in their place, and Catriona commanded herself to keep her mouth closed. This Ewan she had never seen before.

Susanna paused and after a moment backed down. 'You are right. My apologies, my laird. I regret that I could not better control my emotions at the sight of her. It was a shock.' The woman looked past him to Catriona, and the sentiment in her eyes was unmistakable. Was it grief? Sadness?

Catriona could make no sense of it all.

Ewan shook his head. 'Miss Cameron, you are speaking in riddles, and I grow impatient. There is much to attend to this eve, and I would like to celebrate with my bride-to-be. Why are we here, and what is it you want?' A dark edge gave his words an added warning.

Susanna's ice-blue eyes flashed up to match his challenge. 'Surely you remember the summer of 1726, my laird.'

'What?' he asked, his brow crinkled.

'We are about the same age, if I remember correctly, so we both would have been almost ten years old.' Her eyes filled with emotion. 'Catriona would have been about six at that time.'

Ewan stilled; his body tensed. He held Susanna's gaze and then turned to Catriona as if seeing her for the first time. 'Susanna,' he whispered, his voice husky. 'It cannot be.'

'I believe it is.'

'But all this time…' Ewan covered his mouth with his hand and shook his head.

Catriona looked to both of them. 'I do not understand either of you. Brenna, can you explain this to me?'

Brenna's mouth was gaping open. 'The Lost Girl,' she murmured. 'Moira and I never wanted to swim along the loch after that summer for fear of—' She stopped.

Blast. Everyone was speaking in puzzles that she could not decipher. 'For fear of what, Brenna?' Catriona asked, her heart raging in her chest.

'Being lost at sea,' Ewan answered as he took her hand in his. 'The Camerons' youngest daughter disappeared at the beach near Loch Linnhe the summer of 1726, pulled out to sea in the undertow. Word of her disappearance spread to all the clans in the area. We spent months looking for any sign of her. When she was never found, she was believed to be dead.' He shook his head. 'You told us of your memory of being at the beach and being lost at sea, and Nettie's belief that your family had died at sea when your boat must have capsized, but I did not even consider you might have been the lost Cameron sister. I should have thought of it, but I didn't. It was so long ago.'

Catriona stared back at them in disbelief.

'I believe you are my long-lost younger sister, Violet,' said Susanna.

'You believe I am your sister? Why? It has been so long. How—' Catriona sputtered, and then stopped just as abruptly as she became overwhelmed by the assertion.

A smile softened the woman's features and made her even more beautiful. 'It was your eyes at first. My sister always had the most stunning amber-gold eyes, much like yours. And then when I saw the locket about your neck, I nearly fell to my knees. It is the locket I gave my sister before she disappeared.' Her eyes welled, but she blinked back the tears.

No doubt Susanna Cameron was not a woman who cried in public.

Catriona felt numb. Her toes and fingers tingled, and a strange feeling of floating came over her. How could any of what she was saying be true? Was this woman merely mad with grief because Catriona resembled a sister she had lost?

'What you are saying would be most remarkable if it were true,' Laird MacLean offered. 'It would mean she would be a part of the Cameron clan, a sister of the laird, like you.' He came closer to Miss Cameron. 'Is there some way that you could prove what you say may be true other than your memories of her?'

'Does your locket still have the tiny, pressed violet I put in it all of those years ago for your birthday?' she asked, a wistfulness in her voice.

Catriona opened the locket. 'Nay,' she answered, shifting on her feet. 'I am sorry. It contains nothing. It never has. It is empty.'

Susanna's eyes closed and she shook her head. 'If only my brothers were here. I know Rolf and Royce would be able to say for certain. They would be able to confirm or deny my claim.'

'But they are not here, my lady,' Ewan stated. 'While

it is *possible* she may be your sister, there is also every possibility she is not. I know you wish for her to be your sister, but the chances…'

Susanna sighed. 'I know the chances are small, especially after all these years, but there is still a chance. Could you come to us, to our home at Loch's End, so we could talk?' Susanna pleaded. 'Perhaps being there or speaking with my brothers will spark a memory.'

Catriona met the woman's desperate gaze. She didn't know if she wished for it to be true or not. Could it be that she wasn't an orphan? That she had a family? That all this time, she had just been lost to them?

That she could have lived an altogether different life, a better one?

Her stomach dropped, and she felt ill. She clutched Ewan's arm for support. Susanna rushed to her, but Catriona pushed her away.

'Get away from me,' Catriona shouted through her anguish, her voice sounding nothing like her own. 'I do not know you. And even if you were my family, why did you not search for me to the ends of the earth rather than abandoning me? Why?'

Susanna staggered back, her face pained and uncertain as her soldiers rushed to her sides to steady her. 'You do not understand, sister,' she pleaded. 'We thought you dead.'

'You are just one of many that gave up on me, my lady,' she said, gripping Ewan's arm. 'Please take me out of here, my laird.'

'Catriona,' he reasoned. 'If there is any chance that

she is indeed your sister, then you must speak with her. You cannot just run away...'

'My sister, my family, would not have given up on finding me. This is *not* my sister,' she stated, glaring at Susanna. 'I cannot be in this room a moment longer.'

She shook off Ewan's hold and ran past all of them to the door. She moved quickly down the corridor, doing her best to keep the tears and hysteria that threatened at bay. Thankfully most of the guests were so deep in their cups or enthralled by dancing that few of them gave her any notice at all.

When she burst through the door to the outside, she ran down the hill until she reached her favourite spot: a large, flat shelf of a rock that acted as a bench for her to sit upon. She gathered her gown into a bundle and hoisted herself up on the stone. She sat and sighed as she leaned back on the cool, hard surface. The pressure soothed the ache in her chest, and the sight of the stars in the night sky helped her heart regain a more regular rhythm.

Only the heavens seemed to understand her. Other than Ewan. She smiled at the thought of his kindness, his smile, and his support. She knew he had not meant anything unkind in his suggestion to stay and speak to Susanna, but he did not understand. How could he? He'd had a family all his life. Even if they'd been difficult and he'd suffered loss, he'd known them and knew who he was and where he belonged. He was the son of a laird and a Stewart, and he always had been.

But her?

She'd been lost to the world with singular snippets

of memory to tether her to her past and what had been her family. If Susanna's supposition was true, then Catriona was a Cameron, one of the most prominent clans in the Highlands, and she was the sister of the laird. Tears streamed down her cheeks, and she released the sobs she'd held at bay. She wept until she could cry no more. She wept for the life that could have been. For the life lost to the sea.

Chapter Twenty

'How is Catriona?' Brenna asked from the doorway of Ewan's study.

He set aside the map he'd been poring over with little progress. 'As horrid as you might imagine. She refuses to let anyone in her chamber except for Betsy.'

Brenna scoffed. 'Ewan, has it escaped you that not only is she your betrothed, but that you are the laird, own this castle, and can make a demand to see her?'

Ewan frowned. 'I don't think that would be well-received. If anything, that would make things entirely worse, for she would be angry with me.'

'Angry at you for checking on her? Caring for her? That is no crime.' She sifted through some of the piles on his desk, and he playfully slapped her hand away.

'Do you have nothing to entertain yourself with today?' he asked. 'If not, I have many a letter you could draft for me.'

She lifted her brow at him. 'Well, I could do that for you if you would do something for me by checking on your soon-to-be wife?' She sent him a sweet smile.

He sighed. 'You will grant me no peace until I do this, will you?'

'Nay. I will not, brother.'

'Fine,' he murmured. He stood, gathered a pile of correspondence, a stack of fresh parchment, and his ink pot and quill, and set them before her on the large table. 'If you will be so kind as to deal with this, I will speak with her. Let us hope we are both productive in our endeavours.'

'Be sure to straighten your cravat, brother,' she called after him. 'You look like the devil.'

The last thing he cared about today was his appearance. Two days had passed since the celebration, and Catriona had barely left her chambers. And he wouldn't be his father and demand an audience with her. He could, however, insist she speak with him to ensure her well-being. Those two things were different, weren't they?

He frowned. Not really.

Soon he was at her chamber door, so whether they were different or not didn't matter. He was already here. He knocked loudly. When no one answered, he knocked again. 'Catriona? I must speak with you. I need to know you are well. I have not seen you for days.'

'I am well, my laird.'

'May I speak with you, so I can see with my own eyes? I miss you.' The last three words slipped out. Why the devil had he said that? He cringed.

No romantic entanglements, remember?

He was on a slippery slope. He didn't wish to mess up the fine arrangement they had now by loving his future wife. That would only lead to heartache and ruin. He was certain of it.

After a long pause, he heard footsteps, and then the lock on the door clicked. She didn't open the door for him, but offered, 'You may come in.'

He opened the door to find the room neat as a pin and glimmering with sheen. 'Have you been cleaning?' he asked, unable to suppress his curiosity.

'When I am upset, I clean. Is that a problem, my laird? I have already made Betsy cross with me about it. Shall I add you to the list?'

He clenched his jaw. *Deuces.* She was in a fine temper. Why did he ever listen to Brenna? Catriona was in no mood to speak to anyone, let alone him.

Each question she asked was a skilfully laced trap, and he was sure to misstep and land himself in a load of horse dung fit to drown a man. He ran a hand through his hair.

'Well?' she prodded. 'You have seen me. I am well. Is there anything else?' She set a glare on him that would have made his mother proud. He stilled like a deer.

There was no right answer, and he knew it, so he forged on with a truth he would have wanted someone to share with him. He approached her and placed a hand on her arm. She flinched under his touch but did not move away.

'You cannot ignore the issue forever,' he said. 'Why will you not just visit the Camerons? It will help you find out the truth one way or the other. And the answer does not even matter. Either way, we will marry and live our lives, but at least you will know. It will no longer be a question mark in your life.'

She scoffed and moved out of his reach. 'It will not matter? You must be teasing me. There is no winning. If they are my long-lost family, I will know what all I have lost. If they are not, then my hopes will be dashed. Either choice is heartbreak. Can you not see that?' she said, her eyes sparking with emotion.

Bollocks. He saw that now. 'I did not think of it that way, but you're right. I don't know how you feel because I have not lived your life. But I want to help you. To be your partner in this. To try to do what a husband would and support you,' he said, squeezing the bridge of his nose. 'Even if I make a terrible muck of it while trying.'

'Why will no one leave me to make up my own mind on things?' she replied and walked right past him and out through the door, muttering as she walked down the corridor.

'Mrs Gordon?' Betsy called. Ewan turned to find her standing in the hallway with fresh linens, staring after Catriona.

'I came to speak with her,' Ewan offered.

'Aye. How did it go, my laird?' she asked, clutching the linens to her chest.

'Not as well as I had hoped, Betsy.'

'Best give her some time to cool off, my laird. She's not been herself since the ball.'

'Aye. She hasn't. Perhaps some fresh air will do her some good.'

He'd give her time for her temper to cool and seek her out once more. He knew that anything worth having was worth fighting for, and above all things, he'd fight for her whether she wanted him to or not.

'I thought I might find you here,' said Ewan as he reached the top of the slope overlooking the loch below.

Hours had passed since he'd tried to speak with her. He'd even dined without her, but he wouldn't be able to sleep until he'd spoken to her, even if she didn't wish to speak to him.

Catriona faced him, and Ewan's steps faltered. The glow of the sunset cast a golden radiance about her skin, setting her amber eyes and auburn crown ablaze as a few wisps of hair flitted about her face in the light breeze. Despite having been with her for weeks now, the sheer beauty of her continued to arrest and steal his senses in the best and most complete of ways. And she was to be his wife.

'Oh?' she said.

'Aye,' he answered, smiling and closing the few steps remaining between them. He nodded to the wolfhound charging up the hill towards them. 'Whenever I cannot find Rufus, I know you are here with him and he with you.'

Rufus trotted up to him and leaned into his thigh, his pink tongue lolling out of the side of his mouth as he panted.

'Traitor,' Ewan murmured, casting a playful narrowing gaze at his beloved dog, who pressed against him to accept a scratch behind the ear.

'He is a dear companion,' she added, smiling at Rufus. 'I never had a dog before, and I find I might like to have a pack of them. They are fine company. They listen, but offer no advice, which works well for me.' She lifted her brows meaningfully at Ewan, crossed her arms against her chest, and faced the loch and the orange-pink sky.

Ack. Just as he thought. He'd bungled their previous conversation. He should have just listened instead of attempting to solve anything. She'd found out that she might have a family thought long lost to her, a subject he knew nothing about. Rubbing the back of his neck, he stared out at the water. Perhaps he could tell her what he did know. He stilled and his hand dropped to his side.

Or he could just apologise. He shifted on his feet.

'I'm sorry.'

The words felt and sounded like he'd swallowed a fistful of pebbles.

Her form stiffened at his words. Perhaps she was as surprised as he.

When she didn't respond, he wondered if he'd said them at all.

'What for?' she said.

Ah, so he had said the words, and she had heard them. He tugged at his coat sleeve and came a step closer, allowing his shoulder to brush against her own.

'For being an arse. I should have listened to you rather than offered advice.'

He studied her profile as she stared out at the loch, its grey waters as still and smooth as glass despite the light puffs of breeze that ruffled the vibrant green grass along the glen. A bird flew off a tree branch, swooping low and then high. Rufus barked and charged off after it. She smiled. 'Such a simple life, I envy,' she whispered.

'Oh?' he replied. 'Why? It seems frustrating to chase prey one never catches.'

'It is that he is never deterred. Never gives up. Each day is a new start as if yesterday is forgotten. Each eve when we come out at dusk to walk, he charges head-long into this meadow and towards a loch that he has seen a thousand days as if he has never run the track of it before.'

'Such can be your life as well,' he said. 'You can choose joy and let every day be a fresh start and new beginning.'

'As could you,' she answered setting her gaze on him once more.

Her words landed like an arrow hitting its mark. 'You are right,' he murmured reluctantly. 'As terrifying as such a risk for hope might be.' He smiled. 'You have a keen way of turning my own words around on me.'

She chuckled. 'And you hate it, do you not?'

'I abhor it,' he answered, finding laughter tinging the ends of his words as well.

'Why?'

'It quite reminds me of my sister Moira.' He paused. 'And my mother, truth be told.'

'Walk with me. Perhaps you can tell me more about them both. Despite your complaints, I hear the warmth and affection in your voice. It will distract me from my anger at you,' she teased.

He offered his arm, and she accepted it as if they

had done it a thousand times before like Rufus charging along the meadow.

The unexpected feel of her body nestled up to his sent a feathering of desire and excitement along his limbs. His bicep flexed as he tugged her a mite closer, as close as he dared. 'A walk along the loch it is,' he answered, keen to not lose this moment. She'd not offered her touch since the ball, and he dared not lose his advantage. He was keen to win back her favour.

Rufus circled back, whipping past them, and Catriona laughed. The sound tightened his chest, but he spoke despite it. 'My mother and Moira had much in common. They even looked alike. Moira was like a smaller version of my mother, and as the eldest, she could run us about as she wished. I adore her, though. She is smart and clever and knows everything about anything with leaves.' He swallowed. 'And she is brave…and she is a survivor, much like you.' His chest tightened further. 'Mother was the same, which is why losing her was such a shock to all of us. In the blink of an eye, she was dead. I always argued with Moira that she had not died of a weakened heart, but that her heart had far too much love to hold. That when she'd died, all that love went free into the air, the soil, the trees, the birds…and into us. Mere foolish fancies, I know.'

'Nay. Perhaps it is true, and now all her love is around you. Always,' she whispered, meeting his gaze.

His throat constricted at the unexpected emotion coursing through him. His mother had been gone for so long, his reaction surprised him. And why in the world was he telling her all this? He'd never told anyone other than Moira.

Then the truth struck him like a lightning bolt, and his muscles seized.

He'd told her because he knew she understood him and his loss and felt it down to the ache in her soul. It sat reflected in her eyes and in the pulled-down corners of her mouth. Yet despite what it would stir in her, she still wanted to know everything, even if it pained her to walk through such loss because it reminded her of her own.

He couldn't speak, not trusting what would fall from his lips. They stopped and stood in silence, and she nestled further into his body, leaning her head on his shoulder.

Blazes.

Merely the feel of her set his body aflame, and he closed his eyes. He could never let her know the power she had over him or she would crush him, just like Emogene. And he would be left even smaller than he already was.

Or perhaps she wouldn't. She wasn't Emogene. What if she empowered him and made him the best version of himself, making him far greater than he could ever be without her by his side?

He wanted to believe in her, in them, in love…but could he trust it?

He should pull away, step out of their semblance of an embrace. She might soon become his wife, but he couldn't dare love her, could he?

He opened his eyes and shifted on his feet, garnering the courage to step out of their hold, when she spoke.

'At least you can remember her. I cannot remember my mother or father, no matter how hard I try. I squeeze my eyes shut willing just one blurry image of either of them, but nothing comes.'

'Nothing? You can remember nothing of them at all?'

The wind whipped up, and she shivered against him. 'Here,' he offered instinctively. He unbuttoned his overcoat with the intention of removing it and draping it over her shoulders, but she slid under the jacket with him, igniting a trail of fire against his tunic as she snuggled against his side, her arm resting around his waist.

He cleared his throat.

'Thank you. That is better,' she murmured, her voice reverberating through his body.

For her perhaps, but he was in agony. The smell, feel, and heat of her were lancing through his self-control after not seeing or feeling her for days, so he gave in and pulled her closer, his arm embracing her petite waist.

'At least I remember I had brothers and a sister, but I do not know if they were Susanna and her brothers. If I close my eyes, I can smell the salt of the sea air, the feel of the warm sun on my face, and hear their laughter as we chased one another towards the water before the wave crashed over me. They have been lost to me for so long that the possibility of them being alive and in my life now seems like a dream. One that is far too good to come true.'

'I cannot imagine how that feels. I am sorry, Catriona.'

'I know you are, and I am not angry at you, but the situation. You just happened to be there, offering me advice this afternoon that I did not want to hear, so I took my frustrations out on you. I am sorry, too.'

'So, what will you do? You know the Camerons are relentless. They will send you correspondence every day for the rest of our lives begging for you to visit, or they may very well appear on the drive, demanding entry to Glenhaven to speak with you.'

'You think so?' She sighed. 'I would have thought it would not have mattered after all of this time whether I was their sister or not.'

'Look at you. Who would not want you in their life? I know I am the greater man for it,' he offered and paused, turning her in his arms to face her.

'Really?' she asked, doubt in her eyes.

'Aye. You, Mrs Catriona Gordon, have helped me become a better man in the few weeks I have known you. Imagine what you will do for me over a lifetime.' He laughed and tucked a strand of hair behind her ear. 'You cannot begrudge their efforts to know the truth, can you?'

'Aye.' She sighed again. 'I suppose not. And I do wish to know. I am just fearful of how I will feel. Of what it will change in my life. I have had nothing until now. And then suddenly, I have options: I have you, and I have a possible long-lost family. It is more goodness than I can trust.'

'That is how I feel about you,' he replied.

'Ah, is that how you feel about being a laird as well? That it will all be taken from you in a moment?'

He stiffened. Such thoughts he tried to avoid these days. He had far too much to lose than he wanted to acknowledge. Self-doubt began to weave its imperceptible webs. His throat dried.

'You can tell me the truth. I will not tell anyone your doubts,' she said.

He released a breath and a chuckle all at once as unease and relief duelled within. 'Am I so easy to read?'

'You need not pretend with me. We will hold each other's secrets as husband and wife, will we not?' She lifted her face to him, her gaze searching his own for the truth.

Could he pretend and lie to her even if he dared? She would see right through him, would she not?

He nodded. 'I suppose we will, so aye, I have doubts. I am trying desperately to be the laird my father was and to guide our clan to prosperity rather than ruin, but...' He halted in exasperation.

She stepped out of his hold. 'But what?'

He ran a hand through his hair. 'But I do not want to become *him* in order to do that.'

'Who says you must? Can you not be a leader in your own right? You are Ewan Stewart, not Bran Stewart. Lead with kindness rather than an iron fist.'

He narrowed his gaze at her and crossed his arms against his chest. 'Be myself?'

'Aye,' she answered with lifted brow. 'As I've said before, who else can you be? Do you remember your lesson in the barn? It is only by trusting your instincts that you will be able to be the laird I know you can and will be.'

'And what of you? Shall you embrace my advice? Will you find out who you are by meeting with the Camerons and not hide from your fears?'

'I will follow your advice if you follow mine, my laird,' she answered with a smile. 'Agreed?'

'Agreed,' he replied.

The doubt that had tightened like a vice around his chest released him, and he took a full, heady breath before he seized her face in his hands and kissed her. He could feel the surprise on her lips, the shock of his actions in her lack of response at first. But then her lips softened against his own, her mouth yielding and answering his own desire with a matching ferocity. His hands slid back to the nape of her neck, weaving into the silky loose locks of her hair. Her arms slid around his shoulders, her fingertips skimming along his earlobes and neck, sending a crushing jolt of desire through him.

Had he ever felt such a response to a kiss?

Had she?

She shivered against him, and he stepped closer, pressing his body full along her own. Her solid, muscular frame nestled flush with his felt unholy yet necessary, a duality of feelings he was becoming accustomed to when it came to her. His lips claimed her own again and again as the smell of violets and wildflowers and the wind filled his nostrils. All too soon, she pulled away, resting her nose against the tip of his own.

'Well, my laird, I daresay that was a makeup kiss worth waiting for.'

'Aye. I would agree. Perhaps we should disagree more often.' He chuckled.

'Nay,' she answered. 'I find that I have missed you.'

'And I you.'

Chapter Twenty-One

As the carriage pulled out of the cobbled drive of Glenhaven, Catriona clutched her reticule to her stomach. She remained as uneasy as she had been when she'd rode in it for the first time weeks ago with nothing other than the clothes on her back, rescued by the strange laird who had purchased her. Ewan sat silently across from her, his gaze as unsettled as she felt. While they both wanted this visit to the Camerons, so she could truly know if they were her long-lost family or not, she couldn't shake her intuition. Something had changed between them, and she couldn't figure out what it was.

Ewan had been attentive and kind as they spent time together each day riding, and talking by the loch with Rufus. He also provided finger-numbing lessons with the clarsach, which she had yet to improve on. But something had been missing from his eyes since they had set the date for her to travel to the Camerons'. Doubt lingered there, and she had no idea why. They still planned to marry, and they'd had no more squabbles between them, so what had changed?

'Is something wrong, my laird?'

'Nay. Why?'

'You have changed since we set the date for our trip to Loch's End to see the Camerons. I thought you wanted me to do this. That you believed it was important to us both. Is it not?' she asked, twisting the ties of her reticule around her finger.

'It is. I am simply distracted by clan matters,' he answered, shifting on his seat.

She furrowed her brows. 'You can tell me anything. Just as we spoke of at the loch. I will always keep your secrets and share your burdens. We will be married soon, Ewan.' She reached across the seat and took his hand in hers.

He moved forward, his leg sliding between her own, holding her hands tightly. 'I have had this persistent fear that I will lose you once you set foot inside Loch's End. That you are a Cameron, and that you will see all they have to offer you as a family and realise that we… that I cannot provide you all you deserve. That you will choose another. Or that you will choose the life of independence and freedom you crave.'

She gripped his face between her hands. 'Have I said or done anything to make you believe such?'

'Nay,' he answered.

'Then tell me why you fear this.' She stroked his cheek with her fingers, and he pulled the palm of her hand to his mouth, kissing it, sending a thrill of heat and tingles along her entire body.

'Please, Ewan. Tell me the truth. I will understand.'

'Because of what happened with Emogene. She

showed me no signs of leaving either, and then one day she was just…gone. I fear it will be the same with you. I fear keeping you is impossible. That it is far too good to last.'

Aha. The pieces came together. It all made sense. Fear was driving him, not reason or his heart. Emogene had left her mark on him. She was why he had a rule about no romantic entanglements and not falling in love with his would-be wife. *She* was the one that made him balk at their connection and not trust it.

She smiled at Ewan. 'Thank you for telling me. It all makes perfect sense to me now, but you must know I am not her.'

He nodded. 'No, you aren't, and I am ever grateful for that and for you.'

'You are?'

'Aye. Shall I show you?' he asked, sliding even closer to her. His dimple emerged and flashed a warning she chose to ignore.

'I would like that,' she whispered, leaning forward, her hands resting on his thighs.

He picked up a tendril of her hair and let it slide through his fingers. 'I am grateful for your beautiful tresses, and your gorgeous cheeks.' He leaned in and pressed an achingly soft kiss to the apple of one of her cheeks and then the other. 'As well as your amber eyes and forehead.' He kissed her forehead and then made his way to her ears. 'And your ears.' When his lips skimmed the gentle part of her lobe, she gasped.

'Shall I stop?' he murmured in her ear.

'Nay,' she choked out, and she felt his smile against

her neck before he kissed it once and then twice before tracing the top of her exposed shoulder with his lips. She moaned and clutched at the nape of his neck. 'Kiss me,' she ordered.

He hoisted her onto his lap and kissed her. Not soft gentle kisses, but deep, thorough kisses that seared through her body one after another. His hands caressed her bodice, his fingertips skimming over the tops of her breasts just often enough to make her crave more and shift closer and closer to the core heat of his body.

She'd never felt this kind of desire to be with a man, and it raged in her like a wildfire. Nor did Ewan seem able to control his need. His hand slid along her bare ankle up her knee and then along her thigh. She thought she might squeal with pleasure at the fiery trail his touch created, and she tugged his tunic out of his trews, running her palm along his bare back. He groaned and shifted her closer until she thought she might shatter in his arms.

Bloody hell. What was he doing?

What had begun as a tease and way to rekindle their attraction to one another after days of discomfort between them had transformed quickly into something Ewan could scarcely control. His passion and craving for her burned hotter and brighter than any he'd ever known. She lifted her leg, allowing him better access as he clutched her thigh and kissed her, and the movement shook him into awareness.

He wanted her more than he'd ever wanted a woman in his whole life and...his body tightened...*and he loved her.*

The realisation landed on him like an ice bath, and he pulled back.

'I am sorry,' he sputtered, gripping her by the waist and moving her back to her bench seat. His breath was ragged, and the air between them in the carriage was charged with desire. Her face was flushed with colour, and she could not have been more enchanting. He had half a mind to ignore the logic commanding him to control himself and give in to the need coursing madly through his veins.

'Is something wrong?' she asked, her eyes searching his own for answers. Answers he could not give her without revealing the full truth of his feelings for her, which he wasn't ready to confess. He'd revealed enough to her today, had he not? Too much for his liking. He clamped down his jaw, tucked in his tunic, and looked away. Everything was wrong despite everything being so right. How could he explain such insanity to her?

He didn't even try, and thank the gods he didn't have to. The large Cameron estate, Loch's End, rose in an impressive and towering display as they climbed the hillside on the well-maintained road, reminding him of why they were travelling in this blasted carriage anyway: to see if Catriona was a Cameron. He swallowed his fear. And if she was, would she still choose what he offered her as his future wife? Or would she choose the independence and freedom she had long sought and desired since the first day he met her?

There was no denying the weight of privilege and opportunity she would have if it turned out that she was the Lost Girl of decades ago.

He faced her and forced a tight smile. 'We are here. Ready yourself,' he suggested, pointing to her dishevelled hair and now-twisted bodice of her gown. 'I should not have allowed myself to take advantage. My apologies,' he rushed out, avoiding her gaze entirely as he brushed off imaginary dirt from his finest jacket.

An odd quiet consumed the carriage. He could hear her muttering something under her breath, no doubt curses at him, as she adjusted her gown and pinned loose locks of her hair back into their plait. When had he become such a cad and prude all at the same time? Today, evidently. He sighed and berated himself once more. This was not how he had hoped their journey together to the Camerons' would go this morn. He'd hoped to chat with her to help her relax and deliver her with a clarity of heart and mind that would allow her to enjoy her brief stay with them, but also reassure her of his steadfast care and support for her and their future together. Instead, he had bungled everything.

He'd touched his future wife improperly, halted his advance without warning, and was about to deliver her to one of the most cunning and powerful clans in the Highlands unprepared. He rubbed the back of his neck. What should he do now?

'Would you like me to stay after all?' he fumbled out. 'I know we both thought it best for you to be there without me so you could focus your energies on seeing if they or Loch's End triggered any memories, but I'm sure I can stay if that would make you more comfortable.'

'Nay. I will be fine on my own. I will send word to you day after tomorrow,' she said. Her tone was sharp, a clear sign that his misstep was as bad as he suspected. 'You have made your fears clear, and I am seeing how they are ruling over you. I can do without such distraction during my visit.'

'Catriona,' he began. 'I am sorry, I—'

'We will speak of it later,' she interrupted as she smoothed her gown.

'I will plan to send on the carriage in two days' time to retrieve you and bring you back to Glenhaven. I am sure Rufus will be despondent about your absence by then,' he said, attempting to add some levity to the situation.

She was having no part of it. Her gaze flicked up and met his. As the carriage came to a rolling stop, she said, 'I will let you know *if* and when I am ready to be retrieved, my laird.'

He stilled. '*If* you wish to be retrieved?'

'Aye. You make *me* uncertain. I am battling a ghost from your past. I am not Emogene. Love and happiness are not to be feared. Nor am I. If my affection and care for you are too much, then you must decide that. I cannot, my laird.'

Before he could say a word, Aaron opened the carriage door.

'My laird,' Catriona stated with a nod. 'I will send word. Thank you for accompanying me. There is no need for you to escort me inside. I know you have much to attend to.' She accepted Aaron's hand to assist her to the cobbled drive and headed to the front door. Aaron followed behind her carrying her traveling bag for her brief stay at Loch's End. Ewan alighted from the carriage, trying to decide whether to follow her or call out for her return. Surely they couldn't leave things between them like this?

She continued, the distance growing between them, until she'd disappeared behind a bevy of soldiers who guarded the main entrance to the castle. His heart dropped to his stomach as he lost sight of her and realised she'd not glanced back to see if he was behind her as she'd walked on, not even once.

'Shall we return to Glenhaven, my laird, or shall I bring the carriage to the end of the drive and wait?' Aaron asked as he approached, having already deposited Catriona's bag to the footman. Uncertainty registered in his words.

Ewan came back to the moment and steeled his features. 'Aye,' he answered. 'We will return home. Evidently I am not needed here.'

He climbed back in the carriage, settled back into the squabs, closed his eyes, and cursed.

Chapter Twenty-Two

Catriona squashed the anger bubbling in her chest as she heard the Stewart carriage rolling down the lane behind her setting out to return to Glenhaven with Ewan in it.

Blasted man.

One minute he was bringing her to the brink of pleasure, and the next he had set a distance between them as large as the Moray Firth.

Men.

She shook off her frustration as she approached one of the Cameron soldiers at the double doors. She blinked as she brought herself back to the present moment and realised where she was and what she was about to do. She might be meeting her family. A family lost to her. And this sprawling castle was their home.

Could this be *her* home? If Glenhaven had impressed, Loch's End overwhelmed. It appeared to be at least twice the size and reflected all the hallmarks of wealth and power, as well as a focus on defence. Large towers buttressed corners of the huge stone structure with numerous square and Gothic windows, a few of which looked to be battlement-ready. The glass reflected the sunlight beaming down on the dark grey stone fortress. The Cameron coat of arms stood carved proudly above the door, a sheaf of five arrows tied with a band. Before she could take in more, the huge wooden double doors reinforced with iron strips groaned open.

Susanna Cameron stood flanked by the two soldiers that had opened the doors at her side and smiled. She looked every bit the sister of the laird in her forest-green gown, dark hair woven with a golden ribbon through her exquisite plait, and unyielding confidence. 'Come in, Mrs Gordon,' she said. 'It is about time you came home to us.'

The woman's faith in Catriona's lineage far outweighed her own. She nodded a greeting, walked up the large stone steps, and set foot into Loch's End. As the doors sealed closed behind her, Catriona paused, clutching her reticule as if it was life itself. What was she doing here? This spectacular place could not possibly be her home, could it? The entrance had smooth stone floors of a light grey, and two stained glass windows stretched above her. Colourful light streamed in on the stone. Below the windows was a vast staircase leading to the upper levels, and to the left and right of her were large open corridors covered in lush rugs, armoury, and the occasional flash of colour. Loch's End appeared to be as strong and formidable as the Camerons themselves.

'My brothers are awaiting us,' Susanna stated. 'Follow me.'

She had a strange way of phrasing orders as if they were invitations, and Catriona fell into step behind the woman's quick, purposeful stride. Catriona attempted to take in her surroundings but was distracted by her nerves and the pace at which they walked. Before she knew it, they waited outside another large wooden door. Susanna lifted the huge iron knocker and let it fall not once, but twice.

'Enter,' a man stated.

Catriona's heart pounded in her chest.

Susanna pushed the door open, and two men looked up at them. One of them paled as if he'd seen a ghost while the other gasped.

'Lord above,' the younger man murmured as he studied Catriona. He ran a palm down his face as he approached. Standing before her, his eyes welled, and he croaked out, 'Violet, it is you.'

'I… I am Catriona,' she stated as she looked upon him, self-conscious under his assessing gaze and the emotion he was struggling to control.

"I am Rolf," he replied. He was a handsome young man, a few years her junior, with soft blue eyes like his sister's and wild, wavy black hair.

'I…' he started, then cleared his throat. 'I am sure it is you.' He dug something out of his trouser pocket and held his hand closed before her. 'May I?' he asked, gesturing to her hands.

She nodded, extending a shaky hand to him.

'I have waited a long time to return this to you.' He cupped his hand with hers and placed a small piece of blue-green sea glass in it. Her heart pounded in her chest at the sight of it: the very piece she remembered finding that day at the beach and giving to her brother. Could this man have been her brother then? Could he be her brother now?

'It was many years ago when you pressed this wee bit of sea glass in my hand, sister. It was the last day I ever saw you. I have missed you, Vi,' he whispered, his voice husky and low, as he closed her hand over the sea glass and held it in his own.

Vi.

Suddenly, a flash of memory consumed her...

'Do not cry, brother,' she said.

'There are other shells. That one was just taken back by the ocean. What of this sea glass?' she asked, showing it to him.

Her brother wiped his eyes and sniffed before taking the small piece of glass worn smooth by the ocean from her hand.

'It is yours,' she said. *'My gift to my favourite brother,'* she whispered, and ruffled his hair.

He laughed and leaned into her side and hugged her. 'You are my favourite, too,' he said.

A tear spilled down her cheek. 'I remember now. You were sad at having lost a shell to the tide. And I found this and gave it to you.'

'You remember?' he asked.

She shook her head. 'I didn't until this very moment upon seeing it, seeing you...' Her throat clogged. 'Brother.'

She threw her arms around his neck, and he held her tight. 'Sister,' he whispered. 'I always knew we would find you. I never gave up. Never,' he said, holding her close.

'I knew it was you,' Susanna said, smiling at them. 'You see, Royce? We are reunited as a family at last. I am only sorry Mother and Father could not have been here to see it.' She wiped a tear from her cheek. 'Rolf, let me hug our sister. You have had her long enough,' she teased and batted him on the arm.

'Rolf,' Catriona whispered, pulling out of their embrace to look at her brother, wiping a tear from her cheek. It was hard to reconcile the small boy she knew with this young man, but it was him.

'Aye. That is me. Your baby brother,' he offered. 'And this is Royce, our oldest brother and now laird of the clan.'

Catriona's gaze met Royce's. His face gave away no emotion, his hard, unflinching features a sign that he was not as moved by her return or his siblings' joy at seeing her.

She nodded to him. 'Brother,' she said.

'Violet,' he replied with his arms crossed against his chest, his cool brown eyes assessing her.

'Please call me Catriona. It was the name Nettie gave me. She found me unconscious along the shore of Lismore and raised me. I could not remember my name or age, so she gifted me the name of Catriona and decided upon my age, which based on what you have said appeared to be correct.' She worried her hands.

'Royce, what is plaguing you? Our sister has returned. Greet her,' Rolf chided.

Royce moved to her and hugged her, his embrace rigid and void of any feeling, much like she was hugging a large boulder. Catriona stepped back quickly, feeling awkward and unsure after such a warm greeting from her other siblings.

Had something happened between them?

'Thank you for allowing me to visit, my laird,' she offered, attempting to appeal to his position. It seemed the safest way through.

'Aye. We had to know if you were our sister.' He pointed to her wrist. 'And now we are sure of it.'

She looked at her wrist and met his gaze, puzzled by his words. 'That is a scar from attempting to help cook slice up the fruit for a dessert.' He almost smiled.

She examined it. 'Oh, I did not know.'

'I will take my leave. I have clan matters to attend to. I will see you at dinner.' And with that Royce was gone.

Catriona bit her lip. Was it something she said or didn't say?

'Pay no mind to Royce,' Rolf said, casting a glance towards the door. 'He has been in a foul mood for the last decade.'

'Aye,' Susanna offered. 'It isn't you. Come, let us show you Loch's End, and then we can sit down and talk. We've much to catch up on.'

She slipped Catriona's arm through her own and guided her out with Rolf by her side.

While she'd started the day as an orphan, she would end the day with a family, and the realisation of it stung her eyes.

Catriona and her siblings sat outside in the garden, watching the sun set over the loch. Even Royce had joined them, which had pleased her more than she wished to admit.

'So, how did you even come to know Laird Stewart?' Rolf asked. Catriona shifted in her chair. She knew the question would come up eventually as she'd already spent a great deal of time recounting Nettie's rescue of her along the shore, her brief time at the Arrans, and her years as a servant for the Chisholms. She'd counted her blessings that this hadn't been the first topic of conversation at dinner. Attempting to heed some of her own advice, she said the truth of it.

Taking a steadying breath, she met Rolf's gaze and answered.

'My husband, Thomas, was selling me off in the Grassmarket. Laird Stewart offered to buy me.'

They stared at her in abject horror before Royce spoke first. 'Stewart *bought* you? You are a woman, not a mare.'

The anger in his voice cut through the night air, and her heart pounded in her chest. She stuttered out a reply. 'He...he did it to save me. Another man, whom he knew to be cruel, was about to buy me instead, so he stepped in to rescue me. That is all.'

'Who was this other man?' he asked.

'Dallan MacGregor.'

Royce stood, put his hands on his hips, and turned away from them. One curse and then another carried across the breeze, and no one spoke.

'And Laird Stewart's treatment of you since then?' he asked, finally facing them again. Was that anguish or rage she saw in his eyes?

'He has been a kind and generous host. His actions freed me from my husband, Thomas, which I am grateful for.'

'And you plan to marry him?' Susanna asked. 'Are you even free to do so?'

'Aye. Laird Stewart's solicitor was checking into the matter for us, as we did not know if the agreement was even legal. He discovered that even though Laird Stewart purchased me, I was still legally married to Thomas.'

'So, if you cannot marry after all, why was there a celebration of your engagement just last week?' Royce asked.

Catriona shifted again in her seat. 'In searching for my husband, the solicitor found he had been killed by the husband of a woman he was…seeing. I am now a widow and free to remarry.'

He ran a hand through his hair. 'I've never heard of anything so crass.'

'It seems horrible, I know, but I am happy to be free of Thomas. He was…he was not a kind man, even though he did provide me food and shelter. I did not wish him such a horrible death, but I am grateful to no longer be his wife.' She looked down at her hands, tracing the scars along her knuckles.

'Are those from him?' Rolf asked gently, following the direction of her gaze.

She looked to him. 'Only some of them.'

'I can take no more of this,' Royce said, rising abruptly from his seat along the stone wall where they sat. 'We will finish our discussion tomorrow. Good night.' He nodded to them and left, disappearing into the darkening sky.

Blast.

Catriona pressed her lips together in a thin line and worried the edge of her shawl. She'd upset the man again. It was one misstep after another with him. What was she doing wrong?

'He will come around,' Rolf said. 'We are happy you are here and hope you will stay as long as you like.'

'I don't know if Royce would agree to that,' Catriona answered with a slight chuckle. 'He seems...quite unsettled by my presence, and he is the laird, after all.'

'Who cares what he wants?' Susanna answered, standing up and stretching. 'The two of us outnumber him. Don't we, Rolf?' She laughed, reached out, and squeezed Catriona's hand. 'Why don't I show you your chambers, and you can get settled in. You must be exhausted. I know I am.'

'Aye. That would be lovely,' Catriona answered. She stood and stifled a yawn. 'Thank you both for being so welcoming. It is a great deal to take in all at once. I try not to think of all I have lost without you but choose to focus on what awaits us in the future instead.'

'I am just glad you have been returned to us,' Rolf added. 'That day you disappeared, we searched and searched for you. Word was sent to all the clans, and all searched for you as well. We returned there every month, then every year, still hoping to find you, even though we knew you had been taken by the sea. And here you are, returned to us in the same fashion as if you were dropped by the heavens.' He stared out at the horizon.

She followed his gaze and stared out into the loch, its waters lapping softly below. 'I see why this place is called Loch's End. You feel like you are at the edge of the universe. You can see to forever from up here.' And she could. The loch joined the sea, and nothing seemed beyond it but horizon and sky. It made the world seem full of possibilities she'd never even imagined for herself.

'Well, this is your new beginning here, Vi—' Susanna paused '—I mean, Catriona. Think of this as you starting a new life with your old family. Not many people get second chances. I know we will not waste our second chance with you, will we, Rolf?'

'Nay. We won't,' he answered. 'We've missed out on so much of your life. Tomorrow, we will show you the rest of the grounds, so you can see what your life here could be as sister of the laird. As a Cameron.'

She fell in step with them as they walked along, enjoying the fine sights and smells of the garden in the eve. Catriona's stomach flipped at the idea of having more choices. She could scarcely manage the new ones that had been thrust upon her since leaving the Grassmarket and going to Glenhaven.

Glenhaven. Ewan.

It would be the first night she was not under his roof in over three weeks. It was an odd and heady sensation. She missed him. She knew that. But an inkling of an idea was forming as she stared out at the horizon.

Could she finally be free and independent, as she'd

always wanted, as a Cameron? Could she choose to be under no one's control but her own?

Perhaps that would be best for a man like Ewan, who did not want to risk love, and for a woman like her, who finally wanted to see what it was all about.

Chapter Twenty-Three

Ewan grumbled at his writing desk and tossed yet another spoiled piece of parchment in the bin. At this rate, he would never finish balancing the ledgers and sending out enquiries about updating the salon for Catriona as a surprise wedding gift. He paused. He might not even need to. His fiancée seemed to have disappeared by all accounts. Just as he had feared.

Just like Emogene.

He loosened his cravat. Or perhaps his horrid behaviour had driven her away. He cursed at the memory of almost bedding his wife-to-be in a bloody carriage on their way to the Camerons'. He'd then been an arse and pushed her away with no explanation for his behaviour. All because he feared loving her. *Fool.* He loved her already, and nothing would change that. All the lies he could tell himself would not make the truth different or the utter fear such a truth created in him less real.

His pulse increased. And now, he didn't know what to do for he'd ruined it all. He glanced out of the window.

Lightning flashed, and then thunder boomed off in

the distance. His temper was as foul as the dark looming clouds that hung over the valley and the loch. Catriona had been gone for four days without a single word. He'd sent one polite enquiry about when to retrieve her after two days had passed, but his letter had gone unanswered, and his pride refused to allow him to send another. He was a laird, after all. The only communication he had received at all from Loch's End was a letter from Royce stating that she was indeed their sister.

Mrs Catriona Gordon was the long-lost Violet Cameron.

'Is this your plan?' Brenna asked, leaning against the door frame of his study, yanking Ewan from his thoughts.

'Plan for what?' he asked, his irritation blooming back up at his sister's meddling.

'To get Catriona back, of course. What else would I possibly be referring to?'

'Is she lost?' he said, sarcasm dripping off his words.

Brenna came into the room, closing the door loudly behind her. 'You and I both know that if you do nothing, she will never return from Loch's End. She will stay with the Camerons indefinitely. What is wrong with you? I know you love her. Why are you sitting here doing nothing?' Her voice was high and infused with emotion.

He matched her fervour, stood at his desk, and leaned forward. 'Of course I care for her. I love her, which is the whole problem,' he answered, exasperated by the truth and by his weakness. Why could he tell his sister, but not the woman he loved, how much he cared for her?

'So, you admit you *love* her?' she said softly.

'Aye. So much so that I feel absolutely ill at the thought of it.' He slumped back into his chair, tugged the cravat from his neck, and tossed it on the desk amidst the disarray already there.

Not much mattered any more without Catriona here.

Brenna approached him and gifted him a sympathetic smile. 'Then do something about it.'

'Like what?' He shrugged. 'I sent word to her, but my letter went unanswered.'

'Do you know if she even received it?' She leaned against the desk beside him, staring out at the dark rolling clouds. 'You know the Camerons. Royce may be holding her correspondence until they have a better handle on the situation. They may be as desperate to keep her there as we are to have her returned to us, especially after they had lost her for so long.'

'Aye. They might be.'

'Go to her. Fetch your bride-to-be. *Show* her how much you care for her.' She nudged him and smiled.

'And if she will not see me?'

'Then you will have your answer and at least be out of this horrid misery. Although I might suggest a bath first,' she added, sniffing him.

He nudged her back. 'You are such a burden, sister, but I adore you. Even if you plague me beyond measure.'

'What else are sisters for? Besides, be grateful Moira was not here. She would have harangued you even more, and you know it. You would have been begging for mercy.'

He nodded. 'You are right.'

There was a knock at the door. 'Come in,' Ewan called.

'Just arrived for you, my laird.' Mrs Stevens smiled holding a letter. 'From Mrs Gordon, I believe.'

'Ah, perhaps you may not need to pay a visit after all, brother.' Brenna beamed at Mrs Stevens and sent Ewan a wink.

Ewan's heart soared as he rose to accept the letter. 'Thank you, Mrs Stevens.'

She nodded, stepped out, and left them.

The letter had some weight to it, and he furrowed his brow. 'Heavy,' he said as he turned it over in his hand and broke the seal. He frowned when he saw the Cameron crest had been pressed into the wax. A sign that Royce had been involved in the sending of her correspondence. That didn't bode well, did it?

Royce and Rolf had still not forgiven him for what had happened to one of their beloved stallions along their small section of shared border wall that the Stewarts were tasked with maintaining. The horse had escaped through a portion of collapsed stone and not returned. Most likely seized by whomever had been lucky enough to find him. Rolf had dislocated his shoulder in an attempt to chase down the beast. He fell down a ravine trying to prevent its escape. Despite feeling that the Camerons had been at fault by letting it free from their stables, Ewan had repaid them in kind with a fine gelding last spring.

He took a tentative breath and released it. He unfolded the letter, and upon seeing a guinea, he faltered.

He turned over the worn coin in his fingers before setting it aside on his desk. He swallowed hard and read on:

To my dearest Laird Stewart,
I cannot thank you enough for what you have done to free me from my previous situation. You, and you alone, rescued me from my husband in that horrid market square that morning in Edinburgh, and you brought me back to the Highlands knowing nothing about who I was or my past. If I had never returned here, I would not have ever found the family lost to me, the Camerons, and been reunited with my siblings. I am indebted to you for your kindness and for bringing me back to my family and to a life I never would have known otherwise.

Enclosed is a guinea to repay you for the debt I owe you for purchasing my freedom from my husband that day. I hope this will cancel my financial debt to you as it is now repaid in full. I also wish to end our attachment to one another as future husband and wife as I cannot promise to live the rest of my days married to a man as glorious as you knowing I am not allowed to love you.

I have lived far too much of my life without love. Now that I know how precious and beautiful it is, I refuse to deny myself another day of it.

I respect that you do not feel the same, and I wish you every happiness in your quest to find a woman who can match your desire for a marriage of convenience without love. This would have been enough for the old me...for Mrs Catriona Gordon...but it is not enough for me now.

It is not enough for the new me.
With gratitude and love in my heart for you always,

Catriona Violet Cameron

Also, please tell Brenna and Betsy that I will be in touch, and give Rufus, Starlight, and Wee Bit a pet. I will miss them too.

If he'd thought it possible for his heart to stop and for him to still be alive, he would have said that was what happened to him. For he could not breathe or feel anything other than anguish over her words. She had rejected him. She had let him go. Not for more power or wealth, but because he had refused to allow her to love him and him to love her. The very thing he feared would happen, he had created in his own quest for control, and it could not be undone.

'Leave me,' he said.

'Brother? What has happened?' Brenna asked.

'If you care for me at all, sister, you will leave me be. Now. I need to be alone.' His words were hollow and flat, devoid of the raging emotion tightening his chest.

Lightning lit up the sky, and thunder shook the castle. He turned away from her searching gaze. Shortly after, he heard the door open and then close, as softly as a whisper.

He turned to his desk, overflowing with books, papers, and everything else in between. He placed his palms flat on the cool wood, forced a few breaths, and yelled in frustration before sending all the contents on top of his desk crashing to the floor. Panting, he took to the walls, ripping down maps and swords, revelling in the destruction and noise. By the time he was finished, his father's pristine and orderly study was in ruins, and Ewan felt like his surroundings finally matched the chaos within him.

Catriona paced under the covered walkway outside the castle walls, tugging her shawl closer as the winds increased. A storm raged over the loch just as doubt raged within her heart. She'd sent the letter as Royce had encouraged her to do to end this farce of an engagement with Ewan. She knew it was the only way for her to clearly assess her options for the future and decide what she wanted for herself now that she was a Cameron. She could stay at Loch's End as long as she wanted until she remarried, and neither of her brothers seemed in any rush to marry her off. They were both plagued by what had happened to her, so much so that they struggled to say the words out loud.

When she'd asked Royce for the guinea to include in the letter as repayment for what Ewan had spent to safely rescue her from her husband and Dallan MacGregor, he'd blanched at first. He'd paled and left her but returned a few minutes later. He'd lifted her hand gently and pressed a guinea into it without a word, but the sorrow in his eyes was unmistakable. She hoped one day she could speak with him about it, but it didn't appear that it would be anytime soon. Her eldest brother was the most guarded man she'd ever met and kept his emotions close.

Unlike Rolf. She smiled at the thought of her younger brother. He was kind and gentle, and wasn't afraid to show his emotion. If anything, he might be too open to the world, and Catriona felt fiercely protective of him despite only knowing him as an adult for a handful of days. Susanna proved to be a much softer soul as well, although in front of others outside of their family, she was quite formidable, ruling with clarity of purpose and finality. At the moment, all Catriona had was doubt about her decision regarding Ewan. Had she done the right thing in sending that letter to him?

She didn't know.

'What are you doing out here?' Susanna asked. 'A storm is coming. Join me inside.'

'I cannot rest after sending that letter to Ewan. I do not know if I did the right thing.'

Susanna narrowed her gaze. 'What letter?'

'I sent a letter to Ewan to repay him for my freedom and Royce encouraged me to also sever our engagement, so I did.'

Susanna's eyes widened. She clutched Catriona by the arm and hustled her inside. 'Not a word until we reach my chamber,' she hissed, almost dragging Catriona down one hallway and then the next. Their L-shaped castle was deceptively larger on the inside than it even appeared on the outside. Once inside the chamber, its lavender-coloured walls a calming haven, Catriona collapsed into one of her sister's oversized chairs with its floral pattern.

'What are you talking about? What letter?' Susanna

asked, removing her slippers and settling into the chair opposite Catriona. She leaned back and drew down the bell pull behind her to call for a servant. 'Would you like anything besides tea?'

'Nay,' she answered. 'I've not much of an appetite.'

'You didn't at dinner either. Tell me why. What has our dear older brother done now?' The sharpness in her tone sent alarm through Catriona. This was the first time she'd heard Susanna speak ill of their brother. She'd teased him about his difficult and rather cool personality, but there hadn't been any malice laced in her words...until now.

'We were talking about my engagement to Ewan,' Catriona said, running the fringe of her shawl through her fingertips. 'He encouraged me to rethink my promise to Laird Stewart, since my situation had changed. He was looking out for me. He didn't wish for me to make a hasty decision, especially now that I know I am a Cameron and have more options for my future.'

'More options?' she scoffed, a note of bitterness in her words. 'What he means is more options for him as laird. I wish you had spoken to me first, sister, but it is too late now.'

Catriona stilled. 'What do you mean, more options for him as a laird?'

She chuckled. 'I know you are acquainted with the ways of the world, sister. You know that women have little say in their future. You were sold, for heaven's sake.'

Catriona's body flushed with heat, and she looked away.

Susanna leaned forward. 'I do not mean to embarrass you. That is not my intent. I just want you to understand that women have as little power in families of wealth and privilege as they do in homes of poverty. We are pawns to be used for advantage. Nothing more.' She smiled sympathetically. 'The only card you held with my brother was your engagement to Laird Stewart as you had decided upon it yourself, and you have just given that up. Which I believe is exactly what Royce wanted.'

Catriona fought to keep her emotions under control as she searched the castle for her eldest brother, Royce. Susanna had begged her to wait and speak with him in the morn when she was in a better temper, but Catriona had ignored such advice. A servant had encouraged her to seek him out in the armoury, which seemed an odd place to be so late at night. As she rounded the corner and stepped into the room, she saw the man had been right. Royce sat on one of the rock benches as he sharpened a dirk with a whetstone in smooth, rhythmic strokes. The sight of it calmed some of her anger because it piqued her curiosity.

'Couldn't you have a soldier or servant do that for you?' she asked.

Royce ceased his movements, glanced at her, and then continued the steady, recurrent strokes of the stone against the metal. 'I prefer to not trust anyone else to sharpen my blades.'

The sound was oddly soothing, and Catriona felt her temper soften more. She sat next to him and watched for a moment before she asked what had been so pressing moments ago. 'Should I be worried that you will marry me off for the most advantageous match now that I have broken my promise with Laird Stewart?'

He sighed and set aside the stone, dirk, and cloth beside him. 'Has Susanna been speaking with you?' His dark brown eyes searched hers.

Catriona nodded an answer.

'She is hurt by her past. There was a lad she wished to marry, but Father forbade it. Since then, she has resisted every effort to find her a husband. No doubt, she fears the same for you.'

'You did not answer my question.'

He smiled. 'You always were quick. You wish to hear the truth?'

'I would prefer it,' she replied.

He turned his body to face her. 'I *do* wish to find you the best match for your future as well as the future of the clan. That is my duty as your brother and laird, and I can assure you that a union with Laird Ewan Stewart is not such a match. His clan will fall soon. Whether by the British, another clan, or infighting, I do not know, but they will not last. Not without help.' His words were even and unfettered by anything other than logic and reason. While his words shook her to the bone, he was unmoved, as if they were speaking of what new flowers to plant in the back garden.

She shivered. The man had ice running through his veins.

'And if I decide I was wrong, and that I should not have broken off my engagement to him?'

He turned forward, picked up his dirk and whetstone

and began to sharpen the blade once more. After five or six strokes, he paused and looked at her. 'Then you will be digging your own grave, sister. Mark my words. Love is unimportant in such matters. You will see.'

She rose from her seat and backed out of the room, feeling queasy. Digging her own grave? Those weren't exactly the words of support and approval she had been searching for. What did she do now? And who did she believe?

Maybe she'd been better off with few choices. Having this many made her feel addled and confused.

Chapter Twenty-Four

'You would think you were going to a funeral rather than the greatest ball of the summer season,' Susanna teased as she adorned each of Catriona's ears with the most gorgeous emerald drop earrings Catriona had ever seen. They caught the candlelight from her dressing table and glimmered.

She stilled her sister's hands. 'I cannot wear these, Susanna. They are too beautiful. What if I lose one?'

'They were Mother's, and I insist. She would want you to have them. They match your gown to perfection, and the jewellery appears made for you. Look how it brings out the green and gold flecks in your eyes and the roses in your cheeks.' She kissed her cheek.

'I wish I could remember her and Father. I look upon their portrait, but they seem like someone else's parents. Not mine.' She glanced at the small portrait of her parents that Rolf had moved into her room. He wanted her to see if it might trigger a memory of them.

It hadn't. Not yet, anyway.

Susanna sat down next to Catriona on the small bench

seat before the gilded mirror above her dressing table. 'Remembering them does not matter as much as knowing that they loved you beyond measure. Mother spoke of you as long as Father would allow it.'

Catriona balked. 'He did not allow her to speak of me?'

'Father was quite like Royce. Closed up, distant when it related to matters of the heart. I believe losing you affected him so much that about two years after you disappeared, he forbade us to speak of you in front of him entirely.' She sighed. 'It became something special between us and Mother. We would talk of what we remembered of you and what we imagined you might be doing. We never allowed ourselves to believe you were dead, but merely elsewhere living your life.'

A tear ran down Catriona's cheek. 'You spoke of me?'

'Often. Daily at first and then less over time. Sometimes it was too painful, but other times we would laugh over the creative stories we would craft for your new life.'

'You did?' Catriona wiped her cheek. 'What were some of them?'

Susanna chuckled. 'My favourite was one Rolf came up with. He believed you had developed powers as a witch and healer. A good witch, of course, and that you were able to travel through time to watch over us when you wished. He missed you the most. He was utterly lost without you for some time. To see you two together now—' she pressed a hand to her chest '—fills my heart more than I thought possible.' Her eyes welled with tears.

Catriona clutched one of her sister's hands in her own. 'I am sorry for all the time we have lost, but I am grateful to have found you. To have the time with you now. It is a gift I never thought possible. To have a family again.'

'And you shall always have us, no matter what Royce may have said to you.'

Catriona shrugged. 'He did not say I had to choose between Ewan or being a Cameron.'

'He did not encourage you to marry the man either.'

'Nay.' She chuckled. 'He did not. He warned me of what he believed to be the demise of the Stewarts and suggested that I may be tethering myself to a man and a people that will be destroyed in a few years' time. But I cannot fathom it. Glenhaven is large and thriving. It is not as impressive as Loch's End, but I cannot imagine it disappearing or being overcome.'

'I know it seems impossible, but you have met Brenna's fiancé, Garrick MacLean, have you not?'

'Aye,' said Catriona.

'Well, no one may have told you, but that is exactly what happened to him and his people. Over the course of a year and a half, he lost his family, his ancestral home of Westmoreland, and his clan.'

'Why?' she asked, sitting straighter. Laird MacLean appeared a good and competent man. What could have changed that?

'The British. When he was away, his family refused to pay the taxes due. The soldiers made an example of the MacLeans to keep the other clans in line.'

Catriona swallowed hard. She needed no further explanation of what all that might entail. Although she had lived in the south of Scotland for most of her life, she had heard the stories of destruction in the Highlands and had an idea of what had befallen his family and his people.

'And Royce believes that may happen to Ewan and the Stewarts?'

'Perhaps. But Royce always prepares for the worst. It is one of the things that makes him a great laird, believe it or not.' Susanna smiled.

'I hope he is wrong,' said Catriona.

'Aye,' she agreed. 'So do I. But you do not need to make your decision about your happiness based on one man's supposed prediction. It is also not too late for you to repair things with Laird Stewart if you wish it. He will be here tonight. And when he sees you, he will lose all reason.'

Catriona bit her lip. She had tried to forget that he would be here this eve, but there was no avoiding it. 'I do not know what I wish, sister, which is part of my dilemma. I love him, but he does not want love. He wants an arrangement without complications. He told me so the first night I was at Glenhaven, but I cannot go back to having less. I want to marry a man who loves me and will accept my love in return.'

'Have you told him this?'

'I did in the letter I sent him. Most of it, anyway.'

'Perhaps tell him tonight in person. Talk about it. Talk about all of it. Love is not so easy to find. Trust me on this. If I had another chance with the man I loved, I would seize it.'

'And if he decides we are not meant to be after all?'

'Then you will know you had tried. I wish I could say the same.' Susanna touched up her hair and added more colour to Catriona's lips. Sadness showed in Susanna's eyes. 'You will make him swoon. You will make them all swoon, my dear. The choice will be yours.'

Nerves fluttered in Catriona's stomach. 'So, what is this ball we are hosting, and who shall be here?'

'It is the Grand Highlander Ball. The finest celebration of the season. Held here of course, since we have the largest holdings. Royce invites all the clan lairds as well as elders with a few influential merchants and men in industry from Edinburgh. We celebrate the year before and prepare for the one to come.'

Catriona lifted her brow to her. 'Which means?'

Susanna smiled. 'Many deals and alliances are forged, marriage matches agreed upon, ghastly amounts of food and wine consumed, and much dancing had by all. You will love it.'

Catriona laughed. It didn't sound so bad now.

'And you don't have to ride endlessly in a carriage to get there. All you need do is walk downstairs. The music will begin any minute now.'

And as she spoke the words, the fiddles and lutes began to play. 'That is our cue. We are to greet guests as they arrive.'

Catriona froze. 'What?'

'I know,' she said sheepishly. 'I should have warned you before now, but I feared you would claim a megrim and not come down. Once word spreads that you have returned to us, no one else will ask how or why. No man would dare challenge Royce about the matter. They are not fools. They know he can crush any clan here if he wishes it. We have enough power on our own, but we also have more alliances and debts owed to us than all the other clans in the Highlands combined.'

'How is that possible?'

'We know how to utilise advantages when they come our way.' She winked at her with a wicked smile.

Catriona believed her on all counts and followed her older sister down to the corridor and staircase. They descended and stopped at the top of the landing, looking down into a small crowd of guests that had already arrived.

'Some of them you met at the gathering at Glenhaven, but for the others, keep your answers brief and to the point, and do not linger,' Susanna urged. 'Some of these lairds have hands with a mind of their own.'

'I'll remember that,' Catriona murmured. Her worries multiplied as every new person arrived. She had never seen so many elegant people in one place in all her life. Women wore gowns of the finest fabrics and extravagant jewels that caught the candlelight flickering along the wall and from the lit chandeliers above.

Catriona followed her sister down the stairs and headed to the large entryway. 'Go with Rolf,' Susanna whispered as she veered off to the left to stand next to Royce, whose gaze flicked up to her quickly and then away.

Catriona swallowed and stood next to Rolf. He grinned at her and whispered, 'You are stunning, sister. I am so happy to have you by my side this eve.' He squeezed her hand briefly and then let go.

His excitement and joy overshadowed her fears, and she smiled back at him. 'As am I you, brother.'

Greeting the guests wasn't as tortuous as she had expected, especially since only half of them came to greet her anyway. The guests fanned out into two streams upon arriving through the large double door entryway and greeted whichever pair of Cameron siblings happened to be on their side. Once Rolf introduced her as his long-lost sister, the guests were so overwhelmed with joy and celebration that none asked where she'd been found or where she'd been, which was a relief. Or at least, none dared ask in front of her. She didn't know exactly what she would have uttered in reply to such a question except for Edinburgh, which might not have been the full answer they would have expected.

Catriona heard Ewan before she saw him. He was greeting Royce and Susanna. His familiar smooth tone resonated through her ears and made her come alive. Even with his back to her, her body sang at the sight of him, and her fingers longed to touch him. She fought the urge to call to him, and when he moved out of the receiving line towards the main room, a sense of loss whirred through her. She reminded herself it was early as she stared after him. She would have the time she needed to speak with him and settle the discord between them.

'Perhaps you and Susanna would like to dance?' Rolf offered, following the direction of her gaze. 'Royce and I can handle the few guests that have not yet arrived.'

Catriona pressed a kiss to his cheek. 'Thank you, brother.'

Susanna mouthed a thank-you to Rolf as well, grabbed Catriona's hand, and whisked her away to the main hall, where the dancing was taking place. 'And now, we dance,' she said, shouting out a cheer of excitement. Catriona laughed and joined in the reel that was already happening. The revellers absorbed them into their dance with ease, and Catriona smiled. The night of her first ball, she'd found her family, and she wondered what she might find this eve on the night of her second.

Ewan watched Catriona across the room, and his heart filled with such pleasure. She danced and laughed in a bewitching green gown. Her hair was half pinned and half loose, and emerald earrings bobbed from her ears. He had never seen her so happy, so alive, and so free.

Freedom.

It was what she said she had wanted most that night when he'd intercepted her as she'd tried to flee Glenhaven. And now she had it in spades. She had a family, she had choices, and he couldn't begrudge her any of it. Despite the ache and longing in his chest and desire to have her as his own and as his wife, he was content to see her so blissfully happy after all she had been through before he'd met her that day in the Grassmarket.

'She appears happy,' Garrick said, sidling up next to Ewan.

'Aye. And as much as it crushes me to bits to no longer have her as my own, I am bewitched by her joy.'

'Then you, my laird, are in love.'

Ewan frowned. 'Are you here merely to plague me?'

'Maybe,' he said, elbowing Ewan in the side. 'And perhaps to encourage you to speak with her once more. To know for certain if things are truly ended between you or if this is just a misunderstanding.'

'I think she made it quite clear. I either risk loving her, or she is gone. There is no middle ground.'

'You already love her, and she you, if I am not mistaken. What is the risk?' Garrick asked.

'Utter ruin if she rejects me again. She cannot fully know what she wants. She has had nothing and been given the world. That is a drastic change for a short period of time. I should know. It was how I felt when I became laird. How I still feel about it.' He took a long drink from his tankard.

'But that is the beauty of it. You cannot control it, and the more you try, the more you will fail. You can take *my* word on that. Speak the truth to her and just be open to what happens.'

'You always make things sound so blasted simple, when they are nothing but.'

Garrick smirked. ''Tis a gift.'

'Or a curse,' he mused. He glanced back to where Catriona had been dancing and saw that she was gone.

'I will follow your advice, but now I must find her. I lost her in the reel.' He clapped his friend on the shoulder and headed off past the dancers.

Perhaps she sought refreshment or chose to take some air. The room was warming as the dancing continued and more and more guests arrived. Ewan stood in the centre of the room and scanned it for her with no luck. If he remembered correctly, the refreshments were in one direction down the hallway while the covered terrace where one could take in some air and look upon the loch was in the other. Which would Catriona choose?

Smiling, he set down his empty tankard on a side table and set out in the direction of the terrace, knowing how much she adored the night sky and the stars. If there was a place she might try to catch her breath in this throng of people, it was there. What did he have to lose?

He made his way through the first room without much difficulty, but then had quite the time carving a path through some elders recounting the days of their youth and sharing old battle stories and the wounds that accompanied them. Sidelined to hear the end of one such tale, he then carried on, eventually making his way to the terrace. He walked out onto the stone walkway with its cover and scanned the lit area, shadows flickering along the way.

His heart sank when he didn't find her there. Where could she be? He frowned. In Loch's End, the lass could be anywhere. The castle was expansive, and as family, she could travel anywhere amongst its massive maze of corridors and chambers. As a guest, there were only limited sections he could roam. Otherwise he would be at Royce's mercy. And he'd rather that not be added to the list of the man's grievances against him.

Ewan stepped back inside, and then stilled as he heard her voice. He smiled. Perhaps she had been taking some air and had returned only minutes before he had checked the area. No matter. He would talk with her now.

She was set off in a corner, speaking to one of the Stewart elders and his wife. They both smiled as she recounted of the joys of riding and how beautiful she found the daily outings she had taken in the valley. The way she spoke of it moved him. She talked of it with pride as if the land were hers. She spoke of it the way he felt about her in his heart.

As they wrapped up their conversation, Catriona turned in his direction and met his gaze. Although her smile faltered, her eyes brightened at the sight of him, and his heart thudded in his chest, his body feeling alive at being close to her again after so many days apart.

They walked towards each other, and he made a slight bow in greeting. 'Lady Cameron,' he said, acknowledging the change in her name after being claimed by the family as well as the respect she was due. 'You are enchanting this eve, as always.'

She blushed. 'You are too kind, my laird.' Her gaze held his. 'I have missed you.'

'And I you, Catriona,' he replied. 'May we speak?' he asked. 'About your letter...about us?' his voice dropped as he moved closer to her. He revelled in her familiar sweet smell.

'I would like that,' she said. He offered his arm to her, and she accepted. The feel of her hand sliding along his forearm soothed him. Maybe things could go back to where they were. Perhaps not all was lost between them.

'Stewart,' a man called from behind them as they made their way through the gathering. 'Is that you and your new bride?'

Bollocks.

Ewan bristled. He knew that voice. He let go of Catriona's arm and turned to face him.

'MacGregor,' Ewan replied. He glared at the man and walked towards him, placing himself between the bastard and Catriona.

Dallan sidestepped him and set his gaze on Catriona, letting his eyes roam slowly and shamelessly over her. She blushed under his gaze. 'I almost did not recognise you, my dear. But then, when I saw you two together and those bewitching eyes of yours, I remembered you from the market square.'

A few people around them quieted and took interest in their exchange, which was exactly what Dallan wanted. He'd never been good at losing to anyone. He did not care about the shame he would bring upon Catriona. He'd use this moment to embarrass the Camerons. Catriona would be an innocent victim among the carnage of what Ewan knew was coming.

'I am surprised to see you here,' Ewan said. 'Surely you were not invited after the outcome of last year's ball.' He stepped into the man's space and blocked Catriona from him.

'Invitations are no matter. I arrived with my own guest.' He gestured to an older matron of wealth off to the side. 'I don't need to bring rubbish that I find on the street with me.'

Rage flashed through Ewan, and he grabbed Dallan by the tunic. 'You will cease your slander, or I will throw you out myself.'

'What is going on here?' Royce asked. 'There will be no fighting at this celebration.'

'I cannot keep such a promise when you allow the likes of MacGregor in,' Ewan answered, letting go of the man.

'What do you mean?' Royce asked. He stopped short at the sight of Dallan. 'Aye. He must have come in late after we stopped greeting our guests. He is *not* welcome here.'

'I would think I'd be welcome considering what other trash you have allowed in and made a part of your family. Although I hardly recognise you without your harness, whore.'

'Whore?' Royce growled.

Ewan said nothing, but punched Dallan in the face, sending the man back into the sea of guests behind him and skidding to the floor.

The bastard regained his footing and smirked, wiping the blood from the corner of his mouth. 'She must be quite the minx in bed for you to risk peace between our people by fighting me so openly.'

'How dare you speak that way about my fiancée!'

'Your fiancée? You *bought* her, Stewart. I was there. She is your possession, I suppose, but nothing more. No matter how the Camerons dress her up and whatever new name they give her, you cannot change *what* she is, which is rubbish.'

Ewan charged into him, sending them both headlong into the crowd and sprawling onto the floor. He landed punch after punch to the man, unable to stop the fury coursing through his veins.

'Ewan!' Catriona screamed. 'Stop! You will kill him.'

Ewan only hoped he could as he took a blow to the

chin and one to the gut before continuing his assault on the bastard once more.

'Cease!' Royce ordered, dragging Ewan off Dallan with effort. 'If anyone kills him, it will be me. Rolf, have some men bring MacGregor to the armoury, where he will be dealt with. And have them take Stewart outside to cool off.'

Rolf waved over two Cameron soldiers and they dragged off Dallan, who was covered with blood but still arguing his point, through the crowd. The music in the other room still roared, the dancers oblivious to the chaos outside their revelry.

'Let me go,' Ewan argued, struggling against Royce, who had Ewan's arm pinned behind his back.

'Keep struggling and you will tear your shoulder in two,' Royce countered. 'Leave MacGregor to me. We will deal with him. She is our family now and not yours to defend.'

'She is my fiancée. I know what is best for her, and I will protect her.' Ewan stopped struggling, and Royce released him.

'Oh?' he said. 'I believe that attachment was ended, and your debt repaid.'

'Nay. She is my betrothed and under my care.'

'Nay,' Royce argued, gripping Ewan by his jacket, standing over him. 'She is my sister and under my care and protection. I will make her decisions for her, not you.'

Anger brewed once more in Ewan.

Before Ewan could throw a punch, Catriona rushed between him and Royce and shoved at the men to push them apart. 'Neither of you will make any decisions for me. I will make them for myself, and once I have decided, I will let *you* know what they are.'

She sent them both a withering glare and disappeared through the crowd, leaving them staring after her.

Chapter Twenty-Five

'Rolf,' Catriona asked, following her brother down the hall to the armoury, 'what is Royce going to do? Surely he can't kill him for what he said.'

Her younger brother stared straight ahead, moving quickly to keep up with Royce and his men who half dragged and half carried the bloody but still conscious MacGregor down the hallway. 'Aye. He can for what that bastard said about you. Hell, I want to, and I'm not nearly as bloodthirsty as Royce.'

'But what if *I* don't want you to?' she pleaded. The man was a dolt to be sure, but she didn't wish him dead.

'After the things he called you? Why would you *not* wish him dead? He embarrassed you and embarrassed us in our own home. He made a scene. If Royce doesn't respond, then we will be seen as weak, and no Cameron is weak. Not even me.' He stopped in front of the armoury and met her gaze. Anger simmered in his eyes, and the transformation of her easy-going brother into this man was startling. She took a step back.

'Stay here, sister,' he ordered. 'This is no place for you, no matter what you may have seen in your life before.' He walked into the armoury after Royce and sealed the door behind him.

Sickness threatened at the thought of what might happen to Dallan MacGregor, and Catriona rushed towards her chambers. She ran down the hallways as fast as she dared in her fine slippers and long gown. She reached the basin and retched. Just when things in her new life were the best they had ever been, the past yanked her back, reminding her of how small she was in the universe and that good things never lasted. She'd embarrassed her family. Her eldest brother and Ewan had fought with one another over her honour, of all things. And she had been brutally reminded that she was not truly in charge of her own destiny. Even though she was no longer controlled by Thomas, she was still the ward of the men in her life, unless they agreed to grant her the freedoms she longed for, which didn't seem likely.

And any hope she had of speaking with Ewan about a possible future seemed doomed as now he and Royce were at odds. All because Dallan MacGregor had to put her in her place and make a fool of her. Little did he know the shame she had endured in her past. His words were of no consequence to her. If only others understood that. The only words that mattered to her were the words of those whom she loved. Dallan Mac-Gregor would create his own demise; hell, he might already have done just that, as Royce didn't seem a man to grant anyone mercy.

'Well, you certainly made an impression,' Garrick said, helping Ewan up the stairs of Glenhaven.

'Aye. They made an equally memorable impression on me. I believe that might have been my last Grand Highlander Ball at Loch's End.' He nodded to the Stewart soldiers posted outside, and they opened the castle doors for them. Mrs Stevens scurried down the hall and gasped at the sight of him.

'My laird! I thought ye were going to a celebration, not a brawl. What has happened?' She clucked and fussed over him as if he were a chick and she the mother hen.

If he wasn't in so much pain, he might have ordered her to stop. 'Dallan MacGregor happened,' he replied.

'Get some water heated and call for Miss Stewart,' she yelled behind her to the maids.

'Oh, you don't need to—' Ewan began, but it was too late as the maid was already off to fetch his sister.

Garrick cringed. 'You're in for it.'

Ewan cursed, but then smiled. 'Ah, you forget, brother. You will also be in trouble for allowing *me* to get in a brawl.'

Garrick frowned and then dropped Ewan unceremoniously on the closest large chair. 'Deuces. You're right.' He rubbed his forehead.

Brenna came tearing into the room. 'What is this about you being in a—' She stopped short at the sight of them. 'Glory be. Are you hurt, brother?'

Ewan smirked. 'Dallan looks worse.'

Brenna rolled her eyes at him and popped her hands to her hips. 'I choose one ball not to attend alongside you, and this is what happens? And why did you not keep my brother out of trouble, Garrick?' she asked.

'Told you,' Ewan murmured. Garrick frowned at him.

'As you know, your brother manages to find his own trouble whether I am there or not.'

'Are you hurt?' she asked, concern needling her brow. She pointed to Garrick's bloody tunic.

'Nay. I am uninjured. That is your brother's blood that has stained my finest tunic and jacket. He is the one in need of tending to.'

'So, do either of you care to tell me what happened?' she asked, perching on the arm of the chair as she lifted Ewan's chin to look at the wounds on his face.

He pulled his face away. 'Not really.' He wasn't up to another chastisement.

She sent a glare to Garrick who caved under her withering look. 'MacGregor made more than one unseemly remark about Mrs Gordon—I mean, Lady Cameron—and her past. Ewan set him to rights about it. Royce intervened as protector. He then kicked us out for causing a scene at his ball.'

'And Catriona?'

'She is angry at me for trying to defend her honour and protect her,' Ewan said as he touched his swelling lip. 'I have no idea why.'

'You have no idea?' Brenna asked.

'Nay.'

'Garrick, what did he say?'

'He was trying to defend her honour. So was Royce. She lashed out at them both.'

'And?' she asked, tilting her head to the side.

'I said she was my intended and under my care and protection,' Ewan volunteered. 'Royce took issue with that and said she was under *his* care and would make the best decisions for her, not I.'

'So, let me make sure I understand this. You brawled over who was in charge of her in front of a man demeaning her in a room full of people.'

'It sounds worse when you say it like that.' Ewan dabbed his eye with the corner of his torn tunic sleeve.

'Ewan you are a fool,' said Brenna. 'Of course she is angry with you...and Royce. She has lived her whole life with others making decisions for her and controlling her. She wants to make her own decisions and have her own life for once. Can you not understand that?'

He cursed under his breath. He understood that *now*, but it was far too late.

'Deuces. What do I do now?' he asked, rubbing the sore shoulder Royce had almost snapped in two.

'Do you love her?' she asked.

'Aye. I've told you I do.'

'Then you need to think of the grandest gesture you can fathom to make it up to her, and then...do more.'

He let his head flop back against the cushion and sighed. So much for this ball being a chance to win Catriona back. He'd just made his position with her that much worse. He'd tried to control her and treated her like the possession he swore she never was to him.

'Blast. Why didn't you stop me, Garrick?'

'I did, but you tried to punch me in the mouth.'

Ewan cringed. 'Oh. Sorry. I wasn't thinking clearly.'

'Nay,' Brenna answered, crossing her arms against her chest. 'You weren't thinking at all.'

Chapter Twenty-Six

A week had passed since the Grand Highlander Ball, but it felt like a month at Loch's End. Catriona patted her mare's neck. 'Good girl,' she said. The sweet molasses-coloured horse leaned into her touch. 'I know,' she teased. She took a carrot from her pocket and gifted it to the mare, who gobbled it up swiftly.

The ride across the valley and up into the glen was exactly what Catriona had needed. She'd released some energy, and her body felt more relaxed as she stared out towards the rolling hills and glens that would lead up to the edge of the border the Camerons shared with the Stewarts. It would take her less than an hour to make the trek to Glenhaven if she wished, but what good would it do her? Ewan wanted something different than she did. He'd made that plain enough on more than one oc-casion. He'd also not sent word to her at all after what happened at the ball. He had been silent, as many of the members of the Cameron household had been.

Royce was avoiding her, and Rolf had said little to her after entering the armoury to deal with Dallan Mac-

Gregor, who had been returned alive to his clan, but not without injury. Catriona was just glad he had survived. Susanna was almost her usual self, but Catriona could tell her sister was on edge because of Royce's behaviour. She and Catriona whiled away the hours together as best they could. They spoke of what books they were reading and which ones they hoped to read next. They talked about their dreams and wishes and took exercise out of doors by walking the hillsides when they could. But still Catriona missed Ewan. He was almost always on her mind, and she felt like a bloody fool.

The sound of thundering hooves captured her attention from behind her, and she turned her mount. Her breath caught. It couldn't be. Not here on Cameron lands. She squinted.

It was him.

Laird Ewan Stewart was riding Wee Bit, and they were headed this way, like an imagining from her dreams. 'Steady,' she told her mare as much as herself. 'Steady.'

Ewan slowed as he approached, and Catriona's heart skittered in her chest at the sight of him. Had he ever been so handsome? He wore a pair of dark fitted trews with a crisp white tunic and fine grey coat. His hair was mussed, his face flushed with exertion, and his shoulders were set with a determination she had not seen before. He dismounted and walked over to her.

'How did you get here?' Catriona said.

'Rolf allowed me entry. I am rather sure if Royce had seen me, he would have shot me dead with one of his fine arrows, but it was worth the risk to see you.' He smiled. 'You look lovely.'

'Thank you, my laird.'

'May I speak with you?'

She hesitated.

He placed a hand over her own. 'Please. Just hear me out. If you decide to still hate me, the decision is yours, and I will never bother you again.'

She sighed. 'I do not hate you,' she offered.

'That is a fine start.' He grinned, his dimple and eyes flashing with hope. 'May I?' he asked, offering her assistance to dismount.

She accepted and revelled in the feel of his hands along her waist as she slid off the horse and into his arms. A flash of their embrace in the carriage and all that happened there heated her mind and her skin, which made her shiver.

He rubbed her arm. 'Would you like my coat?' he offered.

'Nay. I am not cold, I am just…uncertain.'

'About me?'

'Among other things.'

He took her hands in his. 'I'm sorry to be one of the things you are uncertain of. I'm sorry for a great deal more. For pushing you away in the carriage because I feared you would leave me for the Camerons and never return. For acting like a royal arse by making you feel like a possession at the Grand Highlander Ball. That was never my intention. And I am most sorry for not being the man you deserve. The man I want to be for you.'

She blinked back at him. Such an apology she had never imagined. She was struck dumb.

He let go of her hands and retrieved a fine fabric pouch from his pocket. 'This is for you.'

She took it from him, pulled on the string to open it, and poured a guinea attached to a chain onto her palm. 'What's this?' she asked.

He picked it up from her palm and placed it around her neck. 'I realised there was nothing I could give you that you couldn't get for yourself now that you are a Cameron, so I made you something to show you that you will always have your freedom if you choose me as your husband. That I will encourage you and support you in all your endeavours, even the clarsach.' He smiled.

She laughed and her eyes welled. 'But what of love? I cannot be in a marriage where love is not allowed. That is a rule I cannot follow, for I love you. Dearly.'

Ewan closed the space between them and ran a thumb over her cheek before holding her face close to his own. 'There is one more thing I am certain of. I will love you more and more with each passing day until I am but dust on this earth, Catriona.'

'So you will cast aside your rule?'

'I will cast aside many things for you. My pride, my fear, my pain. All of it. We can build a life together based upon truth, trust, and openness.'

'And love?' she added.

'And love. We will build our life together on that promise as well,' he answered. 'Will you be my wife, Catriona? Do you dare choose me?'

'Aye,' she answered. 'And I will choose you each day over and over and over again.'

He seized her mouth and kissed her.

The rush of knowing that she would kiss him, be held by him, and be loved by him for the rest of her days filled her heart with a hope she had never felt before.

'So, when shall we marry, my laird?'

'Is tomorrow too soon?'

'Perhaps. But any day after that shall be fine.'

He laughed against her lips. 'Then, any day after tomorrow it is.'

Epilogue

Three months later

Ewan watched at a distance as the meadow overlooking the valley below was alive with music, laughter, and dancing. The Cameron and Stewart clans were celebrating his marriage to Catriona earlier that morn. Sun beamed across the grasses, and the sky was as clear a blue as a bluebird's wing. He could scarce believe she was now his wife and that he felt such an unabashed hope for his own future and the future of the clan as he looked along his lands and his home of Glenhaven.

'You have done what we all believed impossible,' his sister Moira said, snuggling up to Ewan and laying her head on his shoulder. He wrapped his arm around her and hugged her. He had missed her far more than he would ever admit.

'Do you mean by finally choosing a bride?'

'Nay,' she said, poking him in the arm. 'I mean how you have kept us all together as a family and a clan, just as Mother and Father would have wanted. It is a miracle, and you are responsible for it.'

His heart tightened in his chest. Had *he* done that? He looked around the field and saw Brenna and Garrick, now wedded and expecting their own bairn, smiling and playing with his nephews and nieces while Catriona stood arm in arm with her sister Susanna. Even Royce smiled as he drank from his tankard and chatted with Rolf, the rift between him and Ewan mended over their common love and adoration for Catriona.

Royce had also finally confessed the reason for his initial coldness to Catriona: shame. He was the one who had encouraged her to chase him into the water the day she disappeared, and he felt responsible for her being pulled out to sea. Of course, Catriona assured him that feeling responsible for what happened to her was foolish and unwarranted, but Ewan understood Royce's guilt, and such an understanding had become a tether between them.

Peace between the Cameron and Stewart clans was restored and even improved, and the Stewart clan elders no longer worried about the future with such a renewed alliance forged. The clan was also making changes to protect its future with Ewan at the helm and Catriona by his side. He had also learned to trust love again and to love as he never had before, and so had his siblings. What more could a laird and brother ask for?

Catriona waved to them from afar.

'I believe your wife has need of you,' Moira whispered. 'Just as poor Rory has need of me. I believe one of the twins just stripped off their plaid.'

Ewan laughed. 'Go then and see if you can gather that tartan before Rufus steals it, and I will see to my wife.'

'Aye,' she answered, ruffling his hair before she left him.

Ewan grimaced and attempted to smooth his hair back down before heading to his wife, who had started to walk towards him as well. When they reached each other, he kissed her and pulled her to his side.

'Do you know what I am most grateful for other than you and our family?' Ewan asked.

'Wee Bit?'

'Other than our animals.'

'Glenhaven?' she answered.

'That too. But I am most grateful that Brenna needed a new hat. Otherwise, I would have never seen you that day in the market.' He smiled. 'Look at our families. They are happy and celebrating in a way I would never have thought possible. And all to honour you, me, us, and our clans.'

'Aye. And I have found a family lost to me for decades and added a new one as well,' she said.

'My mother used to say to not worry because nothing that is meant for you will get past you in your life, even though it may take its time in getting to you.'

'I like that,' Catriona added. 'So, I need not worry about my first riding victory against you. Since it is meant for me, it cannot get past me. I will just bide my time until it is the right moment for it to happen.'

'No rush, Lady Stewart. We have the rest of our lives to get the timing just right.'

* * * * *